LIMERICK

Alan Warner is the author of four previous novels, *Morvern Callar*, *These Demented Lands*, *The Sopranos* and *The Man Who Walks*. In 2003 he was chosen by *Granta* as one of the twenty Best of Young British Novelists.

The Worms Can Carry Me To Heaven

Alan Warner

JONATHAN CAPE
LONDON

Published by Jonathan Cape 2006

2 4 6 8 10 9 7 5 3 1

First published in Great Britain in 2006 by
Jonathan Cape
Random House, 20 Vauxhall Bridge Road, London SW1V 2SA

Random House Australia (Pty) Limited
20 Alfred Street, Milsons Point, Sydney,
New South Wales 2061, Australia

Random House New Zealand Limited
18 Poland Road, Glenfield,
Auckland 10, New Zealand

Random House South Africa (Pty) Limited
Isle of Houghton, Corner of Boundary Road & Carse O'Gowrie,
Houghton 2198, South Africa

The Random House Group Limited Reg. No. 954009
www.randomhouse.co.uk

A CIP catalogue record for this book is available from the British Library

ISBN 0224051105 (hardback edition)
ISBN 9780224051101 (from January 2007)
ISBN 0224071297
ISBN 9780224071291 (from January 2007)

Papers used by Random House are natural,
recyclable products made from wood grown in sustainable forests;
the manufacturing processes conform to the environmental
regulations of the country of origin

Typeset by Palimpsest Book Production Limited, Polmont, Stirlingshire
Printed and bound in Great Britain by Mackays of Chatham plc

for Hollie
this sombre tract

Book One

There was then a nun in the house who was afflicted with a
most serious and painful disease. She suffered from open sores
on her stomach, which were caused by obstructions, and
through which she discharged all that she ate. She very soon
died of this. Now I saw that all the sisters were frightened by
her disease, but for my part I only envied her her patience,
and prayed to God to send me any sickness He pleased,
provided He sent me as much patience with it . . .Well His
Majesty heard my prayer, and within two years I too was ill . . .

The Life of St Teresa of Ávila by Herself

The Condition

The damn weather was strange too. There was no heat in that sun; it was just a big silver light. We had arranged to meet at Cena's. I was at my favourite terrace table with a glass of carbonated water. I wanted coffee but, depending on Dr Tenis's news, perhaps I was not permitted coffee any more? It could be my heart. I had been trying to change to decaffeinated for years. I had also been trying to change from carbonated to still water for around . . . twenty years. I believe carbonated plays havoc with the digestion.

My doctor and old friend, Tenis, walked quickly in his light suit, hands in the trouser pockets, head down as if in constant thought. When he looked up he appeared surprised to see me, as if this were a chance meeting. He was always thus. Even as a kid. It crossed my mind he looked old, so how did I look to him?

'We will walk?'

I nodded to the head waiter, making vague hand gestures which were meant to mean: I will pay for this later. The waiter nodded tranquilly.

'Strange weather?' Tenis said.

'Odd. No heat in the sun,' I mumbled then cleared my throat.

Tenis chose the walk along the edge of the beach by the railings (which are painted silver and yellow in this era) beyond the fountain and the front of the Imperial Hotel which my parents used to own.

Tenis paused for us both to look up at that new, ridiculous kinetic sculpture – an abstract *faux*-rusted thing, the expense covered by Town Hall. It had made the lousy local newspaper. The sculpture had featured hanging wind chimes which sea breezes disturbed. So much and every night until the residents of the apartments across the National road came with a ladder and hacksaw, chopped the chimes down and hid them so they could sleep in peace. We paused briefly to look up at the sculpture's forlorn, stripped frame.

It occurred to me Tenis may not have walked down by the beach-front since we were teenagers, the last summer before we both went away to university in the Capital city . . . over twenty years ago. The year we won the snow race, him driving his father's old van.

We had a tradition in our city of racing up into the mountains on hearing of the first snows there, building a snowman in the back of the van or sometimes even on the roof of a car, then speeding back down to our city to parade through the hot streets, blowing the car horn, throwing fast-melting snowballs at the prettiest girls. There had been no mountain snow for years, I mused.

Dr Tenis now showed a distracted, sort of amazed interest in the people on the beach.

'The Condition,' he almost shouted.

I jumped. 'The Condition?'

'Your Condition.'

'There is a Condition?' I swallowed; rushing seemed to come in my ears as when I am deeply embarrassed. I am a hypochondriac and have always been ready for serious illness. I was made for it. It was gruesome to realise that my dread was not without a certain objective, final excitement and curiosity. The way in action movies, which I once used to watch as a kid, victims would stare dumbly at their own severed limb. I always made the things happen in my life but now something had happened unbidden. Illness which I had always feared had come at last, like a new political regime.

Tenis said, 'The silly blood test we did at the party the other

4

night. Of course I could not believe that, so I had a second and then third test done.'

'What Condition?'

'Lolo,' he said, as if trying out the sound of my pet name.

'What is it?'

'Another of the diseases that dare not speak its name.'

'I do have cancer?' I nodded.

He looked at me. 'What do you mean, "do"?'

'I am a hypochondriac. You told me I had cancer . . . twenty years ago when we were at university. That time in your rooms. As a joke. You are not joking now?'

'I did? As a joke!' He was smiling! He had forgotten.

I said, 'You joked. Just for a moment, back when we were students.' My voice faded as I realised I was trembling.

'You do not have cancer. You have the other disease that will not speak its name. In our city.'

'This is impossible.'

'It does not mean what it once meant.'

'Once meant?'

'This Condition no longer means the end. So many things in medicine once did. That is my definition of medicine: reducing and reducing what means the end. I know you often told me your definitions of design.' He shrugged. 'Sorry. I forgot them. This Condition did mean the end only ten years ago, now no more. It is not the end for you, Lolo. Just illness.' He turned and looked me in the eye. 'Just time to change a few things. That is important. For the poor there is still a danger. Not for a man who is well-to-do. You just need to make a few changes in life.' He went on, but looking over at the beach again, 'This is a mere inconvenience compared to some Conditions. It is almost a Condition to be wished for, compared to those I have seen. It is only what comes with it. You are a free man who has never cared for what society thinks. That just leaves the causes. Of course you will have to make changes. To be bold, I think, in your private life.'

5

What was he talking about? I said, 'This is impossible.'

'Used narcotics, Lolo?'

'No!'

'No needles?'

I shook my head, partly because my ears were ringing.

'Have you donated blood like Aracelli did?'

'You are my doctor. I would never dream of it. I was always too neurotic.'

'Moor prostitutes?'

'Moor prostitutes?'

'Not my concern but you and Sagrana and his circle. Boys? Or men, or boys and men?'

I looked up and down the beachfront. I turned to make sure nobody was at one of the metal tables in the temporary, seasonal café. It was the very café – though structurally changed – where I had fallen asleep on a table in 1978, I was up so early one bright summer morning.

Tenis had his eyebrow raised, the same way he used to at Three Kings, when you recited what presents you had received. Like when I got the model DC-8 *stretch series*. Young Tenis never believed what our classmates from the institute had received for Three Kings. He raised the eye of profound scepticism as we named our lucky gifts. Then one year, I finally realised Tenis's doubt was feigned. A means to be invited round to play with everyone's new toys, just to prove to sceptical Tenis that they existed. We always valued his opinion that much! Hence that terrible raised eyebrow which women all found so charming and I had always hated.

'I am not a butterfly. If that is what you are asking.'

'Lolo.' He turned to face me. 'Not even once?'

'You are ridiculous.' I paused. 'There were times at school when, like all boys we would –'

'You with Sagrana, really?' He laughed. Tenis suddenly said, 'Yes, well, all that does not matter, for as you know this Condition emerged only after our youth was gone. You could discount any activities, no matter what,' he smiled, 'during our youth.'

6

Before I thought about it I blurted out, 'Have you told Lupe?'

He looked grave. I admit I had, by pathetic increments, made it obvious down the years that I adored his gorgeous wife. 'Yes.' He paused, took out a cigar pouch, offered me one.

I said, 'I quit. On your advice.'

'Ah yeah. Wise.' He turned against the wind to light a slim cheroot. He said, 'You are godfather to the girls.'

'I know that. It means a lot.' I could hear how shallow I sounded. I reached out and touched his arm but I felt numb.

'Lupe will still be fond of you.'

'I feel I have let you down. I messed up as usual.'

'Do not be so *bourgeois*. I see many things. And I am no bigot.' He exhaled blue smoke. I stared at him, like a child watching an adult do a job which they longed to do, but could not. Like the lies life tries to tell you in the form of stories: a kid looks at the moon, compelled, decides to become an astronaut and does. Life is just not like that; only in North American movies.

Tenis was going on. I was actually weary of any more dread talk. I just wanted to get on with dying. 'The Condition,' he kept repeating. 'The Condition is infectious.' He was reminding me, perhaps, to keep clear of his wife, though she had no interest in me.

I nodded. 'I understand that.' I was beginning to understand everything now. We both nodded.

The realisations all came in a rush like a good idea at work. 'How long have I had it?'

'Impossible to say until you know who.' He stopped. 'The Condition can lie dormant before it . . . I am not a specialist in this Condition but understand I am recommending you the best one in the country. You have an appointment in the Capital city. They will write confidentially. You will see the best man.'

'In the Capital city?'

'He will prescribe medication. In the meantime, I have to put this somehow, Lolo. You must <u>reflect</u>. Your girlfriends. I know I met some. A process of elimination. You understand? Aracelli does not count. Aracelli gave blood.'

'I could have got it from Veroña or Aracelli?'

'Not Aracelli. That is what I am saying. She was screened. It is on her records. But you do not get the Condition from toilet seats, Lolo. This is not just about you <u>getting</u> it. You too could then have <u>given</u> this Condition. People could have inherited from you. It won't be an easy wait as this news sinks in, so phone me. Here are copies of the results.' He handed me an official envelope which I helplessly took hold of.

He blew out more smoke which was whipped away. 'I have sent out your blood sample to another lab and those results will come back as independent corroboration. You talked about cancer. If it was cancer you would have years. I am giving you decades.'

'Tenis. Is this a joke. A wicked joke?'

'Sorry, Lolo. Get yourself another test. Of course. It will show Positive though.'

'At the party the other night. You might have got my blood mixed up with someone else. Lupe was criticising you about your labelling?'

'That was my hope. Cruel as it would be for someone else. It has not happened, Lolo. We must face the inevitable. But think about those other ladies. The answer is there,' Dr Tenis said. 'I must go to the hospital. Stay in close touch. If you have questions. Otherwise wait to hear from me.'

After he left me, trying to be surreptitious, I repeatedly put a finger to my neck to confirm my racing pulse. Christ, I needed a cigarette but there was no chance of that ever again. I had to keep my health pristine.

I did not want to take the narrow gauge, yellow commuter train, which we locals cynically christened the lemon express, home to my top-floor apartment by the sea out at the Phases Zone 1. After years of perfecting my home, I was now afraid of its comforting silences and calculated familiarity.

Pathetically I felt the urgent need to seek out the proximity of other human beings in cafés and restaurants but simultaneously I was too alarmed to sit still. The idea of a long lunch seemed unbearable. I strolled, aimless but panicked, up the esplanade.

I spied one of our city's shoeshiners all of whom I knew by sight. A curious democracy exists between the *bourgeois* of our city and our shoeshiners. It is an unsaid rule they may discuss anything with us – put across their points (usually outright communist) – and we get the right of reply. I suppose we of the business community use them as a touchstone for expressing the latest public feeling of outrage towards we profiteers.

'A shine please.'

He put down his box, opened the top – you just glimpsed the private, red velvet interior crowded with brushes and tins, the sides stained with black and brown polish blemishes.

He removed some tins, brushes and cloths, closed the box and sat on the plush, red fitted cushion while I lifted and rested my foot in position. He leaned forward, his face intimately close to my fatal groin which I suppose is what gives them the advantage in argument. He began working on the shoe.

'Nice shoe. Italian?'

'Right. What news in our city?'

'Quiet. Strange weather.'

'Yes. Cold one day then warm.'

'The weather does not seem to be as when we were young.'

I agreed. I had a need to keep talking; to say anything. 'True. Then, it seemed cold winters, warm Holy Week, the rains, hot summer, cold winter; now we have rain any time, rains in August. Whoever heard?'

'It is incredible. The climate is destroyed and when it dies so will our city and you know who is to blame?'

'North America?'

9

'You said it, man. Biggest polluter. The North Americans. Pollute the planet, cause the wars and take the jobs. Invented the sports shoe too. Ended my livelihood. Other shoe please.'

'Ah.'

'Yes. It is the end of the world. We all did it but mostly the North Americans. You see it in the skies. Something is not right any more.'

'True.'

'There.'

'Thank you. Great polish. Keep that.'

'Thank you. That is generous.'

'No problem. See you again.' I walked about twenty metres then I turned and came back. He was dropping his tins of polish and accoutrements inside his box. I said, 'Hey, shoe polish guy. Come take a drink with me? Talk about things?'

He looked up, slightly pitiful. 'Sorry, sir. Got to work. Nobody wears leather shoes any more.'

'Sure. I understand.'

'Until next time.'

Stunned, I walked back towards the railway station. I stopped at the kiosk in front of the Imperial Hotel and bought my first carton of cigarettes in two years. Completely alone, trying not to cry, I went home on the local train to my luxury apartment at the Phases Zone 1 to smoke them.

Notes Towards My Own Obituary

The telephone was ringing soon enough back in the rooms of my very large apartment. The inquisitive voice of Kiko Bonzas, manager of my design Agency, with his tones of pleading insistence came through the answerphone which I have connected to a small stereo system with wire-free antenna speakers in four rooms (I dislike music and own no CDs). A voice that still took no responsibility no matter what I paid him. I ignored it. Already it seemed to come from another era.

I take my staff twice a year to the Dolphin restaurant or maybe the Lower Rivers but they are afraid of me on the telephone. I have learned with phones to hang up the moment you have conveyed what you wish. I try to keep all phone calls in my life under three minutes. I knew the staff called me 'the hangman' with regard to my behaviour on the telephone but it made them keep to the point. Kiko was making the best of my answer machine's mechanical generosity and eventually the tape ran out on him.

Mother would have been proud that my annual phone bill had halved since her passing.

I was smoking cigarettes one after the other on my long balcony overlooking the sea above the deserted beach. There was a sudden splash, a glint of something diving down in the clear blue sea water beneath our building. I held the portable computer in my hands, craning up to get a clearer vantage, but whatever sea beast it had been was gone. The cigarettes were making me feel delightfully sickly and light-headed – or perhaps this was the onset of first symptoms? I had been assembling a timid, businesslike list on my computer.

For every man has sat down far too soon – long before the full sunset of their days – to make a mental inventory of the women or girls and the things which have been practised on them and by them. Only a liar would deny such a weakness.

Is this, though, what it amounted to in all of my days? Was this my gallant thread with my pale pearls strung upon it? As a young man I lounged in delusions of myself as a great sinner, but by today's standards I looked positively virtuous. I could be up for a sainthood if statistics like these made it to Rome. The Little Sisters of Veronica's Handkerchief might welcome me as a special dinner speaker in their cavernous rectory. 'My Path of Virtue', Speaker: Manolo Follana.

I found this sudden need to be gruesomely forensic about every detail of my love life unbearably demeaning. Pleasure should never be up for analysis. How can I kill someone by making love to them?

It seems incredible that one as self-conscious as I, and married for years, could find it is impossible to remember clearly a single time I made love – even the more outlandish incidents have become fragmentary in my recollection – what seemed like momentous landmarks have faded and reduced down to a few vague, poorly lit erotic scenes which are increasingly subjective and possibly inaccurate. For instance: the ochre colour of another woman's arm by the light of an unfamiliar lampshade (I recall the lampshade more accurately than the tanned arm) – a woman with dark eyebrows and her sudden, stunningly rich cluster of unfamiliar pubic hair, the utter intimacy of the huge, closed eyelids of a girl struggling for pleasure – the utterly steady, unfathomable eyes of the other girl, watching.

Other participants' memories must be similarly unreliable? All

(!?) that lovemaking I was incapable of taking for granted, and which I thought so very important indeed, has been reduced to mere images. I really should have taken stock of it carefully and savoured it all – or some of it – before.

What a situation. The only thing which now gave reality and solidity to my past was this Condition which finally flowed through the visible blue veins at the wrists.

I held another cigarette in my long fingers and lit it. These hands which touched those same girls and women had once signalled the end of both my marriages. After Aracelli, my second wife, it was worse because I recognised again the same hand symptoms as those similar long months at the end of my first marriage, to Veroña. There was the same nostalgia for that specific sound of my wedding ring clinking in among the dishes and the soapsuds of the sink as I washed up every evening, alone in my apartment. With just a few dishes for myself, I no longer used the new electric dish-washers. A wedding ring on my finger no longer gouged into a bar of soap when I washed my hands, sometimes leaving a greasy and bright-coloured nodule beneath the gold. As I worked on design projects for my Agency, my fingers clicked rapidly on the keyboard of my portable computer, for I was no longer clipping my fingernails weekly so I could rub the most sensitive part of my current wife.

I could simply not accept that my career as a lover was over – such news is despair for any man but especially men of my region who, despite the facts, still insist on being considered great engines to women's joy.

I felt ashamed that in my sickness of this Condition, the healthy, who ream our city's avenues, now would suddenly have a constant, oppressive power over me. All life is not sex – far from it – but at least the possibility and the hope of romance energises a man like me. Believe us, those hopes make we men swing our legs out of bed on many a morning. Daily we have the slimmest chance of making love to a woman of our city with its summer strip of near nudity stretched along the sand, its crowded *discothèques*; the brown arms and legs, blue in the luxury shop lights of the street. Previous surprises show all women are vague possibilities, but just like those fifty-two playing cards inscribed in ballpoint with school-girl names from my institute, possibility itself is the thing. That daily illusion of even the possibility of romance was now dead for ever.

That I had contracted the Condition from one of the names on this list there was no doubt. As Tenis said, you do not catch this Condition from toilet seats. The more I meditated on those words of his the more I became concerned about what <u>could</u> be caught from toilet seats and I made a commitment never to use public facilities again.

In my last hated travels on airlines before I stopped making business trips and sent Kiko instead, I had noted that the DDS touch-sensitive flush systems so popular in European airports were prone to many basic design flaws. At the mercy of local variations in water pressure, small droplets of flushing water were escaping the cistern and spattering out into a substantial area within the cubicle, including, of course, onto one's trousers. Unfortunately, these design flaws do not come within the scope of this account.

I looked again with shrivelled pride at the list on my computer screen. The need to be brutally forensic and recall intimate specifics should have been a pleasure but was now a source of distaste for me. In no particular order and to sweeten the vulgarity a little, I tried to recall instead, with all my memory's power, how each had kissed:

(My accountant Sagrana: who criminally seduced me every sports day at school in the cool, dark graveyard mausoleums – some as big and labyrinthine as houses, lost within them I was led hand in hand from room to room. He was so slim then: girl-like, I would argue. I recall a very slobbery, saliva-heavy kisser – excitable and unable to concentrate for long.)

Enilia Bonvillan: was it me who imposed a middle-class concept of elegance and slow grace on this society woman's leisurely, breath-challenging technique?

Cinzia Carrasco: in the style of Hansa Deprano but punctuated with expected pauses which you could feel were placed there for my appropriate verbal responses, such as: 'You are incredible.' 'You are so wonderful.' 'I am so happy with you.' Etc. etc.

Ann Green: the English: the most erotic women in the world . . . they do not use bidets; their ghostly paleness, their vast stock of natural true blondes, their libertarianism when drunk which occasionally ends in unconsciousness. Those kisses: huge, greedy, entering-into-the spirit, avaricious plummets, like when you bite the apple from a bucket as a child on the Saint Days.

Thinh: a tongue so small it was like a little finger that barely stirred, just lifting itself.

The Young Woman Who Watched: we barely kissed but those few brief kisses: amazed, each bestowed as a testing, astonished dip as if I was the first man or woman who bore another tongue.

Quynh: never kissed a boy before. The tiniest resistant hiss through minute nostrils, bred from practice in private girls' schools.

Aracelli: she never liked kissing. Those kisses were a strangled tongue movement, a painful expression if you opened your eyes, but she withdrew from every kiss with her mouth still slightly open, as if tasting, hesitant, even after years. You saw her pink tongue which was erotic.

Veroña: those kisses methodical/unvaried . . . somehow sensual . . . yes, be honest: noisy

Hansa Deprano: ridiculously histrionic.

Madelaine: those kisses delivered hungrily with a metronomic movement of the head from side to side as if precisely marking time: the tongue excitedly darted as if seeking decent, gold-capped teeth.

It could be only these and one of <u>them</u> had infected me. I was not completely unscientific; it could not have been my early ones – my accountant Sagrana, for instance. Thank God. The Condition had not come to our city then. It was one of the later ones – probably that mad bohemian Hansa. Then again there was Cinzia – or how about that snob Enilia Bonvillan? Who could say what they incubated within them? You also had to consider the mortar and pestle I mashed up that night with the English *Ann Green* and The Young Woman Who Watched. What a stew.

If I even bothered to turn my mind to vulgar details, Veroña would have pinpointed how statistical likelihood for anyone donating the Condition would grow as years went by – as Tenis intimated, some <u>could</u> have inherited it from me.

Already my mind oscillated against my better will: the donor or the receiver, they could not deny me my relevance to them and would be forever bound; and for the lucky one, what a true bond! Not like my broken marriages, withered resolutions, ephemeral vows and gasped hopes. This bond was true. Could I and the one who infected me or vice versa not form our own little leper colony here by the sea and make love with the confidence we were in no way harming one another?

I shuddered as I realised I was making preferences as to who I hoped I had diseased.

My mind was made up in disgust at myself. I was going to take a vow of silence with them all. I was not going to seek out and warn a single one of these women.

I drew the black highlight box right down the list and I hit the button: DELETE.

My Small Blisters

Father, when he was drunk, once told me I was conceived the day the North American president, *J. F. Kennedy*, was shot.

I was born with a caul on my head, a sign of great good luck in our model region. Good luck has never neglected me but, as if to balance it out, I was also born with allergic skin, so sensitive and with such tissue-healing properties that I am a scientific curiosity in the arcane world of dermatology.

As was the fashion in the sixties, supposedly to keep women's busts attractive, I was not breastfed by Mother and only briefly wet-nursed. A child of those times, I was given powdered milk. I was the first of a generation to be exposed to chemicals, pollutants. My skin, today draped in its silks, soft linens and best cottons, rarely troubles me and is as smooth and soft as a rich schoolgirl's. My ex-wives, girlfriends and indeed other men have remarked upon its smoothness and softness. But as if I once stood brilliantly before some hydrogen bomb on a distant atoll, remnants of my lifelong sensitivity mean I still have occasional isolated skin blisters, once or twice a year. A bubble, the diameter of a number 3 cigar, mounds up around my chin area or sometimes on one ear. I have never been able to identify what initiates these blisters. Is it stress or physical contact with something? Or am I just too good for this world in all its rawness which we have ruined?

When I have a blister on my ear I can disguise it with a straw fedora, if it is summer; with a blister on my chin I can always stay away from my office and grow a beard for a week.

I am allergic – not phobic – to cut grass and the smell of lawn-mowers, to fibreglass shavings and to certain types of cheap processed cheese which cause irritation to the roof of my mouth. I am allergic to <u>all</u> man-made fibres (and inexpensive clothing, Veroña, my first wife, would rasp), though I can manage cotton-mix socks! All rougher wool, even lambswool, may be worn over cotton. Only cashmere scarves please. If I wear polyester or nylon against my skin I form a rash where my forearm meets my upper arm. I come out in flaky skin which bleeds when scratched: my wrists, my calves, across my shoulders or the back of my hands. Mother would cry a colourful phrase, which made even me wince: 'His skin has just opened up.'

My small blisters are really quite interesting. They are not particularly painful but begin with a hot, sharp sensation. I must try not to touch the spot but I always do, filled with mournful anticipation: the small red bump arises and, within the hour, begins to weep a little clear liquid. Each pinhead bead of blister spreads, seems to encourage up an adjacent burn, so the blistering expands, pinhead by pinhead, for the next hour, like anthrax, then, thankfully, it stops. After the blister is established, it produces a little orange-coloured liquid if burst and ends three or so days later, in a small terracotta scab. I cancelled the civil wedding of my second marriage, to Aracelli, for a week to allow a small blister on my chin to heal. I am a vain man who stares at himself in the mirror. Strangely for such deep blisters, they never leave any scars whatsoever on my healed skin.

When I was a six-month-old infant, my first ever blister, God's unique gift to me, did not stop. As it spread dangerously, more than 50 per cent of my skin was blistered as if down in kitchens of the Imperial Hotel I had been baptised in one of Chef's largest lobster pots.

I was admitted to the Children's Hospital. In the 1960s there was no specialist in our city so the chief dermatologist had to travel by train from the Capital city to my provincial ward to examine me. She was a lady specialist and fascinated with my case. To this day there has been no diagnosis of my official dermatological condition, nor a satisfactory explanation for the non-scarring of my skin. I still receive the odd request from aspirant doctorates of dermatology, who have seen my records back in the Capital city and are willing to visit if I will submit myself to a series of tests to assist them with their research papers. However, this would need to be timed with one of my rare, small blisters and all the letters have been signed exclusively by <u>male</u> medical students so why would I bother?

In the winter of 1964/65, the lady dermatologist, fascinated by my case, was travelling on the train from the Capital city almost weekly for the months of my hospitalisation; examining me and running tests. Years later Mother explained to me how the lady doctor slept on a spare bed in my private room, before her return to the Capital city. She often carried out her further academic reading in my hospital room, on a desk with an electric study lamp next to my cot. Mother told me the dermatologist's husband became convinced she was having an affair in our seaside city until he too took the train here to surprise her. He was put up in one of the sea-facing suites of the Imperial while his wife slept by my side in the hospital. Still not satisfied, the husband also spent a night on a spare cot in my hospital room. It was getting crowded in there.

Finally convinced of his wife's fidelity, he left for the Capital city. Even as an infant I was making husbands jealous, Mother joked.

I was never a crier. I was very quiet despite my little body gleaming in petroleum jelly, my stubby, fattened limbs moving restlessly on the greasy, pure white cotton, sliding away sections of my curdled skin.

As a teenager I asked Mother if the lady doctor was blonde: truly she was fair as few of our people are. In my imagination I see her unbinding and letting down that gold hair, sitting on the single iron bedstead next to my cot, leaning over talking to me, coming close but of course not to lift me. Unable to embrace me, unable to touch. Are these formative months why I am so desperately drawn to women's attentions in my manhood? Am I still in that cool hospital room, with the fair-haired lady doctor leaning to me, adoring, and I longing to be touched but, with her gold fringe hanging towards my blistered flesh, the woman's fingers always unwilling to make contact?

Then suddenly I was cured of my nocturnal scratchings. As I got older, my skin became more or less normal apart from the occasional minor blister. When I put my trust in Dr Tenis in later years I showed him a blister. Tenis studied it seriously and scribbled a prescription. Outside his surgery, in bright sun on my way to the pharmacy, I finally looked at his prescription which as I should have known, read only:

Job 2:8

I was actually impressed by Tenis's biblical scholarship, which seemed at odds with his show-off and fairly immoral lifestyle – the younger girlfriends, the suede jackets and black speedboat.

On the way back to my place in the Phases, I had to call in at Mother's apartment on Town Hall Plaza to look up Job 2:8 in her big old Bible.

> And he took himself a potsherd to scrape himself withal; and he sat down among the ashes.

Then I had to drop in to the Terrace of the Imperial café where they kept a large dictionary behind the bar for the crossword-addicted regulars. I looked up 'potsherd'.

The Lucky Searcher

After I smoked the last cigarette that first night out at the Phases Zone 1 there was nothing left for me to do. I poured a whisky and ice into my favourite, heavy-based glass and went to bed in a fruitless attempt to sleep. Strange, for I slept with a dreamless peace that surpassed all understanding. I cannot explain it, except perhaps only by way of my realising at last, after all the fretting, after all the pain of rejection and the confusion of acceptance, there was to be an organised end to me. That anxiety about the nature of my ultimate demise, which I have always borne, seemed to have vanished.

In the morning I took the train into our city as I do every weekday, watching the hair of the prettiest secretaries dry out in the warm air and change colour – often from dark to blonde.

Odd Saturday mornings and often local holidays too, I work – sometimes alone – at my Agency offices of Follana Design, 41 Grand Avenue.

It was a Tuesday so round the corner from the Imperial Hotel the small 'antiques' market was set up as usual beneath the porticoes in Town Hall Plaza, under the small balcony of Mother's old third-floor apartment. As was my regular habit on Tuesdays, I walked around there to browse; the Town Hall bell – the only music in my life – tolled its eternal tuneful quarterlies.

I have a wicked affection for old, badly written touristical guidebooks to our city, with their pompously strange grammar, their ridiculous local facts and the repetition of text translated into English, French and German languages – all of which I cannot speak or read, but I can pick out the odd word.

Standing at that old Old Ones' stall I discovered a guide book from 1964. As I was dying, I mused on the logic of pursuing my collecting hobby. What was the point? Then again, what ever had been the point of collecting discarded tourist guidebooks?

I read from the latest guidebook:

In the gulches, in the dry places beyond the outer outskirts of our city there grows the common fern which must be sought out by the rugged slopes. There the lucky searcher must sit down to watch how the little flowers open up at the first light of dawn upon which the lucky searcher's desires will be fulfilled.

Charmed, standing by the stall, I repeated the term to myself: 'the lucky searcher'. My lips almost certainly moved to the words. I had a sudden romantic notion if only once more I could coax a woman with me to those 'outer outskirts' and impose this new homily on her.

Also those phrases, 'the dry places', 'the rugged slopes', evoked Father's old peasant farm before he sold the bottom lands off to the motorway people.

As a young boy, Father and I skirted the orange and lemon trees of his old farm at dusk. Father would machete any snakes in those gulches. I remembered how the jaws of the chopped-off snake heads would still chatter madly. Sometimes, if he had cut them high up, it allowed light through the teeth from their severed necks. Father would kid me that the snake jaws would continue to snap and chatter, never falling still until after moonrise. 'Hoping to give him nightmares?' Mother would scold. But I slept soundly, in those days.

Father was always joking with me. That time on Madeira; just the two of us on holiday so he must have been fighting with Mother again. In a sudden rain shower Father nudged me, told me to cross over and get that taxi to turn round and collect him from beneath the hotel awning. I shyly crossed the road. The driver had his windscreen wipers going. He wound down his window for me. When I spoke to him, in my language and he in Portuguese, the word 'taxi' must have clinched it. The taxi driver began to laugh, showing his white teeth below a moustache, then he turned round on his driver's seat towards my laughing father, who nodded enthusiastically as if they both knew one another! There Father was, across that wet road beneath the pink awning of *Reid's Palace* in his beautiful grey overcoat which I still wear some winters. I looked further along the black taxi and then realised it was a hearse. I felt the blood rise into my face. By the time I had crossed back, the rain hid my tears.

In the stillness of the Tuesday market I could still hear Father's laughter, back in that metallic light with the bone moon high and hidden somewhere behind the scrubby peaks above his farm.

I spoke suddenly in our dialect. 'How much for this?'

Slowly the Old One lifted the guidebook and turned the rectangular pages as if the price was related to some antiquarian expertise of his.

'Five thousand?'

I jerked my head up to the little balcony of Mother's empty place which I still owned, above Town Hall Plaza, at the back of the Imperial Hotel. 'After being raised in that apartment, looking down on this market since I was a kid, you want a local boy's money at tourist prices?'

He looked up. 'It is a nice apartment. And a historical document!' he added.

'Nineteen sixty-four. The year I was born. Am I to be historical now?' I had raised my voice but we both understood the argument was playful. I held my arms out, the way people of my region do. I touched my left hand to my jaw, held the fingers near to my nose

and could smell my aftershave. I leaned in at the shy, smiling Old
One.

His wares were laid out on a trestle table topped with torn blue
baize, obviously from the recently refurbished casino. The wares
were identical to the other traders beneath the portico: Roman,
even Phoenician fake coins, oxidised with a battery and water to
age them – for sale to tourists who think they have made a discovery.
There were banal postage stamps from the 1980s and year-old newspapers, carefully enfolding foreign pornography magazines with
threatening-looking titles. There were useless, arcane books like
'Origin of the Air-Cooled Engine', but mostly I gazed at endless
amounts of photographic albums containing deleted currency in
notes and coins.

This was so typical of our city. Sundays, trade holidays you saw
them: grandfathers and widowers over fold-out tables, swapping
coins and collecting deleted currency by gas camping lamps after
nightfall, cheap chewed cigars rolling in their teeth. These Old Ones:
slippers, trousers too short, broken thread veins like magnified bacilli
on their pale ankles, growling deals and swaps over coin and note
trays. By possessing worthless five- and ten-thousand notes of a
deleted currency, since this crazy euro, these old men won some
hopeless vengeance back over the tyranny which money has
subjected them to all their working lives.

The Old One was staring at me. He announced, 'I knew Mrs
Follana and your father when they had the Imperial.'
I grunted.
'I remember the auction when your parents sold the place up.'
Now I nodded.

I did not like to be reminded. I was sixteen but I had wept, hidden
up in the penthouse above the hotel, while all the silverware, kitchen-
ware, linen, beds and furniture of my youth had been auctioned off
down in the big dining salon with the huge chandelier which faced
the fountain and the sea. Sometimes, ranging across the city,

grimacing on my way to a bathroom at some dinner party with vague business acquaintances, I still come upon the Imperial Hotel furniture: a display cabinet from the lobby, a lounger from halfway up the main stairs, a chair from the television salon where I used to lie on the tiled floor and watch our leader's speeches along with guests. (I can recall the cold tiles on my belly where my little towelling cotton shirt had ridden up, watching footage of the North American, President *Ford*, warmly visiting our fascist leader in 1975.)

Sometimes I would discover an escritoire from one of the sea-facing rooms. Like the night in the fields I met my first wife, Veroña, among her maths teacher father's lavender beds and his insanely painted beehives, the scent hanging like a mist at her bare waist level. In her single bed after our cunning, silent sex, I was unable to sleep as always when first with a woman. I watched Veroña's delicate face. Until dawn began also to reveal, standing on its six legs by her bedroom window: that table with carved elephant heads from room 88 which so fascinated me as a child! Sure enough, Veroña's father had attended the Imperial auction those few years before. Despite the fact she was a looker, I think that ridiculous, ugly table was partly why I married Veroña. And she kept it after our divorce too, though she understood it was once my parents'.

Yet when I think of that table, my eyes always begin to fill with tears and I feel pathetic. In this life, objects alone remain faithful, have mercy on us and survive our ruined relationships. Our emotion is shallow and we have forgotten what we once felt, then some object from the past – a butter dish – the existence of which you had forgotten, is sighted and it all flips us backwards in time, to broken promises. In fact, I would have liked that table returned now that I was ill and I made a mental note to phone Veroña! That hotel's furniture spread all over my city was like some lost Eden I was being challenged to reassemble.

'Ah, the great auction,' I nodded, unfairly angry. 'So, like me, you sleep in sheets embroidered with my father's initials?' I laughed to

26

take the edge off my cruelty but he looked worried and slightly hurt.

'Your father; a real gentleman,' the Old One muttered.

Instantly, his phrasing seemed to imply I was not. He realised that and looked uncomfortable. I knew he was trying to formulate the right words to cover up any implied insult. I do not even believe he meant it, but it was too late. I had taken my hand away from my face to show a vanished smile. I straightened up to my full height for I am tall and make use of it. In that instinctive movement of the wealthy, I took my wallet from my suit's inner jacket pocket. Long ago I realised there is as much aggression lurking in the act of spending money as there is in the act of infidelity. I took out a five-thousand note and jerked it at him. I dropped the dialect. 'May I have a receipt?'

'A receipt?' he replied, abandoning the dialect. He would never have filled out a receipt at this market in his life.

'Yes. Do you not complete tax returns?' I had now dropped the informal mode also. 'It is actually illegal to carry out any transaction without a receipt. I own an Agency so books and items like this are tax deductible. Why should I let any more of my money go to the socialists? Socialists need more money than anyone it seems to me.'

The Old One had nervously produced a piece of card but he was looking around, helpless. I reached in again for the Aurora fountain pen, which Veroña herself gave me for an anniversary and which I still use only for signing the important contracts and shipments.

'Other end.'

He removed the top, leaned over, scratched something then handed the piece of card to me. It read:

Book 5000.

He returned my pen. I felt a spurt of strong sorrow. He had written no date. I could add that later. 'Many thanks.'

'It is nothing.' He was smiling now.

I began to wonder if I had jumped to offence too quickly. Maybe he <u>was</u> once on friendly terms with Father who was no snob after all and would come down of an evening in his black suit, lean against the bar of the Terrace of the Imperial and talk to anyone, usually cleaning between his teeth using a common black thread from Mother's sewing box.

Once, after I had shyly stood by Father's side when he had gaily greeted and chatted with some business associates on the Grand Avenue, he leaned down and whispered to me, 'Manolo, people hold all the secrets of this city. If you do not talk to them you won't find out any of its secrets.'

Now I was holding the piece of card in my fingers. To make sure the ink of my fountain pen had completely dried. My suits are made with no lining for summer and with a very thin silk lining for winter. A dark ink contacting with the silk could be completely disastrous! When I was sure it had dried, I put the card inside my wallet.

I stepped away, holding the guidebook left-handed, caressing it with my thumb, my wide flat nail so similar to Father's. I was stepping ahead, deliberately not allowing myself to look at the guidebook as I moved between the Town Hall clerks' parked cars, making sure I did not make contact with their dusty bodywork. I crossed to that other Plaza side and beyond the tobacconist's at this end.

The guidebook, published in the year of my birth, was a true first-class specimen. A real discovery and maybe the jewel of my collection: wide like a calendar which might fold out; beneath the *Helvetica sans serif* lettering of our city name, it read in higher case: HAND-BOOK, reassuring us that everything in life was now well assured, simply because you held this guide in your hand! On the cover there was a very poor watercolour reproduction of the esplanade: its mosaic pavement, the scallop-shell concrete bandstand, the rows of date palms and the scattered, brightly painted Town Hall chairs for the Old Ones.

The real excitement though was within the cover: the brilliant colour of those inks, the basics of which must surely have been turned out on a hand *Gestetner*. I studied Design at university and I am interested in typography. Though I wrote my thesis on Design Flaw, it is always the perfect layouts and the accompanying signage of motorways, airports and hospitals which fascinate me.

I began looking for a café. Almost exclusively, I only use Cena's café. Cena's is on the esplanade, just down from the Imperial Hotel and the fountain, but it was a little far away. I was looking for some place that I would normally never enter.

A good cup of coffee is one of the central totems of my model region and it is incredible how hard it is to get one. These little cafés do not clean the machine correctly so the coffee tastes burned with little flecks of bean marauding round and round after you have stirred.

Just before the Grand Avenue, on the pedestrianised lane opposite the nougat shop, I saw crazy old 'Hallelujah's' place. He had been a figure around town since I was at school. I noted how the outside café chairs were made from the cheapest sort of white plastic, easy to lift in at night, yes, but with no drainage, so, in a torment, rainwater would gather in the well of each seat. In summer when red African rains come across the sea, I could perfectly visualise how, with this flawed design, the edges of the chairs' swiftly evaporated puddles would be reminiscent of the little ferrous smears of fertilisation you find inside chicken eggs. Also, I could not fail to see the silvery crescent of saliva on the pavement outside the café doorway, spat there by morning regulars so they would not disgrace themselves by spitting on the actual floor inside. I stepped within.

'Hallelujah,' yelled the crazy owner from behind the bar as he raised a bare arm, sleeve rolled up, and yanked a string. A network of goats' bells strung right across the ceiling rafters began to swing and clang together.

I said, not in the dialect, 'Coffee with a cut of milk.'

There were just two other customers at the bar, sitting on stools, each man with the city's morning paper open, spread out at the sports pages so the edges almost touched and either man could easily have moved his head slightly, read the other man's paper and saved money.

I grimaced up at the ceiling; some, linked with strings which hung taut through loops, were genuine rusted goats' bells but others were novelty bells, shaped like bull's testicles or women's breasts. I checked the shoulders of my suit because, with the ringing, little flakes of rust had pittered down from inside the bells in those low rafters. What an old dump.

Lined along a shelf behind the bar was a collection of plaster dildos with grotesque faces painted on them and there were the cliché collages of foreign money bills and, as usual, commemorative editions of our own currency, going back to when the fascists were still in power, with our leader's bald head visible, taped up among the bottles. Hanging above the bar was a fierce-looking birdcage with a stuffed green parrot inside; an ambiguous handwritten card inside the cage read: 'All Complaints to the Mayor'. The whole place smelled of wet wood trying to burn.

The radio was playing loudly from two stereo speakers. The local station was on – at high volume – the low timbre of the presenter's annoying voice, which you could tell he considered irresistible to all women and fascinating to all men, sounded deep from the speakers hung in the ceiling corners.

I find today's popular radio stations sinister. They remind me of the fascist days. Behind all their bluster and highly intense idiocy is a huge distracting silence. Such banalities conceal the dark machinations of the world. The meaningless noise of a radio station is a simple form of censorship. They talk so enthusiastically in order to say nothing. The breathless chatter between pop songs as if to cover up screams of torture in the next room.

I often imagine my ideal radio station. It would have huge sections of dead-aired silence; the rooms of your home would become tense with a kind of expectancy; then the 'presenter', when he or she actually had something worthwhile to say, would speak out a meaningful thought. Perhaps someone else would respond? Perhaps more silence? Perhaps just a ringing, like a Buddhist bell?

The radio presenter laughed. I hoped he secretly harboured profound and disturbing personal problems too.

I took the small coffee glass in its saucer from Hallelujah's hand, over the clear plastic snack display – which had nothing in it – then I stepped to the street window end of the bar. There was a table beside a dated poster of the city's football squad when that Salvador, who was never out of the nightclubs, was in goal. I placed the guidebook down on the table after checking it was clean, brushed the chair with the palm of my hand, then sat.

I began smoking *Marlboro Light* cigarettes with relish. An enormous pleasure had gone from my life these last two years on café terraces since I stopped smoking. In fact, for a brief period, without smoking, cafés came to seem the latest irrelevancy in my life which it appeared I might discard, the way, like old currency, I had deleted expensive cars (I cannot drive), travel, music, cinema, books and then love affairs from my life. But I believe strongly in the café and in café-terrace philosophy. I have learned more about the people of our city from sitting on café terraces than I have during my education or all my years in business.

When I graduated from university, I sat alone on café terraces for six months listening to the businessmen of my city talk about one another after each had left the table. By the end of those six months I knew all their business secrets and everything that was useful to me. In a sense Father was wrong and I was proved right. You need not talk; only listen and make each drink last an hour with two cigarettes, pretending to read a lofty novel, remembering to turn the pages at realistic intervals: then all the secrets of our city will be revealed unto you.

Since the death of my parents – Father first and very soon

after that, Mother – life has come to seem like a beloved jigsaw puzzle but with an irreplaceable piece forever missing. I even talked about it to Tenis, my doctor. He said I was in protracted mourning. I declared I was starting to feel God was fallible, like us; just a failed artist who had been unable to complete His masterpiece: Life. Death was the design flaw in His astonishing creation.

Even after saying that, Tenis did not prescribe me tranquillisers straight away. He did set me up on a date with his Belgian secretary who was extremely pretty but brunette. We kissed for half an hour outside her damn apartment but she never let me upstairs so she does not feature on the deleted list. She spoke our language perfectly and five or six others. She was just depressing.

The coffee was filthy so I only took a single sip. As I held the guidebook up, I made sure the cover was displayed, so to passers-by I would look like a tourist arrived both too early for the season and somehow forty years too late. I did not give a damn what those over at the bar thought of me.

I read quickly, skipping pages in excitement, my smile showing through the lifting degrees of cigarette smoke which was already making my mouth very dry. A beer would have been good but it puts on the weight. When I looked up from the pages I saw my cigarette smoke was at first blue against the clouds visible in that small section of sky at the top of the street window; the smoke changed to white as it snaked into the dark ceiling rafters and innumerable old bells.

Our city in its magnificent and sheltered bay is situated 38 deg. 20 min. and 54 sec. N. latitude and 3 deg. 2 min. and 24 sec. E. longitude and has a Mediterranean climate, and an average temperature of 63.6° F. According to the annual statistics, it has 179 days of sunshine, 144 slightly cloudy days and only 44 days are cloudy. The rains are very light.

This beautiful city was founded by Greek traders 2500 years ago.

In 1900, true progress began with port improvements. Then the city widened and opened new and large avenues and built their municipal buildings. The . . .

I grinned. Here was good bit:

The Typical Quarter at the foot of Heaven Hill with its typical streets adorned with a profusion of potted plants and flowers is very typical and is attractively illuminated at night and provided with many typically typical taverns.

!

. . . on the highway one finds this monastery in care of the nuns where is preserved and worshipped one of the linens on which Veronica dried the face of Jesus.

!

I turned to the English translation to see which words I recognised or even which sentences I might be able to read:

Celebrates . . . artistic groups . . . from midnight until . . . ? Distracting and innumerable all the world? . . . fireworks.

As I did many times each year I automatically thought, I really was going to have to get English lessons. But no. It was all too late. At least that – and damned driving lessons too – was finally out the window for good.

I read on and suddenly burst out laughing. The two men at the bar had glanced across when I chuckled before but now they stared as if it were them I was mocking, which in some strange way, I suppose, my laugh was. As if I considered myself some sort of prince of this unimportant and provincial city to which I was tied in every

33

way and in which I had truly been happy, yet at the same time to which I always felt aloof.

GASTRONOMY

As a main seaport, our city offers to its visitors a great variety of seafood dishes: Local Rice, Rice of Sea, Sea Rice and Fish Rice are popular savoury rice platters.

!!!!

A Beggar

I closed the guidebook then put it in a side pocket of my jacket. I stood, making a point of leaving the almost full coffee glass on my table rather than returning it to the counter. The crazy proprietor would now have to come around the bar to clear the table. If he bothered.

Even though I was obviously not a tourist, Hallelujah grunted, seized his cloth and with a bit of chalk scratched an inverted 150 on the wooden counter so the numeral faced me correctly. I looked at the price then I raised my eyes severely at him; he seemed to be muttering silently. I edged another 'five thousand' (what the people of our city call a fifty euro) out of my wallet and slowly placed it on the chalk numerals.

'Hallelujah!' the owner yelped.

As if I was in the least bit intimidated, the sports-page readers ignorantly chuckled as the owner chinged the till open, countered it with his belly and flicked out four 'one thousands' then picked at some coin. He laid my change across the chalk numbers on the countertop. I removed the 'one thousand' notes, placed them in my wallet then carefully lifted all the coins, sorting them into denominations so they formed a tube in my palm yet making it obvious I was leaving no tip. As soon as I lifted the last coin, old Hallelujah sliced a hot wet cloth across the countertop in an arc, obliterating those chalk numerals and producing that curious phenomenon when the wet shine unevenly evaporates in on itself like a thought being forgotten forever and leaving the dry, flaking, varnished countertop.

I slipped the tube of coins into my trouser pocket but the weight, with an annoying insistence, began to make the soft linen trousers pull unevenly at my belt buckle.

I stepped towards the street door then paused and looked up at the stuffed parrot in the cage. Addressing the stuffed parrot I said aloud, in dialect, 'The coffee here is lousy.' The two sports-page readers burst out laughing in what seemed genuine, enthusiastic amusement.

'Hallelujah,' yelled the crazy owner and I ducked out of the place before the ceiling bells behind me began to clatter louder than ever. Like, I thought, mad water eternally trapped in sea caves.

I looked up and down the Major both ways for no reason. I was weighing the clutter of loose change in my pocket thoughtlessly. I took out the euro coins and examined them. Each coin was of my country alone. The propaganda concept of euro change was that those coins of each country with their symbols would commingle throughout the whole European population – like our very blood in our coastal *discothèques* every summer as we sleep together. In the euro bankers' mad minds a pocketful of change was meant to contain coins from all the other euro countries and those places should have examples of the coin of my country. Other than in the luxury hotels of Europe where our politicians live, this was not happening – even in a tourist city like ours with an international airport, never mind some village in the mountains, the euro coins, like the Europeans, refused to commingle on any large scale. Even the receipts and bank balances of my country still defiantly showed the Old Currency – my accountant, Sagrana, delivered yearly business figures in both currencies. The people of our city all thought in the Old Currency. History and the way people think does not change so easily to convenience politicians.

I turned for a backward glance at Hallelujah's. Horribly, I knew

I would return to the café before they took me up to the ceme-tery on Heaven Hill because I felt sorry for that old man. I never did understand how unpopular cafés made any money. The mystery of their blue, metallic, fluorescent light in their cold spaces on winter nights created a haunted perspective through rigid, angular windows. Lonely figures stood helplessly at their bars. I shivered excitedly. Once upon a time I always used to spend my money in these dirty cafés, owned by widowers who realise they are going to go bank-rupt in a year and cannot cook or keep accounts. When a rare child comes in for a single ice cream, the parents notice whatever is removed from the fridge is well beyond its sell-by date. I feel a pathetic compassion for these men who have let themselves go, eating straight from the pan when they are alone. In truth they are running a sad café because they are lonely and it is the only way they can get company.

I crossed the Grand Avenue, still smoking cigarettes, and saw a young Moor sitting on the pavement against the back of the Dolphin restaurant, begging. He was very good-looking. I felt the change in my pocket which was annoying me. I sauntered over to the beggar's side of the narrow street.

'Spare anything?' he grinned.

I said, slowly and clearly so he would understand me, 'You think you are the only damned soul but we are exactly the same.'

'I bet the contents of our stomachs differ,' he wittily replied, speaking our language superbly.

'You speak well. Do you not have friends whose floor you could sleep on? Do we have to have our conscience pricked just because you are bad company? Mmm? Here.' I was tired of arguing the same points with beggars of my own nationality or illegals.

I took out my wallet and the beggar's face smiled up; he was holding a delicate hand to his forehead, shading the direct sun from his eyes, his palms pink. Folded in a tight square at the back of my wallet, behind a deep line of five-thousand notes, one remained. I took out the clean, folded white square of paper and handed it down to the Moor. Still sitting, without the courtesy to stand, he quickly stretched up a thin arm, the wrist bound in colourful bangles and took the piece of paper.

I walked on ahead – you had to be careful about their reaction – I was jingling the loose change in my trousers. I looked back and saw him carefully unfold the piece of paper as if it contained some kind of valuable powdered drug. When in fact it was an application form for employment in the esplanade *McDonald's*. I had photocopied it thirty times at my Agency, specifically for distribution to the beggars of our streets.

DC-8-61 *stretch series*

I was a spoiled, indulged child. Though I dabbled around the Imperial Hotel, I soon wearied of every little job I was given by my parents. I liked to fill coffee pots from the hot-water boiler, I liked to wash out the silver teapots with that unique, metallic scent of a washed-out pot. I liked to switch on the big dishwasher, I liked to watch Chef light the ovens each morning and peel the potatoes in the shaker machine, or I pretended I was supervising the laundry hampers which the men from the big white lorry brought and took away. I never really <u>had</u> to work for a little pocket money like other children at my institute, who could be found stacking shelves in a supermarket or looking after little brothers and sisters. As an only child I luxuriated in layers of free time and I spent it all in my elaborate childhood games.

Father took me aside one day and said, 'Lolo. Are you going to become a lawyer or are you going to become a doctor?'

'I am going to become an airline pilot.'

Father smiled. On the day of the Three Kings, the Three Kings of the Orient themselves had brought me the plastic model kit of a DC-8-61 *stretch series* airliner. In the toy department of our best department store, I had first seen the big box and, illustrated on its lid, the curiously long, unaerodynamic-looking DC-8 with the English words: *stretch series*. It was soaring through blue skies in airline livery, courting puffy clouds, the ochre grid system of an airport's runways and its *art deco* control tower far down beneath the right wing's engines.

I was in love with that toy jet immediately and lay dreaming about it. I felt my life would be perfect if I could take responsibility for that plane on its stand, sitting on my bedroom clothes cabinet, the DC-8's black nose pointed fifteen degrees skyward. I vowed if I owned the plane, I would polish it devotedly every night with a dedication I could not show to my token chores around the hotel. I talked to my father of little else but the toy jet.

But on the day of the Three Kings when I unwrapped the box then excitedly opened the lid, my face soured, reddened and I was crying. The model aircraft was all in pieces. I had expected the complete, streamlined, strangely overlong aircraft ready-made, there in my hand to fly up and down the corridors of the hotel. All I had were unconstructed wings, lots of silly little parts, a glue tube and tiny paint pots lovingly dropped into the box by attentive sales assistants. I never understood the assembly and painting of plastic model kits using horribly complex instructions was intended to be some sort of pleasure. Greedily, I could not rationalise why young boys would go through all that when, the truth was, every boy just wanted that finished aircraft to play with, looking exactly as it did on the lid illustration. I wailed, tears were on my hot cheeks. What an ungrateful, spoiled little brat.

To try to save the situation and doubtless get some peace, Father descended from our penthouse at the top of the hotel to the dining salon which was packed for Three Kings lunch. The big box of the model plane was in his arms as he nodded to various notable diners. He took the youngest waiter aside. Together they carried in an extra table to the dining room and father ordered the young waiter, who was a student of engineering at the university, to build and paint the DC-8 model aircraft immediately. The waiter pointed out that it was one of the busiest days of the year. Father told him the model was made for children so surely he could construct it between serving tables. 'My son's holiday is tears. Build it. You are an engineer, are you not?'

The unfortunate young waiter assembled the plastic aeroplane in between serving plates held above his head, twisting open wine bottles, fetching more bread and clearing dishes away while shouting bar orders for soft drinks or wine. With grabbed moments he sat alone at the spare table being stared at and catcalled by the diners. Perspiration dripped from his face. He frowned at the assembly instructions, carefully applying the glue to the aircraft parts and shaking the little pots of enamel paint in preparation.

A rear tailplane was found stuck to the side of a dinner plate and had to be recovered. Glued to the side of a wine glass, an undercarriage door was sent back with a complaint. 'Fantastic, part 16, I thought I had lost it,' the waiter called out aloud. The head waiter smacked him on the ear so the waiter's overlong hair jumped. In the young waiter's haste to build the model aircraft, an olive was sealed inside the glued fuselage and for years I could hear its shrivelled flesh and the stone roll from the cockpit to the tail as my plastic DC-8 *stretch series* went into an uncontrollable dive or a steep climb.

The last tables were being brought their desserts and *flambés* but the solitary young waiter still toiled alone at his odd table. His bleached and pressed white tunic had the words 'The Imperial' and the hotel emblem of a big fountain embroidered on the breast pocket. The sleeves and cuffs were dashed with bright blue and silver airline livery paint. The thumbed lenses of his glasses and the skin just below his eyes were marked with paint. With a tiny brush, the waiter applied finishing touches. The model's wings and rear fuselage were balanced on three wine glasses and using *Sellotape* from behind the concierge's desk, the young waiter had made dead straight paint lines out along the big wings. Using ash from the kitchen ovens he had indicated discoloration at the jet engine exhausts; by dipping the decals in a cold glass of wine he had applied the airline name along the side of the fuselage. I stood, my arms held out in joy – it was an exact replica of the aircraft on the box lid which he had used as his example down to the closest detail! Yet I was not allowed to touch the model plane with its wet paint.

41

Perhaps I felt then like my mother and the dermatologist had as they reached out for my little body those years before but were unable to touch my blistered skin which healed so beautifully. With string which Chef normally used to hang a dried leg of gammon, they suspended my DC-8 *stretch series*, out of my reach, from the grand chandelier in the dining salon. This crystal chandelier on the ceiling was so big it had to be brought in by boat when the hotel was built at the turn of the century. Father switched off the chandelier's lights, 'So moths and mosquitoes won't be attracted in and stick to the wet paint tonight,' Chef sombrely noted.

We all stood looking up in appreciation at the DC-8 *stretch series'* silver undersides and the marvel of North American engineering. The last tables of the diners clapped and saw Father slip a five thousand – in those days more than his monthly wage – into the waiter's paint-stained hand where it stuck on the glue.

Cena's Palm Tree

I wandered aimlessly. Along at Encina Real's jeweller's was a balding man who I recognised as from behind the counter in our main post office. He was gazing into the window of the jeweller's. In a telltale move he suddenly held up his arm to read his own watch. Instantly I thought to myself, he is looking at watches he cannot afford. Passing by him and glancing in the window I was proved right. There was a display of *Omegas* hung on a felt tower which was certainly not there last week. He was comparing the time on his own watch to the variety of unsynchronised phantom times displayed by the selection of watches.

And along from the jeweller's was the lingerie shop which has itself paid for the handsome stone bench outside. This is because so many men will not accompany their girlfriends or wives inside, they would lose custom if they did not provide somewhere for the men to sit in the street smoking and waiting.

I turned hard left down the dark passageway towards the light coming off the marina waters. Striations of vertical yacht masts cluttered the white clouds that were out to sea far beyond the angular roofs of the pier development and the huge yellow funnel of the African ferry. I heard the wet slap of the distant ship's ropes as they were pulled aboard then the voice of the pier public address system speaking out a tape of Arabic.

As I came out the lane the upper sky vanished into the palm-tree bushels of the esplanade, their hovering blades just yawing and no more. The long leaves were black against the sun but as always held silver on their edging. There was so little wind not a single yacht mast rope snapped. I remembered the weekend: I had seen a celebratory party on a tethered yacht, figures dancing on deck. That mast had tipped ever so slightly.

I had come to the esplanade but of course, for the first time in my life, I felt no enthusiasm for going to my Agency. The large tube of change in my pocket that I had not given to the Moor beggar was annoying me. The perfect excuse to go to Cena's to spend it! I turned and strode on the landward pavement in the opposite direction of my office.

I passed the hospice, its row of porticoes facing first the pavement then the wide mosaic walkway of our city's famous esplanade with its double row of old date palms. The marina National road was heavy with traffic.

I saw some Old Ones in their pyjamas, leaning over the slightly elevated ground-floor balconies of the hospice pretending they were taking an interest in the passing world, but face facts: they were just keeping out the way of the nuns so they could sneak a secret cigarette. I found myself looking down at the new terracotta paving tiles beside the flower beds where the mosaic of the old walkway began. The flower beds had been watered at dawn, the hoses coiled up for tomorrow at the bases of the palm trees and their reptilian plates of bark. Puddles with dark edges still shone on the mosaic.

I noticed scores of cigarette butts flicked from the hospice balconies had rolled into the grooves between each of the new terracotta paving tiles. The cigarette filters' slim diameters fitted perfectly and deep enough to escape the electric-powered esplanade sweeper machine each dawn.

If those fools at Town Hall and the idiot designers had known this characteristic of these particular tiles they could have, with local knowledge, anticipated this. It was as my thesis on Design Flaw argued. There must be a pre-existing, specific relationship between the designer and the particular environment his design is being imposed

44

upon. Here they did not consider the number of cigarette butts being thrown on the ground due to the proximity of a hospice, and the depth of sealant around the tile was fundamentally flawed anyway.

I realised I had paused, staring down at the ground right in front of an ancient Old One with his threadbare-looking dressing gown over pyjamas; he held his brown face in the morning sun. I was lighting another cigarette.

'Going to be a fine, fine day, son.'

'Looks like it,' I said, not really agreeing, and blew out smoke.

The Old One touched his silver crew cut with arthritic fingers and announced, 'They cut my hair too short.'

'Ah.'

'So they won't have to wash it so much. Iñes would not have liked it this short.'

'It will soon grow,' I said, like an idiot.

'Yes,' he lied.

'Sure.' I wondered if I should tell him. I had seen the same, slightly fierce vigour in the eyes of both Father and Mother, as I sat at their bedsides watching each of them slowly die. I wondered if he looked back at it in my eyes.

The Old One said, 'Yes. Plenty, plenty time.'

He was obviously terrified.

'Hey, be a saint and bring me a glass of . . .' and he said the English words '. . . *Johnny Walker* over from the café?'

'Cannot, Grandad. I do not know what medication you are on. It is not good for you.'

'I have the money.' He nodded his head back to his room behind him.

'I would buy it for you, sir, but your damn doctors would have me shot. I have to rush.'

'Good day, son.'

'See you later.' I stepped onwards.

I walked quickly up to Cena's café, almost opposite the fountain and my parents' old hotel. I had nearly circled on myself that morning. What an illogical route I had taken. A left on the corner, bringing you opposite the side-street entrance of the Imperial Hotel, would take you back to Town Hall Plaza, the porticoes and the Tuesday market where I had bought the guidebook.

I moved in beneath the permanent awning of Cena's, with its specially cut holes to allow the palm-tree trunks to go on up through, dropping their festering dates with reassuring bumps on top of the canvas which draws the tourists' glances upwards while regulars do not even lift their face from their newspaper at the sound. A way of telling if a pretty girl is local or not on the terrace of Cena's; the same way you can tell a pretty girl is not local when she looks both ways stepping out into traffic on the one-way Grand Avenue.

I pulled out then wiped the metal seat of my favourite table by the ice-cream fridge one row in so I would not be immediately pounced on by passing gypsies or beggars, palms held open.

That new young waiter – a slightly superior attitude – began to move towards me but there was old Franco himself, usual stub of unlit cigar in the side of his mouth. He held up his hand when he saw it was me. Franco worked a good few seasons for Father in the Imperial when I was a kid; Franco saved money, sold land from the old farm like all of us original peasants and mortgaged Cena's in the seventies.

Led by his impressive big belly, tight in a button-strained white shirt, Old Franco moved through the down swipes of fluorescent banding. He reached, without taking his eyes from my table, to collect his metal tray which was jammed at an angle into a deep groove cut by a saw in the trunk of Cena's palm tree. There were two further rusted waiter's trays, jammed in the tree trunk above Franco's at about four, then beyond the awning at six metres higher up. Seven metal trays in all are stuck in that palm tree at various heights. These serving trays had remained lodged in their traditional storage slots where, like closing lips, the tree-trunk bark had eventually tightened then seized them forever, even bent one backwards like a wet biscuit – all since the departures of every previous head waiter of Cena's. Right back to Mr Cena himself in 1881. Each tray which jutted out of the big old palm, like a disc of tree fungus, was rising higher and higher with every decade of growth. Cena's own ornate silver-plated top tray, which they say he served King Alfonso VIII off, was now so high up by the date clumps that it was sometimes nested on by the escaped parrots who breed in our city to the detriment of the clean awning beneath.

'Lolo, child, how is business?'

'Mr Franco.' I slid back my chair and stood to shake his hand. You only knew Franco was smiling when you saw the bristly grey hairs on his moustache react first. 'Have you been on holiday?' I said.

'Two months out on the old orange groves tidying up. Television in the garden at nights to watch the football. Heavenly. How is business. Really?'

'Good.' I nodded, solemn and serious as I always am when I talk business, my voice dropping. Suddenly I felt serene. The order and the way things were in our city would go on. Just because I was dying there was no sense being completely crazy. Business had to go on. 'Interiors does best,' I stated. 'Francesco: Kiko Bonzas has it all handled brilliantly. We do three units on the Pier Development,' I pointed over, 'which is difficult trying to get them looking distinctive but each uniquely my style.'

'What is that, restaurants, cafés?'

I counted on my fingers, 'A bar for young ones, a café, and a restaurant that Bonillo's son has, Bonillo: has the Seagull.'

'Yes. Of course. I know him.'

'We do not deal direct with them – it is more simple for us to go through the Pier Development. They get grants from Town Hall anyway. It is Kiko's side of it, not mine, but we are doing the interior of some famous nightclub in the Capital city.'

Somehow Franco whistled around his short cigar stub. 'The Capital city, eh?! Good, Lolo. You do us proud. And our city too. No new Mrs Follana?'

47

I held up both my hands. 'I am the model of innocence.'

'Bachelor life.'

'Not worthy of the word. Cook for myself in the evenings, I am getting good. Mary, a South American, comes to do the cleaning. Life is just perfect without women getting involved.'

He snarled a laugh. 'Will you take something?'

'Coffee with a cut of milk please, sparkling water – no ice.' I looked back towards the hospice. 'And,' I used the two English words, 'a *Johnny Walker*, no ice.'

'At once.' Old Franco stepped away.

I took out my small mobile phone which does not spoil my jacket hang but has to be so slim the dialling keys are minuscule. I scowled sceptically at it as I tenderly pressed in my Agency number. Kiko answered.

'Chief. You are not in again today.'

'Is the new person there?'

'Upstairs going through the computers with Fide.'

'What is she like?'

'A looker, chief.'

'What is she like?'

'I think she will do good . . .'

'What is her portfolio like?'

'Did you not look at it at the interview?'

'No. We talked about *Mies van der Rohe*.'

'Oh.'

'Does she have her portfolio with her?'

'She does. She brought it in on her scooter somehow. I only opened it. I thought the furniture was hippie but I liked her graphics.'

'Really? I am in Cena's on the terrace. Send her over.'

'Send her? To Cena's?'

'With her portfolio.' I hung up.

Old Franco reapproached with his tray held horizontally, the tall glass showing next to the sparkling water bottle, the coffee invisible he held the tray so high, but the rim of the heavy-based whisky glass could just be seen.

'I have a good one for you,' he said, moving the tall glass, then the water bottle and a saucer of little biscuits down with swift darting motions on to my table. 'Three idiot councillors were at table sixteen talking about the doves, how they come and mooch crumbs and snacks from the tables, how their droppings are destroying the façade of Santa Maria's but most of all they were complaining that the doves of our city are not as white as they used to be, when they were children.'

I chuckled cruelly and declared, 'Scientific miracle. Councillors overcome by nostalgia.'

Franco laughed solidly. 'They seriously started discussing how the Environment Department should capture all the doves of the city and shampoo them or even paint them before the tourist season proper begins. Out came the notebooks and they were jotting down the idea to put forward at the next meeting, which we pay for.'

We both laughed. Franco put down the coffee, then neatly arranged the whisky glass in behind the coffee saucer. He trapped the receipt under the ashtray so it could not blow away. I glanced to my right, along towards the hospice. Slowly I lifted the *Johnny Walker* whisky to my own mouth and drank it down.

The young woman in her twenties, I remembered from the interviews, wearing interesting clothes and holding a large portfolio, walked by my table at Cena's. I groaned. She looked delicious, irresistible the way they all do at that age when you first see them, before all their faults are known to you and their faces become familiar and they do not seem as angelic as at first they did. And by then they know your faults and physical imperfections.

She had a brightly coloured motorcycle helmet awkwardly held under her other arm but her name escaped me.

'Hey.' I held up my hand.

She spotted me, smiled, lowered her fringe and moved towards my table. It was then I remembered her name. Teresa. She barged and skreeked through several metal chairs to reach me so I stood up to pull back a chair and assist her to my table. I kissed her on each cheek.

'Teresa. Why did you bring that?' I nodded to the helmet. It had a neon pink colour but at the top was badly scratched and scuffed so you could see the bare alloy beneath. She had obviously had this helmet since she was thirteen or fourteen years old.

'I took my scooter. I thought you were going to sack me so I was going home,' she said quickly and cheerfully.

I was stunned. 'On your first day? Is that what they told you at the office?'

'Yeah. Kiko said that was probably why you wanted to see me.'

Little viper, I thought.

Though the café was very quiet and there were no customers anywhere near us, she put the motorcycle helmet down but on the next table. That annoyed me for some reason.

'They are teasing you.'

'You are not going to sack me?'

'No. I liked what I recall of your portfolio.'

She sat down across the table and burst out crying then moved her arm up to her mouth and eyes. I looked around me. It is difficult to deny I had been looking forward to sitting there with my whisky, pontificating on design theory to my attractive new, young female employee. But in seconds it seemed obvious to onlookers, even to Franco and the young waiter, that Teresa and I had been having an affair and I had broken it off. I was embarrassed. Abruptly she stopped blubbering.

'Sorry.'

I could see Franco did not know whether to approach the table or not. I waved him over, too enthusiastically. My eyes were darting around in an alarmed way. I think I was flushed in my face. It was obvious I cared more about Franco's opinion than the young woman's feelings. So what? That was true. Franco came up behind her.

'Mr Franco. Teresa from work was told I was going to sack her on her first day. Kiko Bonzas has been up to his old tricks.'

The girl smiled weakly. Franco chuckled. 'That cannot be the truth. What would you like to take, dear?'

'You better have something strong.' I lifted my whisky, jiggled it then took a sip.

'Oh, camomile tea.'

I looked at Franco. 'Do you sell such poison?'

'At once.' Franco turned, flicking his tray which flashed.

'Ah, no,' she said.

Franco stopped.

'I will take a little of that stuff . . . whisky.' She almost whispered.

Neither Franco nor I spoke. Franco nodded seriously, then walked onwards.

'Camomile. Dangerous. It slows down the heart,' I said and leaned forward. 'You never heard about the guy up in the mountains in that communist town?'

She shook her head. She was deadly cute.

'Every day for twenty years he had come into the café of the town plaza. He went from two cups of camomile tea a day to four, to ten, eventually he was on twenty cups an afternoon. Then one day, for the first time in his life – for he was a communist – he went quiet. Someone poked him with a finger and he fell off his bar stool. Dead.'

She giggled nervously.

'Camomile tea. Stopped his heart. My best friend knows all the pathologists round here. He is a respected doctor. A specialist.'

'Everything in moderation?' she yelped.

'Sure,' I smiled and I raised the whisky to my lips once more. I stooped my shoulders to feign information imparted in confidence. 'My first wife – I am divorced – she remarried and this was with her second husband. Suddenly she was expecting.' I winked. 'Fennel tea this time.'

'Eh? Never.'

'Well, obviously not just fennel tea but the point is that too much fennel cancels out the effects of the birth control pill. My doctor friend confirmed it.'

'You know,' she turned round, 'I think I will have a <u>very</u> big whisky. It is safest.'

I laughed out loud. 'You seem better now?'

'Yes thanks. Had to find a new flat. And everything. Awful.'

'Where are you of?'

'Here. Here. Our city.'

'You did Design at the university here?'

'Yes. With Mr Cristobel. You know him?' she quickly added.

'Sure. An oaf. What do you think?'

'He has old ideas.'

'He <u>has</u> old ideas. You know I am not impressed by all that. An *Alessi* kettle. *Memphis* furniture. Design is not stuff <u>just</u> for millionaires. Think of your house. Your new flat. Think what works in it.'

'Nothing.'

'Perfectly. Whatever works perfectly. <u>That</u> is design. Everything else is just. Well, it is just. Garbage. You agree?'

'You are a utopian!' She raised her eyes, surprised. 'I . . . can be seduced by beautiful designs, even useless ones.'

'You can be seduced by design in the library but not at my Agency. Sorry but it is true if you are going to work for me. Save your masterpieces for your own time,' I said. 'Name one of your favourite pieces of design. Practical, not fancy high-concept stuff.'

'OK. Let me think.' She looked out across to the marina. She <u>was</u> deadly cute. 'Those metallic, plastic laminated frames which clip on to radiators to hold items: towels or shirts or whatever, close to the radiator to dry, but not resting on the radiator itself and blocking its heat. Completely perfect design. Great for drying knickers.' She sort of sneered.

I did not pause but nodded quickly in agreement and pointed to her. 'You are right. Total harmony between function and design with no frills.'

'You?' She stared at me.

'More of a concept. The designer who decided to dye the last ten sheets of tissue papers in a box a different colour to warn the consumer the box is about to be emptied and it is time to buy another. That is brilliance.' I continued, 'Also, in the sixties, during the race to get to the moon: the North Americans against the Russians; they call the North American space programme, in English, *NASA*; the North Americans spent millions of dollars, <u>millions</u>, trying to develop a pen that would write in zero gravity. The Russians? They used a pencil. That is the essence of good design.' I leaned back proudly.

Concerning The Phases Zone 1

In my neighbourhood, the Phases Zones, there are three small railway 'stations'. All are just a raised concrete platform with a moulded plastic seat and shelter, a route map and timetable. The stations of my neighbourhood are: Phases Zone 1, Phases Zone 2 and Phases Zone 3. I live in Phases Zone 1 but it is actually closer to Phases Zone 2 station so I utilise that but sometimes if I have shopping bags and the train is quiet, I knock on his door and ask the train driver to drop me directly behind my building.

I love the Phases most under the first starlight of dusks when it is the off-season and 80 per cent of the holiday buildings are un-occupied. There is a wonder to this structure, completely abandoned by this sea. I have never seen such clear light, as if I was inside a huge, minutely quivering lens. The rigid cuboids and geometries of the new apartments around me – some with large satellite dishes pointed at the moon and occupying their entire balcony so nobody can sunbathe there – are like a honeycomb of monks' private cells in a modern seminary with private spiritual exercises being conducted within.

Development of the Phases began in the early 1980s when property prices made it worthwhile to blast foundations beyond the pink rocks which curve away at the end of the sand beach. My mother, who grew up in our city, used to say about all the new construction around St Jordi's on the way towards Kilometre 4: 'If you left me out there after dark I would not know where I was anymore.'

My building was the first built of the three blocks, so although less elevated than the other two, my place juts forth directly on to the sand and sea rather than the raised beach of rocks. Several times in the fifteen years I've lived there, high storm tides have pushed up around the base of my building, flooding the cellars. Wet sand has been driven to the height of the reflective red strips on the bollards of the rear car park. We have been trapped behind the waterline, the grey water churning noisily four storeys beneath as if I were the lone survivor on some oil rig. The next day the water would have receded and all the windows had to be washed of salt spray by Mary, the old South American lady who cleans for me.

When Veroña and I married in the eighties we were given the Phases sea-facing apartment by Father – who owned the top-floor – as a wedding present.

We were a young couple who owned no cooking pots. Constant construction was still going on in the areas around the Phases. Father had the apartment interior completely re-formed for us. I believe he was expecting us to have children so a new bathroom was constructed and a room we forever called the 'Nursery', laughing each time we said the word. Father hired builders who were working on an adjacent site until the *faux*-marble stairs to the top floor were so encrusted with thick, dried cement boot-prints that it took years for all the traces to wear away and some still remain.

When Veroña and I lived together in the Phases, remote cranes by the unfinished buildings awoke us, creaking and squealing as they turned out of the prevailing wind at seven each morning. Swivelling skips of concrete floated in ascending sweeps, up towards the shouting builders, shirtless on roofs beside unrendered salmon-pink brick. Mysterious electric wires seemed to sprout from every un-finished surface.

The day's passing was marked out in sudden white clouds of

concrete dust blowing between the buildings. Yellow trucks moved silently and if the wind was strong, top-dust skimmed off their heaped open loads. In the afternoons the sea seemed to grow louder as the building workers took their siesta. They slept, urinated and defecated in the denuded frames of the buildings.

Veroña and I would step naked out the shower — sometimes together — and always feel the concrete dust on our feet from the floor tiles. Our recently completed apartment was bare and echoed. Concrete dust was in our hair, it coated Veroña's and my skin. It made our nostrils itch and dulled the white ends of cotton buds from inside our ears. When we sweated as we made love, we could have solidified into grey statues we were so coated in concrete. It speckled our coffee in the mornings and alkalined our salad in the evenings. As a symbol, concrete dust, with its flat chalky taste, its oddly sharp smell, was a celebration of progress, a drawing under of our past. Instead of floury wafer, our city should have formed a new consecrated Host for Mass from its concrete powders, for we worshipped only the future. The Phases Zone I concrete apartment had been built using Father's compensation money from the huge concrete motorway twisting down our coast. I was a first-year Town Planning student who dreamed of concrete's possibilities — its living chemical warmth as it sets, and I would lick this dullness, the base material matt of our speculative world, from my young wife's arm to see the true burnish of her living skin resting beneath. Our pale tan of concrete dust was a celebration. Veroña and I were physically becoming part of our concrete future, part of the voracious coastal development and the determination of our new society to range us all in a hierarchy of sea views.

The Hatred Of Travel

Teresa held up her second glass of *Johnny Walker* to toast me. 'I grease my ass with soap and slide down a rainbow backwards,' she announced. I lifted my glass deferentially. She took a swallow from her glass not a sip, then quickly spoke: 'I saw you in that magazine. It said you got the Design prize for your thesis. What was your thesis about?'

'Design flaw.'

'In what?'

'Everything. Airliners crash. Doorknobs fall off. There is a consistent philosophy to design flaw. Anyway, I think we need doorknobs but not airliners. I hate to travel.' I muttered the last sentence.

I was feeling my familiar reaction to the presence of young women. That helpless effort to appear attractive and to say exactly the right things.

'You hate travel!?' She paused. 'But I would love to travel, to the . . .' She hesitated, not truly knowing where she wanted to go . . . 'Far East. Thailand, India . . . Australia. Those places.'

I had killed the cat again. I tried laughing as if I were kidding and my beliefs were available for ridicule. Anything for a pretty girl. Why is it I demand that those I am attracted to must immediately share my beliefs? I said, 'Young lady. What the hell do you want to go to Australia for? Nothing there. No history. Little culture. What has Australia to do with you? I will refuse to give you the time off.'

'Have you been to Australia?'

'A twenty-four-hour plane journey! I would sooner do the pilgrim's walk.'

She looked genuinely mystified and began clumsily to light up another cigarette. She said the English words – perhaps trying to be the clever linguist but I knew what they meant.

'*The Great Barrier Reef?*'

'Lousy with sharks. You will be eaten.'

She laughed, as if I were playfully adopting a contrary position.

I was forty. This Teresa must have been twenty or twenty-one – I could not recall from her application form. Sometimes hard to tell with local women. In our city they grow in the sun and on the beach so our women show lines around their eyes earlier than Northern Europeans. She could not have been older than twenty-two, I thought. Murderer.

I shrugged and looked away from her. Dreamily, but anguished, I announced, 'Just this morning, in front of the hospice I noticed that the new tiles the Town Hall have laid down there are not satisfactory.'

'Oh.'

I began to explain the entire conundrum and principles involving the cigarette butts, the new tiles and God alone knows in front of the hospice.

When I finished Teresa only said, 'They are smoking in the hospice?' She seemed to pause for thought, blink and said, 'Such a sad place to die. The view across all those beautiful yachts.'

Interesting. I had not thought of that. I leaned back.

I noticed each and every time before she spoke, how she hesitated on the first word while executing a tiny, prolonged and thoughtful blink. It was a terribly attractive tic. This was unbearable. How could I ever go on in the world? I inwardly admitted. To study that blink up at close quarters. Repeatedly, again and again to make energetic love to my new employee, Teresa, age twenty-something, from about midnight until about one o'clock the following afternoon was the impossibility I needed.

'Do you really hate travel? Never met anyone who hates travel.'
It was true I did.

I told Teresa that even as a child I never felt comfortable when
we went away on holidays to other unfamiliar hotels. Sadly, some
of the hotels were vastly superior to our little provincial place and
our familial pride was always quietly troubled in grand dining rooms
during our time of rest.

As a child, each day away from our city I imagined my toys,
frozen still, back home in my bedroom: the DC-8 *stretch series*. My
die-cast metal cars and the plastic garage, my meticulously planned
road layouts using cleaned granite chips stolen from a roadworks site
– which obsessed me as a child. As an adult a feeling of uneasiness,
of life being incomplete, was always with me until I returned to our
city. I faced up to the fact I was a hopeless provincial long ago.

In my first weeks in the Capital city at university, though I did
not tell my first wife, Veroña, I dreamed – awaking in sweat – again
and again of our home town and its streets, castle and the heights
of Heaven Hill. I saw a conceptual view of our city from the sea
though I had never taken the African ferry out of our city. Why
should I? What was over there in Africa? So few things made by
hands of thoughtful men. If these damn teenagers like Teresa were
so committed to travel, why not step on our African ferry and,
when they disembark, keep walking forever? Rwanda for back-
packers. That would be good for them. They think they want to
see the world as it is but that is a lie. They only want the exotic
edits of the world and part-time reality. Travel is an opium lie.

I leaned forward. 'I detest travel. You know the overwhelming
emotion I feel when I travel? Humiliation. Humiliation in airports
and strange places, all for what? To get back home and momentarily hesitate about where your light switches are? It is one of the
many big fake romances of modern life. The idea that a new landscape will change my life I simply find ridiculous. New landscapes
will change nothing within me. Much as I admire . . .' (and I said
the words in English, though there can be no accounting for my

pronunciation) . . . '*Total Design* signage at *Schiphol* airport . . .'

'Mmmm. Me too,' she nodded quickly.

I continued . . . 'Jet travel has destroyed the world. Do you really think human beings have become better people since the fifties because we can get places quicker? Travel! You would have more true adventures by walking around our city here. Or walking five miles instead of taking . . .' I nodded at the helmet '. . . your scooter. There are tourist ships to Antarctica now. People should be arrested for daring to go there.'

The poor girl. Drinking the whisky, I went on, unable to stop myself explaining it all to her. How she was too young to recall but it was the extension of our city's airport – not travel itself – which had the most profound effect on my youth.

When I was around eight the airport which lies on the salt flats to the south of our city was enlarged. They drained and ploughed over drying pools of Roman origin but that kind of thing was easily covered up in those days at Town Hall.

The investment in tourism development by the fascist government was huge then. The green excavators which put ashore from actual landing craft on Lacas beach were matt-green military ones from anchored navy ships. As if expecting war, they pushed a mile of soil towards the sand dunes at Lacas, extending the old existing runway and widening the taxiways. The old French mail planes to Africa still landed there in the seventies. At the same time, a long, sub-*Corbusier* terminal was constructed with its pseudo-Romanesque mosaics decorating the interior: post-cubist, 'simple fishermen', shovelling a conglomeration of non-species on to the golden shore, the antiquity of the medium jarring with the representation of the wobbly stem of a tourist's sunshade stubbed in the sand.

As a kid, that year, any free moment Father had, my treat was to be driven out to the airport construction down some waste track of red earth where the suspension of my bored, grimacing Father's

Daimler swung us from side to side so my ear hit the passenger window. When installed for the start of that season, the night-time instrument landing system with its high-intensity lights lit up the mosquito pools all the way to the sand dune crests where the new five-storey apart-hotel on Lacas beach had red warning beacons fitted to its roof.

It was an anonymous copywriter at the old Ministry of Tourism and Information in our military government who created that poetic masterpiece: Tourism is the Flower Which if Tended Grows in Every Country. The development of tourism on our coasts exploded in the sixties and seventies along with cheaper jet travel. All the apartment and hotel construction was heavily encouraged and often subsidised by the fascists. As far as our fellow Europeans were concerned, it was a willing exchange of democracy for suntans in those days. Our new airport was one of the main gateways to the foreign package holiday tourists flowing to and from our country. People forget this society was formed by a police state. In those days tourists did not stay. Tourists of the northern countries came for a fortnight each year. A civilisation developed along our coasts based on two-week visitations. We built ourselves a society where all possibilities were exhausted after fourteen nights of sleep. This was reflected in the architecture, design and attitude in the society around us. We ourselves forgot in the 1960s as we adopted features of this two-week world that we had to stay forever.

Then came the villas and holiday homes of the people of the northern countries and then from our own cities – our *bourgeoisie* who wanted to imitate the strangers. Everyone in the Western world today is so vain that we demand to stand above our own little private *St Tropez* as if it were the new Delphic oracle delivering us from office strain. So our country has built a thousand-mile coast made of second- and third-rate *St Tropez's* where people can feel that certain ritual which comes with a sunset in the hills behind us, an ocean's long horizon before us and an exotic-seeming, discount drink in the hand.

It is human nature to wish to gather round a reflective horse-shoe bay. Those people flying back and forth in the airliners rife with design flaws, looking down over Europe today, will see the helpless aesthetic which draws us to coasts where our whitewashed buildings greedily cluster together for the vista around a semicircular bay. Like a morbid jostling at some beheading. It gives promise of a real spiritual nurture and perhaps even some hope that we humans do not completely turn our backs on the beauty of the world and prime real estate.

When I stopped lecturing her, I looked through Teresa's portfolio. There was little ergonomic design but I was impressed by what I saw and the furniture was better than Bonzas thought. We left her portfolio and helmet behind the till of Cena's with Franco, who I tipped heavily, and we walked out onto the piers along the side of the large bingo hall which pulsed and issued figures like some insane new stock exchange. I showed Teresa the new units my Agency were designing the interiors of. The walls had just been plastered with the coloured wires sprouting from the positions where the light switches would be. I was disappointed and annoyed. I should have been consulted on the positioning of the light switches. I turned to her and said, 'Like to eat fish?'

She enthused but I suspect she imagined I was going to take her off to a restaurant for lunch. The Dolphin (or the Lower Rivers). Instead, I bought two very large fresh sole off that morning's boats from the fish stand at the pier end. I asked the old ladies who doted on me for two plastic bags to wrap the fish in so they could not possibly drip onto my suit.

I held up the bag. 'I invite you back to my place for some lunch.' My wristwatch, an *Omega* so heavy it once blackened the nail of my big toe when I dropped it in the bathroom, was at twenty minutes to: there was a lemon express on each hour.

As we crossed by the fountain I pointed to the Imperial. 'My parents owned that hotel and I grew up in it.' Teresa nodded exactly once. I looked to the top balcony windows of the Imperial's rooms, judging how many were occupied by the old practice where, after making the beds and cleaning up, the chambermaids – like Madelaine – would always leave the windows a good few centimetres open for air. It was busy.

I stopped at the newsagent kiosk outside the Imperial and joined the short queue. Teresa stood off to one side awaiting me while she lit a cigarette which I could tell she did not really desire. She lit it just to pass the time. To stand beside me in the queue would make our situation too domestic so soon after our first meeting in life. To stand in the queue beside me would make it seem as if we were a couple, so I understood and respected her keeping that distance.

I could see that girl in the kiosk grit her teeth as I approached, asked for the tragic local newspaper then I said, 'Did you get any of my cigars in yet?' I held out the usual five-thousand note and she had to pick and structure together sufficient change. 'No,' the kiosk girl smiled nervously.

'Why not?'

'The chief never bought them yet. You only asked yesterday and you told us before you quit cigars.'

'The chief never bought them yet? Then think for yourself. Do you not want to make a profit? It is very simple. You go buy seven or eight of my cigars, I will give you the make. They are number 3s. Why are you not writing this down?'

The girl looked at me, smiling stupidly.

'Get them from the tobacco by Town Hall. When I come off the train, some mornings I will want a cigar. Now at the moment because of you, I have to walk to Town Hall tobacco's or over to the new place on the Pier Development.' I went on: 'All that need be done is add on 25 per cent to the price and I shall willingly pay that rather than make the detour. You will make a quarter profit rather than none and yet you will not lift a finger.'

'I will ask the chief again.'

A cough. I turned and saw a queue had formed behind me but there had been nobody there just a moment before. It was as if these people had rushed out from various concealed places to take up positions behind me the moment I had begun to remonstrate with the kiosk girl.

I turned back to the girl. 'This kiosk has been here since I was an infant. If you cannot run this place at a profit you should consider a job in *McDonald's*. Do not bother. I have quit smoking anyway.' I took the change, snapped up the paper then walked away.

'What were you talking to her about?' Teresa asked.

Jealousy already, I thought.

'Oh, nothing at all.'

I nodded to the predictable faces through the windows of the Terrace of the Imperial and I gave my practised, sorrowful look at the café waiter; in one glance I felt I conveyed how standards had slipped since my father and mother sold the place. I saw the waiter actually stiffen.

We stepped into the North African guys' shop on the first corner beyond the Imperial. You might say that I rooted among the vegetables. I found soft-skinned tomatoes and then a local melon. I bought fresh *feta* cheese, but the variety in the packets, not from the counter. I said to Teresa, 'Will you pick six cans of cat food but the most expensive variety, not the cheap stuff. The ones with pull-off tops. Not ones that require tin-openers. And a bag of any cat biscuits.'

'You have a cat? I adore cats.'

I smiled and raised my eyebrows, I realised in imitation of Tenis. 'The sole is for them and I shall make us a stew from the cat food,' I joked.

As we walked out of the shop and along the pavement below the castle cliffs, Teresa by my side carrying the bag full of cat-food cans and vegetables, the two of us made a pretty little domestic scenario I thought, as if we were already sleeping together.

At the far end of the beach, using the ugly new metal footbridge, we crossed the busy dual carriageway over the National road which flows into our city; the road moves on back, past the fountain and the Imperial Hotel, a road which was devoid of heavy traffic in my youth although it was the main route before the construction of the motorway. On the bridge above the traffic and the close, grey or sometimes semi-transparent tops of the speeding trucks, we could glance across the pink tiles of the little railway station roof to the huge concrete cuboids that formed the sea wall.

When we got to the little railway station I bought an extra ticket for Teresa and we sat for a moment on the bench outside. I knew it was not a good thing for a man to talk only of himself in front of a young woman so I had been passing the time politely asking questions of her: what her father worked at and her mother (as if that mattered); what area of our city she had grown up in, etc. Yet I could not help, as I never can, glancing over the ridiculous local paper that lay irresistibly on my lap. I wanted to see if I could swallow down the vomit if Vermici had written every single article as usual. Teresa spoke, I nodded. But I cautiously turned pages, scanning: Traffic pollution . . . dangerous levels on . . . esplanade last . . . writes Paz Vermici. I turned a page: Success of late ferry put down to . . . Paz Vermici writes. At today's meeting of . . . Paz . . . Efforts to start a basketball team at the tobacco factory are encouraging . . . writes Paz . . .

The Monsignor talked to P . . . Arguments over next year's allocation of yacht berths in the marina . . . our maritime correspondent, Paz Vermici. On the sports pages I saw the photographs which had been spread out earlier on the bar top in Hallelujah's place. These blessed sports were the only pages where Vermici's damn slants and opinions were not represented. I tossed the paper in the bin next to me.

Teresa did not notice and was still talking as we stood to board the old narrow-gauge coastal commuter diesel which had come in and stood vibrating on the platform, emitting sweet, hot air from its side radiator grilles with a distant tang of continual electric arcing.

'We need to sit up front,' I told her and we walked through the narrow connecting door of the front two coaches to sit near the top. Teresa was explaining she had never taken this train in her life before and how she could not quite believe that. Since she was fourteen she was permitted to ride her scooter everywhere except when it rained. She told of how she was allowed to drive up the coast to the nightclubs in summer when she was 'at school'. I nodded at her, not concentrating on a thing she said.

Concerning Events

Father and Mother had just sold up the Imperial Hotel and retired early as they deserved. It was my last summer before I was leaving to begin my Town Planning degree at university (I soon changed courses to Design) so I was living with my parents.

On one of his occasional visits, that evening above his village, Father walked out by his old farm and holdings. It was not quiet up there any more.

Father's village lottery syndicate representing every single family had bought many, many tickets over the decades. Though each adult had faithfully paid their ticket money, then religiously followed the winning numbers every week in newspapers, then on radio and finally on colour television in the main café, those winning formulas never did come up for the village syndicate.

One day instead, the surveyors of the proposed toll motorway climbed the curved road, arriving with their measuring tapes and theodolites, moving in yellow reflective jackets in among the olive trees down in the bottom lands by the dry river bed. The dark gloss leaves of those olive trees were dulled by the grey dust of summer.

The government decreed the new coastal motorway was to pass just below Father's village, though it was to be seventeen kilometres before there was any vehicle entrance ramp where villagers could actually utilise this toll highway. The flows of traffic which were to hiss by on those roadways would be like news from another distant world.

When the compulsory land purchase in Father's village was ordered on the bottom lands he had no problem with it. In the normal course of events he travelled back to the locked-up farm at least once a year to visit old acquaintances, reminisce, think about the direction his life had taken and all those things which had befallen him – as all men must. He was uncomfortable and guilty that his brother, Luis, had been reckless enough to sell his own share of the farm cheap to my father years before but that was not Father's fault. After all, Luis had stolen their mother's upright ticking clock.

The bottom lands required for the motorway development belonged to Father and a score of other villagers who had the lower hectares by the river bed: Father's higher farm and upper terraces, the motorway people had no interest in. With indifference Father accepted their compulsory demands: let them excavate the two-hundred-year-old olive trees and flatten the terraces which had been built by hand who knows when – possibly by the Greeks who came before Christ, but certainly medieval. Father never had his accountant, Jesús Two Hearts, ask how much the compensation would be.

The compensation was an enormous amount. European development money, plus central government money, plus local government money, plus local construction interests combined with the fact that this was land not of rich foreign settlers but generational local farmers. It all rocketed that compensation. Shockingly, Father got more, tax-free, than he had received for the sale of the Imperial Hotel and its contents, plus the market value of the Town Hall Plaza apartment and the savings Mother and he had accumulated. In one tax year he was rich twice over.

It might be thought Father would have been delighted to become that rare thing: an innocent millionaire, but I saw the melancholy and dull confusion which overcame him at that time of the motorway compensation.

The money Father had worked for with calculation and effort all his life long – the same amount, <u>more</u>, had now come to him just by random chance. Father was no greedier than any other man. But he wanted a rationality, he wanted rules, where one's rewards were in accordance with the undeniable history of a person's efforts.

Of course Father believed in some luck, only an egotist – who never makes a good businessman – does not. But Father believed in merit too. Secretly I think Father felt superior to those in his village who had never left it. He had departed and he had worked hard and made his money by his wits in the big town, but the same people (as long as they owned bottom lands down by the river bed) who had remained for forty years sitting in the village square by the dripping tap ended up making the same amount of money as Father had worked hard his whole life for. Capitalism betrayed Father. I think all those long years, the countless hours of work in the hotel seemed in vain to him then. It offended Father's morality that money could come for no reason. He had never thought the consequences of lottery through. He did not understand that good luck in life can be as random, cruel and meaningless as bad luck – which tends to get all the attention.

Mother thought him – as usual – an over-hesitant fool and a weakling. She was never extravagant but I could see since the hotel sale and then the motorway money she was allowing herself those things she had once denied. She had lost weight then went to the Capital city with me to secure student accommodation and bought some more shoes and new outfits of fawn suede with startlingly higher skirts. Despite being in her fifties, photos show Mother had good legs then.

Businesswise Father quickly rallied and used the motorway compensation money: the latest *Daimler.* He invested in the Phases a few kilometres to the north of our city. Constructions had not begun but he paid cash in advance to get a discount for all four top-floor apartments on the beach.

If I seemed distracted from Mother and Father's problems at that time, unforgivably, I was. The reason? Our new housemaid Madelaine: confidently breezing into her eighteenth year; black tights, a too-short ex-Imperial Hotel chambermaid's dress from when she had been a junior. Since we sold up she appeared back as Mother's housemaid and home help in our big apartment above Town Hall Plaza.

Madelaine came from the mountains and lodged in a tiny place Mother had specially rented for her a few blocks away from ours. She languished alone in one of those back-facing flats which ignored the ocean: a nondescript 1960s block with too much opaque glass tiling, dogs barking behind doors, children's clothes hanging on every small balcony except Madelaine's, where only a single tiny, vermilion bikini tantalisingly dried.

In her lobby, where I had sneaked around, were scores of dented mailboxes and a jumbling mass of names cancelling out those of ex-tenants on the many door buzzers. Only one name meant anything to me: Madelaine's. Both her surnames were each of a world-famous painter.

I pointed the painters' surnames topic out to Madelaine when she was mopping the kitchen floor one morning. She stopped mopping and looked at me – for the very first time, I felt. Amazingly nobody had ever told her this. She asked if the painters were rich. They certainly were, I said, slumped against the door frame, but after I revealed that they had been dead for some time – one for many centuries – she sighed with an admonishing frown, 'The Host! What the hell good are they to me?' She turned away.

One afternoon my parents were both out, I was reading in my bedroom – a book about the North American city *Seattle*'s monorail system. Madelaine yelled from downstairs. I immediately dropped my book. She was standing by the disused fireplace (the chimney smoked so badly). She had her back to me.

'Laddered my tights.' She turned round. She had. Spectacularly. Above the shin of the left leg and on, up high above the knee, I could see her skin beneath the sieve-like fabric on her thigh. 'That mop handle. I asked your mother to replace it. Could you go out for me, dear, and get new ones?'

'Mop handles?'

'Tights.'

'Use some of my mother's.'

She shrieked a laugh, 'You crazy? The Host! I cannot use your mother's. She is my Madame.'

I had to walk to the Court Shopping Centre. Size B. Must be black, she had explained to me, but really, how embarrassing. Still, I had to admit an erotic charge was to be obtained from purchasing such an intimate item for the sexy chambermaid. I fantasised I was a loving husband, nonchalantly buying an intimate item for his wife, every physical privacy and secret of whom he both knew and cherished.

I bought her the size B black tights, though of course the sales-girl had smirked and managed to get me to blush like a rose, even more when I breathed deeply and spoke out aloud about my 'wife'. As Madelaine had no money on her I had agreed to pay for the tights myself. A pleasure.

When I got out of the elevator back home above Town Hall Plaza I found Madelaine had paused in her cleaning to stare at life going by from out on our small balcony. The quarterly bell from Town Hall tolled. When she stepped back in, I noticed she had taken off those shoes with a heel which she normally insisted on perambulating around on. I had heard my mother darkly discussing with Father how the shoes must be killing her. Madelaine thanked me. I turned to go upstairs.

'Lolo. We need to see if they fit.'

'Ah yes. Of course.' I stood and watched, trying to decide what expression I should have on my face. Her legs were brown from the beach where she seemed to spend all her free time and her thighs moved a little together. Madelaine roughly lifted up her skirt. She was wearing white, brief underwear beneath the laddered black tights which had a dark gusset. I felt the familiar slump of appalling ardour in my stomach. She pulled down the laddered tights, baring her thighs, then she stooped. A knee lifted towards her face, a hand drew the laddered tights off from one foot's curled toes then the other. She quickly flicked the torn tights at me and I grabbed them smiling but still looking towards her. She had fine legs. But I was already familiar with them. I spied upon her and her girlfriends on the beach where they sunbathed by the water's edge; our apartment still gave access on to the Imperial Hotel roof, so with the old 10 x 50 binoculars forgotten by a guest, on top of the elevator winch-gear hut, I viewed girls' sunbathing bodies through a confusion of television aerials.

Madelaine put a foot up on a dining-room chair to slowly pull the new tights on to one leg then the next. When the tights were stretched across between the knees she bent once more and hitched them up with a masculine grunt so her wrists slid the skirt of her dress higher as well. Leaning to one side then the other, actually hopping in the air, Madelaine secured the tights' elastic up above her waist. She smiled at me and patted her skirt down as I put her torn tights in my pocket for keeps then turned away.

'They fit good,' she shouted after me.

In Father's old village after the motorway construction began, things changed. An inevitable chasm opened between the villagers who had benefited from land sale and those who had not. The lucky ones did not do themselves any favours.

Their first act of insensitivity was to withdraw the mere pennies they paid every week into the collective village lottery syndicate! Already with delusions of grandeur, they built a tennis court for the village, though it was obviously a vanity project to turn their grandchildren into the court stars of some hazy future. Also, in the immediate village environs, many of the compensated families built holiday villas with lighted swimming pools and electronic security gates in exactly the architectural style as those dwellings of the foreigners who came to our coast; the foreigners who these same villagers had relentlessly criticised over decades for ruining the coast with construction.

White new villas (which brought drunken and disrespectful Moorish construction workers) peppered the outskirts of the village. Yet soon the old owners of the bottom lands and riverside hectares returned to their houses in the narrow lanes up in the village. Desperate to learn what was being said about their 'success' (as they termed it), they realised the only way to find out was to return among their fellow villagers and play chequers and cards in the café, queue in the morning bakery and loiter in the market square once more, as they always had.

The new villas only a hundred metres distant became the compensated villagers' seasonal 'holiday homes', empty for most of the year, in the same lifestyle as the transient foreigners they blamed for destroying the coastal society. Several outlying villas actually fell into full decay, swimming pools turning green, satellite dishes swamped by gardenia, jasmine and bougainvillea, empty, wind-borne concrete construction sacks swirling on their shuttered terraces.

The 'Motorway People', as the rest of the village cursingly christened them, had ostentatious new furniture delivered to their old village homes. Some Saturdays there would be three groups of men from different city department stores vying with each other competitively in the lanes, carrying huge pieces of furniture and winching them with ropes up on to the first-floor balconies as the assorted beds, sofas and display cabinets could not fit under low lintels or up interior stairs of those ancient houses.

The next craze to overcome the Motorway People – when the access slip was built on to the newly opened toll motorway, seventeen kilometres south – was cars. *Mercedes*, *BMWs*, *Audis* and other makes popular with the foreign incomers were purchased by fifteen or twenty of the compensated families. These large, elegant saloon cars with air conditioning and pale leather interiors did not physically fit into the narrow lanes of the medieval village where the owners of the bottom lands all resided. Rather than park them out at their 'holiday' villas they found another solution.

At the very entrance to the village they paid to have the latest emblem of their success constructed: a bizarre, forty-five-space, tarmacadam car park complete with garage car wash, metallic-style sunshades and crisp white lines defining each numbered car space.

Here the expensive cars sat. Here they gathered dust, were reversed, dented, washed then grudgingly waxed by the bored grandchildren without driving licences who had long ago lost interest in tennis. Finally the cars were sold at a loss, the car wash ran dry and fell into ruin. Weeds grew up between the cracks in the car-park tar.

Since the afternoon of the tights' display, even when Madelaine addressed me she never met my eyes while my parents were in our apartment. I waited to go to university and as my departure came closer I spent my time anticipating when both my parents would be out and I would be left alone with Madelaine once again, like that legendary day with the tights.

Day after precious day it did not happen and in the evening I had to listen to my mother call goodnight to Madelaine as, gently, our young housemaid would close the front door leaving me feeling immature, trapped and with a powerful sexual melancholy causing cruel bitterness towards my parents' homeliness. I even huffily raised the notion of not going to university but staying in our city for another year. This crazy suggestion of mine deranged my parents with fury.

One morning I could take no more and walked to the Court Shopping Centre and bought another pair of the size B black tights from the salesgirl there who this time openly sniggered at me.

I stared at the two famous painters' names on the buzzer, tore the pair of black tights from the packaging and then stuffed them into Madelaine's little battered mailbox with my fingertips.

So one evening that summer before I went off to university, Father stood on his farm above his eccentric village. The steady movement of the air, like the proximity of some boiling insect nest, was the motorway sound. Along the coast, the red retreat of rear vehicle lights was flowing in a slimy way around the mountain and out of sight, like lava in a speeded-up documentary. The receded southbound lanes hid the vehicles but brushed the top of the olive groves again and again with a cast of singular monochromatic headlights.

It was dusk below Father's farm. Halfway up the hill road he could also see the Bonat brothers' garage with lights still switched on in its workshop. Aimlessly, Father ambled down the road back towards the village. As he passed the Bonats' workshop he noticed the double door ajar, the vivid chalky light and hard clear shadows cast by a naked electric light hung from a flex over the roof rafters, the bulb protected by a wire frame. Then Father noticed the figure of the younger Bonat brother – the one in his forties – lying on the concrete floor in his overalls. This was normal as Bonat slid in and out from beneath vehicles on a curious home-made board with fitted castors. But Bonat was lying on his face and still.

Father called out Bonat's name, cautiously pulled the one double door, saw the dark liquid on the concrete was not oil – was not brake fluid. Bonat the Younger had cut both wrists with a specially sharpened strip of dirty-looking metal.

Bonat was still alive and more or less conscious. Father raced to the telephone which was fixed on the wall. Bonat had probably used the same strip of sharpened metal where he had struck the slim wire running up the wooden supporting pillar. The dead receiver tone was irredeemable.

It must have been a strange sight to meet. Dusk had moved into night, the high moon was above, silvering the winding road down

75

to the village. My father, his slim legs quickstepping, Bonat in his boiler suit slumped piggyback over my father's bent shoulders, the mechanic's wrists in tourniquets of oil-stained rags. The garage double doors back up the hill behind them were left thrown wide, workshop abandoned: cold, defined bulb light bleeding out to meet the lunar spill, shadows crawling into the scant dry scrub and cactus that climbs up away from the roadside to the dark mountain.

Soon Father would have been carrying the bleeding man in pure darkness, those arms hanging, the seeping wrist blood plastering down the white shirt on Father's panting chest.

The village was right there ahead, around three descending corners; Father could make out a figure moving on the green- and flesh-coloured surface of the floodlit tennis court; he could even distinguish that the net was still missing but suddenly he and Bonat turned hard left into the obscurity of the olive terraces.

As Father rushed onward holding the weight low, legs speeding to maintain the burden, sometimes the hard dry branches crashed into Bonat's face above him but Father could not step further away from the trees for fear of falling down on to the next terrace a half-metre below.

Onwards, Father and his burden moved. Then the sound of rushing vehicles became louder. The mechanic mumbled something as if aroused from his semi-consciousness just by the very proximity of motor vehicles. The last of the olive trunks were now coiled with oily headlight shadow.

The younger Bonat brother's oxygenated blood was bright red upon my father's white shirt in motorway headlights. Father's good leather driving shoes were sideways for grip in the clay, the slumped body on his shoulders eventually shucked off halfway down the embankment and abandoned. Christ-like, Bonat lay there, head back, arms outstretched. Father gasped air, descended on to the motorway hard shoulder, both his bloodied palms held up, like an exhausted soldier surrendering, the arms high but curiously still as that insane surge of trucks and cars came sweeping through his once-silent olive groves by the dried river bed towards him.

Bonat was rushed from the side of the new motorway to the new General Hospital in the back of a plumber's van, Father by his side.

Father visited his 'fellow villager', as he protectively called him, on a daily basis in hospital and refused to talk to that oaf reporter, Paz Vermici's cheap local newspaper, so the planned feature story of what Mother called 'Father's heroics and the heroic destruction of his best shirt' was dropped.

Mother seemed surprised by Father's Samaritan instincts, but over several evening dinners he explained how the Bonats' business was failing, how the elder Bonat was a brute and a bully to his younger brother and in hushed tones how the younger Bonat's wife had left him to live in the Capital city with one of the damn construction foremen from the new villas in the village.

While this information may have got a sympathetic vote what did not was Father's rash announcement that when Bonat was discharged from the General Hospital his fellow villager was coming to stay with us in a spare bedroom in which I of course had always harboured a forlorn hope that my parents would install Madelaine full-time! 'Is this your retirement hobby, filling our home with failed suicides?' Mother shouted. I nodded in solemn agreement.

Our house guest, Bonat, was less trouble than Mother and I, and an apprehensive Madelaine, had predicted. He was polite, melancholy, quiet, with extraordinarily long cuffs on his shirts, the cruel scratches from olive branches still healing on his forehead. Some days I suspected his quietness was on account of his medication. For a mechanic he was scrupulously clean (all the bedrooms had en-suite bathrooms but I had the full report from Madelaine). He quickly completed all the odd jobs around the apartment which had been waiting on Father or me for a year.

Despite all his free time, Bonat did not linger around the house. Coming from a very small village he was amused by our city's bustle, by the port workings, and could even occupy an hour watching the fountain in front of the Imperial. He spent a great deal of time wandering the main streets and liked to sit in cafés, though I was scornful to learn he had quit cigarettes since his suicide attempt.

Father's new *Daimler* was soon tuned beautifully and in the evening, silently, Mother and Bonat actually played chess together. Mother was surprised to have an able opponent as I have always found board games and cards odious. She knew Father's modest stratagems and predictable breakouts only too well. Some evenings when Bonat reached quickly for a certain move, the long shirt cuffs covering his wrist dressings knocked a chess piece jumpingly on to the board, and as I sat upstairs brooding on Madelaine, that lone click of a toppled queen or pawn was the only sound in our house while Mother and Bonat played on downstairs.

Bonat came to Father one afternoon during that sudden, brutal heatwave and thanked him, one villager to another, for everything he had done. He thanked Father for saving his life at the garage that night. He explained how the bonds of their village had gone to hell since money arrived there and Father was a wonderful example of how the spirit of their village could live on in our cruel and selfish times. Father was told that despite his success in our city he had not forgotten where he came from. Bonat thanked Father for carrying him on his own shoulders through the dark olive groves to the motorway without waiting for an ambulance in the isolated village which would, as the doctors and Tenis later confirmed, have allowed Bonat to bleed out to death. Bonat thanked Father for arranging a single room for him in hospital and for visiting him and then welcoming him into the comfort of his own home, to eat his own food and telling him to take as many weeks as he needed to recover.

'But Mr Follana, I am obviously affected by the new immorality which has ruined our village. I am in love.'

Father said, 'Oh, Bonat. No. Our little Madelaine. She is a heart-breaker and too young with it.'

'I have fallen in love with your wife, sir.'

Father told me he actually laughed at this point, jumping to forgiveness, assuming Bonat's medication was having side effects. But Bonat continued, 'She is waiting for me downstairs now, sir. In a taxi of course. We could never take the *Daimler*. I am so sorry.'

With that Bonat stood, held forth a hand which – amazed – Father took and limply held, then Bonat walked out of our apartment above Town Hall Plaza. Father stepped on to the balcony and, sure enough, Mother, all dressed up in fawn suede and high heels, was sitting in the back of a taxi outside our front entrance as Bonat climbed in and the vehicle moved off. Father shook his head, came into the lounge and called for me. No answer. He looked over at the table by the curtains. The chess board was gone. They had packed it in a suitcase.

That very day on which Mother left Father, I was involved over at Madelaine's little apartment, sitting awkwardly on that damned small sofa through which you could feel metal bars pressing under your thighs and cutting off the blood to your legs.

Standing, she turned round to allow her chambermaid dress to concertina, then slide down her tanned thighs and the back of her knees to the floor while she held a finger to her pursed lips and put on North American movie actress *Marilyn Monroe*-type facial expressions of helpless surprise.

She stepped out the dress and began tugging at the sofa which unfolded into a horrible bed.

'Done it before?'

'Twice.'

'The Host!' Madelaine said to herself in a genuine spirit of curiosity. 'Let me see what you can do.'

That stifling morning at the breakfast table when I was left alone for a moment, Maddy had leaned over to me and whispered, 'Thank you for your gift but today I am not even wearing underwear!' She was clearing dishes from the table, Mother and Bonat were in the kitchen. I visibly jumped in my chair and swilled my orange juice. Madelaine stepped away from me.

Over the following week with Father cuckolded around the cafés and Mother gone with Bonat, I assisted Madelaine to clean our large apartment above Town Hall Plaza so we had more time to make love. Sometimes damp hair was across her forehead by the time she left for her own place in the evening. With our mops swishing we moved towards each other across the tiled floors of the parlour until our two buckets were almost touching then I leaned forwards to kiss her.

I learned how to make a bed correctly; tucked in so the sheets are strangulation-tight against the mattress. Those brief days. Before we made them, we rolled on my parents' bed, on my bed, on Bonat's old bed, on the roof and we fondled passionately in the elevator – and over at her place she finally allowed me into her bedroom rather than on the ghastly fold-out sofa.

Madelaine spoke as well as growled, constantly used the strong curse word, 'the Host', bit me then cried out. She would frequently smoke a cigarette after lovemaking but she would never buy her own, only use mine. When we could lie naked together and look at each other's bodies and smoke in a leisurely way (only when over at her place; in our apartment we both quickly leaped up and pulled up our loosened clothes, giggling in case my parents should arrive), she would say things and I liked to listen to her unfamiliar mountain accent:

'Your father has gone but he will be back and he will tell you. A housemaid can read twenty things into the sheets of an unmade hotel bed.' She would blow out cigarette smoke. 'I can tell by the cotton waves on the rumpled bed sheet if a travelling businessman has slept on his back or on which of his sides. Or I can tell if he slept drunk in his clothes. I can tell if a guest has had a fitful or restful night of sleep. Old ladies for instance.' She blew out smoke again. 'They hardly move at all in their sleep. The Host! It is like they have accepted a place in their coffins already. They seem to slip their little bodies out from a tube between the sheets.' She narrowed her eyes at me threateningly. 'I have often seen the used bed of a little old lady where I have been tempted just to flatten the covers down with the palm of my hand and it would be perfectly ready to use again! Of course I dare not. You must change the whole thing. Another guest might not notice but the little old lady guests miss nothing. You have to make sure their rooms are cleaner than any.

'Young couples or travelling businessmen do not care. The businessman is getting a free meal his company pays for. They are always slobs. The young couples are just there for sex away from usual surroundings. Lolo. I can tell how many times a couple of young lovers have done it all through the night! Even what positions they use.'

I got up on an elbow.

'If they change positions they twist the bottom sheet tight round and around. Even if they flatten it out in the morning, you can see the swirled pattern on it like the rings on a tree which tell its age. If you look closely, you can detect the intervals until the sheet was completely mangled, then if it's summer you can weigh up how heavy it is with sweat as well. A good guideline.

'Your father's hotel was still like the good old ones he used to talk about. Remember at night how we turned down the beds while guests were away at dinners and we placed those little strawberry-centred chocolates on the pillows? Sometimes lovers are in such a hurry to leap into bed together I would find a flattened chocolate with its red insides had melted all over a sheet during the night.

'Some people leave the housemaids tips because they lie in late every day of their two-week holiday and we cannot get to the room. God, Lolo. Some people sleep so much they must think they will never die one day.'

She continued, 'There was this mean businessman who always stayed at the Imperial and smacked my bottom once when I was bent over by the trolley in the corridor – even though I was underage then – the old beast! He never left a tip. He owns a fabric factory up the coast which makes clothes and garments. Well, old Pepa and I had our revenge. When he was at dinners and we were turning down his bedroom we opened his suitcase on the luggage stand to neatly lay out his fine silk pyjamas. There were his pyjamas on the top, but also there were all these samples: shiny nightdresses from his factory and one of them, well!' She gurgled out a bright high laugh at the thought. 'One of the nightdresses was scarlet, and it had a sample cut out right . . . right where the woman's bottom should be. So old Pepa and I laid out the fat businessman's pyjamas on one side of the bed and this shiny nightdress with the ass cut out, right next to it. What a sight. As if we thought it was a . . . kinky married couple. God, we laughed all the rest of our shift together and when we saw the fat businessman in the morning, the dark look on him, but he never bothered me again. You cannot tell your father that.

'Housemaids find everything. When a virgin loses it, the bottom sheet is always missing. You usually find it bound in a tight ball in the wardrobe drawer, the black bits showing through. Once when I was doing a room alone I folded out one of these sheets and as clear as a painting you could see the outline of a girl in her blood: leg, thigh, one side of her bottom, then a cheek and nose, eye socket.' She laughed. 'In the hotel I worked in just before your father's I found most of a toe once; the big one with the nail still attached down in the bottom of a bed. No blood, just as if it had dried and fallen off. The person must have had a leprosy.'

'And, Madelaine, what would you tell by these sheets here in your own bed?' I whispered.

'My sheets?' She dropped her voice: 'They do not have enough clues on them. Yet,' and she kissed me.

I only had two days remaining until I departed our city for university in the Capital. Father wryly said to me, 'Never save anyone's life!' He asked me if I was all right and told me not to worry or let it affect my forthcoming studies. He assured me he and Mother would 'sort it all out'. I nodded and he smiled and said, 'You will get cheques from both of us, trying to be your favourite. Everyone separates these days. Do not be shocked.'

Those who have been through a turmoil of emotions often, completely without reason, assume the object of their feeling has had a similarly turbulent time. Madelaine opened her door with complete calm. 'I am not seeing you today,' she announced.

I leaned towards her small nose. 'Is that a fact?'

Very quickly she sighed and stepped aside. I strode forward, looking at the windows already. I turned. She was wearing her dressing gown and those hideous fluffy slippers with the face of a donkey on each.

I laughed. 'I like your slippers.'

'You told me you hated them. Lolo!' She giggled but tried to resist.

I stopped pulling her and said, 'We are going to sleep together. In the dark.' I stepped over to the bedroom window and began fiddling with the worn canvas straps which lowered the outside louvred shutters on her bedroom window. She reached out her hand and touched mine, which stopped it moving.

I turned to look into her face and I said, 'We are going to be in the dark together, holding each other as if it was all night long though I know you have to go and clean our toilets after siesta – but it is all the night I can make for us together, Madelaine. I had hoped when I went to university you would come and visit me and we could spend a whole night in a hotel together and listen to the scooters and the traffic start up at dawn and hear the water pipes groan and all those noises you hear in damned hotels.'

'I do not think that would be such a good idea, Lolo.'

'I know. So I would like us just to lie down now, quietly in the dark together, and pretend it is night.'

She lowered her eyes and her fingers withered away from my hand then they pushed forward and with familiarity tugged at the canvas strap which allowed the shutters to slowly fall down, the separate strips closed up, making brilliant-white lines of intense light until the entire shutter compressed on the weight of the sill and snapped tightly shut putting the room in gloom. She pushed the bedroom door closed.

'You can see light under the door.' My voice sounded threatening in the dark.

She dropped the dressing gown off her shoulders, moving the air, then crouched and blocked the light coming under the door with the garment. The room was now completely dark. For an instant I was suddenly afraid but I could see her white breasts and then when she stepped to the other side of the bed I saw the pale of her bikini-ghosted buttocks moving. We lay on the bed. There were two soft pats as those horrible slippers fell from her feet to the floor tiles. She giggled and I smiled so she must have seen the white of my teeth. We lay still for some moments and then we were on each other. She allowed me to do things we had not done before.

Afterwards, in a sort of awe, my monotonous voice spoke out in the dark. 'I love you.' She did not reply.

Then we did fall asleep in a darkness so thick it could have been a familiar winter's night. Until the deafening alarm clock, immediately backed up by one awkwardly concealed at the back of a drawer, rang, which she had prudently set at some point beforehand. I listened to the bidet and watched her diligently slip into that chambermaid's dress in the half-light to go clean our tragic home.

The next day I was to leave for university and I sensed Madelaine would not reside in our city by the time of Three Kings when I returned for my holidays. Often she talked, in an ominous way, of her mountain city and how much she missed it.

Unannounced, and to avoid talking to her on the answer buzzer,

I climbed up the stairs to her apartment. I had been smoking cigarettes a great deal, therefore I stood on the landing level beside the door for a few moments, so I did not arrive breathless for that first kiss at her door.

In those apartments a purple-painted door separates the stairwell from the corridor and this door has a tall thin strip of wired, fireproof glass in it.

Standing there, I suddenly heard the familiar echo of the door to Madelaine's little apartment opening, the predictable, hesitant pause of her looking both ways down the corridor and then the breathless silence of her quickly kissing someone farewell at the door, as she did with me every time we had been together in there.

I stiffened and was just about to take a step down towards the lower floor when a figure darted past the thin strip of glass towards the elevators. After a few minutes I morosely followed downstairs and never saw Maddy again. Of course who else could it have been but Father?

Out, Towards Kilometre 4

The narrow-gauge train began to draw out of the station beyond the old brick engine shed. In my childhood before the tracks were lifted, Father would sometimes walk with me hand in hand to see the small steam engine puff out from there to work the barrel and fish wagons on the piers.

Side by side on the carriage seat with Teresa, her bare arm sometimes touching against the sleeve of my soft, airy jacket, we passed beneath the new flyover then the train jerked across to where it became single track by the shore.

Down below my shoulder was a glittering mosaic of bleached plastic bottles, embattled nettings, coloured fish boxes and unthinkably toxic garments left by the high tides. All mingled with the effluvia of sea urchins and kelp pushed right up until against the trackside mesh-wire fence. The train slipped in behind the first block of apartments and the exhaust clattered back off the paint-peeled rear walls.

The buildings were so dense at St Jordi's and on northward along the coast towards the Phases Zones and Kilometre 4 that even with no awareness of local geography, the hysterical clustering of apartment blocks would give you the instinctual certainty that a sea view lay beyond them. A sea that will only be revealed to you, suddenly, glittering in black and silver, wide, when your train comes upon some utilities' land tract or a baffling, high-value gap of wasteland.

★ ★ ★

One hundred metres back from the tower blocks and development of the actual coastline begin those flat indifferent lands, centuries old and so dear to my heart: between wild pampas are sunflower plots, plums and lemons, smallholdings with chicken runs and sudden white piles of abandoned lime or building gravel. The summer houses of the poor. There are small level crossings for grass tracks at which the insistent train driver sounds his whistle though the crossings are never used and lead to one-storey dwellings with bamboo-shaded porches and derelict Seat cars from the 1950s.

Once this landscape was unchanging. The lack of a sea view did not make property development worth it. Recently with soaring property prices, just the proximity to the beaches of St Jordi's has made building on these plots worthwhile. What prevents development is the patchwork chaos of land ownership on the clustered inland side by the railway. One day this strange twilight hinterland, with its lunar, agricultural inappropriateness so close to the sea, will be gone.

What I have loved about this toy railway of the yellow-painted, cruelly nicknamed 'lemon express' is that despite official stops, the youngsters have established several unofficial ones where the trackside weeds are worn away to dust patches. These youths will wave and the driver will stop – unless there is an inspector aboard. Or wishing to disembark at a particular chalet or tower block, passengers knock on the driver's cab door and request him to halt. In summer an entire family in swimsuits, heavily laden with provisions and still inflated beach toys will slowly climb down from the sliding double doors of the train and amble towards their dwelling as stars begin to show above.

The names of these modern concrete platforms I love too. Halts for which the noun 'station' seems too grand – with their coloured maps of the lemon express route in mustard yellow. The English word for the third platform on the line, *Disco*, has been retained – its now bizarre appellation still on the signs despite the closure and demolition years before of the White Windmill nightclub whose beat could no longer be heard on the wind. The youngsters had worn pale chalky paths, which would turn silver in moonlight, through the grass from the railway track to the White Windmill. Paths which have long since been re-covered with rough scrub.

Our city, our model region, our <u>country</u>, excels as no other in producing tracts of wasteland. It is a national art form. A perfect piece of forlorn wasteland for me must always lie near the sea for a direct visual corroboration of sublime nature contrasted with human decay.

Saturday mornings, when I first moved to the Phases Zone 1, the dawn train would slow and stop. The crowd of Friday-night revellers would cheerfully climb aboard. I would often watch from my balconies. The next morning, knowing there were no early Sunday trains, the noisy Saturday-night kids would use the narrow-gauge rail tracks to walk back along at dawn, the girls often carrying their high heels as they stepped from wooden tie to tie. They moved like refugees back into their neighbourhoods of St Jordi's or all the way into our city towards the cathedral bells.

As our lemon express accelerated towards the Phases Zone 2 platform, I stood up from beside Teresa, knocked on the driver's door, pulled it back and placed my head and shoulders in the driving cab.

'Baron. Just before Phases 2?' the familiar driver said but he only glanced at me. He kept his eyes on the track ahead.

Outwith the remit of the windscreen wiper sweep I noticed the driver's windscreen was hideously dirty. He had the city paper rolled up on the control console beside him. I could see that photo from the sports pages cut off where the newspaper was folded. The train was old and I always loved the way you could see individual bulb filaments actually trembling behind those richly coloured warning lights in front of the drivers. 'That would be very good if you can. Thanks,' I said and closed the door.

The train crawled on towards the Phases Zone 2 platform, around the corner after the straight bit where, driven from the beach, sand accumulated, often until only the delicate trace of silver tracks showed above.

When the train was nearly behind my apartment building the lemon express slowed to a stop. The driver allowed the auto lock to come off and when the button glowed green I hit it and the slide door opened. I climbed down first then held my hand up to Teresa but she turned, defiant and dangerously independent, and her foot found the step easily as she climbed down on to the trackside. I painfully examined the allure of her small, tense ass.

The ticket collector at the back end of the train was leaning out and he waved then shut the auto doors. Teresa and I both stepped back from the track, our heads moving quickly from side to side as we focused on one part of the accelerating carriages – usually the wheels or mechanical components of the underside. The rear end passed and the track zinged as the lemon express moved into the distance.

My favourite local tract of wasteland was just behind Phases Zone 1. Before summer in the four corners of this waste, among barren soil, healthy wide-bladed shoots of bright grass bustled upwards like missed bristles when a man shaves clumsily. Across this tract the green overgrown grass vanished in various patches of exposed orange soil. Perhaps where various horrific chemicals from construction activity on adjacent sites or drums of diesel had been kicked over contaminating the soil?

Towards the centre of this waste were two outcrops – little oases of erect, wild pampas grass. One cluster had chosen to send up its golden, eight-metre stalks in the midst of a display of rusted, tyreless wheel rims on which the festered metal was ochre-coloured with patches of intense terracotta. Yet over in the far corner of the wasteland was an even bigger pampas outcrop which served as a shield to what lay behind. In the winters I loved the winded rattle from the hollowed pampas stocks sounding hysterically together as if trying to get my attention when I ignored them and did not glance their way.

I led a bewildered, frownsome Teresa across to the edge. 'This is my favourite piece of wasteland,' I smiled.

We walked across to the far cluster of pampas grass. I could hear the lonely but comforting sound of the lemon express by then accelerating away from Phases Zone 1 towards the next station, Kilometre 4.

At the shield of pampas grass I pushed some aside and asked her to peer in. She leaned forward, her shoulder touching my jacket and she saw what occupied the corner of my favourite wasteland: surrounded by various rusted oil drums and debris was an old abandoned boat.

'This is my yacht,' I smiled.

It was a motor cruiser of about fifteen metres, engine hoisted out long ago. The wooden hull was rotted and in semi-collapse but I waited for Teresa's reaction to what our appearance would surely produce. In moments a brigade of cats and kittens, black, off-white, ginger, ghost-white, tabby or grey, began to tumble out of the galley windows and portholes or the anchor-chain space, out of actual ruptures in the wooden hull, or they just jumped in a steady order from the gunwales on to the tops of the oil drums I placed there for their convenience. Once on the earth they came dashing towards us with tails erect.

'Oh, how beautiful!'

On the days when I attempted to count them, including the two new surviving kittens, there were forty-five or-six cats as well as the two three-leggers who generally stayed up on the decks.

I showed Teresa the tall stool I utilised to dish out the food on so the cats could not leap up. The cats crowded my dusty shoes, circling with anticipation as I gathered the plastic bowls.

'How often do you feed them?'

'Just now, every two days. When it gets colder, daily. Hold this high so they cannot smell it.' I handed her our good fish for lunch.

Elevating the bag up with one arm she still kneeled to caress the latest kittens with her free hand. 'Oh, adorable.'

'Take one for yourself?'

'I have a important job now. I can have no cat. I will be out all day and working late at the office. For my great boss.' she added, turning her head and looking up at me.

I laughed but I flinched a little as she fondled that kitten. Stray cats are not clean. I would need to ensure she washed her hands at my place. I tried never to touch these cats though even I too found it difficult to resist picking up the kittens and holding their new blue eyes close to my face. Their fragile bones you could have crushed in a fist made me marvel at how something so gentle could prevail in this world. Yet I did not like cats at all. Rapacious beasts. From my shoreside balconies I heard their feral screams at night as they mated. Yet I could not endure the thought of them starving to death so close to my home. But the more I fed them the more they bred. Eventually I would have them taken in twos and neutered, I kept promising myself.

I popped and bent the tops off the cat-food tins, then used the silver-plated dessert spoon with 'Imperial Hotel' and the fountain symbol stamped on the handle to gouge out the meat. At first the smell of tinned cat food had revolted me but gradually I had come to rather savour its butch perfume. I poured the cat biscuits into the emptied tins and swirled them around with the spoon to soak up the gravy. I put the smaller bowl up on the deck for the three-leggeds. The cripples ate quickly because the other cats had learned that when the ground bowls were finished there may be more in the bowl on the deck for the three-legs. I placed the other bowls on the earth. The usual scramble went on with some climbing over others – kittens coming off worst. We watched for a short time then I said, 'Sometimes one gets ill and I feed it separately. From a spoon,' I nodded severely. 'Do not get the idea I am a nice guy.'

She laughed.

I placed the empty tins in the bin bag which I would take to the trash skip every week.

We crossed the wastes once again and stepped over the railway line then walked side by side along the beach lane with its speed traps and bollards to prevent parking along it in high season. We did not talk but approached my building in a businesslike silence yet somehow at ease with one another. We used the elevator in silence too and soon I was opening the door of my home for Teresa and we stepped into the porch with its partition wall of coloured, specially blown glass with seashells trapped in it, the light switches and dimmers built into the glass so the wires were visible running down into the floor. We moved around the glass wall into the front salon.

'Saint Mary! You have a beautiful apartment,' she said quickly and stood still to look out along the length of windows. From this height all we saw was the flat sea out to the horizon; a hint of morning orange still seemed to linger at the sky's base.

I pointed out various features about the interiors. 'I had this place made from four individual apartments which belonged to Father. The dividing wall between the two front-facing apartments was here.' I stepped to the point and indicated it by pointing along the ceiling. 'Of course I had to have these supporting columns built in so I took that opportunity to have downlights specially fitted into them. No wires all over floors: those standard lamps there and there which are my own design also have wires which are run in conduits beneath the tiles. I can dim them from there and over there.' I reached out and demonstrated. 'They look good at night. Make yourself at home. Take a seat out on the balcony if you wish.'

I shouted as I moved towards the kitchen. I realised I was excited to have a woman in my home again after so long. 'Of course the disadvantage to a place made out of four apartments is that the stairwells and elevator are still in the middle. You find yourself constantly walking in circles; or if you have forgotten something, deciding if it is quicker to walk round this way or this way.'

'Always a price to pay.' She shrugged.

I paused and looked over at her. 'That is true,' I said flatly. Perhaps she was being wry? I did not need any superior working-class nonsense. Give people money and they all end up with identical concerns. Like poverty, money is an illness with classic symptoms. Soon, with money, she would behave as I and all the rest who have it and adopt at least part of the arrogance money always implies. 'Will you take something to drink?'

'Are you going to have anything?'

'With fish I like white, dry wine. I have some in the fridge.'

'Please. But could I have a glass of sparkling water too?'

I was a bit disappointed by her water request. I have always been unable to deny I feel women should wish to get as drunk as possible in my company. 'You can wash your hands in the bathroom along the corridor,' I called, realising it was an order. I moved to wash my own hands thoroughly and automatically made sure there were no embarrassing items such as boxer shorts strewn in the bathroom or visible through the master-bedroom door. As I would have done if everything were normal.

Teresa sat on the balcony with a glass of wine and the mineral water. I half steamed then swiftly pan-fried the sole in a powdering of flour, lots of fresh caraways seeds and very little clarified butter which I had muslin-sieved myself. I prepared a tiny side serving of egg-pasta shells and rice (which was a little on the hard side but anything is better than too soft), with tiny, glistening dots of a cheap caviar I had. I made a salad with the lettuce in the fridge, the tomatoes and *feta* cheese and my own dressing from the big bottle I have permanently mixed, though I have recently stopped using sugar in it.

★ ★ ★

We ate on the balcony table but out of the direct sun. I have a phobia of eating in direct sunlight. It was bright and she had no sunglasses so I loaned her a pair of my *polarised Ray-Bans* which she kept having to push up her nose. They looked huge but it made her very diverting. Though I was slightly discomfited by the novelty of having to see my own reflection, on my balcony where I was so often alone, in the lenses of my favourite sunglasses.

I had actually done the fish well. We chatted design, jumping from subject to subject a little uncomfortably, skirting around conclusions, testing the ground on our opinions. I defended my favourite architects and designers who I had admired since I was fifteen years old. Why was it I had been more faithful to designers and architects than I had been to my own wives?

When Teresa and I stood side by side to look out from my balconies, where I pointed to landmarks back up the coast in our city, we leaned so close together to follow the line of my arm and finger I could hear her glass of sparkling water tinkling and her watch tick.

We had opened a second bottle of wine. Already I presumed there was an element of conspiracy between us.

Teresa had now noticed the aerial photograph of the Imperial Hotel — showing its roof area — taken by one of the light aircraft which fly low in formation, dragging advertising banners up and down our summer beaches and whose pilots sometimes moonlight, photographing significant commercial buildings or villas of the rich. She walked up close to the photograph, almost with her nose to it.

(IMPORTANT NOTE: I disapprove of conventional picture-hanging on house walls. By hanging framed images on picture hooks: dust, cobwebs or even young lizards can gather behind; also the picture can hang squint if touched or disturbed. I was inspired by the flat securing brackets which are used in new international hotel rooms to affix images flush to walls while preventing their guests stealing those bland screen prints and uninspired reproductions. I have attached all the framed and glassed images in my apartment and in my Agency using these flush-wall brackets.)

She came back out on the balcony. She suddenly asked, 'What was it like growing up in that hotel?' Teresa nodded backwards at the photograph and replaced my sunglasses on her face.

Imagine a little boy growing up in a forty-nine-room hotel with labyrinthine kitchens, elevator, basement, stores, linen rooms and an under-street boiler room with a coal shute. A prince in a palace in some capital city could have grown up with less rooms for adventures. The French *chateau* of an African despot could have less rooms than the building I grew up in.

You would imagine though, I told Teresa, that growing up in a hotel is to do with the influence of large seasonal movements of people; a great coming and going, a sense of many presences. No. Hotels nurture like no other buildings the feeling of human absences. The most powerful season which inscribed itself on my memory was the perpetual melancholy when the hotel was closed to the public. Empty, the bedrooms like wasted opportunities, sheets taken away for storage and all mattresses bound in used newspapers – which I would read – from the first week in October of every year, lodging the disasters and politics of 1970s Octobers in my mind forever.

Even during the season, you hardly see those ghosts who were guests and even if you did you would still avoid them. I only saw them through the painted glass wall of the restaurant and sometimes when I crept into the television salon as a kid. Mother often made the extravagant claim that in twenty years as a hotelier she had never met a guest. She often had the head housekeeper impersonate her when some provincial tourist with airs and graces came to complain about a trifling thing. After all, unlike her, the housekeeper was 'educated', as my mother put it.

In hotel culture guests are – behind their backs – reviled as eccentric, overdemanding, lacking true class and, in fact, seen as something of an encumbrance. It is the truth of capitalism: if the customers did not exist, all would run like clockwork.

So each October when the hotel closed down for the two months of winter repairs and maintenance, I would emerge down from our penthouse and encounter the true nature of hotels as I ambled through empty bedrooms.

I did make a more direct contact with the absent guests in those months. Every year, shortly after the end of season, would come the ritual that I anticipated with more excitement than all my extravagant presents at Three Kings, when we leave our shoes out for the Three Wise Men of the Orient – who brought me the DC-8 *stretch series*.

Father would call me to his office and from the little strong-room he produced the chattels and effects which had been mislaid, forgotten by guests in bedrooms and never claimed. How will I ever forget those snapping chest expanders with one spring in the middle missing? Or the black 'secret agent's' umbrella with the silver moulding on the end of its curved handle? The militaryesque 10 x 50 binoculars in their shiny leather case which I still have today? And that curious box of eggshells, each punctured on the top with a pinhole through which the contents must have been sucked out then each shell beautifully hand-painted and decorated? Curiosity still overcame me though. One day, still a child, I smashed each of the beautiful eggs in turn, just to see their pale, gremial interiors which somehow seemed to have been coated in uneven runs of a resin-like varnish. I sat on my bedroom floor cross-legged, suddenly sobbing at the terrible thing I had done. The feeling of waste, the realisation that some delicate thing destroyed can never be restored, surrounded by a hundred coloured shards of painted eggshell which stuck to my hands. I hid that eggbox wreckage for years.

I took the sliced melon out to Teresa on the balcony using the old plates with the gold edging from the Imperial Hotel.

She wore the sunglasses again. The melon was exactly right, sweet, and full of flavour. We did not talk. I allowed the tension to build.

Suddenly I told her the story in that way which reveals what every story is: a form of seduction. I believe we never tell stories to those we do not wish something from. My father told me hotel stories in the hope of my affection and remembrance; I repeated them to Teresa as I had to others so this would forge some intimacy – however flimsy – between us. When we tell a story to someone we want it to be a form of infection. That I suppose is why I skipped my favourite mechanical stories about the elevator shaft. Instead:

For a decade, each year, before the Civil War, a wealthy old man of the Katta family would come to spend spring at the Imperial Hotel. A widower, he always brought his two beautiful teenage daughters. They would have two suites, one for the father and one for the daughters, always the two corner rooms on the first floor (two of these suites have, since sometime in the late fifties, before my parents purchased the Imperial, been re-formed into three, smaller, single rooms). The old man doted terribly on those two daughters. The rumour was he would only stay on the first floor in case one of his girls leaned out too far and fell from the small balconies. On the first floor he believed they would survive such a fall. In the spring of 1934, on Easter Monday, the two daughters were around sixteen or seventeen years old. Their old father would often eat in his bedroom but he did not believe in such a luxury for his girls. They had been sent down alone to eat dinner in the dining room under the eye of the current head waiter who was a great and humble favourite of the old man. The girls were light eaters but could not be seen to be impolite so they lingered slowly at dinner talking quietly to each other. I told Teresa how, as the girls' desserts were being served, which they were approaching with more enthusiasm than any other part of the meal, there was a loud crack. Voices in the dining room immediately hushed as diners looked up at the glossy ceiling which exploded downwards; lumps of plaster trailing garlands of dust hit the polished flooring between the two main arrangements of tables beneath the huge chandelier. Up on the ceiling there was sense of a large specific, paused weight, ballooning the plaster. A single woman screamed. Men threw down their napkins gallantly and stood as if they had been challenged to a duel. With a sudden, alarming sound first the rusted underside then an entire bath jerked through the roof plaster before falling profoundly vertical; the cast-iron bath impacted and spilt open on the polished tiles of the packed dining-room floor. Its impact threw up a great wobbling column of white water which splashed back down, gushing a soapy inundation out in a slosh around table and chair legs while the dust cloud cleared. It revealed the pale, naked corpse of the old dead father of the two beautiful girls – his eyes wide open. The sodden cigar remained in their father's stiff fingers obscenely echoing his small bared penis where, I suggested to Teresa, both his young daughters' eyes must surely have rested their gaze as they began screaming.

The old man had died hours before, they believed leaning forward to open the hot tap full; poaching him in the boiling water, the big old bath overflowed into the already rotted floorboards beneath. The water had soaked into the horsehair plaster ceiling until the weight of the cast iron, the water and the large old man was too much; tearing free of its soft lead piping, the bath and the old man began their terrible plummet below. I told Teresa I would take her and show her a patch of uneven plaster still visible to this day beneath the paint on the high ceiling of the Imperial Hotel dining room, just next to the chandelier. Exactly where the old man, naked and dead in his bath, crashed down among the diners that night.

We were silent. Teresa had whispered the word 'Never' at the end of my story then tossed her cigarette over the balcony, which failed to annoy me. She looked out to sea. Then she said, 'Never,' again.

'That is true. I promise.'

She looked impressed.

The light had an afternoon feel to it across my open-plan lounge. I said to Teresa, 'Why do we not go for a dip in the sea?'

'Of course, easy for you here, eh?' She lifted herself up a little to glance over the bossed aluminium frontage of my balcony which was always getting stained by the damn salt sea.

'Just downstairs.'

'But what could I ever wear to a swim? Or not wear.'

'Well, I could give you a T-shirt?'

'Mmm. Possible.'

She was suddenly cautious. I tried to encourage. 'I could lend you a dressing gown to put on when you get out of the water?'

'Well, I would need that to go down to the water also,' she said curtly.

'Of course. You can change in one of the spare bedrooms. Let me get those things.' I stood up.

In my wardrobe, T-shirts are neatly piled inside a smooth-sliding drawer. Of course.

I was not that childish as to choose a white one, which would become transparent in the water so I could see more clearly the details of her rubbery cleavage. I selected a dark blue one for her.

I have a winter and a summer dressing gown. The summer one is of a grey almost silver silk. I must admit, I did wince at the thought of getting sand mixed into its vibrant fibres. I wore it with satisfaction each morning. I would need to send it to the dry-cleaner's.

I smelled the dressing gown carefully in case it carried any body odour. To be extra sure I took it to my en-suite bathroom and sprayed some of my usual *Chanel eau de toilette* on it. Then some more. Then I became concerned it would stink of excess perfume which might imply to Teresa an unfortunate gigolo-like aspect to my character. So I opened the bathroom window to its widest position then waved the silk dressing gown around outside in an attempt to dispel any possible intensity of scent. As usual, the old woman in the back apartment block across the railway was lingering near her window and I saw her watch me. She would probably call the damned fire brigade! On winter evenings I would see the old woman spying on me with her telescope as I cooked my dinner alone. I would not have minded had it been a teenage daughter but, really, she must have been eighty. I became so frustrated one evening that with a large marker pen I listed my evening's menu on a big bit of card then stuck it up on the kitchen window. I like my electric blinds but I enjoy the inland views to the mountains too but now I mostly have the blinds down in the evening.

I strolled back through to the balcony and handed my garments to Teresa. I felt I was forcing her into it a bit but I could not help saying, 'There are spare rooms round to the right there.' She just laughed and nodded. I coughed and walked back to my bedroom where I changed out of my suit, which I hung in my wardrobe. I put on my *Burberry* swimming shorts – the only ones I could find to buy with a cotton, not synthetic, lining. Then I put on linen trousers and a light blue brushed cotton short-sleeved summer shirt, etc.

CLARIFICATION: This dressing did not occur quite as casually as I am reporting. I also surveyed my face for a long time in the mirror. I used a tissue to wipe the skin on my nose and just inside my ears. I quickly brushed my teeth. Standing in my rather ridiculous plaid swimming shorts I stretched and sucked in my very small paunch. I was also subject to a wild spray of emotional oscillations. I was aroused by the knowledge a young woman was once again going through a permutation of clothes changing, which would result in her semi-nudity in one of my spare bedrooms. Yet also her over-youthful presence was contrasted with the withering evidence my forty-year-old body was too frequently presenting to me in mirrors. Yes, the muscle was trim where my arms met shoulders, but the skin showed the papery, stretched luminescence of true ageing which still shocked and perplexed me. I was so unfit that I got out of breath shaking my can of shaving foam in the mornings. I knew my old age was crouching just beneath the surfaces which I scanned in my mirrors, waiting to flourish and once again fool me – the type of person who truly still believed old age and illness only happens to others. And if she offered her body to me I could only go so far – but just that far down the road with her would be pleasure enough, I could not resist thinking.

I had sprayed on deodorant but not so much that little fake snow globules would adhere on the underarm hair when I took off my shirt by the waterside and raised my arms. I was also suffering from that nervous rapid liquidity of the stomach which still affects me when I contemplate swimming with women.

I walked back and saw through the balcony glass the new shape of Teresa's shoulders in my silk dressing gown out on the balcony. The dressing gown reached all the way down to her ankles and I could see her bare feet: long toes. She was slightly hunched over, preoccupied with something beneath the balcony. Ominously I stepped up beside her and also looked down upon the beach. Slightly to the right of my building, in the direction of our city, a man stood up to his waist in the sea, wearing purple swim shorts, facing out to the horizon, his head lowered reverentially. He was a Moor.

I thought he was praying, worshipping some obscure maritime sun-god, then I saw the faintly chalky fluorescence bobbing on the gentle water surface around his slim black limbs. I saw both his hands lift up to the back of his head and begin furiously rubbing there. He had a bar of soap. He was washing his short curly hair.

'There is a guy washing himself down there.'

'Yes.'

'He washes a bit then swims a bit to rinse himself. It looks quite nice.'

'Do you want to?' My voice petered out. 'Hey.' I then whispered. 'I know that guy.' It was the beggar Moor from the morning who had been sitting behind the Dolphin restaurant and to whom I had handed the photocopied job application for *McDonald's* hamburgers.

Though I knew it was a useless gesture and that she was young and saw this world in a different way, I smiled and turned to face little Teresa side on. I could not resist saying it: 'He is a beggar.'

'He is very good-looking,' she immediately replied as if in defence – and also as if this were an excuse. She remained stubbornly staring down at him in the water.

I nodded trying not to even reciprocate by looking at that figure in the blue water. 'I saw him this morning on my way to the Agency. Begging.'

'But you never came to the Agency today,' she almost reprimanded me.

'No. I went to cafés, then met with you,' I replied as if I was under an obligation to explain myself to her.

She twisted her hair for a moment. 'I won't go swimming while he is there.'

'Because he is handsome and you want to be seen at your best on the beach, not in my T-shirt?' I smiled as if this were jocular teasing but it sounded like the jealous condemnation it was.

For the first time since that Moor's appearance, Teresa turned and looked at me. 'My, my, Uncle,' she said and did not answer me.

I was furious for a moment. Almost shaking. Illuminated with jealousy and disappointment that she was suddenly slipping away from me because of the handsome Moor and now she called me Uncle, in our region a phrase we only use between old platonic friends and family.

'So we will not swim?'

'No,' she said but she did not get changed either. She sat back on the balcony chair in my dressing gown and crossed her legs so I could see a narrow calf.

I looked back down on the Moor beggar. Now he was leaning forward in slightly deeper water, covering his face in white soap foam. He looked enormously clean. He dived under low swell. When he surfaced I wanted to shout down at him but I felt this would annoy Teresa and I could not choose from a whole library of possible insults. Then he was walking in towards the sand. I could see the orange lozenge of cheap-looking soap in his fist. He dropped it just when the water was up to his calves and he ducked, quick and lithe: snatched it back up out of the small rolls of turning surf.

Making it sound as if I was thinking aloud I said, 'But it feels uncomfortable to wash in salt water. You need to rinse yourself in fresh water afterwards.'

'That is true,' Teresa murmured behind me as if we had solved something and found a chink in the handsome Moor's armour.

I watched him come, bowed, out from the water and move up the beach. There was a plastic supermarket bag there which I had not noticed from which the Moor removed a small bright towel and began drying his hair, looking out to sea.

'I wonder where he is living?' I said helplessly aloud then turned to look at her.

'I think I should go now.'

'I suppose it is inevitable,' I said.

She returned to the spare bedroom to dress without asking permission.

I sat on the balcony glaring over at that bather.

I insisted on phoning a taxi although she objected. I could tell she was anxious about retrieving her portfolio from Cena's. I rode down with her in the elevator.

'I will see you at the office tomorrow then. Thank you so much for lunch.'

'I might not be in at work. For a while,' I said huffily. I nodded and handed the driver a 'two thousand', as though I had picked her up the night before. I heard Teresa's voice babbling objections from the back seat. I entered my apartment building without looking back.

The Moor's Lair

I needed to locate where that cursed Moor who bathed daily in the sea beneath my apartment was living among our Phases Zone 1. Why was I compelled to find where that illegal immigrant beggar dossed?

As I left my own apartment building I turned and walked stridently along the road and the parallel railway, adjacent to the neighbouring apartment block where the nosy old woman lived. I looked up and, remarkably, she did not seem to be observing me but I did see the guy with the long hair who strums at a gypsy guitar on his balcony. He was leaning out from his balustrade concentrating on carefully trimming his fingernails with a small silver flash which I knew to be a little clipper. I glanced coyly for the correspondence but the matching, silver-capped railway lines were not visible above the tips of the verge-side weeds next to me.

To my left was that too-constant sea. I am a trained *scuba*-diver. Usually I loved the sea and what lay beneath but now a dolorous force was within me. That water was glistening like a mass irritation and I felt as if its hopeless volumes might flip on their back giving a disgusting glimpse of the naked, beige seabed and its declining perspectives. My eyelids could not stay open at the surface's scorching silver glint. I put on my *Ray-Ban* sunglasses.

I stalked towards the beach path knowing soon I would vomit below hospital ceilings – I would disgorge real stomach acids, glistening linings, gossamer veinings spat through my teeth.

Stood still on the sand, I loathed the vivid caution of each of my breaths. As I did often, I thought of Mother's death. Now I saw my own diarrhoea and blooded vomit – all those vapours and poultice pastes concealed in the bags and balloons of our own flesh, those stenches from the dark; stinks from drains and bowels – God's little secrets never meant to meet air. Tenis told me that first-year anatomy students fainted not at the sight but at the smell which emanates from split-open corpses. Once, in the days when I was self-important enough to read books, I read that the rotted innards of old *Napoleon*'s corpse itself stunk unbearably at autopsy – after all he did and which those eyes saw.

I stood in the sand by the water's edge where the Moor washed each day. I turned and glared back up the path between two new apartment blocks where he had vanished. I was looking up on the apartment range for the telltale pink of unrendered brick which would show an incompletely constructed building. Sure enough, in the casual fanning of palm fronds on a steeper incline between the brilliant-white masonry coating of two new duplex blocks, I saw exposed brick and a leaning, futile security fence.

I crossed the narrow-gauge rail tracks then stooped over to ascend that climb and was soon out of breath. At the security fence I saw how the wire had been forced back so with a duck of your head you were within the perimeter of construction lands.

Here was the familiar sight that, while not creating wastelands, my region was also perfecting: the salmon-pink, hollow brick blocks which form the jerry-built apartments and villas of our rabid property boom; the spume-like froth of the roughly applied cement spilling from the brick joins, the leaning walls, the amateur finishing disguised with hasty thin plaster rendering, the afterthought of drilled-out canyons in the walls to run electrical cable or plumbing through – the hideous accumulation of dried cement spills, shattered brick and unidentifiable debris on the solid concrete floors – the skeletal stairways leading upwards to other storeys visible, often all the way to the roof, to show the shy illumination of the sky through ducting holes bored into ceilings. Wiring that looks painfully stretched throughout the walls. Glass sheets with manufacture labels still messily adhered to them. The reactive silver of extractor-fan ducts which optimistically run to mythical domestic kitchens.

So much building is speculative in my region that these constructions often enter fallow periods; buildings lie unworked for months, sometimes years, making excellent bolt-holes for their marooned low-paid immigrant construction workers gathered around bonfires with contracts void – or refuges for vagabonds, swindlers, fugitives, freethinkers and picaresques.

This half-built shell was no different. I took off my sunglasses and returned them to their soft, worn leather case which I slid into the breast pocket of my suit jacket and I stuck my head in through the doorless entrance but there was nothing out of place – the usual rubble and paper sacks of unused concrete lay under the rough gash of a window space and I touched one sack with the tip of my shoe. Rock hard. Wind-blown rain in the winter or summer torments had soaked them, thus they lay hardened. All work had ceased here long before because of planning or onward finance problems. I noticed the stairs were suspiciously clear of debris so I crossed to them, my shoes crunching, and I quietly ascended with my head ducked to the first storey.

This was a Moor's lair for sure. It was windowless, lit only by the stairway of ascent and decent, yet upstairs was still low enough to jump from the window gap in any emergency raid because of the steep angle of the raised hill flank behind. Cardboard strips – a large discarded television box – were torn and laid to form a ground base and a garishly coloured sleeping bag was neatly folded on top. Three towels hung from nails which had been fixed into the frequent gaps in the wall pointing. There were those discount shampoo and body soap bottles lined up. There was a small gas camping stove but also evidence of a full fire at one time and scattered charcoal's sour smell after a fire has been doused. Carefully arranged tin cans: tuna, tomato;

a tube of some sort of cooking purée with the aggressive serrated crescents and knife edge slashes of Arabic writing on it; there was a bent saucepan, also a small aluminium Italian style cafetiére, a black dustbin liner containing clothing, and ten or more paperbacks. I could make out a Koran no less, but also academic works in French and English which I could not identify and in my own language a book on the birds and fauna of our model region – I almost leaned over to consult the index for lore of the common fern but then corrected myself, reminded where I was.

I lifted the camping stove and threw it hard against the wall then I kicked the books and cans down the stairs, scuffing the damn leather of my immaculate shoes. I took great pleasure unscrewing the end of the purée-paste tube then stamping on it until all the scarlet content had been evacuated on to the concrete where I ground it in with my heel. I wiped my shoe on the sleeping bag, threw in the shampoo and shower gels with their tops unscrewed and then the clothes. Using it as a container, I began to drag the sleeping bag and its contents down the stairs behind me but I paused, picked up the paperback about fauna and birds and put it in my jacket pocket. I dragged the sleeping bag behind me out into the bright sunlight then I was afraid of being seen by official resident neighbours so I hoisted and hung that sack on the torn, rusted breaks in the bent security fence as a sinister and unwelcoming symbol.

I cleaned my sunglasses and strolled with them on, back towards my apartment building, looking both ways as I crossed the railway. I pulled out the paperback and used the index to read about the common fern but there was only a photo, a dry description of its mode of existence and its Latin name. It was bereft of all its true magic. Furious at the thought of Teresa's perfect rump, concealed beneath that short, swinging skirt, I skimmed the paperback to the verge – not even into a roadside trash bin.

I slept well as usual but the Moor's glistening black body was back there next day. In the morning gentility of the water he was working up a lather on his face and lifting a disposable razor to it, feeling around his jaw over-frequently because of course he had no mirror there to utilise.

Somehow his presence forced me to leave my apartment and walk rapidly to the train halt of Phases Zone 1. I did not return to my Agency that day. I hung around Cena's and other cafés drinking a whisky in each and smoking, not looking at the stampedes of pretty women.

I even entered some newer cafés which I do not frequent – all modern places for a clearly young clientele. I understood the rules of lone drinking. One drink makes you look an intriguing client. Two drinks make you look as if you have been stood up. Three drinks in one establishment are out of the question: people start to look away, purposely ignoring you, taking you for a drunk, or worse: British.

In one establishment that music *MTV* station was on the television screens but thankfully the volume was turned down completely. Some sort of apocalypse was happening on those screens up there. A young pop star came swanning around the swimming pool of a *Cote d'Azur* villa, the housing complex he grew up in totally forgotten. He was dressed in a fortune of jewellery but still managed to look like the pool cleaner waiting to be told to start work.

At one point I haplessly looked back up at the television screens: with a deeply violent competitiveness a teenage girl pop band, virtually naked, were dancing their routines on the silent screen.

By dusk I was very drunk. I marched along the Major. I crossed Grand Avenue where the traffic-light pedestrian crossings play individual tunes to allow the blind of our city to navigate by music alone. I gritted my teeth as I passed the landmarks: Encina Real the jeweller's, the lingerie shop with a mannequin wearing suspenders no girl ever would. Except my ex, Hansa Deprano.

I passed Hallelujah's place without gracing it a sideways look, knowing that to enter it would be, somehow, to seal my doom. I crossed Town Hall Plaza through a tolling of the quarterly bell, walked below the dark windows of my mother's old apartment and around the corner of the Imperial Hotel. The fountain had been switched off but the timer floods had kicked in on the auto clock and illuminated the worn brass piping with a hot, brilliant light. I made it in time to catch the lemon express on the hour.

When I looked up from my shoes and out the train window, a quivering slick of the moon tabbed us all the way up the coast. I was the only passenger who disembarked from the train at Phases Zone 2 platform. The dusk was so brilliant each white street light looked more like whole, two-litre plastic containers of milk hanging there. I walked towards my building along the trackside road in the alternating mix of street- and moonlight, enjoying the crisp sound my shoe heels made on the pavements.

When I reached my building I took from my wallet the flat latchkeys for my ground-floor cellar.

Inside the cellar I switched on the light. All my *scuba*-diving equipment was carefully arranged in the other corner: the tanks, the regulators and my very expensive face mask with its prescription glass the same as my contact lenses, for correcting my eyesight underwater.

In a corner was the speargun which I had never used to spike fish or squid. I preferred to leave all that to someone else and eat mine in a restaurant. I picked up the speargun and I set off under the moon in the other direction, along the railway trackside towards the lair of the Moor.

I took that uphill path slowly, squinting ahead in the right-angled shadows of the fey glow. I stared with real concentration at the ochre band of masonry. I held the speargun down, ensuring it faced away from me, taking care in the climb. I was breathing heavily, almost at the security fence, when I began to detect the cast shadows moving within the lower floor of the brick shell. I was sure the Moor was in there and had built for himself a small fire using the upper stairwell as a chimney.

Sure enough, as I concentrated steadily on the undulating starlight, I could detect drifts of smoke casually shifting. I listened but there was nothing. I swung in beneath the security fence and its rusted links squeaked painfully. I took wide nervous steps to the front door and looked within.

Because of the bright moon it was ink dark in there but I could see flame light showing down the jagged edging of the stairs. If the Moor made a run for it he was going to do it then. I entered the building with my expensive shoes crunching, the underwater speargun held before me. The moonlight was so bright outside I noticed how, in the gloom, it had illuminated the fluorescent hands on my *Omega* wristwatch.

I imagined him sitting still with held breath just metres above. I could hear my heartbeat. I called out, 'Did you get your job in *McDonald's*?' My voice shook with nerves.

There was no reply.

My throat was dry with damned whisky.

'I see you washing in front of my apartment. I gave you an application form for *McDonald's*.'

'What do you want?' came that voice in my language, from up the stairs.

'If I come upstairs will you attack me?'

'Why should I welcome you?'

'My name is Manolo Follana. I thought you might not be alone. Perhaps you have others with you who will try to rob me. If I come upstairs you may have a knife.'

'You may have one.'

'I have better. I warn you, but only for protection. Can I come upstairs?'

'As you will.'

I cautiously ascended the stairs.

The Moor sat cross-legged in the far corner of that room space, his fine features throwing back the flame light of the small fire in front of him. I believe when he heard my nocturnal movements, alarmed, he must surely have retreated there as he was too far from the fire to enjoy its heat. I slowly rose out of the floor as I came up step by step.

I paused halfway up. 'Are you alone?'

'Yes. You?'

'Completely.'

He laughed at my ridiculous underwater speargun. 'Hunting tonight?'

Embarrassed, I lowered the gun away from him. The items of the room had been restored to their former positions except for the sleeping bag. A darker area of the bag had been elevated on a box close to the fire to dry out – he must have tried to clean it in the sea. I felt ashamed.

'I predict one day, Mr Follana, you are going to step into McDonald's and be hit by a hail of hamburgers.'

I laughed.

'There is only one cup left; coffee?'

I nodded and I stepped towards him through the shadow. He stood up and I reacted slightly but he just ducked suddenly to retrieve the cafetière that I had thrown at the wall earlier. He was lightly built close up – delicate. I noticed in the half-light that the plastic handle of the cafetière had been broken and only the rough aluminium mould beneath remained for his fingers to grip.

He handed me the plastic cup of hot black coffee which I sipped while looking at him.

He looked back at me closely. He frowned, his infuriatingly tolerant, smooth forehead wrinkling slightly.

After wanting to say so much I could not think of what to say until eventually I said, 'I need to show you something.' From the pocket of my jacket I handed him the touristical guidebook to our city from the year 1964 and with my thumb I indicated the passage about the common fern, which he read. He nodded.

In that broken house, leaking moonlight through cracked brick as if the building rested on the bottom of a deep milk lake, the Moor was patiently frowning in an absorbed way that was to become so familiar to me, his brow charcoaled by flame shadow and juicy light. He listened intently, sometimes almost smiling as I talked. For hours.

Furtively, like lovers emerging from a dank mausoleum, we moved together under the night an hour before dawn to seek out the common fern using his electric torch among the damp, claylike soil where the new access road was cut high above the Phases, for yet another construction development.

We kneeled on either side of the plant and studied its enfolded flowers. Soon the Moor turned to the sea and whispered, 'The first light of dawn.' I could not believe that old, frayed guidebook could be privy to such a daily occurring miracle as the purple flowers opened too slow for eyes.

'Did you make your wish?' I said.

'Yes.'

'Are we allowed to tell one another?'

'Is what I would wish for not obvious?' he said.

We were brought together into that catastrophic light which seemed to vibrate from within the red soil and coffee-coloured rock about us, from inside complete and half-built apartment blocks below the ridge, rather than come from any single source. Above us in the genesis of day the many stars hung in uncertain white drips.

I said, 'I want to invite you to leave that place. Come and live in my apartment and do as you please there. There is a private bedroom for you and private washing facilities. I live alone and as a free man.'

'What did you wish for?' he asked.

'Someone to listen,' I replied.

Still carrying that ridiculous speargun which he had chuckled at, I had helped him carry his few possessions as both of us retreated down the hillside and into my apartment in the Phases Zone 1.

Then I felt exhausted. I had to put on my *Ray-Ban* sunglasses – the ones so recently worn by Teresa – to step out on the balcony. I noticed the girl's very small greasy prints on the thick black lenses, the conical shape of the tips of her tapering fingers.

I looked out to sea, heard the unsteady horn of the first lemon express of the day approaching from Kilometre 4.

The dusted light of this overstimulated world trembled before my eyes with the certainty of some realm beyond these appearances. I shivered. It was time to sleep. The sea below my apartment was empty of his form. My ears hummed with tiredness in my bedroom as I lay down, sensing him sleeping through the wall near me.

Ahmed Omar The Moor

He showered every morning in his own bathroom. He was a qualified languages teacher from God-cursed Mogadishu. As well as my own language he spoke English, French, Arabic, Amharic, Swahili and Somali. His family and clan had been slaughtered and his city on the great sea had lain in ruins for so long, mature palm-tree crowns showed above the walls within the hollow shells of buildings – a city destroyed first by his own warlords, finished off by North Americans and a tidal wave.

He told me of the days before the wars. When huge white cruise liners came to anchor offshore of his city. He and some boys of his age would paddle out on a raft they had built from wooden scraps and cooking-oil tubs. When they got to the waterline of a huge white ocean liner it was like a city block above them, its reflection in the hot sun so bright they could not look upwards. The rich North American passengers would throw them down single, glittering coins and Ahmed and his friends would dive in a tightened bunch, struggling together beneath the surface, thin arms jutting out for the coin before it twirled too deep into the gloom and away from the bars of sunlight forever. They dived far down until their little chests were bursting, huge propellers the size of military trucks ominous above them, an irresistible force dragging them back up with pleading outstretched hands. Any victor came to the surface with a yell, holding up the bright coin to the blinding sides of the ship – so bright it was a kind of heavenly paradise, the passengers above godlike beings.

Ahmed and his friends gathered again on the raft until another coin spun down to slap or zip the surface and they would knife into the water again after it.

They would dive all day and the rich passengers never seemed to tire of this unsophisticated, budget entertainment. Each lost and sunken coin an agony for Ahmed and his friends, they eventually paddled back with their money towards the city as its lights came on and darkness rose from the cooler sea. The city had electricity in the days of his youth. Often the coins were worthless foreign currencies from countries they had never heard of.

One evening in my low lighting, as I knew he must, Ahmed talked of his night passage, making landfall on the promised shores of my country.

Ahmed Omar said, 'We were gathered in trees close to the beach. We had all paid our money to the city gangsters to cross over to this country of yours, days before. When we asked why we lay out in the open sleeping on wooden pallets night after night, the gangsters said we waited on the correct winds out on the waters.

'Hiding in those trees we were men of old Zaire, Nigeria, Gold Coast and worse too – some, from Rwanda. I was lonely of the men around me. We had just gathered together; though we were all Africans, not one of us knew the other. I shook my head gravely. With much graveness?'

'Gravely,' I nodded.

'Gravely. A man was there with a baseball cap and he looked back at me with a long and hard look but not one that wanted to fight.

'It was an almost full and bright moon; the sand of the beach was white. The gangsters' gold chains shone in the moon and they were helped by local boys who together lifted the wood boat and trotted with it to the surf. We all ran and began to climb into the boat. Almost all the African men had a baseball cap and tracksuits; each carried a plastic bin liner of everything they owned. I had a bin liner too with the rest of my money in it and two books. They told us to sit in positions to even out the weight of the boat. They told us not to talk. Then the boatman climbed in by the engine. He wore a life jacket but nobody else was given one.

'The man who had stared sat behind me. In the noise of the surf and the loading I whispered to him in Arabic, English, then French, and he replied, "I speak French." "Where are you of?" I asked. "Liberia," he said. "And do you know boats and skies?" I asked. He nodded. "I know boats also," I said. "And this is not good."

'He was from Liberia before that country was destroyed and everyone lost their jobs. He could have jumped ship forty times but he had been honest and now ended up on that raft with me. He had sailed from Liberia's port with a berth inside the belly of a huge Western ship. This Liberian was a man of calibre who with his hands had built a platform of wood, and painted it his favourite colours, on the deck of a container ship.

'As that ship sailed to South America the Liberian had built his wooden platform so true. It had to support him above the waters as the ship ploughed the sea with him lowered on ropes, alone on that platform over the bow wake where he painted the rusty metal sides. He told me, since nobody could see him down there, he painted enormous shapes and pictures with his brush first, for he always wanted to be a painter of art, then of course he had to paint a coat over his markings.

'He was teased as the "Red Man" there was so much paint on his black body and in his hair when he went to sleep at nights. When he finished the hull he painted the deck.

'When they were close to coasts a seagull used the ship to rest upon. The seagull tried to take off as the Liberian ran to shoo it from his fresh paint and it flapped its wings but could not fly. Its webbed feet were stuck fast in the paint! So the men of the ship – who apart from the officers and engineers were other Liberians who spoke his dialect – surrounded that seagull and they laughed and taunted it as it flapped and flapped its wings ridiculously and even the Dutch captain came out on the bridge and he laughed down at it too but the Liberian took pity and he came at the seagull from behind, tugged it free and off the seagull flew, back towards South America with dark red feet forever. That Liberian could hold up bread and he could snatch a seagull from the very sky with his hands. I saw this.

'This Liberian who, when a storm came and washed away his lashed-down, beloved wooden platform right over the side, had cried all day until the very captain himself came down to his berth and told him it was not his fault.

'This is a man who, when the captain stopped all engines in doldrums heat with the sea flat like glass, had dived from the container ship in the middle of the enormous ocean with white officers and white engineers too and they had swum together around their vessel laughing and calling out, so their voices echoed back from the huge steel sides across the still ocean. Imagine having experienced such things. The Liberian told me swimming around that ship was as if the whole sunken land of Agharta must lie kilometres below him with its green avenues and boulevards.

'The Liberian told me he floated low, the water at his shoulders and when he turned his head away from their ship to face only the ocean, he shook uncontrollably as if a spirit had entered him and he became afraid and he said the feeling was the same when he crossed the flat sands of the Sahara with nothing anywhere an eye could see or rest upon. When he turned back and could see the ship and the rope ladders tossed down the metal sides of his own neat painting, he stopped shivering.

'I often thought the Liberian must have feared that if he spilled from the little launch, crossing the Straits to your country, that same fearful spirit would enter him, feeling part of the ocean, no longer of the world of men – which was just a faraway small thing – and this malign spirit would be the last thing he would know.

'So this was the calibre of the man who sat behind me that night with the boat's engine noisily running as we moved away from that shore which we had been trapped on and towards your country.

'Soon enough the hated coastline we had left behind sunk beneath the horizon and we were left alone with just the moon which seemed to move with us above, leading a swarm of stars over a white sea on either side of our boat. It grew colder. The sea was so smooth it seemed a piece of the sky had actually fallen into the sea until you leaned out and touched the cold surface with your fingers. On out and across we went and again I shook my head and I turned and looked at the Liberian behind me.

'Time passed as we made that terrible bright scar of whitened froth behind us and I kept looking up. Eventually the pilot waved to all of us in the boat and you could see the orange colour of his life jacket the moon was so bright. He smiled and made a motion with his arm to the coast of your country which was now clearly coming into sight. I felt the other men around me tense up as we approached. We came closer until we could all see the shore and the boatman cut his motor and the boat slunk down into the dark surface and I turned to the Liberian and I nodded up to the moon and he nodded back.

'"Go, go, go, swim for the shore quickly," called the man in the life jacket to the men around us. As if it was a race, the Africans hurriedly slipped over the sides – some had removed their track-suits but they all kept their baseball caps on. I felt the boat rise in the water as each passenger got off. I reached into my bin liner and I grabbed my cash notes in my fist and pushed them down the front of my trousers to a private place, then I knotted the bin liner with my books within, so it was full of air. I climbed over the side of the boat into the cold water. The Liberian was there in the water next to me, thinking of his huge ship on the ocean, and we began to kick to shore.

'The boat motor burst noisily into full life behind and whined away. Immediately I called to the Liberian in a low voice, "Do not swim for that shore, stay here with me." His face was wet and his teeth chattering but he nodded and we watched the set of baseball caps pathetically racing towards the beach and soon – as we floated out there holding on to my inflated bin liner – the first Africans stumbled on the sand and, in clear moonlight, figures led by swinging long shadows that made them look like spirits ran from out of the treeline shouting and we saw the baseball-cap men hold up their hands in surrender.

'"We have returned to the same coast," I whispered.

'"Yes," said the Liberian. "We could tell by the moon and the stars but these men are fools. How did they cross the desert? Now they are being robbed for the rest of their money. What if the robbers see us?"

'I said, "In this moon they will. I will have to let them kill me if they try to take my money because I must cross the water." I let go of my bin bag and said, "Take your money with you and if the boat returns dive and surface, again and again like a hunting bird does for fish."

'Sure enough the Liberian and I soon heard the boat returning after its fake departure so we let go of our bin bags and I dived the same way I did for coins as a child. I kicked and I kicked and because it was a moonlit night I saw the boat cross over where I had floated above and I saw the Liberian's twisting, swimming body off to my side but not as deep as me. I knew I would have to surface then so I kicked quickly up. I surfaced noiselessly.

'Because I am a black man with shaven head, then I would be very difficult to see but I understood not to open my frightened eyes or they would be like two white lights in the dark. I grabbed a full meal of air and I dived back down again, trying to pretend I was chasing a twinkling, slinking coin. The boat came back yet again but not as close this time. I surfaced, again sucked air and tried to dive but I was getting tired so when I came up under the sky again I floated for a moment and tried to squint from one of my white eyes. The boat was there with its chugging engine and the gangster aboard was shouting to shore, laughing, "The bastards could not even swim," and I dived again. Under the water I heard the boat accelerate away. I came up for the last time I could have managed and the boat was making its white trail away along the coast.

'For a long time I was concerned for him then at last I saw the Liberian's head floating as silently as me. At first I had thought he was my floating bin liner. I swam quietly to him and whispered, "Do not smile and show your white teeth, turn your back to this shore and quietly swim with me."

'So the blackness of our black faces saved us. We swam for hours. Our fake *Omega* watches had stopped working in the water. We climbed ashore two kilometres upcoast where we could see the electric lights of a road and we hid on the rocks there until morning, then began our journey back to the city.

'We heard the gang killed one man on the beach who was very angry and would not hand over his money. We learned two other African men happily moved off penniless into the interior, firmly believing they were in your country and it was months before they realised the place they were in was still the place they had come from.

'The Liberian and I stuck together and of course we had to pay all our money again to a different gang with no guarantee these men were any more honest than those last cheats and killers.

'Some days the Liberian and I would stare at the sea all day and pray it would just open up for us so we could walk across the land beneath the sea as did the man in your Bible. I know your people think badly of immigrants in their poor boats who arrive on your shores but there is something none of you understand.'

'What is that?' I asked.

'Our navigation is not good. Every one of us was aiming for Monaco and its casinos.'

I laughed. 'What happened next?'

'Another night came for us to cross. We knew this night was real because there was no moon – it was as black as my skin – the wind was blowing on to far shores and the boatman was risking himself by being in the boat that night rather than on a calm, moonlit night.

'By then we had learned no real human-traffic boat tries to land in your country on a night of full moon. We could also tell this was a real boat from how crowded it was. There were even three old women in African robes. The boat sat only twenty centimetres above the water. The Liberian and I looked just once at each other then took off our new, fake *Rolex* watches and dropped them over the side. I had only one book with me but I still threw it over the side and pleaded with other people to throw useless things over as well, but none would. They clung on to the junk in their bags even though its weight might kill us. One of the old women had a plastic deckchair.

'The boatman laughed – again the only one with a life jacket – and did not mind us talking so I asked why he risked overloading the boat – was he really being paid that much? He said he had already been paid, had given the money to his family so it did not matter to him if he died and that life was a curse and he laughed again.

'All was well until we got closer to the middle of the Straits where the two oceans meet. Out in the darkness the surfaces of the seas began to swell up and the top of these hills of water – which one could only sense and hear – were so close-sounding I thought I could reach out and slap their cold flanks. Suddenly we could actually see the frightening breaks and boils of white froth – way, way up completely above us as if we would be inundated and pushed beneath. As if we were all riding on the backs of enormous whales.

'The old African women began to wail as they had never floated on water before and people prayed in a mix of languages. Water was sometimes gushing in two or three centimetres over the sides of the boat then thankfully not again for many minutes but each time we believed we were doomed. We all had to bail out using anything we could – cups, baseball caps, hands, and I angrily grabbed the old woman's plastic deckchair and I cast it over the side. I remember it hit the water with a wet, cold smack and though it was coloured bright white and surely slightly buoyant, it became invisible in a single instant as surely as if I had cast it into a sea of molasses.

'Finally the other Africans understood and they too began throwing excess items and soon everything out of the boat. Shoes, tins of food, a dead chicken, an electric torch, rolls of blankets, sunglasses, Western fashion magazines with – for a floating instant – thin, near-naked pale women on their wet pages, clattering cassettes and several small portable radios, a big bundle of wool with two protruding knitting needles. Yes, into the darkness I saw float the largest bailing bucket, drinking glasses and mugs that also could have been used to help us bail. I called out but it was too late and our mad captain laughed. I saw a *thermos* flask go into the sea, the young man just in front of me wearing a Brazil football top panicked wildly and made the ultimate sacrifice: he peeled off his *Nike* training shoes and they went overboard. Someone tried to throw over the fuel tank but the boatman screamed at her.

'After an hour the huge flanks of water that lurked on either side of us seemed to be going down and the Liberian and I slumped, leaning forward exhausted, our fingers bleeding from being dashed again and again against the rough wooden boat bottom in the centimetres of water, and flipping handfuls out – knowing that if a large flood breached us, a centimetre of water could make the difference between the boat sinking beneath us or gaining those vital seconds to bail out more.

'The boatman kept assuring us it would not be long but then things changed. There had been the lurking slopes of water and their swirling, terrifying summits but then our wet skin and hair suddenly cooled and we began to shiver as a wind hit us. There had been no wind before; that was what was eerie about the stubborn drops and huge lifts of the conflicting sea surrounding our tiny vessel.

'I saw the boatman mutter to himself and look at his compass using the tiny torch he carried round his neck. Then I thought he had pushed his face into a big plate of soup he was eating. That is what I thought but his face had dipped into black water. I saw colour and light for the first time in hours because the boy in front of me with the Brazil football top had been pushed by the water and the back of his skull hit my forehead and teeth and I tasted salty but deliciously warm blood in my mouth. I tried to shout to the Liberian but I was alone in the cold dark sea.

'There was an explosion of white right in front of my eyes or I would not have seen it. Brazil was the only word I saw. The boy had not parted with his leather football with Brazil written on it and I grabbed out and held on to it tight. I was astonished – not to be sunk – but at how all others had vanished in seconds. As if they had been made invisible. Since everything had been thrown from the boat, nothing floated or could be seen. I shouted out.

'I never saw anyone again. What I did see in all that black was a faint light. Without that light I would have been lost but there it was, watery weak and distant with the impression of being squeezed down by a low sky of clouds. Sometimes I thought it was an illusion. Or the dying soul of the Liberian expiring on the water surface. I cried out his name into the dark. I did not want him to be wide-eyed, looking around, fearing the same spirit was coming for him. I wanted a good angel to come for my friend.

'Even through tears for my friend and the sad-faced old ladies I had to keep that light before me as I kicked. Even to take my eyes off it for a moment might have meant disorientation and death. Yet I was no longer afraid. I was cold but I was in no pain. Of course I knew I had nothing to lose and this gave me strength. Once you know how death feels, Follana, you cease to fear it as much.

'Sometimes I still dream of that light. I swim and it warbles before me but it gets no closer. But in the black sea that night the light really got closer. I swore if I made it to land I would identify

that single light and kneel before it and bless it and thank it forever, but gradually it multiplied into two, three, four, many lights –
too many to worship. The lights of your city. I swam in with the
football stretched in front of me and I came ashore near here on
rocks with sand between them. I tried to find the exact place again
but I never could.

'I shook the white foam from my body and I fell on the sand
which I swear had the heat of day still in it and I rolled until it
covered me like dried mud. Or when I was a boy with my swimming gang and we found that old dead elephant covered with a
layer of flies so thick they were like a sheet of black satin and we
all ran away screaming when the sheet lifted as we came too close.
That poor old elephant had come to die in that place, standing in
the shade of a tree, but as he slept, killer ants climbed up inside his
hollow trunk and ate him from within.'

Book Two

There is nothing in myself that can be relied on.
St Teresa of Ávila

That *Hollywood* Movie With That Shark!

Through sunglasses I saw the tea-coloured arms of two Chinese or Japanese girls; they were my age – fifteen or sixteen. It was that great year when things were changing in our country, or in the interior at least. Our touristical coastal town showed little outward sign of the political changes. Just two Japanese-looking girls leaning against the eternally chipped paint of the railings (which were blue in that era), both their firm backs to the realm of beach and sea with all that damned watery, sandy toil.

The Japanese girls had challenging expressions, which seemed to combine complete boredom and utter contempt. I could tell I was going to have to use ice-cream and boutique technique.

I removed Father's *polarised* sunglasses which were far too big for me and fell off when I smiled. The girls became even paler. Strikingly so with cloth caps pulled down on their hair which was folded up and invisible within. They were of identical height so perhaps neither was the dominant character? I remember thinking that even then.

In the imitative way of adolescents, both girls wore above-the-knee dresses: one of flowers, one of a geometric pattern, both with very delicate straps over their bony shoulders. What those straps immediately reminded me of was when in the beachside cafés, a schoolboy of our institute (often Tenis) would sneak up behind a schoolgirl of our institute (often the Macero girl), gently drape a green, slender tendril of slimy seaweed over her shoulder so care-fully she would not notice until she turned her chin and screamed,

127

shaking the seaweed free. That is what those little dress straps on the two Japanese girls' shoulders looked like to me: slender hanging tendrils emphasising those sunken hollows around their collarbones. Imagine when they touched them off each shoulder with a finger at bedtime.

I walked up to the two Japanese girls and bowed slightly. They looked at each other for support. They laughed even louder when – like a second-rate magician – I removed from my inner jacket pocket the menu displaying eleven ice creams and I turned and pointed grandly to the Imperial Hotel, which belonged to my parents – across the roundabout, behind the elaborate white spume of the unpredictable fountain which was in full surge that day.

Eventually the Japanese girls followed me, cautious but fascinated by my absurdity which made them laugh together. Yet, like other girls, they were quietly impressed by the long Terrace of the Imperial café with its linen tablecloths and the non-matte, sparkling light bulbs on the receding series of baby chandeliers; the old dining salon with the huge grand chandelier, tables set up neatly for dinner behind the ornate wooden screens. I showed the girls to the quiet table up the back of the café under the knowing smirk of our then head waiter.

I believe, despite their prettiness, what drove me to be sure I could make a connection with these two girls was language. I am a terrible linguist, which really means I have never learned to speak, or even read, English or North American or whatever it is called. My first wife, Veroña, would later argue that my hatred of travel and my love for our model region was not healthy natural pride but an affectation on account of my inability to speak English. Veroña would loudly remind Dr Tenis that even when we were all together in the Capital city as young students, shy about my provincial accent, I made Veroña do all the talking. Tenis would roar with laughter at this information even though it was said to him more than once.

Back then in the seventies, damned English was always my worst subject at school. Class would laugh at me on all those words that it was impossible to know how to pronounce. The word for sugar is *sugar,* the word for surgery is *surgery*, yet though both words begin with *su*, the first is pronounced *shh* and the second *soo*. Or perhaps it is the other way round? The vowel sounds would change in accordance with different spellings. I trembled on the first day with old *Meester Jeffreees*. He tried to sell English to us on how simple verb conjugation was and even drummed some into us. I still remember, perfectly: *I say, you say, he says, she says, we say, you say, theys says*, for instance.

Jeffreees destroyed English for me, revealing that the word to cry could also, in his example, mean to have a hole in your trousers. The actual word – this living danger I shall never forget – is spelled: '*t-e-a-r*'. Even then I thought to myself, Good God, imagine saying to a girl, with the slightly incorrect pronunciation, at a delicate moment: 'My darling, you have torn trousers in your eyes.'

The English language. What complete soup. Why have one word when seventeen will do? Every English word seems to mean several different things through obscure changes in pronunciation. It was the ultimate diplomatic tool for politely expressing neither one thing nor the other. Also the size of the vocabulary was alarming; even if one had an understanding of basics, how on earth to choose the word from so many when it is the word that counts? Especially for meeting tourist girls.

I realised there and then at school, I would never master English language or any foreign one. Like my parents before me, I speak none. I retreated into the castellated, Latinate certainties, even clichés, of my own repetitive tongue with its darting, fiery imperatives and the dialect of this model region where each orchard or olive grove once had its own name but on no map. I used to know them all around Father's farm – where an immovable stone in a meadow could name the hillside. Now, all forgotten forever, because no one dared write the names down in forty fascist years when our dialect was outlawed and we had to whisper it in our homes if we thought the Civil Guard were passing the window.

English is the language of corrupt big-money deals being done in every expensive hotel lobby of the world; the language of bad movies and fame. It is the language of North American lies. In South Korea they are so desperate to speak English, young women are slicing away the frenulum – the skin tissue from beneath their tongues. They believe it helps them better pronounce those strange single 'l's and 'r's. Maybe it will help them swallow the American lies better too.

Among the promenade cafés of my not-so-hot youth, where foreign girls from the beach would be briefly free of their parents and in search of ice cream, I struggled so much more often with the cursed English language than I ever did with any brassiere straps. My tongue too clumsily munched at ponderous Anglo-Saxon words rather than getting pushed into any girl's mouth. Swedish, Swiss, French, German or Martinique: it was only cursed *English* they spoke. Tenis and even Sagrana in those days could babble away to them. I soon realised, unless I could find a way around language, into the relative silence of physical intimacy alone, I was not going to struggle with any bra straps at all!

Yet when the two Japanese girls tittered quietly together, turning their almond eyes to me, I saw how they politely covered their small mouths with their hands; it was like later, when I discovered Design at university (I changed from Town Planning). I moved into a pure world of forms and colours alone; language fell away from me like my blistered skin used to.

When I saw these Japanese girls' expressions I idealised that they were an embodied escape from English, from Europe, from local mores; they quietly leaned close and uttered only their own strange, soft sounds to each other, as useless to me and our city as the cackles of the escaped parrots up in the palms.

Access to the free ice cream at my parents' Terrace of the Imperial gave me that immeasurable superiority over my male contemporaries when it came to 'picking up' girls of my age. I simply carried a copy of the ice-cream menu with me, removed from its plastic cover and folded up in my linen jacket pocket. This is why when all nineteen tables in the Terrace café were occupied there was one ice-cream menu missing and two tables had to share.

In those days before desktop was invented, Father had simply asked reception to scissor out the coloured illustrations from the ice-cream packaging then glue the pictures of the eleven ice creams onto each menu. Except for the Lemon Jelly Bomb, which, incredible considering its name, had only a black-and-white picture on its packaging. Looking back and considering the politics of the faraway days it is remarkable the name of this ice cream made it past the official government censor at the Tourism and Information Department. Hotel reception tried colouring in the black, inky image of the Lemon Jelly Bomb with yellow felt tip but this produced a messy, unpleasant green quality, I remember.

In our language-less tourist culture which I celebrate in the world of signs at my design Agency, we move among symbols and runes; tourists need not speak our language nor we theirs for a tolerable fortnight of coexistence. Could the warring world not learn the silence of signs – making all utterance unnecessary? Visual illustrations of food are essential if one is to eat. Research has shown if tourists think they must speak rather than point they will move on to another establishment. In cheaper restaurants all the dishes are displayed above the counter in overenthusiastic, richly coloured photographs insanely enlarged and displayed against a looming lightbox with the changeable prices handwritten beneath. A gesture and a grunt and we are fed. The Stone Age returns to Europe.

That day the two Japanese girls spooned up Father's ice cream. The fountain's heavy rush outside the opened windows drew both their sets of eyes and sometimes the breeze moved the very top turns of the smaller water jets but not the large central one. When one of the city buses on the 112 route circled the fountain, the long body of the bus, like a screen, subdued the water's rushing noise for the brief moment it passed and then, like a theatre curtain, opened up the full sound of the fountain once more inside the Terrace café where we sat.

I was very happy being in the company of these girls without language. I looked at them: two little black-eyed rabbits, I thought. I wished I could take out a cigarette and smoke it – a habit I had begun to cultivate but it was not possible in a place where my parents would come to hear of it. Worse, I sensed these two girls would not approve of me smoking.

This was the problem as they sat smiling politely, clinking their ice-cream spoons on the plates after four scoops each of different flavours, only talking to each other and pointing to something outside the window in low words. These girls had the sinister air of Bible-study class. They were so demure, polite and compliant. Neither that one in the flowery dress nor the other in the pattern was going to stand by politely as chaperone while I kissed, corrupted and finally removed the bra strap of her friend up against the popular shadows of the wall on the dark path below the Meliander. For this was my purpose in life that summer. I was not progressing satisfactorily. I am ashamed to admit that despite a strange reputation in later life as a ladies' man, I was a very late developer. I had not even kissed a girl and I was beginning to panic that once more this attempt was not going to work out for me and that my tastes in girls were fundamentally and fatally flawed.

I experienced the familiar sinking, weary melancholy that we three were going to part with perhaps only a vague commitment to some negotiated rendezvous arranged with both girls later in the week. I just knew one was <u>not</u> going to go on a date with me without the other as chaperone. The mournful anticipation of a platonic history with these two was fast approaching.

Already there had been an ominous moment of actual communication between us! The usual tapping of watches, the gesturing towards the Typical Quarter of the city and then to my shock the use of the word, '*Grandmere*'. With horror, I mumbled, '*Français?*'

(my French is worse than my English). No. They glared and shook heads once each as if trying to jut a wasp from their fringes.

At an absurdly early age I learned to take any girl who was willing to look at clothes shops. In my linen suit I looked like a real rich kid, maybe off a yacht in the marina, with my sister and some of Daddy's money, so the assistants were falsely attentive to whatever few girls I occasionally led there.

Women's clothes shops are another realm beyond language. Teenage girls love to look, pick up, touch, long for then hold garments against their hard small breasts (or they looked hard; I had never touched any). Girls walk away and leave you glancing at yourself in the full-length mirrors within moments of entering any good boutique (as they were all called in that era). This is an advantage as the girls do not talk and they certainly do not expect you to talk back with any opinions of clothes because you are just a boy. Thankfully on account of our ages then there was no adult-like expectation I was ever going to buy them anything either.

So those Japanese girls and I moved between the usual three boutiques I took my fruitless pickups to. Through the streets between, they walked side by side with the unbearable self-absorption of adolescent girls, both falling silent when they passed any male of roughly our own age.

I remember that day as slightly blustery but it seemed to have a disproportionate effect on these petite, fascinating girls. Constantly, until they reached indoor sanctuary (though even there, they stumbled upon unexpected blasts of several portable fans as the blades dolefully turned on counter ends), they were reaching to hold onto their cloth caps. The wind would buffet their dresses, push both the front then the back fabric through their legs so they would suddenly grab down and hold their skirts in place with ever-so-briefly goose-bumped arms. If this was some sort of modesty it was ill-considered; you saw far more of their figures during these gymnastics than you would if they had grinned and borne the occa-sional breeze. Any outlined contours the tightened cotton did reveal were teenage-slim. They spoke single words directed at nobody each time the wind flurried them. Next, a breeze on a corner would excite the cloth on their bare shoulders where they had put so much white sun-protecting ointment you could see minuscule hairs sealed flat for the day. So their hands and long arms reached here then there then here. Whether they walked or stood still they really looked as if they were being molested by quick-moving rodents that were unpredictably darting along their torso and limbs beneath those dresses. I had never seen anything so diverting. There was also this feeling that nature itself, not just I, was trying to undress them as they walked on either side of me, talking incomprehensibly and grabbing at themselves in reaction to sea breezes.

When we emerged from the final boutique I sensed an ideolog-ical movement towards the Typical Quarter and a return to their mysterious *grandmere*. My heart was glum as we began to move through the old lanes into the Quarter, the girls on either side of me, one saying an occasional word to the other. Loud budgerigars in small coloured cages were attached in clusters around the windows on the whitewashed walls above us. Television sets were speaking out the same dreary afternoon programmes from deep within the houses. When we rounded Gold onto Pinero the girls' attentions were suddenly directed forwards to the large afternoon queue for Gilliemetro's cinema.

Today I dislike the cinema very much, as well as music, and I am proud to say in later years I came to learn to dislike books also, but in those days I treated the cinema with only a mild indifference.

The cinemas of our town were curious, furtive places, their small frontages on our narrow streets disguised cavernous interiors which pushed back, often through the cross-sections of several older build-ings. Gilliemetro's was an institution, especially in the afternoons, to escape the summer heat. It was popular with rich and poor alike and also with mountain people who came into our city on rare occasions and considered it a great event. Sometimes, even in the seventies, the visiting country peasants handed about a *Kodak* to have their photograph taken standing together outside the cinema.

As we drew opposite the cinema entrance the two Japanese girls saw the title of the picture which was showing and the outside lobby cards displaying images from the film. Both girls pointed and began excitedly chatting together.

It was that *Hollywood* movie I had heard schoolmates at the institute mentioning with great excitement, about a big shark eating people. One had to admit one's interest and admiration for such a theme but what surprised me was the way the girls turned and spoke their words quite beside themselves with enthusiasm. My heart slumped. If we had been able to go into that cinema together then it would extend afternoon to early evening in their blessed company and I already felt physically sick at the thought of parting from them.

However, the queue for the *matinée* stretched right down Pinero and around onto that little cross-street. I knew the notorious Mr Gilliemetro permitted the queue to build up, then in full evening dress he would emerge from the back office behind the ticket booth where his wife waited. He would slowly walk down the line savouring his power, ignoring the wisecracks and jibes, secretly counting very accurately but without moving his lips. As he arrived at the farthest reaches of the queue, which meant the cinema's capacity, about twenty metres round the corner from Pinero, he would *karate*-chop down a cuff-linked wrist and announce, 'End. Go home and arrive earlier next time.' Unless it was an adult with a child who stood there in which case it would be a more sympathetic commiseration. If Gilliemetro noticed in the back queue an adult from God's Work with a couple of grandchildren, or an off-duty Civil Guard or some official from Town Hall, he would chop down the hand a few bodies early with a wink to those bastards whom he would gently escort back round the corner to the entrance, arm in arm, and there admit them to those seats stolen from legitimate customers.

Gilliemetro was no fool; he had already wormed his way out of a prosecution – with season tickets – for locking emergency exits to stop kids sneaking in. He would patrol the aisles with his torch during the rowdier comedy features and happily eject any children he found misbehaving and then try to refill the seats at a small discount which, daily, caused youngsters to linger outside his cinema for the first twenty minutes or so of any screening. He was especially vigilant towards couples he judged were being over-amorous, unless of course they were God's Work or Civil Guards in the best seats with their mistresses.

Yet that day with the two girls, the cinema was so obviously full. There was also that most crushing and always final problem. Ice cream in my parents' hotel and tours of the boutiques were, despite their obvious exoticism, free of charge. I had no money whatsoever, having spent my savings on cigarettes and a *Dunhill* luxury refill lighter. I did not have time to run to the hotel and beg to my mother (who would be in the hotplate room making up side salads for dinners) that I had two Japanese girls, more beautiful than ever before seen, waiting for me outside Gilliemetro's.

Still, I was prepared to gamble. I held up my hand to the two girls indicating they should stay by the wall. Already they were attracting stares and wolf whistles from the rabble. One lad put a finger each up to the edges of his eyes and pulled them back in the classic imitation of so-called slant eyes. I felt like going over and boxing him. I strode to the cinema entrance and around the crimson rope set up there. I had hardly stepped into the small lobby with Madame Gilliemetro behind her glass booth before she started repeating, 'Back of queue, back of queue.'

'Madame Gilliemetro.' I bowed slightly. 'My father said the tickets for my cousins and I would be with you.'

She looked puzzled. She was trying to put a name to my face. As always my linen suit, absurd for a sixteen-year-old but what my parents insisted I wore, was having its useful effect. Sometimes it brought me scorn, and I cursed it, sometimes advantage.

'Tickets?' she said in a low, cautious drawl.

'Father sent a man round to purchase them, they should be here in an envelope, three tickets with my name on it. Follana. The best seats.'

'The Fronts? Oh. You are the Imperial Hotel boy?'

'Yes.'

'Mr Gilliemetro,' she croaked. Her husband emerged immediately from the back office in his evening dress and bow tie. She turned. 'It is Mr Follana's son from the Imperial Hotel. He says his father sent a man around to buy three tickets in advance. The Fronts.'

Gilliemetro squinted at me. I knew Gilliemetro's politics well even then so I clenched my fist: 'That Red of a kitchen porter it would have been.'

I could see Mr Gilliemetro cheer up and nod.

'He looks very respectable,' I heard Madame say. She was partially deaf and seemed to believe this allowed her to speak out things in front of people without them hearing.

'There are no tickets reserved, boy. You do not come here much, boy.' Gilliemetro was unsmiling. 'We need to be seeing more of your sort here. You will learn from the cinema, boy, even the funnies.'

'Yes, sir,' I snapped.

He looked at me. 'Three tickets?'

'Yes please, the best seats.'

'You may go in and take your seats now but you must pay. I am sure your good father will understand.'

I knew any hesitation would be the end so I smiled cheerfully. 'Of course. But may I change a five thousand?' Bluffing, I reached in and began to remove my slim, empty wallet. Madame looked both offended but also impressed; she puffed herself up. Though they considered themselves of the upper class, the Gilliemetros were still just a shady step away from show business and although my father made no secret that he was just a peasant made good, the Gilliemetros were certainly not as wealthy or prominent in our city as my parents.

'A five-thousand note. You should not be out at your age with that size of note,' Madame Gilliemetro snorted as if her handbag was stuffed with them.

As I was to learn later in business, once you start to appeal to people's snobbism, taste goes out the window and the sky really is the limit. I said, 'Father gave me the five-thousand note to take my cousins to the Dolphin or the Lower Rivers for lunch but they wanted to come to your cinema just to see this film rather than eat.'

'The Dolphin. Wonderful. We go ourselves often. Do we not? Mr Gilliemetro?' She coughed then lowered her voice: 'You are our first customer, dear. I do not have change of a five thousand.'

'Oh? I shall go back and see if my cousins have smaller notes, Madame, but I doubt they will.' I looked over at the girls. At their Oriental features. 'They are not my real cousins, but orphans. Father pays for their religious education and they come from a very modest home. Overseas. A mission.'

'Oh, Holy Mother. Pay on the way out, child, when we will have more change.'

Mr Gilliemetro quickly added, 'You can pay me when you come out. Change galore then, boy! You would not believe what we turn over with this film. It is a worldwide success. You can tell your father that. And you can forget about filling your faces with sweets, we won't have change of a five thousand in the sweeties drawer either. You can come out for your sweeties after the film has started when we have change. Watch your pockets in there. The Reds are everywhere.'

'My cousins never touch sweeties, Mr Gilliemetro. They consider them ungodly.'

Immediately on these words came the sound of the smiling Mrs Gilliemetro's auto-ticket machine ratcheting out three of the yellow ones for the best seats. Joined together in a strip, the tickets emerged from the flat, fanatically polished, metallic surface of the mechanism. She slid them across to me through the little bevelled hole in the glass. I took possession of the tickets between my forefinger and thumb. I walked back to the door accompanied by Mr Gilliemetro about to conduct his queue patrol.

'Wait to pay me here after the show,' he repeated. 'We will have sufficient change.' He pointed to the corner of the lobby.

I thanked him and waved to the girls though my stomach sunk at the thought of the inevitable, embarrassing confrontation with the cinema owner. The girls stepped quickly towards us, smiling.

'Sweet little heathens,' Mr Gilliemetro groaned. 'Saved by your father's kindness. Remind us to your father for a good table when we are next at the Imperial. The table beneath the chandelier please. We like it there as well as the Dolphin.' He nodded.

'Of course,' I smiled. I had never known the Gilliemetros to eat at our hotel restaurant. I was manoeuvring the girls in past him and I remember touching their bare arms as we three moved towards the back of the lobby.

'Be waiting right here for you when the show finishes,' he repeated again, then he walked over to the red rope and began to remove it. I heard the queue cheer behind us.

In the cool, empty semi-darkened cinema the Japanese girls paused to sit down in the central section of the stall seating but I touched the one in the flowery dress on her bare arm once more and shook my head, motioning to the front.

The entire cinema consisted of stalls on a single floor, there was no upper area or balcony but that did not hinder social segregation. Right at the front, below the screen, were four rows of large leather seats with metallic, imitation scallop-shell ashtrays built into the front of each armrest. I motioned to the girls to enter the second row together. The girl in the flower dress did so but the one in the patterned dress hesitated and permitted me to step into the row before her. I did, but considered this remarkable, for its implication was this: I was going to sit in a cinema in the middle, with a girl on either side of me!

There I sat in the middle of the row on the leather seats between two girls, the one in the floral dress to my right and the one in the pattern to my left, the sharp creases down my trouser legs close to their bare knees. I felt my breathing change with this thrill. Occasionally, as if I was not there, the two girls would lean slightly towards each other and whisper something across my lap, their little voices had moved up into a pitch of excitement.

Things began to get even better. The noise from the rest of the audience behind us was growing and the rustling attacks on sweetie bags were evident yet nobody was settling into the best seats around us. This was often the case with expensive seats; they were popular in the evenings with the *bourgeois* of our city, but the *matinée* audiences were office and shop workers on siesta or youngsters sent out the house for the afternoon but due home by early evening. These empty seats all around us were superb as it gave a heightened impression of exclusivity to the girls; but for the noise behind we were so isolated down the front we might have been in the cinema on our own! On the other hand it would be untruthful to over-romanticise our surroundings. The scallop-shaped ashtrays embedded into the armrests were filled to overflowing as usual and as we had made our way to the centre seats of our row, our feet had kicked sweet wrappers, drink cups and cans. The Gilliemetros themselves did the cleaning.

I deeply wished to light a cigarette but again I was intimidated to smoke in front of the Japanese girls. Then there was the appalling prospect of what I was going to do when the movie finished and, without money, I was confronted by Gilliemetro. I could perhaps conceal from the girls what had happened but long-term my doom was certain. I may as well just enjoy these last few hours with these girls, then, as they say, face the music.

I took out my packet of Fortunes and to try and normalise the activity I offered them to the girl on my right as if this was the most natural thing in the world. To my astonishment and without hesitation she took a cigarette. I whisked the packet to her friend on my left and she also nibbed one out with her delicate fingers. Using the leather-covered, gas *Dunhill* lighter which I had spent a large chunk of my savings on, I lit both their cigarettes and then my own. With great satisfaction I smiled to my left, to my right, then leaned back watching our combined smoke arise into the delicate shifting blade of the blue projection beam above us as Future Presentation trailers were shown with those usual curlicues of trapped hairs and mysterious blips or oily distortions in the corners of the images.

I was really watching the girls out of the corner of my eye. Their curiously flat faces held up, they concentrated fiercely on the screen. Their smoking was inexpert but steady and with little rapid and deliberate movements of gusto as if not wishing to waste valuable tobacco. I blew smoke rings, smiling warmly as they tried to copy my quivering hoops. I was thrilled at the anticipation of the hours we could spend together in future, smoking rather than communicating.

They had taken off their cloth caps and shaken out their straight, jet-black hair down their bare shoulders, I guess out of consideration for viewers behind us? It is true they were not blondes but Jesus Wept. You cannot have everything. Relax and enjoy these two hours, Lolo, I thought.

I relaxed. The movie started. What happens first is these electronic fish squeaks come out of the dark like in the horrible shark's mind which has not morals nor conscience; this is all it hears as language: pips and squeaks of fish sonar indicating prey, while you saw what that marauding shark was seeing: the eerie seabed, but you did not see the shark yet.

There was this hammering music and a blonde North American woman threw her clothes off and ran beautifully naked with swinging breasts and legs that folded back divinely beneath each buttock into the night sea. North America: what a paradise.

Then something happened. The camera moved from the perspective of the shore, across the water to in front of the woman's face where she had swum way, way out and floated in a leisurely way.

You felt uneasy. Then you saw underwater what the shark saw again, in a sort of generous cathedral of blue light closing on her softly moving legs. You could see <u>everything</u> on the naked North American woman. I looked carefully on either side of me to gauge the reaction of the Japanese girls, whether they were shocked looking at something forbidden like this, but they just stared on up ahead, rapt and seemingly liberated.

The naked American woman was thrown everywhere by the invisible shark but you never saw what it was doing to her under the water surface, you just knew it was terrible. That is why this movie-maker was smart. He realised he could not show us a shark straight away so he made us afraid of the seas and what it is that lies beneath them. I was quite shocked when the woman's head gurgled a final time then slurped under the oily water.

Then you saw this cop and his all-American family. He drives an enormous North American police utility vehicle and discovers what is left of the young woman washed up, crabs clinging all over – really horrible, all you see is a woman's fingers clenched in pain and then the cop turns to the sea and looks towards the horizon and you know the shark is out in that somewhere. My heart had speeded up.

All their talking in the film had been made into our language with the usual incongruous accent of our Capital city but you could see the actors were mouthing crazy English language at a slower speed. Once again I looked on either side of me wondering, as they did not speak my language, how much the girls could understand of this because the cop wanted to do the correct thing: stop all damn swimming, but it was a holiday resort like our city here, dependent on tourism, so the local business heavies stopped the cop from closing the beaches.

Then it must be weekend and everyone is on the beach. This young kid swims out on a lilo and the cop is right there with his wife and sons and he does not swim because – like the audience are now – he has always been afraid of the water, but that shark comes anyway.

This time I felt the girls stiffen on either side of me and the whole cinema gasped it seemed so real. The shark hits the kid on the lilo and you do not see it but you sense that shark's enormous size as it rolls over like a big cat, showing some fins, and this fountain of blood just spurts upward, probably as the shark mouth squeezed down upon that skinny kid who you would not have believed could contain so much guts.

Again, the camera goes to the edge of the water which is pink with human blood and half the kid's bitten lilo. The water's edge was the dividing line. This damn movie-maker knew all of us in Gilliemetro's were now uneasy if things were off land and on water. I certainly did not want the film to go on water again.

This brilliant tough guy comes and offers to kill the shark but they are too dumb and advertise a hunt so all these horrible people in small boats tip blood and guts into the water; they catch some other shark and hang it up. You see right down its open throat and the girls beside me put their hands to their eyes at this view.

So the cop goes with a shark expert on his fantastic speedboat to look for the right shark at night on the foggy water, which is madly reckless, then they find a boat all smashed up with a bite out of the side. My stomach sank as that crazy shark expert put on a mask and dived down into the night water. Was he insane? He is looking through a hole in the underneath of the boat and he gives it a tug to see what is in there. A dead man's head with its eye gone comes out the hole.

Well, I had screwed my eyes shut in fright and my ears rung but each girl on either side of me screamed, left the seat and bumped back down again and a huge shout of fear came from the cinema behind us then they let out a breath and laughed. I did not laugh and found nothing amusing in all this terror. I had to force open my eyes again in case the girls witnessed me with my own eyes squeezed shut like a coward, but that horrid, pale white head was still there with alarming, squealing music. I looked to my right and the flowery-dress girl had lifted her hand up to her chest where she was holding it; she appeared in clear physical distress.

I felt something on my leg and glanced down. I saw a small hand which felt around for a moment, discovered my own hand and then took a tight hold of it. I looked to my right but she was not looking at me, she was just gripping my hand, terrified, staring ahead. The girl to the left in the patterned dress had slipped low down in the seat and raised her knees on the seat back in front of her as a measure of protection from the screen. My heart had stopped for a moment then I squeezed the other girl's hand back and I soon began to caress it gently with my free thumb. I wanted to turn and look into her face but I could not. I just gripped her hand and bit my lip staring up at the film.

Up on that screen were hundreds of people on a huge beach, all screaming and crushing each other to get out of the water and cross that magic line to safety, but it was only some kids with a fake shark fin but then the real shark slipped slyly into the salt-water lagoon. The girl holding my hand let out a moan as the real shark's fin sliced through the water heading for a guy in a little rowboat. I swallowed as the rowboat man screamed. His whole leg was bitten off and spun to the lagoon bed. The man had tried to pull himself up on his capsized rowboat and now, for the first time, we saw the grizzled maw of the enormous shark, its wicked sneer as the mouth opened to bite just below the surface. I could not help myself: I spoke out aloud, 'It is the Devil.'

Because that is how it looked. The fingers gripped in my right hand tightened and now the girl on my left slid inside her patterned dress and grabbed my arm. With one of her hands she squeezed around my left biceps and with the other she dug her fingers into my lower arm at the same time burying her face deep in behind my shoulder.

'It is the Devil,' I nodded again in a certain whisper. The beast's huge fin was now sneaking back out to sea and the cop once more forlornly looked towards the ocean's horizon after that creature.

The three of us knew from the lobby card pictures that these lunatics were going to get in a boat and go out there after that shark. I was drained at such a prospect. The girl who was holding my hand saw her friend had pushed in close to me. She copied and pushed her face into my right shoulder protectively and as the film played on she alternated between grabbing my knee or covering her eyes. The girl on my left moved her face in and out of my shoulder cautiously glancing at the screen.

When something alarming occurred on screen, like a boiled set of shark jaws being removed from a bubbling pot, the two girls squeezed in on me from both sides, compressing me in the middle. I placed a hand on one each of their thighs. I kept my hands there tightening my grip on the dresses so they slid over the skin underneath.

The three of us had sunk lower in the seats. Sure enough the cop and the shark expert had finally joined up with the tough fisherman to go hunt the shark but in that old boat! Surely they should call in the army or the air force or something in the name of God and bomb the monster? I had begun to tremble now as this boat – ridiculously close to the water – bravely steamed out to a desolate, fearsomely open sea.

And there it bobbed: a flimsy old fishing boat. You could hear it creaking as it swayed out on the wide ocean – hopelessly exposed – with that thing down in the water waiting somewhere beneath. Despairingly a hand gripped my left knee, a mouth muttered, 'Noh, noh, noh, noh.' I turned my head both ways to the girls. We looked each other in the eyes and I nodded grimly. I slid lower. By that point both girls had leaned in on my chest, virtually lying across me where they gripped each other's hands as well as mine for support. We looked like <u>we</u> were aboard a foundering ship, clinging to one another in our last moments.

The shark suddenly stuck its head out of the water and grinned at us. Both girls screamed. I screamed. The one on my left began crying. It was the final blow. When they both looked at me in appeal I held up my hand in submission as if we were *scuba*-diving and communicating with only gestures. I pointed down to the floor beneath our seats. We looked up. Night had fallen on screen.

Gently, all three of us slipped off the edges of our leather seats then slid, lowering ourselves downward into the darkness and moving shadows of the litter-strewn cinema floor where we could have peaceful sanctuary from this relentless terror on the screen. We slid our legs out ahead beneath the seats before us – theirs were bare in the blue light – our feet rolling paper cups and crisp packets aside. We sighed with relief down there and leaned against each other exhausted. We could hear terrible crashes, splashes and despairing shouts above us from the three men on the doomed boat.

At first we recoiled and jumped at each noise but slowly we calmed. At one point the patterned-dress girl whispered something to her friend then slowly raised her head above the parapet of the seat in front but the two of us tugged at her dress until she snapped back down again and buried her face in my shirt front. She shivered and murmured words to herself at whatever horror she had witnessed up there. She held her cheek to my chest; I stroked the back of her neck for a few moments then at some point the patterned-dress girl quickly leaned in, close on my face – above her friend's head – and kissed me. On the mouth.

My shivers of fear subsided to be replaced by new ones as I was the kisser and toucher of them both. We were frolicsome down in that dark. As the screams and destruction from that forgotten screen somewhere above us rose in volume, I vowed there and then to make this an ideal for my life, to hide from the true horror of the world in the company of the fairer sex. I kissed those two girls so long, I counted to fifty in my head each time, moving from one to the other then back again, my eyes open, theirs closed and sealed by lashes. And they kissed me. I seemed to be allowed to touch anywhere but I did not risk obvious limits. It was a fragrant wrestle.

Eventually the other girl was behind and pushed right up so her bare legs passed under my arms. She was resting her head between my shoulders, her arms tightly around my chest. I touched her slim ankle. Her friend turned to get into a new kissing and touching position. One of the slender tendrils of the dress strap on her shoulder had fallen aside; I took my hand from the other girl's ankle to touch that shoulder and there was a shift in the light from the screen. There was a sweetie wrapper stuck to the bare skin of the shoulder, adhering to the sun-protection cream they both had on their upper backs. I lowered my finger to knock away the bit of paper and then I saw what it was. It was a five-thousand note, once lost on the dirty floor and now stuck to that beautiful, pale, bare shoulder.

Addendum

In that brilliant light in the blue hour of evening, the three of us emerged from the cinema after paying off Gilliemetro with the famous five-thousand note and offering him a humiliating tip from the change which despite himself he had to refuse.

We walked the steepnesses together to where they were staying up in the Typical Quarter, each of us with eyes downward, shyly concentrated upon our shoes – they wore open-toed sandals – but the edges of our mouths held smiles. My testicles were starting to ache in a unique way I had never known before.

As we were passing the type of large furniture store in which our city and indeed our country abounds, the flowery-dress girl stopped then pointed to the shop window and made a quiet exclamation to her friend. They entered the furniture store with an intense, combined concentration and indicated I was to follow.

We walked through ugly, ostentatious empire furniture to work our way back to the window. There was one of those large, imitation sixteenth-century globes of the world, in polished dark wood. The girl in the patterned dress spun the globe slowly then smiling at me moved her finger towards Japan. I nodded enthusiastically. For someone who was to grow to loathe travel so comprehensively, geography was my star subject at school. I leaned forward. Was it the northern or southern island of Japan from which they came? I sensed something awry. The delicate little finger was pointing. To

Vietnam. I said the word out loud. All I could think was, they are communists. This was too fantastic.

Back outside on the street they were talking to each other gaily. They pointed down below the Quarter towards the beach and sea. Using their arms they signed the universal cutting-through-water: 'To Do the Breaststroke.' After that shark film they wanted to go swimming tomorrow. I laughed, nervous, but I nodded energetically. We bowed and they – in turn – awkwardly stepped towards me, retreated, came towards me once again and each pecked on my cheek then on lips. I touched their waists tenderly with just my fingertips but the motion felt slightly awkward and thus melancholy.

They walked ahead but still I followed them dazed, unable to let go of my wonder as they turned the corner. I stopped there and saw them both enter the apartment building with bright orange awnings. Those now-faded awnings are still there to this day. We waved and smiled. I blew kisses, a gesture they seemed puzzled by.

I thought of the beach tomorrow, but as I raced back downhill, my spirits rallied until no thing could ever damage my joy.

Swimming With Vietnamese Schoolgirls

Go to the beach swimming with my two Vietnamese girls in the morning. The horrors!

The first horror was that they both could even contemplate swimming in the sea after watching that *Hollywood* movie with that shark. The second horror: that we had not agreed a specific time to meet up.

This had seemed cool and casual that dreamlike afternoon before. But all through the night in our penthouse of the Imperial as I lay without sheets in my bedroom which was filled with a seductive blue light, I worried. What if the girls and I missed each other on the beach; how would I then find both of them? After all it was a long beach and I was unable to know which end the two girls would arrive at as they descended from the winding lanes of their Typical Quarter. And if I were to take up a position of vigilance at a promenade café on this end of the sand I could miss them at the other end when they came down on to the beach. And vice versa. It was also at this time in my life that my eyesight was starting to weaken, which I had sensed but, not wishing to be required to wear spectacles, I was in complete denial as I squinted at bus numbers and distant café televisions. I finally had to relent and become a spectacle wearer by the end of that year, though I later had the infuriating (to my first wife at least) habit of whipping my spectacles off to appear more attractive when I espied any pretty young woman passing a café terrace and Veroña soon forced me to get contact lenses.

That day I knew I would struggle to accurately identify the girls across the huge sightlines of the beach.

If I took my towel and lay down on the sand of the beach, the girls could settle together at the other end. Even if I sat in the calculated, precise middle of the beach I could see myself: I would be forced to sit up on my elbows under endless heat with Father's *polarised* sunglasses firm on my unsmiling face, my restless head turning from side to side. I would be required to rise again and again from my chosen place and patrol up and down the sand, stepping around the many bathers' bodies like the man who sells the ice creams and cans of cold drinks with his burdensome cooler box.

Urgency was obvious. Curse that bloody beach, source of so much pain to me. It was simple. Without me quickly there, I estimated the beautiful Vietnamese girls would last alone about three minutes together on their beach towels before they were surrounded by settlements of other boys who, with that suffocating confidence I knew and resented so well, would chat then disgustingly – I could feel my fury rising and clenched my fists in bed – those boys would drag their towels over and presumptuously settle on either side of my Vietnamese girls.

Those young long-haired guys from the straight streets behind the castle; boys I could not compete with who arrived at the beach by bus in the morning already in their swimming costumes; they have no bags, just a football among ten of them, and I have also noticed they seem to drink nothing from the cafés all day long; they pummel their wiry bodies under the sun, they throw themselves into surf, then emerge smiling with a violent whip of their head which lashes an overlong dark hair-length aside. Their hard brown torsos glisten. I guess you would call them the working class.

If I were to arrive later than the girls, despite our intimacies together at the cinema the day before, I could visualise how those charming, constantly fidgeting, rapid-talking boys with their non-stop athleticism would infiltrate then drive a barrier between my lovers and me. Though I was ashamed at my horrible and jealous possessiveness, I had to prevent this scenario at all costs.

So I arose at 6 a.m. the next morning, alive with excitement and motivation. I began my grooming which went very quickly. I wore beach trunks beneath a pair of linen trousers and a short-sleeved shirt. I concealed my smoking paraphernalia in a white, rolled-up hotel towel with the fountain symbol of the Imperial embroidered upon it. The notes of change from the legendary crisp five-thousand note were in my pocket. I combed back my hair with water and I would have wished to sneak into my parents' bedroom to pilfer a palmful of Father's hair tonic in its blue bottle which I sometimes splashed on my chest like aftershave. However, the hour was so early my parents were still asleep, so I sneaked downstairs and the night porter released me out into the light where I put Father's *polarised* sunglasses on.

All beachfront cafés were still closed. The lifeguards' high watchtowers empty. The green Safe Swimming flag hung limp on the summit of each. The Town Hall tractor was towing the wide rake trailer across the beach to sieve out cigarette butts and litter. The grooved sand was darkened from the lightest morning dew. The Town Hall street-washing truck had just made its sweep down the promenade tiling which was heavily puddled so I had to step carefully. Seagulls were black against the pale dawn light out to sea.

I walked up and down yawning. It was not even twenty minutes after six. For hours the beachfront cafés did not open so I walked back and forth. I felt faint then realised I had taken no breakfast. I smoked a cigarette.

When the first of the beachfront cafés did open I asked for a coffee. The owner looked at me as if I was crazy. Next thing he was pushing me awake. I was slouched at a table, my torso and arms thrown out across it, my cheek against its cold metal. He told me to get out of there, he said I must be on narcotics or something.

I stumbled down the promenade. Rising sun was now glancing, shining brightly on the puddles. Still not a soul was on the damp sand of the beach. I sat on the tarpaulin heap of brightly painted sunbeds and deckchairs until the tanned guy arrived and started to drag the sunbeds out, organising them in lines. He asked if I wanted to help so I did. It was a good excuse to watch the beach. Though I needed to save as many as I could for the girls, I gave the sunbeds guy one of my cigarettes. We smoked together and he laughed at anything I said. I did not mention the girls. He announced I was a very serious person for my age.

It was going to be a hot day. Slowly, then more rapidly, the sand on the beach of our city was covered with humankind in all its varieties: slow-moving families with inflated lilos under many fathers' arms, large grandmothers with a gathering of little granddaughters close around their granny's collapsed and hanging thighs; all purchased sunbeds for the adult number of their groupings. Then came moody, hierarchical gatherings of young local girls who laid out patchworks of towels decorated with cartoon characters. Fat, laden tourists waddled to the sea edge and constructed small domestic scenarios with folding tables and chairs. They stabbed the sand with umbrella points, arranged iceboxes and radios, triumphantly winded in their temporary chairs they snapped out wide newspapers with headlines bold in many foreign languages all of which I could not read.

Though I preferred not to have to step out deeper than a few centimetres in case of shark attack, I walked in my swimming trunks and shirt along the water's edge in the sharp, right-angled shadows of the beach. I had removed my canvas shoes, tied the laces together and draped them around my neck as, strangely, was then the fashion. My trousers were folded neatly and rolled inside the towel. I was pacing the water's edge as this is a recognised activity and as long as I did not move up and down the beach rapidly enough to become comical, I could observe the entire stretch of sands strolling back and forth from one end to the other. It was also a good method of staying awake.

I looked out sorrowfully at the heedless swimmers. Poor fools.

Did they never visit the cinema? I shivered, waiting for shark fins gaining on them, then turned my full attention to the beach.

I kept close vigil, having several serious false alarms; once when two black-haired girls, lying on their tummies, were mistaken as the Vietnamese. Later I panicked and rushed with a splash from the water's edge when I saw a girl stepping along the promenade in front of the beach cafés, her face turned downward as if scrutinising the palm of an upturned hand. As I came closer I realised my mistake. In fact, she was a girl I vaguely recognised from my school institute.

My situation was made all the more nerve-shattering as I was in no way familiar with what beach attire the girls might wear: the colour of their towels nor, for example, the way they might pin their hair — which is how you identify female acquaintances among the near nudity of beaches. I glanced up jealously at the lifeguards below their flags on their high, white metal ladders and pedestals with their sun umbrellas secured to the superstructure, whistles ready for shark attack and mass evacuation. What a fine view they must have of the beach, I thought.

By early afternoon, when the low wash had advanced then retreated a metre down the sand, a melancholy equilibrium was overpowering the beach; things had remained the same for too long, so people retreated up to the cafés and hotels for a long lunch; some paddled or swam out to the boundary buoys. The younger kids chased one another noisily and scuffled in the water's edge.

I tried to remain calm as I finally spotted the two of them walking slowly past the beachfront cafés, alongside those painted railings (blue in that era). The girls were casually wrapped in sarongs. They had woven, colourful shoulder bags at their sides. Best of all they had their faces turned to the beach as if looking for me alone, among all these bodies. I felt an enormous emotion, a helpless rush of gratitude towards both of them just for their very existence.

I had to step cautiously between the annoying crowds of sunbathers towards the two girls, restraining myself from waving wildly. As I moved further from the sea where I had so gingerly paddled, I began to notice how hot the sand was on my bare feet so I moved quicker than was graceful, coming up awkwardly behind the girls at an angle, running on the burning sand and hopping in a curious dancing fashion to keep the heat off my soles. I raised my arm and saw my ridiculous shadow before me. I called out a hello then both girls spun, almost alarmed. I heard the nearest one let out a long 'Ahhhh'. She smiled.

There was a prolonged awkwardness as I stood moving from one leg to the other on the hot sand beneath, staring up at them about three metres above me on the sea wall. I looked up at them both as if I were considering a crucifixion painting in some baroque church in Rome. They looked down upon me through their matching sunglasses which reflected my figure on the white sand.

I noticed their little swimming bikinis beneath the tied sarongs; of course the girls were smiling wryly, I suppose at me moving from foot to foot below. The one who had worn the flowered dress the day before motioned with her arm brusquely for me to advance up the ramp and join them. I moved forward onto the pavement and suddenly found myself standing before them. They nodded quickly and allowed me to kiss them on each cheek. Immediately I became disappointed at the formality the three of us demonstrated.

Carefully I removed three cigarettes from my pack. Each of the girls quickly took one and I cupped the lighter to their mouths, lit my own, then without hesitation I pointed at the beach, shook my head in distaste, smiled hugely and nodded instead as I pointed over at the then-new Meliander Hotel. I had to sit to rub sand from between my toes and relace my canvas shoes. The girls said some words to each other and seemed a little cautious but again they followed me.

With guilt because of my parents, I still recall how secretly impressed I was with the extensive construction of the Meliander Hotel. It grew out along the old railway pier during 1975. For my parents in their Imperial Hotel opposite, this new, modern, three-hundred-room hotel seemed a grim omen for our future and I was barely permitted to mention its construction.

The architects and Town Hall had displayed an irresistible scale model of the projected hotel in a clear *perspex* box on the prom-enade when I was in the depth of my scale-model-building period: the DC-8-61 *stretch series* era. The hotel model's elongated double V shape jutted out on the foundations of the old pier at right angles to the historical esplanade. Those new aluminium railing balconies boldly looked up the beach coast or over the docks. It was an inspir-ational development for me; as important as the expansion of our city's airport! Most exciting of all on the hotel model with its tiny cars and miniature people were the TWO swimming pools, the stepped depths clearly delineated, minute diving boards poised over their waterless lozenge, each pool to be positioned in the chevron dips of the double-V-shaped design.

Up in the penthouse of the Imperial, every morning before school, I watched the Meliander Hotel construction advance. With my 10 x 50 binoculars, I observed the largest crane's operator busily climb the ladder to his suspended box.

By the end of that winter the new hotel was completed, the palm trees lowered into place at the drive-in lobby, and the forgotten *perspex* display box of the architectural model proposal, full of condensation and trapped, dead insects, was hoisted away in a van.

The Meliander's opening never did harm our hotel's revenues. Many of our guests were regulars who holidayed at the Imperial for the same weeks every year and did not cancel even after my parents sold up. With the advent of cheaper air travel, eventually a whole generation of respectable families who holiday in their own country vanished. Though I was not to know it then, even the future of the new Meliander could not be assured. Soon the Meliander was attracting a specific clientele: with the growth of business confer-ences came those men in suits, and transient, haunted-looking airline crews were the mainstay of its tame, predictable pleasures and bland kitchens. Even in high season, management found they had too many rooms. The Meliander Consortium was eventually taken over by a national conglomerate and the farthest wing of the double V shape was closed down, the legendary second swimming pool drained to gather debris and dead seabirds. The rooms of the far wing were allowed to decline and took on a neglected, sometimes shocking air, with broken windows appearing right into the mid-1980s. Rumours had it that escaped criminals and illegal immigrants were hiding in those rooms in the closed-off section of the Meliander Hotel. Schoolgirls spoke of it in hushed tones.

Smoking grandly the two girls and I walked among the disappointing herbage outside the lobby of the Meliander, withered and neglected since the hotel's first season. A girl on either side of me, we coasted through the lobby by the magnified brilliance of those walls of tropical fish tanks, we moved towards the chiming elevators and my target upstairs: the remaining large triangular swimming pool for residents and, importantly, patrons of the poolside restaurant. Here, I surmised, the girls would be free of the predatory city boys and all three of us would at least be definitely safe from shark attack.

As the two Vietnamese girls and I stepped from the brass-doored lifts at pool level, the ambience of the Meliander Hotel – in its heyday – was still firmly aspirant: splashes and cheerful calls from the fluorine blue bustle around the pool. The restaurant had a glass wall overlooking the pool, piped music, a colourful, long bench of buffet, towering in the centre of which was a high display of imitation fruit, the dining tables had yellow cloths.

They were so excited, both girls rushed poolside, then stood on their tiptoes peering over the wall and its crawling foliage, laughing together down at the dark path, beach and sea below.

I stepped into the restaurant and spoke to the head waiter with the moustache who knew me from taking the odd coffee in the

Terrace of the Imperial. He gave me a table by the pool window where I sat and openly smoked. When the head waiter brought the menu, prophetically, I asked for the dessert menu as well. I waved in the girls who shuffled round the door in their sandals, warbling together – like the pool pumps – placed their woven shoulder bags on the table, on top of the cutlery even, then sat accepting more cigarettes.

As I had predicted they ordered only ice cream and *Coca-Cola*s while I had an omelette then coffee which revived me and allowed me to light up more cigarettes. The girls produced a piece of paper and a pen from one of the bags then pushed it before me but, changed out of their own curious tongue. They tried speaking French language to me.

I grimaced. I did not wish to be able to communicate any more than we had in the cinema. I wanted us just to smoke and look at one another and I knew what it was they were saying to me in French. They were asking what my name was! As if that mattered. Flowery-dress produced a ballpoint pen and passed it to me. I had to smile and, on the back of the bill, draw a silly little drawing of me walking arm in arm with each of them (I am a passable drawer, but I played it safe on their eye shapes). I put an arrow to my figure and wrote: Lolo.

'Looloo.'

I spoke out my name and they slowly repeated it, trying it out, each time showing the coloured ice cream resting on their little tongues, then they each wrote down their names, frowning in concentration. The flowery-dress one stood up and came around the table to place the paper the correct way up in front of me then, annoyingly dragging her sandals on the tiled floor, she returned to her seat across from me and sat dreamily.

There were two names written on the paper in pink ink and innocent girl's handwriting: Thinh Tram, Quynh Hoang. I looked up and blinked towards them. I felt I was in English class once again. How to pronounce such stuff? I mumbled out the names and they laughed at each other. I cleared my throat, tried again and they repeated how the noise was meant to be. Correctly pronounced, their names sounded like hovering mosquitoes.

Thinh was flowery dress and Quynh was patterned. They carried on drinking *Coca-Cola* with great enthusiasm, tipping the glasses back hungrily so after the ice cream was gone I asked the head waiter if we could have more drinks out by the pool. This was fine but I had to settle that initial bill. The head waiter became more lively and amicable when I effortlessly produced my collection of four one-thousand notes then casually handed him one, leaving the change as a hefty tip.

There were many free sunbeds around the pool. To my complete disappointment Quynh and Thinh chose sunbeds and spread their towels on them next to each other so I found myself sequestered on the end bed, beside patterned dress or: Quynh.

Had a decision been made between them about who I alone could possess? I felt an oily grief and confusion mixed with guilt at my greed.

The *Coca-Cola*s arrived on a tray from a white-jacketed waiter. I handed out cigarettes but the girls refused them. They were standing, removing sarongs, dropping them softly to the sunbeds. This was the life. In bikinis, first Thinh then Quynh both dived at steep angles into the pool from the edge just in front of me but causing no splashes they arrowed in so smoothly. They surfaced together and shouted loudly at each other in their language. They began to swim back and forth doing the style called the crawl.

I watched how, with their faces in the water, the shining liquid of the swimming pool poured around their black hair, flowed between their shoulder blades then swirled in little pools above the smalls of their backs. They swam identically as if once coached by the same instructor. In fact, I could see the young bored lifeguard watching their style (or more probably the loose wet fabric on their buttocks) from his tipped-back seat at the far end of the pool. I hunched on my sunbed and almost growled possessively as the girls swam too close to that lifeguard.

Blind, the thin arms reaching up yawingly, jabbing into the water with sharp elbows and cupping backward hands, Thinh reached the end of the pool. She submerged herself then with upward propulsion from the water, slapped her wet palms on the dry poolside stone and heaved herself high with trembling arms to swing her bottom round into a sit. She rested, kicking her toes in the surface as water running from her body spilled black on the pool edge. Shoving out a hand she helped pull up Quynh.

Then they both stood, dripping adjacent to the diving board. My jealous heart lurched as I saw the lifeguard's mouth move. The girls nodded and then strangely their mouths also moved. He replied. They seemed to be having a conversation. How was it possible? Perhaps that swine spoke French language? I felt a pure hatred for the man. Could he not accept his damn position as an employee and cease trying to fornicate with under-age patrons of the poolside restaurant?

Because I was trying to do that.

The lifeguard had blond hair and a thin gold chain with some symbol attached, glinting on his bare chest above the zip of his white tennis top. After they talked and nodded for minutes I accepted that for sure he must speak the damned language. Finally the girls each dived from the board and torpedoed underwater along the pool bottom, their limbs suddenly retracting then propelling them up towards my end. I continued glaring at the lifeguard from behind my father's *polarised*.

Thinh's head popped up; she placed her hands on the poolside, resting her chin on the stone, and breathed heavily looking directly at me. She pointed into the swimming pool indicating for me to join them in that inviting water. I could see Quynh, concentrating and serious, climbing the ladder out of the pool by the diving board with water pouring down her shining legs. Using a hooked finger round her rear, she unselfconsciously pulled her bikini bottoms out then let them silently ease back.

I stood and removed my shirt. My skin was going through an especially benign phase and I felt confident about my semi-tanned torso. I seriously paced along the pool edge towards the diving board as if contemplating something when there was a commotion to my immediate right and a delirious scream. In the seconds I had taken my eyes from them both I felt first the bony grip of their wet, cold little thin fingers then the weight of them both combined as they charged me off from the pool edge: I felt the strange power of my own weight as my legs then all of me plunged into that shocking water which squeezed up my nostrils. I recall a retreating necklace of bubbles coil around my upstretched arm, the fingers of my hand reaching for the silver froth of the surface. I sank until I simply sat on the bottom, mouth open, legs splayed out. What I had been unable to confess to the girls so I could be with them that day was that I could not swim.

Uncle Luis's Funeral

One evening in my apartments at the Phases Zone 1, Ahmed Omar leaned back as usual, comfortable on the calfskin sofa by the panorama window. I was drinking whisky.

'I want to tell you about my Uncle Luis's funeral,' I said to him. 'My Uncle Luis had led a quiet life since the Civil War. Because of his service he got his card for the Falange and thus could be some kind of clerk in the Tourism and Information Ministry. At a desk with an electric fan, he worked his way up through the hunger years of the forties. In the fifties he married red-haired Aunt Lucia. They never had children. Uncle Luis helped Father settle when he first left the farm after the war and came to our city as a waiter. And dropped all the dishes.

Father and my Uncle Luis had never been close. Yet it was not the war which led to their fallout, like in so many families. It was the famous dispute over my deceased grandmother's upright clock (it lost an hour a week) that stopped them talking to each other. War, a clock? Brothers will find something to hate each other about.

Like so many things in life, Father and his family's good fortune in the Civil War was just a chance of geography. On their high farm in the country, up the bend in the road from the village, they were never very clearly associated with either faction in the war. They supplied olives and small amounts of grapes, raisins, oranges and lemons to the losing side then, after the victory and persecution, they supplied the same comestibles to the winners. Food supply was considered such essential work and my grandfather was so old, Father, who was just sixteen, escaped any type of conscription. Later, Father would ingratiate himself to the fascists of our town; who did not? In our country, my generation are all in some little way the last of the fallen angels and we have the religion to go with that. It can be a good place to start from in life: without illusions about your virtue. Like Father said on his deathbed, 'I know I am a bastard, but I do not deserve this.' True, Papa.

Like the European democracies, Father's family, who never read newspapers, remained steady-eyed and indifferent. With the same tolerant resignation that he displayed looking out across the full dining room, I can imagine – as a young man – Father looked out on his country's warring factions and the maddening slaughter around him. If it interfered with gathering the fruit, it was bad, otherwise, down in the village, the shootings, throat cuttings and the priest who had the rosary beads forced into his ear with a hammer were nothing to do with Father. Like people who paid over the odds for dinner, Father thought war was for fools. He did not have to see the murdering to believe that. Fugitives would pass through, hungry and afraid at the start and again at the end of the war. They were not invited to stay in the outhouses but fed with soup and given fruit and water to go on their way. Though they were one side's fugitives at the start of the war and the other side's at the end, both were treated identically.

Our region was on the losing side but by the time the uniformed victors came up the dirt road, inspected Grandfather's well-tended terraces and fruit trees and noted my uncle's war service on their side, the farm was left alone to do what was best both during war and victory: produce olives and fruit. It was only in the sixties that Father had learned, while his country starved, most of his village's fruit for the next few years had been exported to *Nazi* Germany. In my student days when we talked politics, I asked him if he felt guilty about this; he shrugged, ever the artisan, and remarked, 'A well-tended orange will taste as sweet to a *Nazi* as to anyone else.'

It was different for people in the cities in those hunger years; like Mother. Such are the bounties or betrayals of geography. Mother grew up hungry in our city, which was among the last to fall. The prime minister, who had taken refuge, fled our city. Then Mother saw the shifty, desperate men hanging around the pier cafés, including the Terrace of the Imperial, trying to get boats out.

One evening, when she was a little girl standing near the fountain in front of the hotel – which she would one day own – Mother watched a fishing boat put out, overloaded with men and even dragging fifteen uneducated communists in old, damaged nets. Naive of geography and the size of the sea, they believed if they swam for it and the skipper cut the net free after steaming an hour east, they might float north to a safe country. Perhaps they thought they would wash ashore in the Soviet Union? The skipper Olienzo shrugged and took their money, watches and the least ruined pairs of boots. It was a better way to go anyway. Once they were cut free they must have floated together like a group of swans until dawn; still asleep, the salt sea bore them down, a dozen men tangled together in the torn net, spinning slowly away from the last surface light into benthic darkness, comrades all the way into the depths.

My father told me Skipper Olienzo felt that the military should actually give him a commendation for his actions. The skipper boasted he had killed more Reds in one evening than many of the heroes who fought at the front; he used to brag nightly at the seamen's mission bar. Before he was stabbed up an alley one night.

How our Uncle Luis came to be in the fascist army was a standing joke in our family. Father enjoyed telling me how, as a boy, his elder brother was excited only by mechanical cultivators, engines and tractors. Somehow, my uncle obtained a manual for *John Deere* tractors from North America. Quite a feat in an area where there was no postal service. This manual – with vivid colour diagrams – was one of the few pieces of print in the house, and it was Uncle Luis's obsession; he would turn the pages from cover to cover then back again. He had successfully memorised all the engine components which my father was expected to regularly test him on in the evenings. Shy of working among the trees and on the olive terraces, Uncle Luis's only desire was to travel to towns and walk in circles again and again around any rare cars, trucks, buses or, preferably, tractors that could be found.

Just before the armed rising, Uncle Luis in his first time away from the farm had travelled to the north to visit a distant relative. All that excited him about his forthcoming journey were the trucks and tractors he hoped to encounter.

In that region the rebels had control within days of the rising. Where my uncle was, nearby rebel forces were only one ancient tank in strength and mechanical-mad Luis walked eleven miles just to step round and round that tank again and again, like a dog about to lie down.

In days Uncle Luis was dismantling and reassembling that tank engine, telling the officers in charge what maintenance was required and boring them with the theory of the internal-combustion engine. In those days he could have been shot just for boring them with the theory of the internal-combustion engine but instead he was commissioned and ended up as a fascist mechanic on the northern front.

Like so many fools, I do not believe Uncle Luis saw any bigger picture. I do not think he believed for one second in the holy, nationalist crusade he was meant to be a part of. He was just delighted to be on the side with the best tanks. Especially when our German friends arrived with their splendid armour to fight for our Christ and Country. Uncle Luis was lucky. I believe if he had been faced by an enemy with more gallant tanks an irrepressible melancholy followed by desertion would surely have overcome him.

★　★　★

So in later years, Uncle Luis and Aunt Lucia lived in a small apartment with many canaries, four streets back from the esplanade near Algoroba Plaza. Uncle Luis drove a motor scooter. Its engine was sometimes lovingly dismantled in the salon with various components laid out precisely on torn strips of cloth. Aunt and Uncle were never well off and had become envious of my father and mother's growing business: their little shop in the lane then the petrol pump back in the village then the two ex-military trucks delivering round our city then finally mortgaging the Imperial Hotel and quickly owning it.

Grandmother died. In a rash effort to get ready cash — ironically so they could show off to my parents — my uncle sold his share of the old farm to Father, cheap. Uncle Luis and Aunt Lucia made their Sunday passage in fine clothes while my father and mother shuffled around the hotel in patched affairs with threadbare cardigans, but they were the wealthy ones. When my uncle took Grandmother's clock without asking — saying to Father, 'Oh, but you are rich enough to buy your own, I should get it' — the two brothers hardly spoke again.

Though my father and mother did not talk to them I was still expected to make the odd polite visit to Uncle and Auntie, keeping up the pretence of being a family. My memories of Uncle Luis and Aunt Lucia when I visited their apartment are the dismantled scooter engine, the canary noise, the uneven ticking of the infamous clock and Lucia's famous red hair.

Lucia was always standing by the windows in front of the brass canary cages with their domed minarets; the sun was behind her so the canaries were black apart from the kernels of their feed which the sun glinted through when the seeds shot up as the birds fluttered from perch to perch. Above, the light moved through Lucia's endless cigarette smoke and turned red as it tried to struggle through her thick hair. I guess by then her hair had really turned grey because Uncle's was grey, but Aunt Lucia dyed her tresses with fierce, poor henna the colour of first rains which rush in a dried red-soil river bed.

Aunt Lucia passed away first. I was engaged to Veroña when Uncle Luis died that hot, hot July. Veroña's family were not churchy, they were liberals – her mother died when she was an infant and her father was a maths teacher. Veroña was studying mathematics at university in the capital where I had changed from Town Planning to Design.

At that time, in the mid-1980s, our country was changing so quickly in so many ways. Yet even I was shocked at the length of the skirt Veroña wore to Uncle Luis's funeral. Despite her mother's early death, I understood how sad but deeply erotic Veroña found funerals. I strongly feared she was wearing no underwear for spontaneous convenience later on. I furiously rasped in her ear to go home and change – that Uncle Luis's home would be full of religious Old Ones and most of them pious ex-Falange, but that news made her more determined. Veroña and I had shared some whiskies in an old café and we were both tipsy by the time we got to my uncle and aunt's old apartment off Algoroba Plaza. Aunt Lucia used to boast how much that apartment was worth but it was difficult to suppress emotion when we learned they had only rented the place for the last twenty-five years. The landlady had concealed this new fact to allow Luis to lie in a grand overnight vigil using the big bedroom upstairs.

Mother and father (who were separated at this time) were too impatient to sit in an overnight vigil so two ghastly old nuns had taken their place until the late morning. The nuns still sat together like caryatids in the corner of the bedroom when Veroña and I unsteadily ascended those steep stairs, my mouth touching her eighties permed hair, using my body as a shield so some relatives behind us on the steps could not look straight up her skirt.

That bedroom was airless in the heat, crammed with people standing in various relays of obscure prayer. There were many women of the type who had come to pay respects but also to judge the furniture. All around that chamber, chairs were positioned at odd angles where older vigilants slumbered. Poor dead Uncle Luis in a suit lay still on the large old bed at the far side, his white cuffs and bloodless hands lay upon his chest. He had been dressed by the mortician, Madame Solielian, wife of the crematorium owner; Mr and Mrs Solielian both stood solemnly in a corner. I could see Uncle Luis's face was heavily made up.

My mother and father nodded from the far corner, glum but more in outrage at Veroña's skirt than at Luis's passing, I do believe. Then Veroña herself looked around, the skirt mercifully fallen those vital three centimetres lower because we were off the stairs. She anticipated the pious, agonising wait in the room wearing her red, very high heels. When would that abstract moment arrive, at which it could be said we had paid sufficient respect and we could file out to lumber towards the cemetery on Heaven Hill where I too would now soon lie?

Drunk, Veroña just did not see clearly in the dark room after the bright streets – she moved politely to sit somewhere and lowered her ass gently down. She lowered it on to Uncle Luis's cool, rouged and powdered face, the prominent, slim family nose pushing coolly between her bare buttocks and the shock of his icy forehead vivid as she sat on the dead man. The bed creaked at once.

Veroña sprang up violently with the tiniest squeak when she realised she was sitting on the face of my uncle's corpse. Despite the legendary exaggerations over the years, I believe only my father and mother, the two nuns and a few at the front saw what happened clearly. But we all heard the nuns take in breath and mutter frantic prayer. I tried to lunge for my embarrassing fiancée and pull her upwards but I realised this would only draw more attention so once she successfully raised herself, stepped slightly to the left and sat on the vacant chair she had originally aimed for, I just stood and perspired consistently in mortification.

I could not look at Veroña for the hour we remained in that room and I knew she was trying not to look at me. I did venture to glance towards my father. He turned at one point, his brow held low, his forehead slimy with sweat, his mouth set in a curious way. After a moment I suddenly realised my father was trying to hold in the most profound and genuine laughter that can overcome a man.

Tears of laughter moved along the wrinkles by his eyes. Father used both his arms to pin Veroña and me against the wall in the downstairs bathroom where we locked ourselves after the vigil. Veroña just put her face in her hands and kept repeating, 'Oh my God, I am so sorry,' but Father, anxious nobody see him laughing when he was in mourning for his brother, tore at the tears on his face with a handkerchief. Looking up at Veroña when he sat on the edge of the bath he hoarsely whispered, 'The happiest day of Luis's life, girl, and you had to make it today!'

He choked back laughter in the rear seat of the vintage limousine all the way up to the mausoleums and cypress trees of the old cemetery, that haunt of Sagrana and I as schoolboys high on the side of Heaven Hill by the castle and garrison.

I remember heat and high sun. The hour when shadows of the darting white doves of that cemetery are mistaken for wasps buzzing around your feet. There were dark red roses in vases by many crypts. There were vast old family mausoleums as big as houses. Cicadas drilled furiously out in any unmanaged overgrowth. In our mourning clothes we were a black line walking alongside whitewashed walls of corpses sealed in stone caskets up to and above the height of six metres.

Uncle Luis was to be interred in the south wall which formed a surrounding enclosure of caskets. We gathered around: Priest, Solielian the undertaker, family, relatives, demure retired clerks from the old Ministry of Tourism and Information. Father and Mother actually holding hands stood next to Veroña and I.

The bearers had opened his carrying coffin and were lifting Luis onto the stretcher to hoist him up to the open, waiting, black hole of the wall casket. Mr Solielian and his attendant stood by in readiness to seal the slab. Veroña clung to my arm. I looked at my fiancée, suspicious that she was aroused and on our way back to the limousine may jump me in that mausoleum which Sagrana and I haunted, but Veroña's head was still, her face earnest as when she considered her student thesis in third year.

Suddenly I saw Father jerk and take a step back, his shoe heel caught a piece of dusty kerbing and he toppled, but Veroña lunged out and caught him by an arm. Father was staring ahead, glaring at something. I saw it next – what I thought were rags – lying stretched out on the ground: that unmistakable hennaed red hair but now only attached to the pale skull and the shrivelled face mask of Aunt Lucia, as if she had dried brown paper pasted over her features; her nose had vanished. Then I saw the long white dress which I remembered from when she was interred. The fabric was stained brown – and there was a skeletal foot from which a jewelled sandal had fallen off.

Aunt Lucia and Uncle Luis had wished to be buried together, possibly for reasons of economy, and this was being done quite literally. Mr Solielian and his grave worker had simply opened their tiny crypt and slid my aunt out and left her lying in full view there beneath the uncensored sun.

I could see Father was shocked but he recovered himself. Veroña was having quite a day of it, putting her varnished nails to her forehead, her spindly fingers forming a caged frame around the brow and eyes which cast a network of shadows on her face as if calculating one of those theorems.

After Uncle Luis was finally slid into that lozenge of blackness, sure enough the withered corpse of Lucia was hoisted up by Solielian and his grim assistant and it was shudderingly forced in next to Luis. The stretcher she was on gave some resistance; Solielian shrugged apologetically, raised his boot and aggressively shoved Aunt Lucia home. His assistant picked up that discarded jewelled slipper and carelessly spun it into the black hole after them.

As we all walked away I turned. Mr Solielian and his accomplice each lit cigarettes which rested in the corners of their mouths as one held up the seal stone and the other started slapping on wet concrete with a trowel.

There is no wonder I fear death so much, for what is it about my region and my country that makes death such a crude exhibition each time? Air-crash corpses adorn our magazines in doctors' waiting rooms; on a piece of wasteland in the middle of the Capital city I once saw a white, dead horse rotting over a period of one month and no attempt was made by authorities to take it away. Innumerable dead insects and rodents are to be seen in full daylight besieged by regiments of ants and maggots.

On the National road behind the Phases Zone 1, my second wife, Aracelli, and I once saw some tourists get out of their hire car with a video camera to film a dog spectacularly crushed on the tarmac. The dog's top half tranquil, its expression smiling, its rear torso perfectly flattened and the contents of the ribs squeezed out to one side, looking like salmon *pâté*. Aracelli told me the tourists were saying in English as they filmed, 'You could not see this back home.'

Tenis was full of stories regarding inconvenient human corpses and there was to be the same macabre farce with Father's death.

When we got back to town, after Uncle Luis's internment that day, Father and the other oldies lifted rattling iced brandies to their mouths at the bar of the Dolphin.

'Did you see her hair?' Father shook his head. 'It was unchanged.'

'I wonder where she got her henna. Good quality,' Mother whispered.

Father turned to Mother and me: 'Do not let that happen to me – cremation, anything, but not that.'

At the Meliander Hotel the sweltering night of Uncle Luis's funeral, Father had booked for Veroña and me, infuriatingly – to show his power – a room with twin beds.

We sweated heavily in our lovemaking. Veroña was predictably inflamed; at some point in the darkness (for we had a sea view so there was no ambient light from our city) I heard a bed sheet literally slap the tiled floor in its sweat-soaked state. When we lay still between bouts there was something unfamiliar about the heavy wetness of sweat which clung to us. Veroña switched on the bedside light then screamed. The single sheet and bed were dark with a frightening quantity of blood; our naked bodies were wreathed in black slobbers of it, mixed with our sweat.

Eventually, after I had calmed her, Veroña stood in the bath touching blood-clotted hair out of her face as red trickled out from within her.

My voice trembled, 'Darling, I think you are having a miscarriage, we had better phone an ambulance. Perhaps I should phone Tenis at his halls and ask for advice? Three in the morning?' I mused stupidly.

'Lolo, are you sure it is a miscarriage? Blood is . . . everywhere in me.'

'Do you feel normal?'

We were each breathing fast and hard from both our earlier exertions and adrenalin shock, mixed with something ancient, primitive: this vivid blood mercilessly revealed under fluorescent light – like Lucia's dried corpse in the bright heat that afternoon.

Veroña said, 'I feel good. I think it is you.'

It was true. My foreskin had torn about half a centimetre at its base. It healed in a fortnight and never troubled me again.

We showered. Sympathetic yet mocking, for a moment Veroña cradled my crippled penis in her fingers – with those forever-painted nails and she mumbled playfully. I felt less of a man.

I used a wet towel to wipe the tiled floor. I balled up the bed sheets. I did not try to hide them in the wardrobe drawer as Madelaine the chambermaid had spoken of those years before. Instead, I threw the bloodstained bundle of sheets out into the darkness from the window of the Meliander Hotel beyond the dark path below. The blooded sheets fell to the sea where they unfurled on the surface but eventually rocked and slapped out beyond the odometer, the green warning beacon then vanished.

After his death, Mother and I had Father cremated by the Soleilians, but we ensured Father escaped their burial plots on Heaven Hill. One February evening his ashes were packed by The Pyrotechnic into the largest firework money could buy in our city. Father was shot up into the air in a rocket from the water's edge on the beach just down in front of the Imperial Hotel. Over a hundred people drank the best French wine with sand in our good shoes. Tenis stood on one side of me, Veroña on my other, Sagrana next to her.

It was a pink trail Father left behind him and at some point which could not be defined, maybe three lengths beyond the green beacon and odometer on the farthest pier end and as high as our town's castle behind us, Father exploded very loudly and became a football-pitch size of golden tears and blue stars which, as they fell quickly down towards the black sea, were reflected upon it, revealing small metallic waves. Father's colours became invisible before they touched water, and when I blinked, my father became greenish amoeba shapes sliding slowly on my black retinas.

Learn To Swim

I remember all too clearly my eyes open, my body suspended help-lessly for a moment at the bottom of the Meliander Hotel swim-ming pool with my legs stuck out among the rising bubbles of my own calamitous descent. I commenced to float back upwards and was about to find my feet on the tiles of the pool bottom.

It was clear I was easily within my own depth at the point where Thinh and Quynh had playfully pushed me into the pool. The water would have come up to my neck and despite my humiliation I could have clung to the sides of the pool then cautiously edged my way to the ladders in the shallow end to climb out. However, events piled up on me. The French (as he turned out to be) life-guard was just trembling to commit a heroic act.

Down in the shadowed turquoise of the deep end, my bulging eyes registered a tremendous commotion of bubbles, the explosion of ballooning white tennis clothes, healthily sweeping, tanned limbs entering the water. The lifeguard had made a spectacular and perfect dive into the pool and he came slithering towards me beneath the surface like the worst kind of shark. His eyes were open and I could swear the lifeguard was smiling, showing his white teeth. I broke surface and took a swallow of air but the lifeguard violently grabbed me around the torso and wheeled me so he was invisible but somewhere behind. He seemed to have his arm jammed under my chin. For a moment I wondered if I were being arrested as well as saved?

Even though I could have stood on the bottom of the pool, he dragged me backwards, his powerful legs thrusting us up into the shallow end so quickly my feet slipped on the tiles of the pool bottom. I tried to call out in protest, 'I am OK, I am OK, just allow me to stand,' but I had swallowed a mouthful or two of disgusting pool water and was generally spluttering and spitting while trying to speak. Before they would just allow me to stand a moment in the shallow end with the water level at my knees to gather breath, a porcupine of arms and grasping hands were jabbing down and hauling me from the swimming pool as if my fall through its waters was a kind of suicide attempt I may immediately repeat. I had to be whisked from the area like an old president who had just taken a potshot in the gut.

I was hoisted away from the poolside and held down on the ground. I saw the lifeguard leap up with one thrust of a leg, trailing shoots of water from all over his white tennis clothing; he dashed to a sunbed, whipped the long cushion from it, sending a pair of someone's, possibly valuable, sunglasses and a shirt hurling into the air. Then I recognised it as my own sunbed and Father's *polarised* sunglasses. I recoiled in fear as the lifeguard's tanned legs approached, the horrible hairs plastered flat. I tried to turn my head and look around. In all the scrum of over-helpful men, Thinh and Quynh seemed to have been pushed away while I had been carried horizontally then laid down on the paving tiles upon that cushion. I could feel myself needlessly soaking it. As I suspected, the lifeguard approached my chest with two flat palms ready to begin breaking my ribs in an attempt to evacuate water from my water-free lungs.

Then came my finest moment. With a firm gesture of the hand held up vertically as if I was refusing any more carrots from a silver-service waiter, I stopped the lifeguard descending on me. Majestically I arose unsteadily to my feet. I coughed briefly and announced that I was all right, I was all right.

I swear there was a murmur of disappointment. My triumph was short-lived. Suddenly disinterested in my well-being, the crowd took its eyes from my dripping, sorry figure and turned them instead to the upright French lifeguard *par excellence*, athletic in his plastered

175

tennis whites which in their transparency showed the darkened hairs of his hard chest and his gold, slightly off-centre crucifix – his bleached fringe was glued slightly to one side.

Enthusiastically, every person around that swimming pool – the middle-aged couples, the younger men who had hoisted me out, the entire restaurant staff present to watch (even, I noted, Chef in his tall hat), the diners away from their abandoned tables clearing their palates with the sight of my ignominy – every set of hands burst into a rapid, deafening applause at the quick-acting and professional lifeguard.

'Do you need a doctor, young fellow?' asked some interrogator when their applause lessened.

'No. I am quite all right now. Thank you.'

Someone said something to me in damn English language. I frowned testily, ignoring him.

'What happened?' another demanded.

I said, 'Oh, we were just fooling around and I slipped and fell in. Startled for a moment but I am fine now.'

'You looked like you were in trouble in there, fellow,' that interfering oaf added.

The lifeguard chose his moment. He announced, loudly, 'He cannot swim.'

'He cannot swim?'

'Can you swim?'

I saw Father's *polarised* sunglasses on the wet tiles near my feet. I bent to pick them up. I had to move some of the observers aside but they actually resisted me kneeling in, with my outstretched arm, to retrieve the sunglasses. Clearly they thought they deserved some kind of an explanation. One of the lenses was cracked on the sunglasses but I put them on anyway.

'Hey, he could not swim,' someone called to the rear.

'Can you swim. Can you? You were just flailing about in there,' the lifeguard smiled.

I looked around. I still could not see the girls but I had flushed deeply like a rose with true embarrassment. Everyone was staring at me. I was shivering but hands had dropped a towel around my shoulders. I looked round and there was Thinh. Her arms were reaching up around me, adjusting the towel. Dazed, I stared at her. Quynh approached carrying some of my things. Their presence gave me a brief taste for frankness so I turned to my onlookers. At least nobody from school was here. 'Right. I cannot swim.'

'Call them friends. I saw them push you in,' croaked an old, over-tanned xenophobe, holding out a shaky, accusing finger towards the girls in their bikinis.

'There was a language misunderstanding. They are from Vietnam. They speak only French.'

This was a mistake. The gathered Old Ones looked at the girls suspiciously.

'Drowning is drowning in any language,' muttered the xenophobe.

The lifeguard turned to the girls and in French said those fatal words to them, 'He cannot swim.' He pointed at the pool, held up an admonishing finger and shook it, though he was smiling.

The effect on the girls was as I suspected, a sort of contained hysteria with lots of fingers held to their mouths, then quick-talking to each other in their strange language; like their reaction to that *Hollywood* movie with that shark the afternoon before; mingled with a complete, disbelieving pity for my remarkable inability to swim. They were grabbing my arms and simultaneously saying things to me then they turned to the lifeguard and spoke in French to him. He nodded and spoke out the side of his mouth to me, 'Sorry, they say. They ask why did you not tell them? Do you know one another well?'

My mouth dropped at the effrontery. I turned to him, 'Sir. Is there a charge for your services? Now you have saved my life am I required to fill out some form or answer all your questions towards some kind of official inquiry?'

The lifeguard shut up.

The fat wife of one of the men actually gasped when I said this. She was wearing a one-piece bathing costume which really looked as if she had been hit by fertilised ostrich eggs travelling at great velocity. I saw the mob narrow its eyes. They were aghast at my ungrateful statement and cynical manner but I saw also how they swiftly turned their eyes from me to the girls with the clear implication that these foreign teenagers were somehow responsible for everything that had taken place here; these strange-eyed, non-Catholic communists had bewitched and corrupted a countryman in the proximity of their enlightened poolside.

With as much dignity as possible, deliberately lingering to try and put some division between my plunge into the pool and our shameful but inevitable departure, the girls and I tidied and gathered our things. Then we paused to haughtily light up cigarettes. Though I was still dripping wet, I pulled my shirt on, the buttons undone, hanging open on my chest. The girls studiously wrapped themselves in their sarongs and gently placed tanning lotions into their shoulder bags. The crowd dispersed and the noise of luncheons regained the pool terrace but everyone kept staring over at us.

The lifeguard, who sensed the girls' sympathy towards me, wisely took up his seat by the diving board again.

As we retraced our path towards the elevators, passing the poolside restaurant windows and the diving board, a man with an enormous paunch, a bald, tanned head glistening with suntan oil, turned his face aside at me and growled, 'Learn to swim.' Some people laughed behind me.

The girls both looked at me questioningly, puzzled by the man's harsh command and the resultant laughter. As we crossed towards the elevators Quynh touched my arm, nodded backwards and said something in French then changed to Vietnamese. By the rising intonation in both languages it was clear she was asking what the fat man had said. I pointed to myself then put my palms together beneath my chin, fingers facing forward and I motioned the gesture 'to swim', pushing out in the classical arm motion of the weary breaststroke style, pulling back hands, cupped.

In the elevator as we rode down I stood dripping. Thinh, with a look of real sympathy, touched my arm.

For our city is a city of swimmers. The beach with its sand is the sacred ground of our modern, heathen society and we tend it lovingly with the Town Hall's mechanical rakes, sweepers and sieves to withdraw cigarette butts, condoms, impurities and the flotsam of the sea.

We nurse the beach back into shape with mechanical diggers which rush to it like ambulances after the winter storms. We replenish the beach with clean white virgin sand. After all the beach is a kind of metaphysical material itself: for sand is rock on its centuries-long journey towards invisibility and we celebrate it: as kids we dig and play in it, building castles with towers; in our youth we shower it from our private parts after we have made love upon it, drunk. We caress sand through our fingers, crunch it between our toes, and when it is warm we let the soft bodies of our lovers and our dearest children lie down upon it. On the beach we remove our clothes, show ourselves as we really are, appendix scars on the prettiest girls. In our city the beach is our one true bed where we all sleep together under the common sun. If only I could have joined this celebration as a youth. Perhaps I would have been a different human being? As a youth I began to long for my own little private kingdom of beach and freedom on some far tropical island. How I used to dream.

Cruelly positioned as the Imperial Hotel was, I lived out every summer of my lonely youth within earshot of the joyous calls of frivolous teenagers yelling from an ocean's edge; of screaming girls with brown limbs being thrown through walls of surf.

When I was young, nobody found out I could not swim. It was my gravest secret. Thankfully at my institute, since every single person swam from an early age, swimming was never part of any sports curriculum and every spare moment of physical training was spent on our national obsession: soccer.

Every Friday afternoon, the Master ordered me and my future accountant, Sagrana – who was as useless at soccer as me and just as unwanted by both teams – to run to the top of Heaven Hill with its black, leaning cypresses and enormous crypts and wave our arms in the air from there.

From the summit of the large pink sepulchre we swung our thin arms for a full minute towards the soccer pitch and the Master's hysterical whistle far below us. This regular, intended punishment became a heavenly diversion for Sagrana and I each Friday and we rushed the dusty lanes and open fields to gain the deserted cemetery where we could enter the cool shaded crypts, smoke cigarettes and tarry there.

Sagrana was smoking professionally already in those days, with his husky voice, long fingers, girlish looks and those dark bags beneath his eyes. Already he was showing the talents that would define his destiny. He would describe his painfully precise regime to make his cigarettes last. As we lay together on a long tomb in the urine tang of a crypt, Sagrana would describe the intricacies of our town's bus fares and how, by changing buses twice, one could actually cross the city at little more than half-price. For his own reasons – girls were not his concern – and greatly to my relief, Sagrana never showed a moment's interest in beaches or swimming either.

Since the beach was the only way to meet girls in those pre-discothèque years, girls were a pleasure I had to forfeit. It was assumed among girls from the institute that I was bookish, eccentric and profoundly disinterested in them and that I spent a suspiciously unhealthy time with effeminate Sagrana, prowling among the tipping cypresses and racing leaves of the windy cemetery.

Yet I had huge crushes on each and every girl in my institute. Enough to write in pen each girl's intimate-seeming Christian name on a pack of playing cards which I kept in a wooden cigar box beneath my bed. I remember I never even met some of the girls so named and only admired the prettiest from a distance.

I would shuffle these cards every night, pick out one at random. I did not care about the card's suit of clubs, swords, golden coins or goblets, jack, queen or king. I was interested in its handwritten, neat Christian name to bring forth the completely specific image of that particular girl's smiling face, her precise mouth or her bare legs in our institute's skirt as she had dashed by me on a rainy day. I pleased myself with my own hand as other men do.

Even today I retain precise, specific images to go with the names of at least thirty of those once-teenaged beauties; my dream lovers: the Mª Rosa girl, for example, as she lifted herself over the back seat of a scooter one grey day, graceful legs revealed, the spectacular curving indent of the small of her back visible above the elastic waist of her black skirt. Those young girls must now be mothers. Heavier, their younger looks expunged. May I say I feel I almost do them a tender honour by holding those cherished images in tribute; inviolable within my saddened mind, their lithesomeness lives on.

I swore to myself in my life as a man I would sleep with exactly fifty-two women as per the number of cards in the pack, to make up for the desperation of my lonely youth. Of course, as has been set down in this account of what has befallen me, I did not achieve anywhere near this score.

Still dripping from my plunge to the bottom of the pool, Thinh, Quynh and I crossed the road towards the Imperial Hotel. With the cracked lens on my father's *polarised* sunglasses, a bright line of harsh reality leaked through the cosmetic sepia which I so preferred the world reduced to. As we paused by the big fountain outside our hotel to let the 112 bus pass, I turned to the huge concrete fountain basin with its lapping waters. Again cupping my palms beneath my chin, I pretended to dive in and swim. The girls burst out laughing loudly, obviously finding this impossibility very funny.

Once across the road we rounded the newspaper kiosk to the Terrace of the Imperial doors. The girls hesitated but I gestured them inwards. I led them on through, nodding to the waiters who winked rudely. I knew Mother and Father would be downstairs supervising the kitchens for lunches so I led the girls through the hall and reception.

They looked up admiringly at the paintings – mostly very good (almost illegal) imitations of Botero and originals by forgotten provincials – which had hung up the walls of the high stairway since before my parents owned the hotel.

We passed by the varnished reception desk and the huge double doors where a horse coach could be backed in at the turn of the century. We passed the glass case where the government-controlled hotel rates – which were just about to be abolished – were strictly displayed. Then we three ascended the stairs together, up past the television salon and the billiard room which I let them stick their heads in even though they were girls. Finally I showed them up our private stairway which led to the penthouse and they followed me to the 'blue' front room with its glassed-in window view of the Meliander Hotel and the silvery sea beyond.

The girls whispered together as we stood in the modern kitchen. There were bottles of *Coca-Cola* in the fridge, so I poured two glasses with ice and lemon.

With the girls following, ice tinkling in their drinks, I led them down the corridor and showed them my bedroom. I instantly bit my lip for of course I had forgotten that on the cabinet of drawers still stood the model of the embarrassing DC-8 *stretch series* which looked a little too boyish to my eye but the girls did not seem to notice. Thinh turned to me and spoke in French and I sadly understood most of her strange question. They wished to see my parents' bedroom.

I led them along the curve in the corridor and cautiously opened the door. The girls looked into the bedroom and 'Ooohed'. They seemed impressed by the lacy decor, the bedcover with its cushions and the long fitted wardrobe with its varnished sliding doors. I walked straight in and motioned for the girls to follow. They stood in the middle of my parents' bedroom in their sarongs, nodding and openly talking to each other. I could feel a touching breeze on my wet shirt coming through the window behind us.

Quynh nodded to me and said, '*Toutes Mama . . . ?*' and she lifted up her slim leg from the knee and, twisting it slightly aside, she alluded to her slip-on sandals.

'Shoes!?' I said and repeated our word for it in our national language. I slid open the wardrobe door and pointed to its base. My mother insisted on keeping her shoes in the shoeboxes they were purchased in although this took up more room at the bottom and rear of their wardrobe. Witnessing this archive of footwear, the girls began chattering in Vietnamese and lowered themselves to their knees to remove the topmost shoebox, gently as if it were some fragile religious artefact. They opened the lid of the shoebox. I peered over their shoulders. The shoes were swathed in strawberry-coloured tissue paper so they unwrapped this with their little painted fingernails (I tried to ignore that they were chipped and scrappy), then reverently lifted out one of my mother's shoes.

Excitedly they leaped to their feet, kicked free their sandals and Thinh dropped my mother's shoe on to her turned-up foot then stood in it. It did seem a little big but not so very much and I was startled by how much taller Thinh suddenly became. Putting her weight on her foot and lifting higher with her hand on Quynh's shoulder to steady her, they both laughed loudly.

I sat on the edge of my parents' bed to watch some more shoes be removed from their boxes and tissues then tried on by both girls who walked unsteadily over to the mirror and back, circled like fashion models and laughed in my mother's expensive high footwear. I was careful, however, despite my good humour, to note as best as I could the order the shoeboxes were coming out in.

Until both stood before me, Thinh wearing a golden shoe with dark red balls of glass on one foot, a black high heel with a single purple bow on the other. Quynh wore the other shoes of the pairs on the differing feet. I laughed at them then I stood up dramatically and the girls froze. I pointed to the ceiling and I made the gesture to smoke.

If I wished to smoke I had to do so on the hotel roof or my parents would smell the tobacco. The girls nodded. They helped me put the shoes back in boxes, still admiring them. We replaced the shoeboxes in the correct order but then I slid open the next wardrobe door and I leaned in among the hanging garments where there were even more shoes in their boxes. From right at the back where it appeared the shoes had not been disturbed for a great deal of time and were unlikely to be missed immediately, I prised out four boxes then pushed my mother's blouses back in position. I handed these four pairs of shoes to the girls, closed the wardrobe doors then checked the room was undisturbed, patting the bed smooth where I had sat.

Closing my parents' bedroom door softly, I led the way along to the utility room with the washing machines and there I pointed to the ceiling and the wide ladder to the 'secret' hatch above which led to the hotel roof. I climbed first, opening the noisy hatch, then I lithely hopped up onto the roof. The girls passed the shoeboxes upwards then I took each girl by the hand and helped them ascend.

It was very hot and bright up on that ochre-painted roof; simultaneously we all replaced our sunglasses. The sounds of that elevated world were a mixture of semi-distant traffic accelerations, brakes and horns from the vehicles below, the bluster of the light breeze carrying the mash of both the fountain beneath and surf from the beach beyond, combined with those fluctuating cries and bursts of distant laughter from youths at play in the seas.

We three slowly crossed to the waist-high, crenellated roof walls with their uneven plaster and paint blisters then we looked down, disorientated above the big blue, now inverted, Imperial Hotel letters of our electric sign which illuminated at night.

The breeze moved our hair which for each of us had dried from our experience over yonder in the Meliander swimming pool, slightly changing its character. Below us, small heads and sunhats moved on the pavement around the newspaper kiosk. We turned; off to our left was the dark crown of the cypresses on Heaven Hill, to the right our city behind us climbed up to the Typical Quarter and then: the huge yellow cliffs, the colour of dried-out dog dirt, below the castle rock and the battlements one hundred metres above.

However, my eyes rested on my chosen destination. I crossed over to the door of the demurely spitting and seductively hissing concrete room of the hotel's huge reserve-water tank.

A Supplemental Chapter. Its Title:
The Reserve-Water Tank

The reserve-water tank of the Imperial filtered through every drop of water which was used down below in the hotel. Using a system of ballcock fillers from a boosted mains pressure, the tank always remained filled to the same level. When a hot-water tap was turned on downstairs, more water was piped below to the boiler in the basement to heat. When a cold-water tap was turned in a room, the flow came direct from the tank and once again the ballcocks opened to quickly replace an identical amount from the mains system back into the reserve-water tank using electric booster pumps.

A good hotel must maintain a large private source of emergency water in our region because of summer heat and the unreliability of the mains system in drought or high-tide storms. A hotel without any water simply grinds to a halt in minutes rather than hours. Food cannot be prepared, guests cannot bathe and the hotel cannot be cleaned. The guests leave and demand refunds, nothing is earned, wages have to be paid: disaster looms.

My father fitted this new tank when he bought the hotel in 1963 and installed the booster pumps in the mid-1970s. If the mains failed, even with a fully booked hotel there was at least two days' water supply stored in the tank.

The reserve-water tank is not unlike a swimming pool. But because there is sufficient space on the large roof area – and also to distribute weight – it is shallow, never exceeding a metre in maximum depth, thus it more resembles a very large bath.

The tank is constructed from heavy, welded metal side and bottom plates. The secure concrete building housing the tank serves various practical functions: it prevents any ingress of nesting birds such as our city's white doves which would contaminate a water supply; it is ventilated by insect-proof curving vents in the ceiling to prevent access to hornets, roaches or worse: breeding mosquitoes could contaminate a tank of even moving water. Also, in the unlikely but potentially disastrous event of the tank leaking or bursting, as well as the emergency drain system plumbed into the floors around the tank, the concrete walls would prevent the huge volume of water spreading out across the roof and destroying the hotel below. Any leakage would be safely drained off by the plentiful waste sinkholes on the floor walkway which leads around the tank.

As a child the allure of this roof world was huge. Obviously I was deeply prohibited to go on the roof with its myriad dangers: falling from the battlements, decapitation or electrocution in the elevator winch rooms and of course drowning in the reserve-water tank, which was strictly padlocked until I was a teenager – as was the roof hatch – with only Mother and Father having secret keys.

When I was very young this aura of danger from the tank room both frightened me and attracted me to it. My parents tried to destroy the magic of the roof by taking me up there quite frequently to watch a cruise ship dock, its masts garlanded with bulbs, or for firework displays high on the castle cliffs above us during the June festivals. What happened on these occasions though was that in between the ship's whistle or the muffled explosions of rockets I heard the call of the reserve-water tank room.

High up on the concrete walls of the tank room, to let in light, were a series of little sealed windows, but above them were the vents. Through the vents I could hear the exciting hiss of incoming water and the rich swirl of a substantial but invisible mass of water. When the intake was not pumping, one heard a peaceful silence within the tank room, then every so often the most deep and echoing drips or mysteriously rich plonks and plops. Combined with this, on hot bright days the reflection of the invisible water's surface trembled in wormlike rings on the inside ceiling visible through the side windows, teasing me towards that aquatic grotto.

I begged Father to permit me to see the tank room and when I was around eight years old he showed me inside. As he turned the key in the padlock it was of course the start of a great love affair for here was a private swimming pool all to myself in a green, shaded place, casting patterns on the ceiling and the wooden structure built a half-metre or so above the water to permit access to the pipes and areas inside the tank. The tank was surrounded by interesting masses of pipes and excitingly urgent-looking cock taps, including a big one painted gloss red!

Finally Father said I could have access to the tank room when I learned to swim but of course my frustrations in that area have been well documented. Eventually we came to a compromise. I would be allowed in the reserve-water tank room when my height, without shoes, was thirty centimetres <u>above</u> the tank water level.

Like the simpleton I was, I beamed at thirty centimetres on my school ruler only for me to rush back through to Father and ask, 'But what height <u>is</u> the water level?' When I learned it was a metre my joy turned to rage then tears as I caught my parents laughing at me. Father took me on the roof and with chisel and hammer, since he anticipated foul play if he used a pencil, he chipped a groove at one metre thirty centimetres into the wall beside the water-tank-room door.

For a birthday and a half I would often troop my poor parents up on the hotel roof for a measuring until the day came when I was tall enough, without shoes, to be allowed in. Mother did not approve; I still could not swim so I had to climb into the cold-water tank to prove to Mother that the bottom of the tank was not slippery and I could not knock myself unconscious.

My kingdom and desert island became the private, flat roof of the Imperial Hotel! Up there away from all eyes, below the ramparts of castellated walling. Up there on the flat ochre red of the water-proofed roof with its untidy jumble of TV aerials, both elevator winch houses, the huge cold-water tank enclosure and eventually air-conditioning units and unreliable solar-heating panels. The creaking metal hatch gave warning of any approaching intruders – usually just Father opening fifteen centimetres of roof hatch to yell me to lunch, the crack of darkness showing the white false teeth of his moving mouth.

I would get so hot sunbathing on the roof some days that I would climb into the cold-water tank and sit, hanging onto a sweating side pipe with one hand.

Often I would just stretch out up on the wooden platform above the water where I maintained a collection of books, comics and some sunbed cushions. I even carried up an electric fan, the type which scans languidly from side to side.

When the hotel guests came back from the beach in the late afternoons there was so much activity in the water tank just below my prone body on the wooden platform that small splashes and cooling water vapours would arise from the busy surface filling the air with delicious fizzing sounds as I read and mused in the remote fan breeze.

I opened the door to the reserve-water tank and led Thinh and Quynh inwards to my special and deeply personal world. I had never admitted any other person before: not Tenis, not Sagrana, but these girls finally seemed worthy.

As I stood aside to indicate for them to step forward, I glanced down nostalgically at the little one-metre-thirty chisel mark in the wall, still clearly visible beneath newer layers of whitewash.

Thinh and Quynh edged to the tank sides and peered across that broad, green-tinted expanse of water held within. Perhaps they looked a little less impressed than I had hoped so I announced, '*Pour moi, le mer superieur.*'

They laughed.

I had led them up the stairway to the sunbed cushions on the suspended platform and flourished the pack of Fortunes. We sat. I switched on the electric fan and passed around cigarettes as they put their shoulder bags aside, but immediately they turned their attention away from the reserve-water tank, and me, knocked the top off the first shoebox and lifted out another of Mother's pairs of shoes.

It all finally caught up with me: the six-in-the-morning rise, the long stressful day on the heat-blasted beach, that humiliating hurtle into the swimming pool and my ridiculous rescue, combined with all the strain of trying to keep up appearances to these two irresistibles. After having finally enticed Thinh and Quynh to my secret lair, I simply fell asleep on one of the sunbed cushions above the tank.

While I slept I imagined the movements of the Vietnamese girls around me. Their rare and slow activity must have been almost without intention and random. Water would have dripped restlessly then buzzed in that cauldron below. Sometimes the girls' eyes would have followed sounds like the eyes of puppies in a cage at the pet shop. Of course we know they opened those other shoeboxes and must have held pairs of my mother's fine shoes up close to their flat faces in a sea-cave light. The soles of each shoe would have been only slightly scuffed by its occasional passages out onto the pavements of the esplanade as far as the thick carpets of the Dolphin or the Lower Rivers restaurant and no further.

Eventually, as afternoon heat climaxed outside on the roof, Thinh and Quynh whispered together, slid those silent airy sarongs aside and used arms and upstepping legs to entwine themselves down around the banisters of the platform stairway, stepping slowly over rivets and metal plate into the cool water.

They moved with smiles, lowering themselves down into the tank water as I slept. Perhaps cupping palmfuls upwards to trickle from their shoulders and, after kneeling there, silently stretching themselves out in the reserve tank.

Inevitably, testing buoyancy on their backs, their legs, which looked pale green, obscured by black ripples, floated up until scrappily painted toenails broke the surface. Suddenly they rolled and swam, their unique splashes echoed. Pushing out they got two or three good strong strokes each to take them across the reserve-water tank. A head turned aside dipping black hair into water which soaked it through. They moved beneath my sleeping body which was suspended just above them through the centimetre gaps in the boards, as if they were levitating me on a cushion of air from their circular swimming beneath.

When my eyes opened I saw the glossy black hairs out-of-focus close. They had pulled the other sunbed cushion alongside mine and Quynh was almost against me, both hands sandwiched beneath her cheek, and Thinh against her back, still managing to fit in on the long slim cushion. The bundles of the trembling electric-fan air moved down our bodies before the blades obediently halted on our feet then felt their way back up the length of us in faithful motion. I immediately held my breath then took a long desperate inhalation. I wanted nothing to change. I did not want the world or my emotions to oscillate onwards from that moment. I wanted all to cease. Just lying together, water whirlpooling below us, the sleeping girls already adapted to the noise of our new world, was enough. I did not want them to move. This moment was the end of my lonely waiting. I wanted no more.

Yet I reached out eventually to their rubbery skin. On each of them it was wet when you put your fingers right into the nape of their necks, deep into the hair.

Initially I experienced pinpoints of concentration deeply focused on a shoulder then involuntarily my eyes would be unfocused. I began to close my eyelids, drift to more abstract reflections. So ironic when I wanted to be no place else yet undeniably I used to visualise myself in those other times. Actual historical times. Times of the Moors before Christian victory often came to my excited teenage brain: palaces full of flowing water and reflected light, harems and swishing cloaks.

Inevitably we shifted position, rolled over, paused on one elbow for a fascinated moment as the fan added a fourth presence, spraying us with bulletins of goose-bumping air: it was after some time I frowned and saw the substance on their bare bodies. I thought it was peeling paint but the wooden stairs and platform had never been painted. Every tiny fleck seemed to be broken from a larger mass and each morsel had the luminous, varnished, slightly transparent quality of parchment. Those reflective specks were glued to the girls' smooth wet skin, to the smalls of their backs, around their amazingly compact, visible ribcages. These bits on them were like my peeling skin; flakes were down Thinh's shoulder and some pieces in her hair. For an instant I wondered if they were afflicted by some spectacular Vietnamese skin condition themselves and they were truly my sisters in every way.

Thinh suddenly sat up, moving away from me, then stood wiping at her arms. She quietly said something and looked at her friend. Quynh had her bare legs out before her and stared mutely down at a crushed shoebox. Both of them had rolled over or lain on top of this shoebox. I presumed what coated the girls was some kind of painted decoration from the expensive shoebox. With a mystified, slightly distasteful look, Quynh cradled up a piece of the coloured tissue paper from the crushed box. In her hands was a shattered, hanging cocoon. It was the dried and brittle lucky caul I had been born in which Mother had proudly displayed to me years before and must have preserved ever since in a shoebox at the back of her wardrobe.

Thinh and Quynh's rolling and substituting bodies had mostly pulverised that shrivelled, transparent silvery leaf of prenatal skullcap.

Holding hands, I led the girls down into the reserve-water tank and they let me wash the dried membrane which had enclosed my foetus from each of their pale bodies, dissolving my caul into the tank water to move through the pipes of the Imperial Hotel, into the kitchens, the sauces, the coffees and the baths of our guests.

The following day when I led them back again to our secret roof, Thinh carried their *grandmere*'s old French dictionary for translating into my language. I was in the huff a bit; I did not want any languages, only what our bodies did.

They both lay side by side up on the platform above the water tank on a single sunbed cushion, the dictionary opened beneath each of their chins, their legs turned up from the knees towards the ceiling vents, sandals dangling. They were smoking my cigarettes. Two bobbing, empty *Coca-Cola* bottles would chung against the metal side of the tank. The girls would stretch down an arm from the platform; their fingertips could just play with the surface.

At first I resisted the single words they would fire out at me. Soon though, I fell in with the game of using the dictionary and I would lie between them, pointing to words and trying to put incorrect, impossible sentences together in our languages. Their sentences were always so beautiful compared to mine and they made me laugh. One concocted that second day in my language, they spoke together in chorus: 'Now we make some delight upon you.'

For the first week we came up to the roof in the forenoon. We would also sunbathe on towels spread among the television aerials then, when we were flushed with heat, I began my swimming lessons in the reserve-water tank. I would swim towards one girl away from the other, across the large shallow of the water tank. The girl in front of me, usually Quynh, would hold out her hands and I would reach at the last moment with shaky arms and take those small fingers. Thinh called out commands in French language and, when she got excited, Vietnamese. We sneaked away at dusk when my parents were down at dinners, working hard.

The final bathers were leaving the beach clear and huge just as the three of us arrived there. It was getting darker by each wonderful minute. The sand seemed purple, its indentations scattered with black shadows like fallen leaves. I endured the jealous looks of some boys my age passing a football to each other but once the girls and I stepped beyond the low surf it was quite black out there in the water. The attention span of the beach is short. We were forgotten. People could not see us. We stopped walking when the surface reached our three belly buttons.

I lowered myself down in the salt water.

I floated and then I began to swim, my feet lifting clear of the solid, sandy bottom. I let out a yelp of surprise and the girls clapped and quickly ducked their shoulders beneath the surface to coast off and swim alongside me, elegantly, with one or other of their cheeks held in the water as they watched. I tasted salt and my eyes stung but I shook out my fringe and kept breaststroking forward.

I turned not towards the beige shoreline and the small but brilliantly white surf with the very high street lights suspending their tense, flushed light above the sand; nor towards the faint geometric illuminations of the Meliander Hotel's ranked bedroom windows, but instead I headed to the pitch-black ocean so I would be out of my depth. I imagine I swam a little like a dog, my head held erect, making movements in relation to my submerged limbs and my breathing not relaxed but hissing and jerky.

I stopped and we three were treading water together: a means of remaining in one place without sinking, moving legs and arms in rather desperate circular motions in the invisibilities below, our feet sometimes suddenly touching, gulping breaths and somehow more intimate than any of the sexual things we traded. We floated – a small distance between us – breathing towards each other's faces on which beads of sea water darted like maimed insects.

I looked up to stars, circling seagulls, their underbellies cast with the sodium lights from the docks, the clouds above stained brown.

The girls made me lie on my back, long and stiff like a canoe they escorted me inwards, their salvage, one on each side they swam

and steered me towards shallows and we laughed as the surf carried
me that final distance and I stood trembling back on sand, a swimmer,
exfoliative water gushing down my thighs like runny diarrhoea from
a desperately sick person.

Ahmed At The Phases

During those valuable bright days that I talked constantly of my life to Ahmed, over his strong coffee in the balmy changing light of my apartments above the sea, all that I kept from him was the Condition. I felt humiliated before him to admit that. But everything else he devoured and listened to and questioned, to define particular accuracies. Everything that had befallen me I laid before him. Of my small blisters and the DC-8 *stretch series*, my feelings for the Phases, my hatred of travel, Father's village, Madelaine, Thinh and Quynh and learning to swim. He often lifted his eyebrows knowingly but laughed shyly.

In the daytimes, Ahmed regularly accompanied me down to feed the cats of the old boat on the tract of wasteland.

One day as we approached together I knew something was wrong. Rather than appearing dramatically, stretching themselves into arches of electrified hair as I approached, all the cats were already out, lined up along the edge of the deck, their attention rapt and suspicious. When I moved through the pampas grass I saw two guys in the corner of the wasteland who the cats were watching. The men had reflective vests over their dress jackets and theodolites were set up on tripods. One held a clipboard.

'Good afternoon,' I called.

'Good afternoon,' they both promptly replied.

They barely glanced at me as I approached with the carrier bag but for some reason one of the men stood and stared – no, squinted – in the direction of Ahmed who, rather timidly I thought, perhaps afraid of their official appearance, came just forward of the pampas grass then halted. After looking in Ahmed's direction the clipboard man looked away towards me again as if nobody else was there.

'What are you guys up to?'

'We are Lombos Construction. This land is sold and plans are going to be submitted for residential apartments.'

'Oh.' I looked over at my colony of cats in their boat. 'Oh. I feed those cats,' I gestured towards them. 'I mean, just damn strays.' I suppose I seemed rather ridiculous.

'We saw them there in their boat,' the guy nodded and chuckled.

'Damn it all,' I said. 'I know you guys are just doing your job, but hell. What will become of the cats? When is this being started?'

'You know what planning clearance is like. Weeks? Months?' The guy shrugged.

'Damn,' I repeated. 'That old boat cannot be lifted. It would fall to bits. Hell. I will need to buy them a new boat and put it somewhere else.' I looked around. 'They are just damn strays,' I mumbled again.

'Shame. I mean, it is all equal to me, friend, but strictly speaking this is private property now.'

I nodded. I was astonished to find I could not reply. My throat was jammed up with a huge emotion. Eventually I said, 'Yes. Of course. When do you think it will be fenced off?'

'Could be any day.' He shrugged.

'OK. Sorry to bother you. Thanks.'

'No problem.'

I crossed to Ahmed and explained the situation to him and he helped me feed the cats in the normal manner as Teresa had before, but I was stiff and uncommunicative, anxious to get away from under the eyes of the surveyors who were looking at us and I believe they were whispering and laughing. They made me angry.

When we left with the cats madly crowding the bowls of food

197

I said to Ahmed, 'Perhaps you could feed the cats from now on?'

'Sure. I like cats.' he said.

'Be sure to always wash your hands after being with them,' I said.

A warm spell of weather came to us when Ahmed Omar and I could swim together and float in the sea beneath the glass and concrete of my top-floor home. Ahmed was happy just to carefully swim beyond the small surf line.

I had shown him my *scuba*-diving equipment down in the cellar but he displayed surprisingly little interest.

We laughed a great deal together. And how I talked – for garrulous men fear nothing so much as solitude.

Poor Ahmed. I was his book. There was not a single thing for him, in any language, to read in my apartments – it was his fate to wash ashore into my wreckage, patiently accepting the words of my confession.

Books Became Of No Use To Me

I used to have books. Laughable to think of it. God, at university in the Capital city, where I changed from Town Planning to Design, I would move addresses with suitcases of the things. The heaviest articles I ever carried on public transport; my shirts and spare suit all pressed into hideous shapes. It was acceptable when they were just books of design. The classics: *Lewis's Typography/Basic Principles* (an old English edition I could not read and a separate translated copy for me); *Tschichold's Typographische Gesaltung*, a 1935 edition which I could not read, only look at the texts. *Hoffman's Graphic Design Principles and Practice* (in translation), *Dreyfuss's, The Measure of Man* (in translation). Anything to do with the Dutchman *Crouvel* and his amazing Agency: *Total Design. Corbusier's, Five Points of the New Architecture* (in translation).

But then as I spent time in the second-hand bookshops of the Capital city under the thumb-tacked signs for *Architecture and Design*, I got into the bad habit of buying other books that I thought would give me an air of moral improvement.

In all my spare time during my Town Planning terms I designed gleaming new settlements with perfect traffic flow and logical railway termini; yet I also had an idealistic apartment – for myself alone of course – in my mind. In contrast to my dream apartment's austere, modern lines it would feature several walls of old distinguished-looking books which would round off my urbane humanity. From the presumptuous age of eighteen I began to collect these distinguished volumes for my idealised apartment library: some history, some science, but to get volumes of matching bound leather at budget prices it mainly had to be collected works of fiction – of tales, stories and novels which was not my preferred reading. Yet bound collected editions by these famous authors looked attractive. I bought them in translation of course, where the foreign authors were concerned. I recall the first Collected Works I bought (in translation) was the North American author, *Pearl S. Buck*. I read my way through her many strange books, in cafés of the Capital city, for a great deal of my university years. Then I began to buy more, always in alphabetical order. Oh, I remember the <u>names</u> of the authors' matching volumes for sure.

Easter, Three Kings and the start of summer holidays too, these books were slowly transported back on the train to our city in straining, heaved suitcases with my clothes in those odd shapes for hotel laundry to wash. Yet even when I returned to our city for ever, swore not to travel (I detest it) and vowed to make my future, dare I say my <u>destiny</u>, in this place – my income increased and I came to make hasty deals or bulk bargains in Jotun's and Lullil's second-hand bookshops. I even mail-ordered several rather over-bossed collected editions of classic writers.

The modern world has created its own dumb literature the sole purpose of which is to kill time. An endless supply of thrillers and romantic entertainment which expects nothing and dulls the head with meagre pictures. If we could connect every one of these books into a fabulous, giant volume we would have a work of complete hellish madness. We would get no *Decameron*.

For years I had most of my unread book collection of bound classic volumes stored in one of the upper rooms in Mother's apartment, above Town Hall Plaza, until I moved into the Phases Zone 1. Though I had my big apartment at the Phases Zone 1 (eventually four knocked together), I began to have doubts.

If you have to work to build up your business and then to live a little where does one find time to read so many books? I had tried to make attacks into my volumes, or at least the A and B author surnames. The As and Bs were quite enough. My vision of sitting on café terraces reading my way through a famous author's final volume then, over a cigar, coming to some pithy conclusion about his/her philosophical significance was fading. I was increasingly busy at my design Agency with contracts pouring in.

I recalled reading at the beginning of his <u>vast</u> Collected Works that when the French author, possibly, of *The Phantom of the Opera* – perhaps Gaston Leroux? – completed writing a new novel, he would step out on to his balcony as the sun was rising and fire a pistol in the air to let all waiting Paris know it could look forward to another of his books. What a presumptuous son of a whore.

I slammed his first volume closed. It had got to the stage where if I found time to actually read to the last page of a damned novel I felt like stepping out into the moonlight on the long balconies of my place at the Phases and firing a pistol in triumph over a deserted beach and the gently mashing nightwaves.

After I had hoisted them up into three walls of book spines on shelves of olive wood I began to view my volumes as only a future pleasure, which must be reserved for retirement, reflection and old age alone. Some nights I sat on the calfskin easy sofa in my large place just looking at those many hundreds of books. Gradually they were taking on the look of an obligation and then, soon, a torment. They reminded me of the idealism of the DC-8 *stretch series* model. I had believed if I possessed it my life would take on a new and purer meaning. My marriages to Verona and Aracelli had been based on the same idealism. Each new wife gave me a chance to be good again. The books were the same. I had believed they would make me a better person.

Still I would persevere. A random volume; an out-of-sequence 'Collected'. I chided myself with the usual: if they could find the time to skilfully write all this down surely I should find time to read it?

I was managing to read about a book every two months if I was lucky. I tried changing over from fiction – from made-up stories that never happened – to the rarer biographies in my collection.

These biographies were actual descriptions of real people's lives; they were much more absorbing. I could read more of them quicker. *Napoleon, Woodrow Wilson, Gandhi* or *Einstein.* However, I soon found out that no matter who the subject was, regardless of the life they led, virtuous or in most cases deeply flawed and despicable, their deathbed scenes always moved me to tears. It was pathetic, this glut of humanism in my throat, but each time without fail, after having followed the twists and turns of these lives, the grimaced ambitions and the thwarted lusts, as that inevitable moment of the end appeared, my hands began to shake. In those early hours of dawn, being the only person still awake in my block of the Phases Zone 1, I swallowed back hard on the tears and placed the finished biographical volume aside, exhausted with a draining emotion.

Very late one evening after my second marriage – to Aracelli – was over, I sat down. I began to count my book collection. There were one thousand two hundred and twenty unread books on the walls of the library in the Phases Zone 1. I telephoned a taxi to Mother's apartment above Town Hall Plaza. It was around three in the morning. I had not been in that house for six months but I set to work on my knees on the dusty stone floors.

How did I ever gather so many of those damn books full of promise and good intentions but ultimately devouring these valuable days of your life? There were a further six hundred and forty-two single books and paperbacks in boxes which had been stored because these modern editions did not look so good up on the shelves as my bound cloth and imitation leather volumes. I discounted the few cookbooks, maps and atlases, manuals, illustrated books on design and architecture-related reference books. Thus, as Veroña might have calculated in her tiny handwriting:

Total unread volumes = 1862
Reading an optimistic 3 books per month = 36 per year
Years needed to read all my books, calculated by number of

books (1862) divided by annual reading score = 1862 divided by 36 = 51.7

Fifty-two years were required to read all these books.

I would die before I could read them all. They would beat me. I would need to stay alive into my nineties to read all these books. There was too much great literature in the world – more than could be consumed in one human lifetime. What a swindle.

At dawn it was cold and I locked up Mother's place above Town Hall Plaza. I was the first customer to edge my way into the Terrace of the Imperial café which my parents had once owned. I ordered black coffee and then sat out on the bright terrace. The roaring sounds of the coffee machine were away back behind me. After I received my coffee I stepped over to the public phone kiosk and got Sagrana, my accountant, out of his bed. I said, 'Sorry to bother you so early. This is urgent. Phone Jotun's the second-hand book dealer. Sell all my books to them. Tell him he can come round to my places any time. They can name any price, I am not looking for profits, I just want them out of my life.'

I have not attempted to read a book since. My empty, polished olive-wood bookshelves gave me an immense sense of well-being, of leisure, and had given me a sense of having a future though this too was now ended. When I have spare time, I rigorously complete those cheap Puzzle Compendiums that you can buy at the kiosks and then throw away in a common litter bin when solved.

A Tribute To My Accountant, Sagrana

Sagrana's books of his clients' affairs were models of accuracy and order. Sagrana's office, right from the start, was a modern series of rooms just off Catalina Square. On the windows he had old-style, sun-blistered wooden shutters so the light sliced in downwards at angles and long white beams of it always rested on his desk fan or floor in different places according to the hours of the day one would visit him.

Ever since school when our physical education teacher would send us running up Heaven Hill to the cemetery because we were so bad at soccer, Sagrana was my friend and dear to both my wives so we visited often.

Amazingly, accountants, like mathematicians, have their own professional jokes. Sagrana's overused favourite was: 'There is no accounting for taste and I have a taste for accounting.' Eventually he had the legend embossed in gilt and hung framed – with flush-wall fixings, I advised him on – behind his desk. Tenis, on a visit one day, cruelly warned Sagrana that the sign could soil his serious image with potential clients. 'Do you think so?' Sagrana asked, suddenly grave. So when my accountant interviewed wealthy new parties seeking his services he started removing the framed legend from the wall and concealing it in the bottom drawer of his desk where he also stored the newly acquired electric screwdriver which he was not skilled in using. Consequently the plaster around the plugholes grew powdery. One day I saw the holes in the wall had been plastered over then painted and his framed motto was balanced, temporary and precarious, on his bookcase which showed no photos of a wife and children but many framed qualifications and refresher diplomas. Within a year his framed joke was gone forever.

In that office Sagrana would run his hands over the red, imitation leather notebooks he used for his clients. The books would be laid out on his big desk when visitors like us, in search of stories – not gossip (for there is a distinction) – called round. Veroña the mathematics prodigy liked to listen to Sagrana's beautiful voice while she would slowly turn random pages and look through his neat columns of numbers. We would notice her silent lips helplessly move as she checked a column and Sagrana gained satisfaction from her little shy nod of confirmation. We were still young and in Sagrana's office we smoked, talked and circled the books on the table. Sagrana in his grey flannel suit would lower his eyes at me so the pupils used to sink into those now enormous dark rings above his cheeks. We could smell his aftershave, the oddly cheap cigarettes that were his brand – the tobacco packed so tight when you accepted one you had to knock the cigarette repeatedly on a table top to get a decent draw.

It was Sagrana's habit when an elderly client passed away – though not necessary for any fiscal means – to use historical and held records to total up that client's earned income using inflation-adjusted figures and conclude just how much that client had earned in an entire lifetime. I soon realised that, for Sagrana, that final inflation-adjusted figure he arrived at was as important to him as a priest's blessing on the deathbed.

Sagrana confessed when I was later married to Aracelli and we were having dinner together one night that an inaccurate or flawed account book or a missing VAT receipt seemed to him to disturb the very universe. He said he found inaccuracies in his accounts more important than his income. Often he had awoken in the night convinced he had added up a column incorrectly or forgotten to include a certain deduction. He had dressed and crossed the dark, windy square (when he still lived up by the fire station) to click on his desk lamp and go through his client's books once more. He found the mistake. He was never wrong. Where a mistake lurked, his very subconscious found it in his sleep. He told us he had stopped working for various clients because he knew they were submitting erroneous income figures. He had no moral position on this, cheats being common currency; it was just that it physically disturbed Sagrana to know his books contained untruths.

Sagrana could stroll by a potential client's house, look at their car, see their furniture and smell they were earning more than their declaration. He said if he worked for the 'Mendez's People' at taxation he would rise to the top in years but his devotion was, alone, to that elegant curve of a story which every one of his red books told of his clients' lives.

Sagrana went further. If his collected red books did not reflect the absolute truth, the individual fluctuations and wavering destinies of an individual's life, he did not want to keep their books. Sagrana believed that he was assembling a sacred truth about a human being more profound and more beautiful than what God (and here he crossed himself for, with all his contradictions, Sagrana went daily to Mass 'for the aesthetics') would tally up as the condition of that person's soul. Sagrana's collection of grim government payments and deadly accurate accounts told the story of his clients' lives with more clarity than any of those novels or stupid biography books that I used to become teary-eyed over.

Admit it. Most of us do not even know where we were during what month on what day of our lives, ten, six, two years, even two months ago. Yet Sagrana's quiet red books will 'account' for your whereabouts. They will show what you bought, what you believed, what you tried for and what you failed to get.

Across town was a more attuned figure in your life: Sagrana at his Agency. Sagrana's neatly preserved envelopes of business-related receipts will tell us that at 11.28 on 28 March 1986, I visited the newsagent kiosk by the Imperial Hotel. In the evening, at 19.09, from my Agency I ordered office supplies to a large specific value. On my way home, in the supermarket at 21.01, I bought an interiors magazine – this was a business-related expense so I had retained the receipt. Sagrana had extracted the price of the magazine down and drawn it up in the column as a non-taxable expense. But there also, preserved on the actual receipt in his VAT records, were the other things I had bought in the supermarket that forgotten evening twenty years ago. Sagrana's books and records could tell me what I had for dinner that night (I notice a bottle of my first wife's favourite wine) whereas the best detective in the world could never have found that out. Receipts from secret *rendezvous*, telephone calls to lovers, credit-card bills of presents, travel tickets, agency invoices, tax forms – pious but accurate expenses explanations! Items flagged by Sagrana and questioned under the possible conflict of dual purpose such as restaurant bills. (Why two desserts and two coffees? Are you sure you were not joined by somebody towards the end of that meal? My God, he was right!) Signatures that slowly changed with my maturity suggesting I felt sometimes more sure of myself than others. All was stored there. Sagrana was correct. He was calculating a more accurate picture of late-twentieth-century man than any sociologist.

So Sagrana would touch a red book softly with his hand then tell Veroña and me a great story that he could piece together from his language of legislatures, figures and columns, double entries and line accounting: 'Think your father's story and his motorway money is rare? Look at these figures here. Old Polthus's place out in the groves with his water windmill pumping for two hundred years and the old estate house painted blue. His family were citrus millionaires for three generations.' Sagrana would nod. 'He was broke on his estate for three years. I noted his sole income as the occasional sale of a bit of antique furniture to pay his maid, the electricity and food bills every month. Slowly he was emptying the old place. The house echoed more each time I visited and sat on the terrace with the old man. Quietly I stopped billing him for my services but I kept the faith and I filled out the nil tax return each year. His friends vanished, even the minor aristocrats from whose stock he came. One day at his estate a foreigner pulls up in a car, walks slowly down the driveway looking up at the birds in the trees. "A foreign ornithologist, but at least a visitor after three years. Perhaps a flamingo obsessive from the salt lagoons or searching for Audouin's gull, but a mile from the coast?" Polthus puts down the old tele-scope saying this aloud from the terrace to the ancient maid who has stuck with him, taking her wages in sacks of oranges and lemons. The old mission bell rings. After politely being served iced tea on an unauctioned silver tray, the stranger starts asking questions about the forty trees which line the Polthus driveway to the estate. Turns out the trees are a rare strain of wood best used for the produc-tion of very high-quality musical instruments: violas, basses, cellos, violins. And only a few of these mature trees are left in the world. The rest are still growing and will take forty years to mature before they are ready. Total value of trees after local and central tax? Three hundred and sixty-two million. Enough to make Polthus rich again and truck in forty new, common dark cypress to replant down the drive. Two years later, the foreigner brings a string quartet, using instruments cut from the very trees of Polthus's driveway, to the estate so the old man throws a party in honour of the story. Champagne, *Schubert*. I was there. Nobody else. The string quartet, the tree buyer, me, Polthus, the ancient maid. That old guy listened very carefully to those instruments playing out their beautiful tunes about the strangenesses of fate.'

Our Citrus Coast

In answer to Ahmed's questioning of two childless marriages, first to Veroña and then to Aracelli.

One evening after Veroña and I had been married about two years she invited me to dinner. We were both still students but she was making good money from moonlighting computer projects despite all the work on her own mathematics research. We were back in town for a weekend from the Capital city so she took me to the Dolphin, or was it the Lower Rivers?: the magnificent, lonely desert islands of each table centred with ridiculous coconuts and pampas grass trimmed to look like palm trees as the natives bowed their heads on the glistening shores of cutlery; a panorama window of the marina with its dead forest of pale masts. We could only afford the cheapest bottle of local wine but the food was as usual. I have forgotten what, but the usual. She waited until the fish then she said, 'I have something to tell you.'

I moaned and said, 'Who is he?' It would be that intellectual bore Bartolome she worked with, constantly, late into the nights. He had no good looks at all but they were always making private, crushingly boring mathematical jokes together. Veroña and Bartolome loved variations on stories where they had witnessed a great professor of mathematics from the university, caught making a mistake at the supermarket cheese counter on weights and prices.

Though Veroña was way out of Bartolome's league and far too fast and dangerous for him, I had long been prepared for them to have a stupid one-night fling, both drunk, all caught up in their work – talking so endlessly then just leaning together to kiss for no other reason than they knew not what to do next. I was panting to enjoy forgiving her and also pleased that it was such a non-threatening (and ugly) rival I had to brush aside. Although he was hopelessly stuck on Veroña, aghast she had married so young and to a non-mathematician, I had an affection for Bartolome as he was ultimately protective of her.

Veroña leaned over the table.

'Watch your hair on the candle.' I nodded.

'You will be angry.'

'Not unless you really surprise me.' I took a swallow from the wine glass and wished we could afford to order another bottle to get through this.

'Even if I have gone behind your back?'

'We have talked about these things.'

'No. Not men, Lolo, silly. Something else.' She lowered her voice terribly. 'For the last six months I have lied to you that I was on the pill.' She leaned back quickly and did that expression where she dropped her head slightly to gauge my reaction to a provocation.

'You are not. Are you?'

'No.'

I lowered my voice. 'Why would you endanger our studies this way? Can you afford more wine?' I shook my head then looked around. 'Why did you do that? I thought you loved your research.'

'It was exciting for me in every way. I _am_ back on it now,' she added, childishly.

I frowned. I was angry but I was also flattered. 'And nothing happened? Do you think there might be something up with . . . our health?'

'I thought it was me but I went to the doctor. No. Not Tenis! You and me did it at the times when I am most ready as well as all the others. I am perfectly OK. I thought maybe it was a message so I went back on the pill. I was not going to say anything to you then I thought it best. It was difficult to tell you.'

'Oh come on! After misleading me so completely you say you were put in a difficult position?'

She moved fish bones on to the edge of her plate. I kept noticing how precisely they were placed there. I straightened my napkin. 'I will see someone,' I said casually, already embarrassed because I knew who it would be.

On the way back to the lemon express station we went up the stinking alley by the sex shop where for a phase she loved to go, in the hope we would be discovered. She always deliberately made so much noise, both her palms against some back-exit door she dreamed would open. I know sometimes she went into the sex shop alone; just to excite the old perverts she would flick through dirty magazines then leave.

Back in the Capital city I went over directly to visit Tenis in the grim medicine residences. It was that place with its minute balcony opposite the old man across the narrow street who kept a single lovebird in a cage on his balcony. The lovebird sounded piercing cheeps all night in lonesome despair.

Tenis was sweating, smoking, bags under his eyes with sleeplessness. That same day I accompanied him to the pet shop where we bought a lovebird in a cruel little cage, baulking at the price. We went for a few whiskies in a grand café with our caged friend – which drew taunts – then we drunkenly gained access to the stairwell opposite the medical residences and left the bird anonymously outside that old man's door.

Next morning the two birds were together in the big cage, indulgently grooming one another and they were silent from then on, leaning together in melancholy as Tenis slept well and studied his medicine volumes.

Thankfully drunk, when I told him my predicament that day he went rosy with laughter. 'You and her. Parents!' We were back in his small room just as you would imagine: anatomy books and other texts all round him, smoking the most expensive cigarettes. 'I am not putting my face near your inadequate equipment, Follana. I will be unable to have sex for a month. Are you sure it is not a straight case of impotence? No worry. I will marry Veroña when she divorces you. On second thoughts this might be amusing. Come into the shower.'

'Are you serious?'

'Sure. Anything for a laugh. But not near the window, for God's sake.'

Mortified, I stepped forward. It was cramped in there and I had to actually stand in the shower cubicle holding the curtain aside and drop my trousers while Tenis kneeled incriminatingly down by my crotch. He had gone uncharacteristically quiet which made me believe I must have a larger manhood than him otherwise he would have confidently mocked me straight away.

Tenis had actually adopted a very professional and serious air – probably to concern me – and was pulling on those thin plastic gloves. 'I take packets of these gloves home from the medical faculty for my mother,' he pointed out. 'They are excellent for cleaning out the litter trays of all her damn cats.' He gently explored my testicles, moved them aside then grunted. 'It would be easier if you were lying down but our affair has gone far enough, old friend. See this?' He was holding my left testicle slightly to one side, pointing to the floppy sack of flesh.

'No.'

'Cancer. You will be dead in a month.'

I raised my eyebrows.

'Ha!' He smiled instead and pointed to a raised series of veins and purple lines. 'OK. What you have here is an unusual meeting of the different veins. A lot of blood supply in this part of men, so many veins and blood vessels. This is not abnormal; however, the testes are incredibly sensitive to temperature change.' He stood up and peeled off the gloves, tossed them in on top of tissues and used disposable razors in a small trash can under his sink. 'A clustering of veins like that raises the temperature within the testes and can affect sperm production and thus fertility.'

He began washing his hands with his back to me. I quickly kneeled to pull up my trousers. I recall my bare ass touched the cold tiles at the back of Tenis's shower. I was shocked he did not make smutty, personal remarks. The realisation Tenis was going to be a very good professional doctor came to me for the first time. Tenis said, 'You should go see a local specialist. Get your father to pay for it and give them a sample. I suggest Mata. Not just because she is a woman which should hopefully embarrass you but she is sympathetic and teaches here. She is one of the best for couples. You and Veroña should go together. Mata will arrange a sperm count and you will have to take things from there. Unlikely at your age you are completely infertile but possible with that vein clustering that your count is low.'

I waited for smutty remarks but no. Tenis was completely straight-faced.

'I mean, God, I know she wants kids.' I shrugged.

He nodded. 'Has Veroña been checked?'

'Yes. Perfectly healthy.'

'You will be able to have children for sure at your age. All sorts could be done. She is not to worry,' and he stepped into his study. I followed. He produced a quarter-full bottle of whisky and we smoked together and drank a short measure each from the same glass as he only seemed to possess one, talking of home gossip and our parents.

When we first came to the Capital city to commence our studies, Tenis and I met at least once a month for a cheap student dinner but as he became more and more involved in the medical faculty and its social life, I saw less of him. Medical students, quite rightly, considered themselves a legitimate *élite* and were difficult to socialise with. They all knew they were going to escape military service and be there for seven years to our three so what was the point in getting to know Town Planning students? They had to get almost twice as many points as Town Planning entrants like myself; only Veroña's mathematics mob came close. The medics worked harder than any other students and of course their final kudos was they chopped up dead human beings. Legitimately.

I went to see Mata. I was completely infertile with a minimal sperm count. When I showed the results to Tenis he patted me on the back and called me 'The only orange with no pips on our citrus coast'.

Tenis's Party On The Seventeenth

Setting: Tenis's villa on the coast, past the airport.

Dramatis Personae: Beautiful Lupe (Tenis's wife), Tenis himself, their young pretty nanny whose name I forget, the two girls who are my damn little god-daughters, that architect of the villa, one real nurse, one pretend nurse (both in full nurse dresses with white stockings), Mendez of 'Mendez's People,' (the district's Chief Tax Inspector), his wife, our city's Fire Chief, his wife, the local Police Commissioner, his wife, a local butcher (in a neck brace), Sagrana (my accountant), Solielian, owner of the main crematorium and his icy wife – our city's leading mortician.

The only relief I could gain from such company was reflecting that my dentist, in fact the dentist of all of us, Villon, did not appear to be present.

Tenis's villa was built into the sand dunes along the beach from Lacas and our city's international airport. Tenis claimed he liked aeroplanes though he had shown no enthusiasm for them when I did, in our youth. He had become bored with his course in flying lessons after two circuits of his villa in a blue Cessna.

He was one of the few who had managed to get planning permission approved for a jetty to tether his speedboat to, which, when he was consultant at the General Hospital, he sometimes used to take to work. Until it all became too much of a bother for him, changing clothes and berthing at the marina.

Even Tenis could not get permission for a jetty directly on the beach but a spur of pink rocks jutted out just along from his home where the coast ended in a small promontory before the coastline cut back in again to form another sandy bay further south. Moulded, dark-painted aluminium gangplanks with handrails had been welded onto the pink rocks to form access to a small jetty where the famous black speedboat was moored. Famous because once when bad high-tide storms were forecast, Tenis had the engines taken off and the boat was carried up and lowered into his huge swimming pool for sanctuary – though the little girls played in it. It was saved from the storm but somehow fuel leaked out of the pipes, the entire swimming pool was contaminated and had to be drained, scrubbed with washing detergent, then refilled. Ultimately the fuel stained the new grouting between the tiles and Tenis had to have the pool stripped and completely retiled. He had come to despise the black speedboat but was forced to keep it for his growing children's amusement.

The architect there that evening had been chosen over me to design the Tenis place, which was still a source of tension – and the real reason he invited us both. Yet there were so many problems with the sliding doors, access from upper floor to lower, the coldness in winter and the cost of having the place wired for computers when all the walls had to be torn out and cavities created, it actually meant Tenis had come to hate his chosen designer. I was glad I never got the commission for I was younger then and I am not even an architect so I would have made mistakes too.

On the night of that party on the seventeenth, my accountant, Sagrana, had picked me up out at the Phases Zone 1 in his car and driven me to Tenis's villa. It always amused me to see my accountant drive hunched over the steering wheel with his crucifixes and rosary beads swinging between us from the rear-view mirror. Perched on his nose were these glasses with curiously flat lenses which he insisted he needed to drive but he never used glasses at any other time, especially for his meticulous bookwork.

It was a beautiful sunset and my contemporary and I fell silent as we drove beyond the now built-up shoreline at Lacas near the bottom of the runway landing lights, then two kilometres further south we turned onto the long, tarred straight road towards Tenis's place.

Each airliner of the busy evening period, curving in over the black dusk sea, could be seen miles out, the intense white navigation lights, which seem to hang from the forward-landing gear and in at the wing roots, trembled in the mild atmosphere as if they were silver drops which could fall loosely to the sea.

The long straight road led to a colony of rich people's houses but Tenis's neighbours' extravagant, pseudo-modernist villas were mere summer homes. The neighbours spent most of the year in the Capital city which was good because it meant they would not be there. Unjustly, as locals we all looked down on incomers from the big cities.

There were already cars parked outside. In the generous parking area I noted that not a single car was parked directly next to another. Every saloon car had at least a space between or had been twisted into an original but awkward angle in relation to the adjacent vehicle. I realised the arranged positioning of the guests' parked cars already predicted the uncomfortable body language they would perpetrate at the party this evening, each cautiously keeping his distance from the other.

As we made our way through the house and down onto the blue stone of the poolside terrace, avoiding any of the insane and possibly violent peacocks which wander Tenis's grounds, the incoming jet liners were even closer. Perhaps they were just larger aircraft? I gazed towards them and when I grabbed a drink off a tray held by a completely striking girl dressed as a nurse, I stood alone by the railing above the beach watching the planes come in one after another.

I glanced at the women in the nurses' uniforms too. I wished something outrageous would happen. I wished this evening I would receive the erotic fuel of a glimpse of the top of a nurse's inevitable white stocking. I saw beautiful Lupe and Tenis were up the pathway struggling with the barbecue trays and Sagrana, drinking *Perrier*, had immediately dived into discussions of import with the Chief Tax Inspector.

I felt lonely. I saw four or five of the insane peacocks were clustered at the bottom of the garden unsocially avoiding us all. They used to be based in the aviary section but somehow they all got free and interbred which made them go mad. They would leap onto the roofs and could be heard parading on the tiles of the guest rooms at dawn. In truth I had stopped staying over on account of them. Lupe's magical presence and my awful, guilty crush on her were just too much to be awoken by a peacock staring at me as well.

I turned and watched the aeroplanes as I had since a child. The jets were so quiet compared to the days of the DC-8 *stretch series*. These violently computerised *Boeings* and *Airbuses* had their flaps splayed fully down, stiff with resistance, their noses raised in both a haughty and hesitating manner. They seemed to be restrained by invisible tethers from behind which made them tremble lightly like horses. Somehow almost silent, the airliners moved into the palm breaks at the edges of Tenis's property and one never saw them or heard the reverse thrust again. I walked back towards the guests nodding and smiling and at an amiable trot took the curving steps up round the cactus garden illuminated by green spotlights.

'Lolo darling,' Lupe called and slapped a silver oven glove towards Tenis.

I kissed Lupe on both cheeks. I was very fond of her. No. I was in love with her. She wore heels but with a sort of carefully cut white tracksuit which hung all over her slimness, in cotton too it appeared, if I could have touched her. For a brunette – not my ideal – Lupe Tenis was one of the most physically attractive women

I knew. I hated to sunbathe and swim with her around her husband's ridiculous speedboat because she was so beautiful it always seemed she was being intimate by displaying herself just in a bikini bottom. Of course she was not. It was because of her black eyes placed among the smooth flat cheeks and the angular sides of her forehead that she always looked interested. Her lashes snapped constantly in the light. She showed absolutely no trace anywhere I could ever see of having had those children. Miraculously, being married to Tenis who socialised with cosmetic surgeons, her breasts were small, real and hardly bounced when, topless, she played volleyball in the pool with us. Yet I had seen her with my own eyes breastfeed the younger girl.

Darkly, Tenis announced, 'Lupe put petrol on the barbecue.'

One of my god-daughters, that eldest one Eva, laughed excitedly and ran around and around my polished Italian shoes shouting, 'Petrol!'

Lupe said, 'None of the canisters are labelled in the garage. I am sure Lolo would have his containers labelled. You are meticulous, Lolo, while this idiot who people trust with their lives cannot think to label the canisters in his garage. Well,' Lupe whispered, 'we'd better consult the Fire Chief.' She trotted off down the stairs as we both watched her.

'Can you believe she invited the butcher just so she could get fresh sausages and burgers?' Tenis pointed to a large metal tray with a sheet of semi-transparent greaseproof paper resting upon it, the circles and tubes of meat adhering underneath.

I chuckled. I fawned pathetically over every little thing Lupe did.

'It is so obvious why we invited him. Him in the neck brace. When he delivered all that this morning, Little Claudia – our youngest, Lolo . . .' he raised his eyebrow. My disinterest in children, even my godchildren, and my inability to remember ages, birthdays and even kids' names was notorious. For people without children time seems to stand still; your own ageing is less clearly spelled out than by the furious growth of sons and daughters around you.

'I know,' I insisted.

Tenis whispered, 'Little Claudia pushed him down the steps yet he still came back tonight. With a neck brace. I feel so ashamed. I could have recommended someone better for his neck too.' He turned to me. 'How is business, Lolo?'

'Good. You?'

'Same. What do you think about my nurses. Beautiful?'

'What one is your <u>real</u> one?'

'Guess.'

'No idea. They are both enchanting.'

He tipped back his drink and used that eyebrow.

The Fire Chief, standing by the pool down below with his wife and Lupe at his side, waved up to us. 'Just leave it a while to evaporate,' he shouted.

'Right,' Tenis called down then said more intimately to me, 'Idiot. Imagine the scandal if there was a fire.'

Lupe came back up the steps. She is deeply clumsy and in moments dropped a lot of burgers and sausages on the rustic bricks of the patio. She had jerked up the greaseproof paper hurriedly and the meat had momentarily adhered to its underside then fallen to the ground. 'Oh no,' she hissed.

I kneeled and helped her gather the raw meat. She turned her eyes, the irises so dark in all the white, and goggled down the stairs. 'Shhhh.' She smiled. I watched her lean over and remove a garden hose from the trunks of the young palm trees and she turned a tap there which was shaped like a frog. Lupe used the garden hose to wash the grit off the meat. 'We shall give these to Mr and Mrs Mendez.'

I laughed.

The downstairs toilets were busy with those babbling wives so I went upstairs to use the one I knew in Lupe and Tenis's bedroom with its salvaged ship mast used to construct the bed. As I stepped to the en-suite bathroom I could not help notice, and indeed pause to study, the profusion of women's clothing and underwear – more than one woman's − on the bed, including torn-open packets of white stockings with their glamorous illustrations. Some of these garments had been crushed and flattened by the weight of bodies on top of them. Some vestments and cellophane packaging were pushed off the bed and lay on the floor around the bed. With a sinking feeling I was sure some of those mixed-in underclothes were Lupe's.

When I returned to the pool area the landing jets had become just lights but they were so close you could see the dimmed cabin windows. We had been standing around the pool chatting, drinking, enjoying the mild evening. The nurses were bringing out more cocktails on trays and the Tenis's daughters had become bored, following and whispering at the stiff gait of the butcher in his neck brace who glanced at them despairingly until they had gone upstairs to play or hopefully to be put to bed. I went out of my way to chat to the butcher and he seemed a sensible, fine fellow to me. I must have been in an expansive frame of mind for I even spoke to the architect of the villa; specifically, we talked about the horror of the new bingo hall on the Pier Development.

There was some kind of new music of a type I did not under-stand − a discovery of Lupe's who was modish − playing on speakers that were waterproofed and permanently hung around the pool. The drinks trays seemed to shuttle out quicker. There were some appetisers: Russian and good *Waldorf* salad which we were serving to ourselves from a long buffet table just inside the sliding door of the huge downstairs salon.

Suddenly Tenis materialised with his stethoscope. As each one of us came to the end of the buffet table in the queue, holding our plates of food, Tenis insisted on carrying out individual medical examinations.

Tenis made us sit on the edge of the table and took our blood pressure using that ridiculous armband which always reminded me of the hateful swimming lessons my father tried to give me. One of the nurses inflated the armband tightly by squeezing a rubbery teat as the other scribbled our blood pressure down in a book under Tenis's frenetic, joking supervision. He made us open our shirts and he listened to our chests; even the wives of the Police Commissioner and the Fire Chief had to part their blouse buttons so he could pop the warmed stethoscope in there.

Then Tenis asked us all if we had any specific complaints that we would like him to conduct a closer examination of with the help of his 'beautiful assistants'.

Perversely there were a number of volunteers with concerns. The butcher's neck was felt and his brace adjusted with a nurse on either side of him. A worrying small lump under the architect's arm was merely an inflamed sweat gland which we all got to examine. The cop had complaining ulcers so Tenis gently felt and probed, lectured us quite fascinatingly on ulcers then, to the delight of the cop and disquiet of his wife, Tenis demonstrated to one of the nurses how to feel for general problems in the abdomen.

Things had been amusingly macabre but took a distinctly sinister turn when Solielian, the owner of the crematorium and graveyard with his wife the mortician, measured each of us with a long tape, only half jokingly, for our coffin size. Then, instead of another tray of drinks, the more beautiful of the nurses, the one I suspected of not being a professional – or at least not of nursing – brought out a tray of sterile syringes and plastic phials.

Tenis gave a speech on how admirably low the cholesterol levels of our model region were compared to areas (he named them) in Northern Europe. He lectured on how accurate cholesterol readings are and what a useful tool in predicting future health dangers. He asked for volunteers to provide blood samples which he would have analysed at the lab.

'Hey. This would cost you sixty thousand anywhere else.'

Immediately damn Sagrana was first up! I felt a little betrayed but it all seemed professional enough. Tenis carefully swabbed the arm and suggested the patient look into the eyes of his beautiful assistant. The blood was drawn then transferred into the phial, the arm swabbed with antibacterial fluid and one of the beautiful assistants put a little transparent plaster on the 'patient'.

It was a brilliant stroke of Tenis's usual genius. Everyone was alarmed yet none could admit it and we were forced to join in this gruesome charade so we could be seen socialising with an acclaimed doctor and cardiac specialist. Grizzled machos like the cop and Mendez could not possibly refuse the blood sample, especially in front of their wives, who were offered the chance to opt out by Tenis, but, drunk like all of us, those ladies gamely volunteered up their fat arms, grimacing and giggling their faces away from the needle as the deed was done. Yet I was convinced their husbands had turned pale.

Sagrana and I made eyes at one another. It was hard not to be delighted at Mendez's presence there that night. We knew the slug had hopeless designs on the Mayor's office and we could just imagine those danger words already repeating in his ever-calculating mind: 'girls dressed as nurses', 'alcohol', 'perverse medical examinations', 'Hypodermic Needles'. Perhaps he was already paranoid that Paz Vermici at the dreadful local newspaper would get hold of the story and print it in the worthless publication.

A queue had already formed for the blood samples.

I had hung my jacket in the grand hallway so I rolled up my shirtsleeve and joined the queue. As it got closer to my turn I noted how Tenis carefully disposed of the used syringes in a plastic bag held open by the beautiful nurse. I noticed how she stood, both her arms held open with that plastic disposal bag but her legs apart. She must be the fake?

As I was having my blood sample taken, to my horror Tenis began telling all the guests – who stood holding their hands to their small arm plasters – about my terrible hypochondria which I have suffered from all my life.

'Lolo was at his Agency one day,' Tenis loudly said. One of the nurses gently swabbed my arm. 'He began to feel a tightness in his chest and a pain right here, in the sternum.' He pointed to the middle of my chest with a gloved hand then he puckered up the skin on my arm. 'Lolo is such a coward and the pain got no better. In fact as the morning went on the sensation became worse and the dull pain increased.'

I looked into the eyes of the beautiful nurse. Blonde of course but surely dyed or a wig for her eyebrows were dark? I felt an intense tight little pressure on my arm. I was sure my internal pressure dropped as I was punctured. The nurse smiled.

Tenis's voice still went on: 'Lolo phoned me. First time around ten o'clock that morning and the calls kept coming in at thirty-minute intervals. By siesta Lolo was describing to me sweats, increased heartbeat and now sharp chest pain, convinced that he was about to have a massive heart attack. I finally gave in and told him to come round from his Agency to my Consultancy. He arrived terrified, the pain in his chest still there. I made ready to examine him and asked he remove his shirt. Right in the centre of his chest he had a large red and yellow pimple that needed to burst.'

The company all shouted out, laughing like a television audience on a cheap Saturday-night show – which was what the evening was becoming. I smiled. The story was completely true. The beautiful nurse laughed in my face. I felt her soft breath. I had definitely glanced towards Lupe. She was laughing and nodding too although she had heard the story more than once. With her black hair and brown face her white teeth matched her bright clean tracksuit.

'Lolo Follana. The only man in medical history to confuse a heart attack with acne.' Tenis carefully labelled the narrow sticker with my name written upon it, adhered it to the side of the phial of my blood then placed it next to the other blood samples.

'If only he labelled the petrol so carefully, Lupe,' was all I could think of adding. I strolled away as cool as I could. (Later, when I sneaked to the kitchen on my own to find *Perrier* for Sagrana, who rarely drank, I was amused to open the fridge and find all the gruesomely dark phials of our blood with their name tags on them, stored in there beside chopped limes, lemons and mineral water.)

Tenis held up a device towards the chief cop. 'Be careful how much you drink tonight, Commissioner, I shall be breathalising you all before you leave, and <u>you</u>, especially, have to pass!'

Our Military Service

After university when I graduated with high commendations and completed my thesis on theories of design flaw I had to face up to my compulsory Military Service.

My wife Veroña was going to continue with her doctorate in mathematics, spending more years in the Capital city. Thankfully, Military Service had just been reduced to nine months, but I faced it with the common anger and dread of every young man plus my own especial fear. After all Military Service and barrack-room life is no place for a man who uses women's moisturisers on his face and sensitive skin each night and who can only wear the smoothest cotton or linens next to his body. They would eat me alive at the military and I knew it. I am not the kind of man who folds his trousers neatly before making love to a woman, but really, there is no need to be a savage.

Conscription in my country was almost universally despised. The pay was non-existent, barely covering costs of nine months' writing paper, envelopes and postal stamps to some girlfriend back home – who is being diligently ravished by every man who knows you are away for nine months, while your letters of longing slide under her bed unopened.

The only person I ever saw prepare for his Military Service with any joy was Sagrana who was no admirer of our military. However, the thought of being sequestered in barracks surrounded only by young men was heaven-sent to one such as he, and indeed, he had many adventures which do not – I hope – have their place in the scope of this account of the few things which befell me. The air force? Oh no. Sagrana put in a noble request for soldiering and soldiering alone, sir. He assured the senior officers he wished no favouritism in the army but wanted to start at the bottom and work his way up – in every sense.

Military Service was basically like the world – one law for the rich kids and another for the working class. I was a rich kid. I do not deny it for one moment.

There were two ways out of Military Service: be a rich kid and get a cushy number organised by your influential parents so you ended up in the Red Cross or an office in one of our big cities – or in your home town. The other option was outright refusal as a conscientious objector. I knew many kids, from rich and poor, who claimed to be conscientious objectors and got out of the army. All the conscientious objectors I know these days spend their nine months playing highly violent, war-orientated computer games in their bedrooms.

When I was young, in our armed forces there were twenty-two thousand officers including an incredible three hundred 'generals' who could not command a septic-tank-emptying operation, yet over after-dinner brandy could be heard to proclaim loudly, 'When we drove *Napoleon* out of this country in the War of Independence . . .' behind the bombproof mesh of the requisitioned Carlton Hotel salons.

Despite Father keeping his distance from the regime – as a man who had once dispensed good tables in the Imperial dining room beneath the huge chandelier at the last moment – it was not long before he was offered back favours regarding my placement for Military Service. This also happened to Sagrana who of course swung it for the basic soldiery. Tenis, I recall – whose own father had to give up the study of medicine in the hunger years and who owned two delivery vans – was not such a rich kid as us and his father had no swing, but as a medical student, Tenis's Military Service was exempted and eventually he escaped just by attending some three-week battlefield medical corps course.

To my horror, suddenly Father telephoned me in the Capital city one day to tell me he had managed to organise for a naval position. We all knew at that time the navy did not have enough fuel to put half the fleet to sea and I envisioned early-morning *reveille* on a tied up, non-air-conditioned warship in the southern port. At first I was aghast but Father paused on the phone − which meant he was tapping the side of his nose − and told me to wait and see at the evaluation being conducted in the Capital city.

By that time I was of course a swimmer and a thorough advocate of beach life. In front of the Imperial Hotel, Veroña and I spent our summers on the sand which I had been exiled from as a kid. Ironically I had flourished into what I took as a reasonable swimmer. I often beat rivals in the races out to the marker buoys. Veroña and I also took up self-contained underwater breathing apparatus diving, called after its English acronym: *scuba*-diving. In those days *scuba*-diving still had a pricey, vaguely exclusive *cachet* about it. The qualified instructors were local guys who had known the rocks and cliff bases since they had been kids, before all these stupid young British and North Americans came down with experience in the oil industry and started getting people killed.

I can never forget the wonder of my first *scuba*-dive. Plunging backwards off a *catamaran* then descending down the anchor chain to silty white sands charged with lurking skate and sand sole which would skiff away in a milk cloud at a fingertip's touch, a looming emerald cliff base above us patrolled by overhead squadrons of bright-coloured fish. I was sure I had found the sanctuary I had sought all my life: not a desert island or the roof of our hotel but secret inner space which hides close, all along our benign coast. I was always afraid of what lurked beneath seas since that *Hollywood* movie with that shark I once saw as a kid, but that day I first *scuba*-dived, I saw there was nothing to be afraid of: it was beautiful down there under the sheet of invisible water.

★　　★　　★

In the Capital city I went along to the Military Service evaluation. To my amazement my letter instructed me to bring swimming trunks.

I was lined up with thirty or so other guys along the side of a public swimming pool. One look and I knew most of them were city kids with fathers in high places. A shrill whistle blew from the naval officer who was dressed ridiculously in full uniform and gold braid as if he was going to sail a toy yacht across the pool surface.

We dived in and swam up and down without stopping.

There was the sharp whistle. 'You. Name?'

'Manolo Follana, sir.' I blinked up at him.

'Good swimmer. Out. Sit at the side.'

I sat through the other tests. Most of the boys were commanded to sit on the opposite side of the pool to me. Only three other boys, good swimmers I noted, sat on my side.

One of my number was sent to the middle of the pool. He had to scream and struggle and our mission was to get a hold of him with our arm under his chin and swim him backwards to the shallow end. Myself and the other boys were asked who wanted to go first. I timidly raised my hand, already feeling aggressive.

The guy pretending to drown would have made a good movie actor the way he was carrying on, but I got behind him in the centre of the pool – thinking of that damn French lifeguard and all his applause. I got the mouth jammed up clear of the surface and he relaxed as I pulled him in. It was a shame I had volunteered to go first because when I was struggling with the lad, I noted his shoulders were festooned with yellow pimples and my brown arm swept them all off in various small, watery puffets of blood.

Finally the naval officer with his clipboard announced across the pool to all the other lads, 'You might all think you can sit out your Military Service getting a beach tan and chasing foreign girls but you at least have to be able to swim for this one. Get out of here and take a shower. Go to the air force but do not crash in the sea.'

The rejected boys trooped out in their own echoes through to the showers.

The officer turned to us. 'Lucky boys. You four are lifeguards for your Mili.' He produced a large map of our country and its coasts and asked each of us where we wanted to be placed in the available lifeguard stations. There were scores of locations dotted around our coasts and I noticed a few strange ones positioned around inland lakes. The purpose of this was simple. One guy was so dumb that he had to ask where his own home town was. The sailor showed him and he pointed to the nearest lifeguard station. With a huge sense of relief I looked down the coast to our city, saw positions were available and pointed firmly to it.

So it was, on my nine-month Military Service I lived at home in the Phases Zone 1, joined by my student wife at weekends, and commuted on the lemon express daily to the beach in front of the Imperial Hotel where I perched up high, like Simon of the Desert, on my own lifeguard watchtower.

An ironic fate for a boy who never learned to swim until he was sixteen, tutored by soft-fingered girls with little coloured bikinis in a huge water tank, then after nightfall by sense of touch in these very beach waters.

High on my lonesome watchtower was the flagpole which each morning I would hoist according to the size of the waves and occasional jelly-fish shoals. The green flag: Safe Swimming; the yellow flag: Take Care; or the hated red flag: No Swimming Permitted. A red flag meant standing up on the tower which swung in the gusts with a hooded sports top, blowing yourself hoarse on a whistle as the suicidal wet-suited surfboard kids ignored you all day and paddled out into the high breakers, which tipped over frothy summits smeared with oily wires of loosed black seaweed.

All summer long, while the other four lifeguards of the beach sat, literally high in their elevations smoking marijuana, I had a different set of motivations. My compatriots would have been hard-pressed to see an elephant having swimming difficulties – they used the *walkie-talkies* between us to arrange the drug deliveries and report the colour of that day's bikini on the prettiest girl of the beach and her minute-by-minute progress along the water's edge or up to get an ice cream.

Our radios bristled into life when any young girl removed her bikini top to sunbathe. My fellow lifeguards developed a points system both for the progress of their own suntans and for the bare breasts of topless sunbathers. They took bets on which girls were urinating in the sea rather than padding back up to the toilets in the bars and restaurants. They arranged to meet girls in bars on the front while still on duty. They wore mirror sunglasses so they could doze up on the towers unnoticed.

You were only going to get saved from drowning by my crew if you were a topless, pretty girl. All binoculars from the ladder towers or the Red Cross *Portakabin* were levelled at your bared breasts. The merest scream as your boyfriend surfaced from underneath you and every lifeguard on the beach simultaneously jumped forward with anticipation then stood down with regret. Men and ugly women were left to the hazards of fortune.

I, however, was completely diligent and mocked by my fellow lifeguards. I was sober, alert and constantly on watch for swimmers in difficulty. All I wanted to do was emulate that stinking French lifeguard, milking the applause around the Meliander swimming pool after he manhandled me from it. I fantasised about saving a babe from the waves, of handing a little girl, dripping and gasping, back to her weeping mother, about grabbing a little boy thrown from a burning boat. Each of my heroic fantasies ended with a crowd of observers applauding in a wide ring around me.

I never had the slightest chance to be a hero. In reality I was called down the beach by desperately waving hands to find that a French family were having an argument with an English family over the positioning of their deckchairs – I had to explain, through the language difficulties, that those were not my duties.

In my 100 per cent cotton Red Cross T-shirt and my swimming shorts (which I had to provide myself to get 100 per cent cotton), I was often photographed smiling with my arm round a giggling, seventy-year-old granny.

I was asked to give advice on sun-protection factors and to spread sun-protection creams on to the shoulders of fat, middle-aged mammas who shrieked in laughter by the busload when I refused. I went embarrassed, like a rose.

Fathers walked up to me and demanded I explain to their little boys the workings of my *walkie-talkie* then allow them to use it. When I was at the top of the watchtower, an aggressive gang of pre-pubescent girls often gathered at the ladder bottom and tried to look up my shorts.

We had two drownings that summer during my tenure which I can never forget. They were low on possibilities for heroism. What shocked me about drowning was how useless and token our services were, how quickly it all happened and how heavy are bodies when they come dead out of the sea.

From movies and books you believe drowning happens over long dramatic minutes but it really happens in only scores of seconds. Bang. Head is glanced by boat. His face slumps forward. Water in lungs. He dies with his head only barely submerged.

One guy disappeared that day a red flag was up. He had his collarbone broken on the sand bottom in less than two metres of water by a huge breaker and was rolled in dead at our feet just half a minute later by the waves. I was hardly off the ladder screaming for my colleagues. I was frozen in shock and that wastrel from Gacinto who had let his hair grow all summer unchallenged by our inspector tried resuscitation for twenty minutes – we were taught never to give up. I had to admire the long-hair's determination.

The autopsy report, which I alone requested, still showed the cause of death was drowning but I had seen the man step into the water only thirty seconds before he died as I blew with all my strength on the whistle and yelled on the radio that an old nutcase was going into the brown waves.

Afterwards I had to sit in a bar and have a brandy to stop my hands shaking and still the nausea in my stomach, but I noticed the other lifeguard boys merely crossed themselves and gathered, talking for a while before they returned to their positions. The police did not write down anything we said in any officially recorded way, they just nodded and took our word for it.

Drowning is a very public death. As the boy from Gacinto went through our regulation attempts at resuscitation to the man in a swim-suit with an ice-cold paunch, whole families with young children stood round watching as if a mermaid had washed ashore. In fact, our main duty was to hold back the crowd from prodding and nudging at the dead body – as they will inevitably do – until the Solielians came down on to the sand, incongruous in polished shoes and mourning black, to carry away the dead man and take him to his rightful place in the cemetery high up above our city on Heaven Hill.

The Embedded Christ

Now a citizen who frequented it with a pretentious familiarity – making up for lost time – I met the Romanian artist Hansa on the beach of our city one white sunny day. Hansa was a penniless artist. Her latest phase was shining slide projections of her enormous brown eyes in close-up at whitewashed brick walls in doomed galleries.

My first marriage was gone, destroyed by the faults of my character. Veroña and I had just divorced. My parents had sold the Imperial years before.

The tricks of the beach I had learned from my lifeguard colleagues in my Military Service days, from Tenis and even Sagrana. I asked Hansa, who sat alone on a single white towel from her hostel, if I could leave my house keys with her (I had many copies at my Agency) while I went swimming but, hardly wet, I immediately returned to the shore before some other man got to her and then I began talking. I refused to move away back to my own towel. When I finally did collect my own towel it was to pull it over beside Hansa while still casually talking – the most obvious move for a man in our city. She wore and even replenished after swimming – lipstick. On the beach!

A beggar from North Africa was pestering the hot beach that day, swaying up and down the sand trying to grab handbags. I was grateful to that beggar as he created some drama for Hansa and me to talk about. The beggar stamped up along that sand followed by a group of jeering local lads who shouted out warnings each time he moved to grab at some middle-aged lady's bag. Occasionally a local urchin would rush the beggar as if he were going to strike him but the youth of our city would never connect, just stop short and retreat to rejoin the pursuing group, and one had to admire the beggar's tenacity or his desperation – this thief would not be put off – he circled, threading the sinuations of the beach, followed by that swarm of abuse.

Yet I was becoming weary with the entertainment by the time I felt properly attached to Hansa. This beggar was becoming a positive distraction. In fact, when Hansa made an admiring comment about him I felt a lush wave of furious jealousy. By this point our entire end of the beach had sat up on our towels, deckchairs or sunbeds and were watching the thief.

Anything for a pretty girl or woman. I stood and walked directly up to the beggar, unafraid that he might have a knife as most of these guys did. My trick was to open my palm for him so he saw (and nobody else could) what I held there before I reached him. I transferred the five-thousand note into his hand. He turned directly and marched off the beach. The following gang of ruffians looked at me in admiration. It appeared as if I had muttered some dreadful imprecation or physical threat at the man or that he instinctually sensed me as an obvious grand master of black-belt *karate*.

There was a smattering of applause for me – as on that day of the cursed French lifeguard – though the applause was not as decisive, enthusiastic or final as that fool's share. Hansa smiled admiringly and clapped. Though Hansa interrogated me in bed, all through our relations I never revealed what magic words I had 'said' to that beggar.

Hansa Deprano spoke our language very well in an over-formal, almost literary manner – with an accent from the Capital city though she had never been there. She spoke cursed English as well of course, which she claimed she spoke more fluently – though she spoke our language note-perfect – except for that odd overuse of the formal mode. Her grandfather was of our country – an old exiled communist who after the Civil War had headed east for a reasonable climate and ironically found himself living under communist weather soon enough. He never lived to experience the joys the *Ceauşescu* regime. Hansa's father was of the German-speaking minority so she spoke that language also. Really – how do these damned multilinguals keep all those words in one head?

It was out of nostalgia that I took Hansa up for ice cream in the Terrace of the Imperial. She was wearing her brief aqua sarong, hung with little seashells on its hem. She followed me there with the tenderness of a new wife while the sands were too hot and still haunted by that beggar's powerful and desperate spectre.

Ice-cream and boutique technique still worked after all those years. Listening to my stories of growing up in that hotel she was later seduced by Western plenty in the expensive clothes shops which I paraded her through. Each item of luxury her greedy eyes fell upon was a hook attaching her more to me. We arranged to meet in Cena's that night for a glass of something.

In its enticing shades of different light sources I arrived on the café terrace of Cena's early that evening and took my favourite table. I wore my latest linen suit. I was gently bruised by the day's sun. Hansa was late. I tried to pick out her elegant, modestly breasted figure among that throng of evening passage walkers, promenading along the esplanade.

I had spent the day with Hansa in the state of semi-nudity of our modern beaches so I naturally wondered what she would wear that first evening date and how she might appear. Suddenly I felt a slight hush descend on the tables around me. I turned to my right and my glass nearly shot out my hand. I did not recognise Hansa at all standing there, enormously tall at my side. She was wearing a bright green miniskirt of such shortness her crotch was nearly visible; white, insanely heeled boots came high up her bared legs and she had worked bright blonde clogged weaves into her piled hair. I had to speak quickly to cover my *bourgeois* shame at her appearance. My God, her trying to sit down at the table in that skirt was an operation. As she strained downward I longed to hold up the tablecloth to shield her from the popping eyes of the men of our damned city as she finally managed to fold her legs, kneeing the table beneath in the middle, so the ashtray jumped in the air and the saucers crashed.

For the rest of the night, I was anxious to remain in the same establishment because her entrance in each new café or bar created such a novelty among the young men but she insisted on us constantly moving on. I was filled with lust for her but a conflicting anxiety to get her out of our city to somewhere else rumbled hypocritically beneath my every response.

I walked her back to the cheap hostel in the poor area through catcalls of damn youths. I kissed her hand, longing for the next day on the beach when being stripped to her normal bikini would prevent her from standing out so clearly from the crowd and drawing such attention to me.

Lingering lunches in the Dolphin (or was it the Lower Rivers?) followed, over which she explained how as a family with a foreign grandfather they were suspect under *Ceauşescu*. In that regime at the Collection of Rumours Department there was an official Inspector of Typewriters. Typewriters were strictly controlled and if you owned one – as her father did – you had to register it with the State. When it was properly registered an official came to your home or office and told you exactly where the typewriter was to be located. From time to time the Inspector of Typewriters called to spot-check the typewriter was exactly where it was meant to be. I recall I trembled with fury at such a regime.

Within two nights I had Hansa installed in my apartment at the Phases Zone 1, making love until the mattress shifted. I even had her shipped to Villon's dental surgery for a filling she could not afford. This was love. This was it. I was sure.

★   ★   ★

The final item I paid for during Hansa's tragically short holiday that summer was the taxi on the tearful night she departed our city – all the way to our airport at Lacas, detouring from the National road and using the new toll motorway bypass to catch some charming Romanian charter flight at around 3 a.m.

In the taxi I felt ill with the love and the huge future prospects for Hansa Deprano in my life. We had been up for the whole previous night at a *discothèque* and I slumped in the passenger seat next to the insensitive, garrulous taxi driver so she could rest in the back. When our taxi paused in the sobering, curious sepia light of the motorway toll stations the sound of summer crickets flooded through the driver's electric window as it went down. I turned with despair to see Hansa's bare and now brown legs, which had been pale the day I met her on the beach, stretched all along the back seat. I noticed, as we slowly drew up to every glum motorway toll attendant, the garland of dropped coins permanently entombed by the summer hot tar beneath their serving window.

Hansa and I both cried our farewells and kissed again and again at the entrance to Departures.

My three-minute phone rule was long abandoned and my bill happily spiralled as I lay on my calfskin sofa talking to Hansa, in mysterious *Bucharest*, every single night of the months which followed. I had to complete an important project, the old conversion of the merchants dealing hall in our city for which my Agency won the regional architecture award, details of which can be found on their website.

Despite my hatred of travel, after two months I flew to see her in Romania. I could not book a scheduled flight in those days. When my twenty-year-old Romanian *Boeing* 737-100 (at least not a Soviet-era aircraft, one type of which was so unstable it had to have a ballast tank of water fitted in its nose) lurched into *Bucharest* airport, I was terrified to see the speed at which thick white snowflakes were rushing by my cabin window while we were still in the air. Each flake glowed with a hideously brief and horizontal luminescent intensity.

So quickly off an aeroplane and into a taxi then a basement bar with blonde Hansa Deprano, her arm chummily thrown around me, I was still deaf from the air pressure.

I was in the 'new, free democratic' Romania with Hansa leading me down metal steps of a beer cellar just by her fingers so I could feel all her rings, down into the noise and smoke through squeezes of young Romanians in dark clothes and black leather. Then I had a huge beer in my hand and we were on the bottom floor, pushed right up against the cold, wet, brick wall. Hansa Deprano kissed me. I had waited months for that kiss and to be with her again and I had imagined our reunification with great lust but what did I say to her after all the waiting and anticipation? I said, 'Hansa. There do not appear to be any fire exits in this place. How do we get out of here if there is a fire?'

Then she led me back, drunk, across a snowed-out *Bucharest*. Through icy winds we leaned together in love, back to where she was living in those days.

I was faced with a student place: up and up we went into one of those tall thin buildings which you imagine some idiot composer must have resided in, freezing to a thankless death over an out-of-tune piano. Hansa Deprano was in front of me, ducking her pinned-up blonde hair to ascend the stairs. It was a honeycomb of art-student hovels, and as we climbed, each empty dark room we passed had its door flung open wide showing *Baby Belling* two-ring electric cookers sitting on cheap, dirty carpets.

Hansa's room was at the summit, up in the very source of the snow. It was freezing. The first thing I did instead of watch her unzip and drop the daring, short leather skirt and black wool stockings, was cup my hands to the glass of the small, snow-plastered window and peer out. I was looking for a fire escape.

'Look, my tan is not all gone,' she growled behind me.

All night long, despite Hansa's considerable and liberated distractions, I found it impossible to concentrate on lovemaking. Again and again my body went rigid, then Hansa's too, as I listened to yet another drunken student thump up the stairs below us. Within moments the odorous certainty of late-night cooking would manifest itself from the bright gap under our bedroom door.

Hansa Deprano had sat on me backwards. She gave me her black lipstick and I had to scrawl the forenames of women I had been with across her undulating shoulder blades. I wrote VERONA and then, rather cleverly I thought, I used the 'A' to form MADELAINE downwards in curling letters with the E almost on to Hansa's right buttock. By turning herself slightly to the candlelit mirror which leaned against the wall, Hansa could decipher and greedily pronounce the names. I was interrogated and had to describe everything. Hansa wanted to know so much dirty stuff you soon ran out of facts and had to make convenient things up. Soon she was handcuffed and tied to the bed – as was her latest pleasure. I was not enjoying the liberties of her helplessness.

I believed Hansa, being tied firmly to her single bed, would impede the speed of our exit in the event of fire. In the rooms beneath, so many different midnight feasts seemed to be cooking all at the same time that I kept glancing over my shoulder which annoyed Hansa so much I put that blindfold back on her. We then had an argument as I absolutely refused to allow her to tie me to the bed. I tried to convince her that this was not a moral or judgemental stance but there was a fire-safety issue involved here. She scoffed and called me a 'typical Catholic mamma's boy'.

It was then Hansa raised her voice and said aloud, 'Lolo Follana. You are less a personality than a collection of phobias.'

The only advantage of Hansa's new tastes for ropes and handcuffs was that while she was bound and blindfolded on that narrow bed it was impossible for her to prevent me pulling on her Chinese robe and tiptoeing away. I slowly crept, shivering down the stairway, through that student ghetto and sniffed outside strangers' rooms for the scent of real fire: the scent of plastics or wood. 'Lolo?' I sometimes heard Hansa call wonderingly from back up round the stairs as I inhaled deeply on a lower landing. When dawn began breaking I had not slept at all but felt I had survived a great mortal danger.

When I did doze off once I was awoken by her mouth around me. I was so tired I only wanted to sleep but she had brought a cold mango from the fridge to join us.

Later I watched her dressing in the half-light, the smeared name of my ex-wife still across Hansa's back. She was surrounded by her huge Byzantine gold paintings propped against the torn wallpaper of the walls. There was a potted peace lily, somehow still alive in that frozen room, growing in the corner and when she bent over to pull on her bright yellow, soft wool stockings, the back of her naked thighs touched those dark leaves and they seductively stirred. I fell asleep.

When I awoke she had left me a drawn map and note in stunning calligraphy of how to find her painting studio which, ominously, was far out in the suburbs at the end of the tram routes. Her note ended, 'My underwear will be yellow all day from mango. x x x.' In daylight I now noticed the wooden floorboards of her room were crowded with her naked, gold-paint footprints.

On my way to her studio it was time for me to write some post-cards from that dreadful country to our sunny city by the sea, for which I was utterly homesick already.

Near Hansa's fire-trap home, along the pavement heaped with frozen snow, there was a tiny door-in-a-wall comestibles shop with potatoes in cloth bags leaning against the walls. On a rusted stand, which squeaked then stubbornly ceased moving when turned, were ten or fifteen postcards of strictly two views: a cluster of brutal, Soviet-style high-rise blocks – the dyes and techni-colour pigments betraying a photo from circa 1968; and a diesel mechanical tractor in a bright yellow cornfield followed by smiling, traditionally costumed peasants, holding sheaves to their bosoms.

I selected two high-rise block cards and three of the tractor cards. By looking at the old woman at the mechanical till and pretending to lick something then affix it to the rear of a card, I managed to communicate that I wished to buy postage stamps. Of course, like every establishment that sells postcards, it did not sell stamps.

I found a grubby café to sit in shivering and managed to order an expensive ice-cold beer.

On a card of the Stalinist high-rise blocks, to my Agency staff I wrote:

Our new *Bucharest* branch. Opening soon to which you will all be transferred. I will be back on the 12th, or maybe the 14th or maybe the 9th, so don't relax.
Chief

I selected a tractor postcard for my accountant Sagrana.

Thriving business seeks immediate audit. Accommodation provided. Daughter available for marriage.
Back on 12th.
Follana

For Tenis I also selected a tractor.

This year's model, available in three colours.
Death to Capitalism.
Love to Lupe.
Follana

I was left with two postcards but was unsure who I should send them to. A postcard to my just-divorced wife would have been a little premature in the fields of amicability. I opted to send one to her best friend from their girls' institute, Aracelli. I then wrestled with the decision of what image on the postcard to choose and in the end settled for a tractor.

I am actually abroad.
It's snowing. What a dump.
Hope you are well and Veroña OK?
Home on 12th.
Lolo. x

I had hesitated, but eventually committed to the kiss symbol. An unused postcard remained but no matter how I racked my brains I could not conclude who to send it to. I would need to get one of the city's grandest hotels to send to my mother's grave. If they had any grand hotels. I placed all the postcards in my jacket pocket for Hansa to post later and pulled my jacket tight around me.

I managed to follow the multiple tram changes from central *Bucharest* out into the far-flung conurbations but when I stepped off into the snow at some crossroad in the suburbs I was intimidated. Night was falling as I had risen from bed too late and exhausted. It had taken me much longer than I thought it would to reach that suburb.

I consulted Hansa's drawn map and walked on ahead, the new experience for me of my feet sinking into the snow which I only knew from my youth when we raced to mountains to build snowmen on the roofs of our cars and drive back down to our coastal city.

I took the wrong street twice. The third time I got the correct cross-street but then Hansa's map was unclear if I should be taking a right or a left. I tried the climb to the left, ascending slowly in case I slipped in the snow, broke my leg and was condemned to certain death in a *Bucharest* hospital.

Darkness had fallen completely. When I rounded the corner on to a long, deserted street — wide, with almost chalet-like buildings on either side — up in the air I saw Christ himself deeply embedded in the ice, looking straight at me. The guttering of a house corner above had blocked and the overflowing rain had frozen, completely entombing a plinth and stone statue of Christ beneath — huge icicles hung from the fingers of his welcoming hands, black eyes stared blindly, his diseased cheeks seemed to fester in blue beneath that glistening, transparent layering. I felt he was suffocating — dark branches above him had fused with a cone of ice that stood unceremoniously on his head and the twigs were festooned with thousands of tiny mini-icicles.

I must get out of this uncivilised, savage country and back home to my own, I involuntarily thought, and a welling homesickness arose in me.

I struggled onward up that deserted broadway — its house numbers were in the tens of thousands. I did not want to be at the wrong end! At the extremity of the road, I saw a Soviet-era car revving high to turn the corner and come towards me but in a dreamlike way it slowly began to turn in a long slow skid until it faced the way it had come. Illuminated bags of exhaust smoke stopped and its headlights went out. I squinted, mystified. I walked onward into the dark.

There were the lanterns of some kind of café or tavern ahead. It was undoubtedly snowing heavier than when I got off the tram. When my slow, cautious walking allowed me to reach the car I saw the reversed slashes its double tyre tracks had scored in the road where the car had spun around. I could hear its warm engine tick and tinkle within the bonnet.

I turned and looked at the building with the lanterns. I saw shoulders shift within the steamed-up windows of that establishment. I stepped inside and a bell rang. After all the sheer white outside I was dazzled by a jungle of colours and plants within — a small, fully stocked flower shop in the midst of all this blizzard. I held out Hansa's map towards a man in an imitation leather jacket. He pointed back in the direction I had come from and said many words to which I nodded and replied English '*yes*', again and again. The man shrugged and turned from me, carried on smoking.

I pointed to some red roses and the ugly woman from behind the counter took the flowers from the metal bucket – the water was so cold, condensation showed on the speckled aluminium sides. I paid with the strange currency. The woman behind the counter bundled coins into my hands. Hansa would be impressed for me to produce these red roses in the midst of such frozen wastes – yet what a strange place for a flower shop in the midst of this idle, shabby suburb.

I stooped and ducked my head beneath the shop bell, back into soft, large, airy gaps of black night, between each large quivering leaf of fallen snowflake – as they tickled down my face, my eyelids fluttered in reaction.

The woman in the shop had wrapped the lower sections of the rose stems in common newspaper to shield my hands from the thorns and as I held the flowers to my chest it was fascinating to see a white snowflake lay down on the rich dark flesh of rose petals and transform into three or four tiny, precise spheres of water.

There was an oppressive intimation from the blacked-out tundra ahead; something uncanny I could not decipher. The wide avenue before me ended and turned to left and right in a T-junction but my eye had become used to the urban expectation of buildings and built-up areas. At the end of the boulevard everything seemed to stop. There was a wall then everything beyond was dark. What was this region of complete dark?

I walked onward to the left then came to a gate. But from there I could see small electric lights within, which covered the dark grounds as if it was a park with illuminated yet unsymmetrical walkways. I entered through the large open gate and saw the first of the gravestones.

It was a cemetery but an enormous one; it seemed to stretch to the dark, snowed-out horizons on all sides ahead of me – like an enormous battlefield – yet the contours were dotted and clustered with weak, minuscule, fading lights.

As I came closer to the first headstone I realised what these faint lights were. Perhaps that day had been some sort of Name day or Saint day as small candles had been placed on the ground with curved transparent covers, some in different coloured glass, some just pickle or jam jars. But as the day's snowfall had accumulated, the snow was gradually burying the candles, some just showed the very tip of flame but some candles were already fully submerged and their subterranean glow was visible through bluish, Antarctic, illuminated snow before their flame was fully asphyxiated.

It seemed wrong to back up now and leave the graveyard with the roses – which explained why that flower shop was so close by. I lay the bouquet down on the nearest grave and crossed myself. I stood still a good time longer watching time kill one candle light after another until that land of the dead was returned to complete darkness under the suffocating snows.

The next day my already heavy cold developed into mild pneumonia. I rested in Hansa's deadly bedroom, eating bean soup after bean soup, their surfaces dusted with archipelagos of hot paprika. I was comforted just by the feel of my passport in my pocket.

No matter how I tried, I could not persuade Hansa to return to our city on the sea with me. She still had her mother there in *Bucharest* and her art career. I explained to her she would not need to concern herself about money again if she came with me. She spoke our language so well surely fate was urging her to run away with me and live by the sea where she could get a studio somewhere in the Phases, work at her leisure and live in love with me?

For another week that long, visceral girl lay beside me in her tiny bed heaped with garish overcoats and awoke me daily with her mouth into the cold. I had to wear one of her wool hats as I slept.

I broke her down two days before I was due to depart for home. Hansa Deprano agreed to move to our city with me. I was overjoyed. I almost tried to persuade her to let us leave together immediately I was so anxious to escape that oppressive place, but she was offended. She explained she would need to close down her life in *Bucharest*, rent out her flat, arrange her art world contacts. It would take a few months.

At 5 a.m., outside those death-trap apartments, the taxi driver removed two bricks from behind the rear tyres and dropped them aggressively in at my feet in the passenger foot space. 'The handbrake is not working,' Hansa explained blankly behind me.

Exactly repeating her tearful departure from our own city in the summer, Hansa stretched out on the back seat of the taxi and slept, leaving me unable to speak to the glum driver next to me who produced an incomprehensible commentary all the way.

I recall we overtook a car being driven by a man with wide, constantly startled eyes, more afraid of life than me.

We met a police motorbike convoy and a darkened *Ceauşescu*-era limousine, blowing horns aggressively while speeding the wrong way up the dual carriageway, forcing all vehicles aside into the hard shoulder. It was the new leaders, rejoicing in democracy and returning from a luxury meeting in the West after cutting a few infrastructure deals.

Capitalism, like the new Crusades, had steamed into *Bucharest*. The snow had broken midweek, the huge raindrops fell so vertically and so heavy I had seen the sheltering beggars dumbly watch their small copper coins on the black slabs of pavement begin to shift or be slightly adjusted among the rivulets and rushing gutters.

'I will come to you soon, Catholic mummy's boy,' she wept. After finally kissing me goodbye at the airport, she handed me early desktop brochures about her and her artwork to give to local gallery owners in our city in preparation for her arrival.

*   *   *

In the bleak cafeteria of *Bucharest* Departures where the few who looked like we could stretch to the price of a cup of coffee assembled, I sat smoking the foul local cigarettes.

Groups of peasants clustered outside with their belongings defensively bunched around their legs, glaring in at us. I noticed a bored-looking security guard circuit his way through the cafeteria and yawn. He was about to leave but he strolled up to two men in business suits who were chain-smoking and gulping short coffees. I could not understand a word, but it soon seemed the two men objected to being asked for identification and they raised their voices at the security guard despite him being armed with an automatic weapon, slung casually under his arm on a shoulder strap. His slight patience exhausted, one of the seated men in the dark suits suddenly stood up. He was tall and he punched the security guard hard and square in the mouth. The other suited man threw back his chair and jumped up on to the security guard's back and they spun round and round together, both shouting in unison, as the attacking man's polished shoes swept items from the surrounding table tops.

As the gun, which was facing backwards under the man's arm, swung wildly, I saw the amused peasants sneer at me as I instinctively cowered beneath my table.

The tall one repeatedly struck the security guard in the stomach as he wheeled round, still bearing his colleague. It was only then I noticed the bracelets of gold around the cuffs of the two men's jackets. These two brawlers, overwhelming the armed security, were our pilots that morning.

Our flight was delayed as two substitute pilots were summoned to replace the originals who had finally been arrested and led away in handcuffs. I noticed the two replacement pilots who arrived at our gate after two hours did not seem to have shaved for several days.

Uneasily aboard the airliner, I glowered at a huge-shouldered, large-nosed peasant who sat in the window seat blocking the emergency exit. He wore another of those thick black fishermen's jumpers with a high neck; long-dried food dribbles went down over his enormous paunch. I was positive I could identify the familiar bean soup with paprika.

Just at the instant we became airborne I leaned a little over the big man to peer out and down through the window to confirm to myself we were safely ascending. My last glimpse of that country was a turnip or potato field, its cultivated rows showing through the broken, dirty snow. Just about to pass under the wing in the very centre of that huge field was the unmistakable posture of an old crouching farmer, his trousers down as he defecated.

It was with a surge of powerful homesickness that we came in towards our city from the east over the small jetty and large swimming pool of Tenis's yellowish villa at Lacas. Sun had been drumming a flashing rhythm off the sea swell then the aircraft sketched its own hawk profile in fast shadow over a petrol station's dirty roof. We moved into our own cast profile and were down on the runway with dirty desert scrub between the taxiways.

I was astonished. My ex-wife's best friend Aracelli was waiting for me. Shyly hidden against the glass window behind the Arrivals barrier – she suddenly looked beautiful, piled chestnut hair with sprays coming off, the birdlike face, the long overcoat hiding that body.

I actually said, 'Hey. What a coincidence. Who are you waiting on?'

'You. I got your postcard.'

I immediately knew something was terribly fractured in my plans, the way Aracelli and I were both too afraid to greet each other by kissing on the cheeks.

'Has something happened to Veroña?' I hopelessly asked.

'Nothing. She is seeing someone else. She is in the Capital. Yours is the only flight today from where you were. I waited. For hours.' She shrugged.

I looked down at her.

We could both feel the sudden, almost swooning and deeply selfish instinct of our bodies.

We began tearing at one another inside her car in the dank gloom of the new multi-storey car park then we drove to the apartment above Town Hall Plaza where Aracelli and I made love all night on the mattress I keep upstairs. I knew with Aracelli's pale body I also got our city, my home.

When I telephoned Hansa with dread the next day she carefully wore me down. I confessed I was seeing someone else. I lied when she asked when it started. 'Twelve hours ago' did not seem like the truth of a good human being. I carefully put down the receiver.

Inside my travel bag were Hansa's brochures written in our language but with missing accents, diacritics and punctuation indicating she spoke our language much better than she wrote it: 'Hansa Deprano's work employs materials such as tomato sauce, sugar, chocolate, syrup and soil to create striking images which challenge our ways of seeing . . .' I tossed her brochures into the litter bin at the front of the Imperial Hotel. Within six months Aracelli and I married in a civil ceremony at Town Hall, beneath the quarterly tolling bell.

An Hallucination?

Daily, Ahmed and I would feed the cats and then walk together through the Zones, often as far as 3. But one afternoon he shyly apologised that he would remain in the apartment.

I left the apartment building and walked up the railway side. I was sure I sensed Ahmed was watching me from above in my bedroom window. Yet I was drinking quite a deal of watered whisky with ice and using some old tranquilliser pills from the bathroom cabinet. I looked across to the apartment building opposite. The old woman was standing at her window but she did not seem to be watching my progress along the shore road. She was staring intently across that air which separated us, towards Ahmed. The gypsy guitar player was not on his balcony but the glass sliding door from his salon was slightly ajar. Inside I heard a child cry or was it a small dog's bark?

I took in a breath and surveyed around me. When I got to the uphill path I crossed the railway. I was surprised to see human figures up in Ahmed's old lair as I ascended to it.

The yards around that building shell had been cleared and the security fence dismantled and stacked. Two South Americans were barrowing rubble out of the building shell. I watched. A large concrete mixer truck, the holy cow of our coastal society, was parked on the road behind and above, the rear hopper turning and mixing in readiness. They were going to complete the building.

I climbed up to the higher road and took it as the route back down towards the Phases Zone 1.

When I reached the boat in the wasteland I was shocked. The cats had already been fed. A generous amount too – some meat still remaining neatly scooped in the plates, the Imperial Hotel spoon cleaned off. The emptied cans put into the bin liners. I checked the price tags on the dumped cans and they were from the North African's place by the Imperial Hotel. I looked around the waste-land suspiciously, I eyed the higher ground of the apartment range above this for a watcher but could see nobody. 'Teresa has been here,' I said out aloud.

When I closed my front door behind me the flat had that soul-less feel of human desertion. I was now sick, for sure.

I called shakily, 'Hey. Illegal Immigrant. Guess what? They have started work on your old place up on the hill. Hey?'

Ahmed was not there. I had a sudden attack of chilling loneli-ness.

I hurriedly searched through my big flat. Sometimes Ahmed sat in my design room for hours with one of my laptops, surfing the Internet which he was skilled at – I can barely operate it. He would sit at my technical drawing table, angled and secured horizontal.

But Ahmed was not in my design room. Eventually I stepped out on the balcony and I groaned.

He was swimming in the blue sea beneath me, beside the petite but perfectly formed figure of Teresa. She was wearing a bikini. Brightly coloured but I could not say what colour. The light shining around them was so strong I was forced to retreat inside to get my sunglasses. I returned holding onto the railing to watch both Ahmed and Teresa swimming, lingering close to each other then suddenly darting off in playful directions, breaststroking side by side.

Ahmed and Teresa's lips were moving – I could not watch. It was too painful. I just turned away. I walked back into the house.

Lying on the terracotta-coloured sofa, I waited for them both to come upstairs but when Ahmed came through the door he was alone. He smiled. I asked if he had enjoyed his swim. He said he had. I nodded morosely then suddenly I did not care so much. Teresa might be good for him but as long as he kept her away from me.

We both testily avoided each other into the evening and I went to bed early. I heard him go to his own bedroom much later after he had spent hours with his fingers clicking on the keyboard. I had to smile at my teenage jealousy, lie there and savour it with a grim smile. Like a night cramp that you feel beginning to pass, I enjoyed its familiarity if nothing else.

Why Yes?

Ahmed was questioning me about the end of my first marriage. Sometimes I was sure he was going to instinctually reach out for the pen and paper pads by the telephone and jot down notes but I was not (he might have been) weary with my confessions yet. I still believed when I had confessed everything to Ahmed our relationship could commence.

When we were young students in the Capital city, my first wife Veroña's work was based on her early ambitions as a statistician. The stuff she took home was work-overflow from various companies. Soon she was doing extra-governmental work. As her studies in the Capital city progressed and her talent was acknowledged by the professors she started to lean more and more towards theoretical mathematics and fell in with what I thought of as a dull but eccentric clan of maths heads.

Veroña's research seemed to be financed by what I took as a suspect government agency. She started to come home to our already cramped student apartment in the Capital city with bin liners full of confidential documents which had been shredded by machines. (Man, the bidet was so close to the toilet in that dump you had to sit sideways.)

This government agency needed to know how many times their shredded documentation had to be sliced so it could never be reassembled according to mathematical probabilities. It was fascinating – at the time – how Veroña demonstrated her conclusions, which depended on the size of the document lettering and numbering used. If every shred was separated, one after the other, into four separate bags it rendered the pages beyond any probability of reconstruction but she also recommended geographical dispersal of the four divided bags, which was adopted. Surely anyone in a café could have told them that? Yet my wife got a hefty chunk of taxpayers' money for her report. Highly confidential government secrets and corruptions were shredded – split four ways and the lots taken to be burned in different locations – all on my young, first wife's recommendations. What an achievement for new democracy and open government.

But I noticed after that contract Veroña herself bought an electric shredder machine – which were still very expensive in the eighties – and despite the lack of any possible interest in it, she began to shred all her own discarded research documentation: A4 sheets of unsuccessful calculations, massed with her neat formulae in black, fine-point pen. She separated every fourth strand into different carrier bags marked discreetly 1, 2, 3, and 4. She deposited the supermarket bags in different wheelie bins around our neighbourhood. Sometimes I would catch a sudden view of my new young wife from our little kitchen window, with her hair up, in that favourite orange overcoat, moving stealthily from neighbourhood bin to bin with her collection of bags. She looked more like an eccentric down-and-out vagrant than a mathematics prodigy.

As time went by Veroña's research became even more occult in my layman's opinion. She was involved in obscure numbers systems, convinced that mathematical patterns could be found in all places. She analysed and successfully contrasted the patterns of pedestrians moving on the pavements of New York and Rome using footage from security cameras. She told me she had once recognised an old acquaintance captured on film in Rome. When she told her friend the precise time they were in a definite street location in Rome they thought she was a magician with powers.

Veroña talked – with her mouth always full though she was so thin – of reincarnation, of the movements of ant colonies and locust swarms and of the German philosopher with his belief in patterns of eternal recurrence.

She was fascinated by the numbers system in poker and tried to get me interested when it is well documented how much I detest card games (other than my old holy tarot pack, with fifty-two schoolgirls' names inscribed upon them).

I had to spend several uncomfortable nights drinking with grey-haired poker cheats who had never seen the sun, banned from the Capital city casinos for using the numbers system. It was clear they were all trying to sleep with Veroña as she scribbled notes about their dime-bar philosophies and torched egos.

Eventually I could not understand even the basics of her research any more because by this time Veroña was using early *IBM* and *UNIX* systems which no common mortal understood.

I saw in later years, though we both could not perceive it at the time, that the real crisis in our marriage came when I graduated and Veroña was awarded a scholarship to continue her mathematical research. I wanted us to return to our city and base ourselves there, but for the advanced level of computers required for her research, my wife needed to be in the Capital city. So I went home to our city for my Military Service – albeit on the beach – then began to build up my design Agency.

Of course, as has been previously stated in this account of the things which befell me, for sixth months after my Military Service all I did was sit on the café terraces of our city, playing the part of an idle graduate with time and a few pennies on his hands relaxing after Mili Service, but secretly I was eavesdropping on the big-mouthed businessmen, contractors and Chamber of Commerce blowhards who barely cast me a glance as I lapped it all up.

With my face in some pretentious novel I never completed a paragraph of, they spilled the beans at the next table. It was from excitedly gossiping estate agents I learned of the prime office site that would be soon be coming up – and where my business is still based – worth a packet in real estate alone. I had borrowed money from Father and put a deposit on the place from the café telephone before those show-offs swallowed their third aperitif.

Understandably, Veroña and my parents took me as a wastrel. Nobody was as shocked as my wife when almost overnight I was suddenly in business at a Grand Avenue office, starting out with laminated menus, luminescent frontages and my own invention which never quite took off – remote-controlled illuminated night names for houses up in the villa ranges where I distributed leaflets through doors by hand – plus my first two interior-decoration commissions.

I have to say I worked hard, was focused and applied, perhaps for the first time in my life. Only Town Planning, great designers or architects, *scuba*-diving and pretty women had motivated me in life before but suddenly I thought business through carefully, operated on my hunches and beliefs, stuck to my guns and it all worked quickly and very successfully.

I knew I had been very lucky and that made me grateful and cautious. A businessman who is never grateful is a bad one. And you need luck to be grateful otherwise, like all the big shots, you think everything happened just because of you and, thus, that you can never be wrong. Then you make big mistakes in business. I met a lot of parrots like that at the Commerce Club and soon dropped my membership.

For a person who had been profligate and unconcerned about money in my past (as long as it was available to me on a modest dripping tap) I was surprised to discover I was an astute businessman. I never failed. Everything I touched became a hopeless success and made profit. I even appeared in design magazines and sometimes in large-circulation national newspapers as if I were some kind of talent, which is nonsense.

The great design talents change everything. They come along and the whole landscape is transformed, *Leonardo* who the Pope asked to design his mausoleum then decided it was bad luck and cancelled the order! *Bernini – Frank Lloyd Wright –* they are their own fountain, they dominate and make the form their own and weirdly they leave us, their inferiors, with no way of following them.

I was never going to change or even dent the language of design. I was a mediocre talent from a provincial town with a good business head. Yet it would be possible to say my work, and by some horrible adjunct I myself, became fashionable and in the mode for a mercifully brief time. After two years I was nationally known within the industry. Money started to come in.

Veroña seemed to lead a weirdly separate life as a penniless student in the Capital city who did not cash the cheques I sent her but shredded and distributed them in four different dustbins and, worse, had almost completely lost interest in *scuba*-diving.

My life had moved on but hers had not. I was paying bills and tax, meeting with the local commerce organisations and employing people who depended on my Agency for their livelihood. I was busier than I should have been as a new husband yet to me it was Veroña who seemed lost in irrelevant and obscure maths research. She lived with the conviction her research was the priority in our relationship while I was not only supporting us but making us both grow wealthy.

After my mother's death, I owned the apartment above Town Hall Plaza, the four at the Phases, which I would start converting into one gigantic place, and I had poured all profits in to pay off the loan on the Grand Avenue office of my Agency.

This was an obvious time for me to open a branch of my Agency in the Capital city but I decided against that. The Capital city was not my home turf. I never felt comfortable there and I was a controlling boss who liked to see with his own eyes what was going on in an office so I decided not to open there. Everybody criticised me: Tenis, Sagrana, my employees, but I knew my own strengths and weaknesses and I was no empire builder.

I may not understand the oscillations of my emotional life but business is a different matter. I was a hard-working, precise local boy and I knew by instinct a branch in the Capital city would be a failure both financially and also in terms of aesthetics – I refused to water down the quality and precise application of my work which I felt would surely be compromised by another branch.

The person who was most angry about me not opening an office in the Capital city was of course Veroña, who seemed to treat it as a personal insult that I was not going to spend a fortune of our money building a fancy office in a high-value real estate area of the Capital city just to be near where her research was. Veroña did not even enjoy her life in the Capital city any more – she just worked on her little sums.

When Veroña did return home during term holidays, she had a full-sized blackboard bought from the schools authority placed in that lovely spacey salon at the Phases Zone 1, blocking the view, massed in coloured chalk with her calculations and theorems which she would furiously erase. She laid layers of soft, coloured chalk dust on every surface throughout the whole apartment – and we had just succeeded in getting the place clean after years of concrete building dust.

I made her replace the blackboard with a whiteboard but there was an enormous argument between us about it. Up went the whiteboard, twice as big. It might have made no dust but I had not realised the bright-coloured pens squeaked so infuriatingly on the smooth surface of the board as she aggressively scrawled out her frightening symbols, wearing a football scarf that winter, and I had to go for a walk or ride the lemon express into our city while she worked.

I visited her in the Capital city one day and she drove me for hours out past a beautiful university town and into a bleak desert upland – completely ochre – villages on the horizons as flat as cowpats with a single church spire, like a rogue sprig of straw stuck up.

'What do you think?' she asked, leaning on the hire-car roof, not wearing her contact lenses but silly sunglass clips on her spectacles.

'You do not want us to build a house here, do you?'

'Know what you are walking on?'

'Cow shit?'

'Death. This was a battlefield.'

'Yeah? The Civil War?'

'Certainly not. War of Independence. 1812.'

And the rest of the day we had to speed from one strategic crisis point to another then over hills to more featureless dry tundra which created a dust cloud behind the hire car – even on the tarred roads.

She had a map of the battle's hourly developments – I walked with her a bit but it was a hot day and it was boring. Finally I just sat in the car with the air conditioning on trying to understand how this could relate to mathematics research. Veroña's form was a black dot high on the ridge where she had gone to see the small cliff – do you not know the soldiers had to put down their weapons on it then clamber up under fire?! She even came back covered in dust with a spent musket ball, slightly indented, and she got deliriously excited about it.

The following day she took me up to the university with her research partner, that idiot Bartolome who she never even slept with, to show me the computer programs they had been running. They seemed to have a room all to themselves full of huge computers. I was polite, but as a businessman I could not help wondering about who was paying for all this.

I was disturbed by what was shown to me. It could all easily have challenged the later conceits of Hansa Deprano and her experimental galleries.

Firstly, as if I were a prospective financier (it had not struck me yet that is what I <u>was</u>), they switched on a video monitor which displayed movie clips of old *Napoleonic* battles which had been edited in with police footage of violent rival football fans surging backwards and forwards along the terraces.

Then the olive-green computer screen showed plotted masses of coloured dots moving on a plan of the football terraces overlaid with a grid in a scale of metres. The red dots surged forth then the yellow dots flooded the other way. Clearly they represented an exact synchronisation with the figures on the video monitor. Mathematical formulae were displayed.

Then the computer screen showed the massed ranks of what was obviously a vast simulated battlefield, precisely scaled with many contour lines. I recognised the two peaks and the villages of the bleak plain where Veroña had driven me. A huge range of coloured dots moved in ranks and flank positions, some merged and some swirled away. I was reminded of tropical fish but I realised they were a representation of troop phalanxes and swift cavalry. In a bottom section of the computer screen, various mathematical formulae responded to the mass troop movements and the formulae seemed to come to some kind of conclusion.

The computer screens blipped out and the lights came up. I was shocked. To audition as *MTV* pop-video makers, Veroña and Bartolome had real potential, but I feared what their mathematics professors would say.

'You are my husband and not a fellow mathematician. You must not breathe a word outside this room. Bartolome and I have proved in our conflict models that human figures are following a pattern of movements that can be mathematically predicated. Or in layman's language you could phrase it another way. They seem to be moving to a plan.'

Bartolome leaned towards me threateningly. 'These researches are at the very edge of theory.'

'Do you not see, Lolo?'

Bartolome added, 'There is what you might call a pattern. A mathematical harmony. We have demonstrated a predictable pattern of movements in our model conflicts. We cannot say what the pattern means but it is there.'

Veroña looked more passionate than I had seen her in a long time and I felt a sadness for us both. She said, 'We are following a plan that might not be apparent but is revealed in conflict. Those soldiers on the battlefield: there was a plan operating there which we can only call a mathematical one. We are mathematicians, it is not for us to speculate.'

'Let me try to get this right,' I said, picking out a cigarette.

'You cannot smoke in here. The computer sponsors will not permit it.' Bartolome shrugged.

I returned the cigarette to the packet. 'Let me try to understand. Your calculations have arrived at some kind of correlation between the movements of football fans running and the soldiers on old battlefields?'

'Correlation is just a word. As mathematicians we do not have any use for spoken language or any mathematical equivalent. We search for repeatable calculations. We have detected patterns. Mathematical formulae that can be used to predict the most likely movements of these troops and violent outbursts behaving in a predictable manner.'

'Could these patterns not be due to your models? I mean, how do you know the accurate troop movements in those old battles?'

They both looked at me threateningly.

'The battle models are calculated on huge probability of troop locations and well-documented movements and of course we tested our formulae on other conflicts – we just felt these conflicts were . . .'

'More colourful.' Veroña smiled and nodded.

I relented. 'Absolutely incredible stuff,' I also nodded. Trying not to laugh.

I let Kiko Bonzas take over the Agency for three weeks that summer so Veroña and I could spend a full holiday together at the Phases Zone 1. I believed Veroña needed a long rest. Veroña's old high school best friend, Aracelli, and her latest Then Current boyfriend visited and lived with us for three weeks.

They were boon companions. The weather was exceptionally beautiful, many hysterical nights – which though I refused to sing, even I found very diverting – took place around an insidious *karaoke* sound system Aracelli had brought us as a gift for the apartment.

Aracelli's Then Current was an engineering graduate. He and I had some long dinner conversations which terrified the ladies. The history of concrete and the chemical properties of its setting, for instance. He had worked in a subcontract office on the new super-railway project so obviously that was fascinating. For me.

When the girls raided the clothes shops of our city the Then Current and I drank rum and *Cokes* discussing our respective female partners' sexual preferences.

When we were bored by the sea in front of our apartment at the Phases we four would take the rattling lemon express into our city. Veroña and Aracelli would sunbathe topless on lilos floating out by the rocks below the Meliander Hotel. The Then Current and I would laugh because if teenage boys snorkelling over there got too close you saw the girls both pull their bikini tops back on.

Veroña was always wearing high heels. Always. She would carry a pair – expensive Italian ones I paid for – in her beach bag and step into them with sand still between her toes the instant we came up off the beach by the cafés and railings (which were painted green in that era).

After a first, particularly vicious, week of partying, Veroña went through a craze of putting her aching feet in a basin of glass marbles back at the Phases Zone 1. She got Aracelli to try it too. She claimed moving the feet noisily around massaged them gently. Years after Veroña and I divorced, I would occasionally still find a single, blue glass marble in the dust under an old cabinet and smile fondly.

One night at the now-defunct waterside *discothèque*, Light of the Moon, along from the lemon express station – little more than flashing lights, stacked beer crates, a bamboo roof, mosquitoes and music — Veroña led me off into the shadows of the reeds where she tasted me.

I was still buckling my belt but, holding her breath, she took my hand and led me immediately back towards the beat of guitar music. Straight away my wife grabbed and slow-danced with Aracelli's Then Current boyfriend, suddenly she was kissing him as Aracelli and I swayed and watched — the Then Current, Aracelli and I were all silently accepting of this occurrence and never mentioned it again but I remember the young man reacting curiously to that taste being pushed into his mouth by my wife's active tongue.

One day the three of us left Veroña smoking a cigarette in the salon of the Phases and we went to the farmer's cart that used to set up in summer along the road and we returned carrying ripe honeydew melons — so many they would not fit in the fridge so we had to put them in the spare bath with water and a bag of ice. Veroña was still seated in the salon. Her cigarette had burned out in her fingers and the ash fallen to the stone floor tiles. She had been watching a fly circling in the room all that time. 'It is following a pattern,' she quietly announced.

Although the apartment at the Phases was large, often during those three weeks of doing as we pleased it was possible for Veroña and me to overhear the sounds of the other couple making love.

Veroña and I tried to make love as quietly as possible. That horrible stray cat Veroña had adopted over the summer, and which had got too bloody used to sleeping on our bed, glared in at us for half an hour one night as we made love then it vanished for good.

Another night after the candles long burned out, Veroña and I lay listening to the soft sounds of those other lovers nearby. I observed, ever so subtly, my wife's lips moving. I knew what she was doing immediately. Veroña was imagining the other couple but only relatively aroused. Her imagination assessed the likely angles of their moving limbs and bodies together, her lips murmured silently as they did when she was calculating mathematical formulae and I knew that she was visualising that discovering and returning of pleasure next door, reducing those human physical forms to pure geometric symbols in her mind.

That winter we were back to the usual. I was very busy at my Agency and Veroña was lost in the Capital city in her own research. At the Phases, I called hello from the kitchen when she came in but I heard the car keys crash into the metal Indonesian bowl. The flick as she snatched up a magazine and I knew the mood was bad. I had not seen her in two weeks and this was us reunited.

I felt oddly combative, as if the electrons in the air around us were reacting, so I sat down beside her and said, 'What?'

'Nothing.' She shrugged but looked hard and long at me.

Then just as quickly she leaned over and said, 'Have you been with Aracelli?'

I had not. I had not been with anyone. I remember a sensation like pulling my whole self into my sternum then expanding outwards. A tremendous dissatisfaction. Then it happened.

'Yes.'

To this day, occasionally, I still turn over that 'Yes' in my mind. In my defence it was a foolish stab at general truth. I had thought of other women. Of Aracelli, Thinh, Quynh, Madelaine, that French waitress in Cena's, doubtless mused on schoolgirls from the cards, Lupe the television presenter and those three pale English girls who were on the beach the weeks we were, but got disappointingly pink then brown. And did Christ not say just to think about it was sin enough? So our marriage was not biblical.

Conversely the 'Yes' was a setting out, a stepping forth towards nowhere but other women. I was using a good and truthful act to allow me to achieve something bad. And since Christ was not taking any notes it was a lie anyway. Suddenly I invoked strict rules Veroña and I had never lived by, just to push her away from me.

Also I was sabotaging their good friendship. It was all so reckless of me but as she screamed and wept I remained head down, tight-lipped, not looking at Veroña. I felt a huge pity for her. Did I think I was so superior? Even the way her hair did not perfectly fit in behind her ear made me want to groan and lean out to touch it into place but I refused myself the familiar relief of any reconciliation.

Veroña stood and snatched the keys to the car from the bowl. On her way to the door she jammed on the system, snatched up the radio-controlled microphone, and snarled at full volume through the *karaoke* system, 'You damage me, Follana. You do need a psychiatrist to bang.'

The neighbours downstairs must have sat bolt upright.

'Aracelli is a psychologist,' was my infuriatingly quiet response but the microphone had smashed on the wall and the door had slammed, cracking the new plaster.

I sat still for a long time shaking my head. Why did I say yes?

Then I phoned Sagrana to ask about divorce law.

Veroña went back to the Capital city directly to sleep with Bartolome at long last, doubtless mumbling fractions and integers while nibbling at one another's ears.

The next day she telephoned Aracelli, screaming at her, who, of course, was shocked, furious and embarrassed. Aracelli turned up at my Agency and we crossed the road together and walked awkwardly to Cena's side by side in silence, somehow only able to talk over beverages. I tried to explain to her why I had said the Yes. Embarrassing and absurd as it was, that was obviously what Veroña wanted to hear, and if I said it, it might make her realise how wrong she was.

I recall, touching her hair away from her face and nervously sipping at her coffee glass, Aracelli was suddenly confident everything would be repaired. I was shocked to find my emotions oscillate and surprise me – in fact, I was infuriated at Aracelli for uttering such a feeble optimism. But my 'Yes' – just that tiny word – put a whole wide river of debris into motion.

★   ★   ★

Veroña broke with me. It was a separation that lasted two weeks then became a divorce. She did not want any of my business or property. 'You worked for it all.' She said she wanted cash to continue the research. The bloody research. I had a lot of cash at that point so Sagrana gave her most of it and I bought a small apartment in the Capital city in her name, paying it off for her in three chunks over the next two years. Bartolome moved straight in so I subsidised their lovemaking. None of it was a very good advert for fidelity. I offered her a much larger apartment at the same price in our city but she refused to come back until the accursed research was finished. I suppose her absorption in mathematics saved me a localised ex-wife.

About a year later, Sagrana heard Veroña's research money had been withdrawn by the university and her work mocked in a respected journal. I felt awfully sorry for Veroña. I felt more sorrow then that at any time, for while I may have chipped and dented her as man and woman do, the rest had burrowed deep into her.

We had reports that Veroña was to be found cross-legged with scissors in the apartment I bought her, cutting A4 sheets of her calculations and her own personal documentations, such as bank statements and letters, into thousands and thousands of strips then sorting them meticulously into plastic bags which she would distribute at specific refuse bins – becoming hysterical if their location had been moved – and the maddening thing was she kept that table from room 88.

Within a year of Veroña and I divorcing I was married to Aracelli in a civil ceremony; as witnesses just Sagrana, Tenis, Lupe and definitely no Then Current, Now Former boyfriend of Aracelli, who was furious.

I can remember Lupe's short mauve dress but not my bride's. Here we go again, I thought, and I never ceased harbouring a sickly attraction for my best friend's wife.

Just before we married, in the bed together at the Phases Zone 1, Aracelli grabbed my hair and snarled, 'I know what you are like,

Lolo. After we are married you will go with a few women but I only ask this – I have pride – not with some girl I have to face every day because then I feel I am being laughed at which just about shows you I care more about being laughed at than I do about marriage. There are millions of women in the world, why go with one *I* know? Not the girl who works at the next desk from me, or the waitress in my café, or the woman at my bank or the ice-cream parlour. I have seen it happen with my girlfriends. They say to their guys, "Oh yeah, these are modern times, we go with who we want as long as we are together," and they mean it, but the very next day their guy goes straight out and sleeps with their younger sister. Go find your bitches on the beach but make sure they are leaving in a fortnight and not coming back again.'

'Same goes for you too then,' I grimaced.

She let go my hair. 'If you want to see some hairy ass on me, fine.'

'Hey. There can be no kids with me. That will lead to trouble.'

'If I ever get the urge to totally ruin myself we can adopt or get a really pretty schoolboy to knock me up.'

'A schoolboy with a rich dad.' I added.

'Richer than you, Mr Pasta.'

After that conversation with Aracelli, to my own amazement I found my mind shrugging women off for the first time in my life. I stopped looking at them over the top of my newspaper when I was in Cena's.

The freedom she gave me made that freedom irrelevant. Aracelli and I suddenly got happy together and it took us both completely by surprise. Our happiness was like a bouncing baby we did not know what to do with. Sometimes I stared at her across a dinner table in the Dolphin (or was it the Lower Rivers?) and I felt a sudden shocking fear of losing her.

Again in my life what I wanted so badly – the infinite variety of other girls' bodies – had suddenly oscillated into what I wanted the least.

The Solielians

I was at my Agency when my mother phoned, hysterical. I immediately telephoned an ambulance then Tenis but he was in the operating theatre. So I called the ambulance service once more. In our city then it was best to phone an ambulance several times. It was quicker for me to run up the Major to the apartment in Town Hall Plaza than consider any alternative means of transport, so I ran.

I was panting as bad as him. Fully dressed, Father was on their big old dark bed which we had brought over from the Imperial Hotel. I was alarmed by his appearance; both arms thrust skyward – as if he was fighting off an invisible *djinn* – Father was shouting and repeating, so Mother shut the window, 'You are going to lose me, you both are going to lose me, what will you do without me, both of you? The pain is awful. I want it to stop. You are going to lose me, the money, get the money and look after the money, you are going to lose me.'

Tenis told me in his early doctoring days when he was doing a ghastly spell in Accident and Emergency in the Capital city, 'Our country is impressed by drama, doctors too. When they come in screaming and shouting – even those with a leg missing – I've noticed those screaming suckers always live. It is the quiet bastards who nurses and doctors ignore that die. They are always the ones who are lowest and in the greatest danger and have no energy for screams. I've started attending to them first; leaving a queue of

269

screamers. The mortality rate since I've been doctor of the floor has halved. If they are screaming they are not going to die.'

Father shouted and roared. I was convinced that he was going to be OK.

'What happened?' I asked.

'He fell over in the salon, chest pains. Oh, the struggle to get him here,' said Mother.

'Right. Father, calm down. I have phoned Tenis who is on duty and an ambulance twice.'

'Never mind Tenis. Get me Jesús.'

'Jesus will not help you now. You have not been to Mass —'

'My accountant Jesús, you stupid bitch.'

'Jesús Two Hearts is miles away.'

'Get Lolo's accountant then; that Sagrana.'

'Sagrana?' I said.

'He is sensible. Not like you.'

'Oh yeah. I doubt you would approve of him in every way.'

'You are going to lose me, boy. Phone Sagrana.'

'I will. Try to relax.'

I phoned Sagrana who went into a panic and I heard him knocking things from his desk.

'He wants to talk to you.'

'Why?'

'God knows, but he looks a bit rough.'

'I will be right there.'

I phoned the ambulances again and the operator was rude. 'You have already phoned twice.'

'Where is the damned ambulance then, you witch?' I slammed down the phone and I tried Tenis again but he was still in theatre. I wondered if I could get his pager number so I phoned Lupe who kept repeating 'The Host, the Host' in a breathy and — I suddenly felt — incongruously sexy way. She assured me she had a secret pager number for Tenis that beeped even at the theatre table and she would contact him immediately.

'Tenis to the rescue.' I announced back in the bedroom. Mother wept. Sagrana arrived in moments (before the ambulance, please note), kneeled solemnly by my father like a priest and took his hand. Father visibly calmed.

'Mr Follana, you must be calm until a medic sees you. This is not the time to worry about financial matters.'

'It damn well is, boy. Two weeks ago I took everything out of the dual account and put it into my own account – the interest is a point five higher.'

Sagrana's face suddenly became grave. 'Oh,' he intoned.

I piped up, 'So what?'

Sagrana looked at me, annoyed.

Father ordered, 'Help these two idiots and get me down to the bank and we will transfer the money back to the dual account now.'

'Mr Follana, it has passed into siesta,' Sagrana immediately whispered. 'The bank is not open until morning.'

'Get me down there to talk to the manager.'

'The bank is closed. For God's sake,' my mother yelled, 'Not now. Now is not the time to talk money, we need a doctor.'

'Explain, explain,' he gasped, exasperated, eyes bulging towards Sagrana.

Sagrana turned and spoke in a calm voice. 'Were there a . . . loss within a family the bank will withhold monies if the victim was a single account holder in his own name but legally cannot do so with the dual account of a married couple.'

'Does that matter?'

'Yes. The money can be trapped there a long time – sometimes years – while taxation issues of the individual are looked into.'

A low, depressive ambience filled the dark bedroom. I was not making big money then, so even I felt a twinge of selfish need for access to my parents' money.

Sagrana continued cautiously, 'If it would lessen the stress on Mr Follana just now, obviously it would do little harm –'

'Yessss, yesss, you tell them, lad . . . give them some sense.'

'– to transfer the money over to Mr and Mrs Follana's dual account first thing in the morning.'

'Yesss. That is sensible.'

Still holding Father's hand – stroking it indeed – my accountant lifted his other hand to consult his watch. 'It is nearly three o'clock now. The bank will open at eight thirty in the morning. As a precaution I will accompany Mr Follana then.'

So I sat on one side of the bed, Mother on the other, both of us stroking Father's liver-spotted hands. The thumbnails so similar to my own. Sagrana moved position and sat at the foot of the bed in one of the slim-backed ebony chairs from the television salon of the old Imperial and pulled close to the bottom bedboard.

'Sagrana,' Father called and grimaced.

'Yes, sir?'

'Smoke if you wish. You need not leave the room.'

'Really, sir, that is not acceptable with you feeling unwell. I will just step outside.'

'Smoke, man!' he commanded. 'You too, Cinderella,' he growled out the side of his mouth at me. 'I can see you are too well bred. You did not get it from me.' He chuckled then gulped. Sweat was pouring down his face.

Sheepishly Sagrana removed his cigarettes so I followed.

'What brand do you smoke, Sagrana?' Father asked.

Sagrana showed him the cheap fishermen's packets he bought.

'A good smoke. A man's cigarette. Look what Lolo smokes. North American girl cigarettes. You know why? Because he has seen the North American actresses smoking them and he thinks by smoking them he will get in the pants of the first one to come to our beach!'

'Father. Lolo is a married man now,' my mother snapped.

I laughed to try and brush it off.

'As if a famous actress would come here,' Father slyly muttered and caught me out.

'Actually, that . . .' I could not help butting in . . . '*Ava Gardner* . . .'

Father burst out laughing at me then coughed and to my horror I saw Sagrana's crossed leg jump as he chuckled too.

'Poor, poor Lolo, eh? I never wanted a daughter but I got one in trousers, eh? What a boy. The money of mine he went through in that Capital city, Sagrana.'

'Oh no, Mr Follana. Lolo is prudent with money,' Sagrana defended.

'He is not with mine. Christ. What was he doing with all that money in the Capital city? I do not know. Most of it went on fancy books, I think. Books. He had enough books to build a house with. What did he want more books for! Know what you are, Lolo?'

'What, Father?'

'The Frenchies have a word for it. A *bohemian*. Know what that is?'

'Yes, Father.'

'That is what you have always been. A *bohemian* in an expensive suit I had to pay for. I suppose you were smoking hashish through there with the other *bohemians.*'

'I never touched drugs, Father, and you know that.'

'Never? Never?'

'I told you I tried hashish once and I felt I was at the dentist. I am far too much of a hypochondriac to try anything else.'

'So you did not spend all my money on the North African boys selling hashish? I thought that was where all your mad ideas came from. Town Planning indeed. A man who cannot keep his bedroom tidy designs a town,' he chuckled cruelly. He looked at Sagrana and he winked.

'Shhhh,' went Mother.

'Hey, Sagrana. Go over to that wardrobe there and take a look in the bottom. Go on, man, do not be afraid.'

Sagrana crossed to the wardrobe and opened it.

'In the bottom, man, take it out.'

From the shadows Sagrana retrieved a dark bottle of wine.

'Bring it over here. Look at that, you lot. *Latour* wine 1961. The

273

Frenchies are not good for much but they know wine. And *bohemians* too, eh, Lolo?'

I nodded.

'Sagrana. I stole that from the idiots who bought the old Imperial next door. It was on the bloody inventory: three crates *Latour* '61 and the fools never came back at me for it. How can you respect that? They were not hoteliers. Just idiots. Look what they've done to the place. Cheapened it!' He shouted and coughed.

'Father, calm down.'

'Poor Mama.' He ran his hand through my mother's hair. 'Poor silly Lolo and poor Mama. Too good for this world the both of them,' he said quietly. 'Sagrana, go to the kitchen and get a corkscrew and four glasses.'

'Father.' Mother scolded.

Father said nothing private or loving to us. As we heard Sagrana crashing in the kitchen and dropping things, Father looked at me and said, 'Sore, son. Real sore.'

'Hang on, Father.' I squeezed his hand. 'Tenis is coming. And the bloody ambulance. I will go phone again.' I made to stand. But he waved me down with a hand.

He grimaced. 'I know I am a bit of a bastard but I do not deserve this pain.'

'I know, Papa, I know.' Tears started to push into my eyes at the thought of him being in pain but I did not cry because Sagrana came back into the room.

'Here, waiter!' Father called, immediately brightening when Sagrana appeared. 'Give it to Lolo, son. I taught him to open a bottle of wine. He has always been good at that. Especially if Father is paying for it.'

I opened the wine and tipped some into each of the four odd glasses.

'Papa, you cannot drink until the doctor arrives,' whispered Mother.

'Listen to that, Sagrana. Do not marry young. You are sensible.

Lolo has married as you know. She is great to look at. A lovely girl but no business sense. Head in the clouds like him. Cheers, all.'

Solemnly we all took a sip of the strong, fuming wine, watching him. He tried to sit further forward but all he could do was wet his lips. Still, I saw his tongue shoot out and taste it.

'Oh yes.' He sighed. There was a long silence. Ominously, Mother sensed something and got off her seat and lay down on the bed next to Father with her arm across him.

'Drink up, man,' he nodded at me. 'Who is making money in our city then, Sagrana?'

Sagrana coughed. 'Estate agents outside town are raking it in, Mr Follana. Pusol and his crew.'

'What is that bastard Seraini doing now?'

'He sold up.'

'Ah. Always hated the shit. I was hoping he was doing bad.'

The doorbell rang.

'Thank Christ,' I said out loud and I walked off down the corridor to the intercom.

'Yes.'

'Is it you called the ambulance?'

'Get up here, third floor, my father has had a heart attack. What kept you?' I slammed the handset down and left the front door open, returning to the bedroom.

When I re-entered the room Father looked worse. I could see from the angle I was at now he seemed to be constantly straining to rise from the bed.

'Relax, Father. That is the medic now.'

'Do not tell me to relax, boy. I have to get through this till the morning. Do not tell me to do anything about relaxing. I have a job on my hands. I curse you, Lolo. I really do curse you. Damn you, Lolo. You steal my money and you tell me what to do.'

'This guy will help.'

He burst out crying. I was shocked.

Mother wailed, 'Oh Papa. Do not cry. What are you crying for?'

I heard the ambulance crew shout from the corridor so I dashed through. There was only one guy and he had no bag with him.

'Where is all your stuff?'

The guy looked at me. 'I was trying to say.' He lowered his voice. 'Is this patient still alive?' he asked incredulously. 'I am the meat wagon ambulance. I am not a medic. I only pick up those who have passed.'

'You are joking.' I hissed. 'Get on your radio and get a doctor here now.'

'Lolo!' Mother screamed.

I stepped to the bedroom. Father seemed asleep at that point. Sagrana sat on the bed beside him and tried to lift Father's shoulders a little forward. He also used two fingers to force Father's mouth open a little and check his tongue was not blocking his air passage. Father coughed and he seemed to revive a little.

Sagrana turned to me, his face wide, full of a kind of excited passion I had not seen since our hours and hours in the graveyard together as lithe schoolboys – the dark bags under his beautiful eyes seemed to have vanished in the panic. 'He is in real trouble. We must get a doctor here, I think he is going unconscious. You were a lifeguard, maybe you should check his breathing.'

I whispered, 'That was years ago. That damn asshole was the ambulance for the dead. They sent the wrong one. What should we do?'

'Get Tenis. Tell him to organise something quick.'

'I tried. I phoned Lupe.' Clear panic was in my voice. 'She paged him but he is in theatre.'

Father had opened his eyes and I felt relief. He looked stronger and he motioned me towards him. 'In the name of God, get your hair cut, man,' he whispered to me and he seemed to fall into what I thought was a sleep but he jerked in little spasms and his eyes opened once more, briefly. They were horribly distant. They saw nothing of this world – they had moved to another.

Then he went still. Sagrana started to whimper, putting his soft hair onto Father's shirt.

'I do not hear breathing.'

I fumbled with the bedroom window to scream down at the orange-topped ambulance I could glimpse below but the window was too slow so I ran through the corridor. The driver was still there, just standing idle in the kitchen.

'Help us. Help. He is unconscious. You must have some training?'

'I just started the job.' The ambulance driver came into the bedroom and Sagrana stood aside.

To my surprise the driver immediately responded, trying various recovery actions and the kiss of life. He did it very coldly but efficiently. I noticed how, as he pumped my father's chest with a palm – both arms formed into a pillar – the ambulance driver's eyes had a faraway, distant look across the bedroom – I was reminded of the eyes of a copulating male dog which had mounted a bitch, as I watched, on a piece of waste ground near the Phases Zone 1.

I crossed helplessly to Mother and put my arm around her shoulder; she had put the knuckles of a hand in her mouth and was biting them, looking at the horrific sight of the quite violent actions of the ambulance driver pumping on top of my stricken father whose shirt he had torn open (he had carefully place Father's gold St Christopher pendant to one side) to reveal a powerful mat of grey chest hair. (I myself am strangely hairless. As is Sagrana.) The mattress complained in a smutty rhythm. I found it impossible not to let my mind oscillate to the memory of me kneeling as a teenager, efficiently shoving at Madelaine from behind on that very same bed, her chambermaid uniform bunched up well above the small of her back.

Father was not responding.

Mother wailed and fell onto the bed beside him repeating his name. Sagrana was shouting at the ambulance driver to get help. The ambulance driver nodded smartly and dashed off again.

Amazingly, in seconds, the ambulance driver rematerialised with three real paramedics in wildly bright reflective jackets which seemed to light up the dark bedroom.

Now they moved Sagrana, Mother and I completely out of the room and surrounded Father with full electronic equipment in shining metallic boxes – including those electric-shock pads they place on the chest. As well as this they were shouting into *walkie-talkie* radio sets. I noticed the bottle of wine had been knocked over on the expensive bedside rug and was glugging itself empty onto it, but then was not the time to stand it upright.

After ten minutes of us trying to calm Mother – who was hysterical through in the kitchen – the paramedics emerged with lowered heads.

I was taken aside. I was shaking.

'Look. No chance. After this time. I am sorry. If we had got him to the hospital we would have done just the same. The law is now that we cannot move him without the doctor being here to sign the death certificate. We cannot sign a death certificate so we need the doc to come here to do that. Understand? You have my sorrow, sir.' His two assistants nodded and they trooped out.

My mouth felt numb. I embraced Mother in the kitchen then I led her slowly through to the salon and left her sitting to collect herself. I walked back to the kitchen but suddenly the first ambulance driver wheeled his trolley through and down the corridor.

'What are you doing?' Sagrana asked.

'If a doc cannot make it here I might have to nip up to the hospital with your father.'

'He is not <u>my</u> father.'

'To get the death certificate signed there but I will bring him straight back, I promise. I need to put him on the trolley now. I shall just put the trolley in the bedroom.'

Sagrana growled, 'Let the lady of the house in with her husband first, man. For pity's sake.'

Mother and I went through together to see Father and we lay rather peacefully together on either side of his dead body for some time. I found that lying in that position, with the body of my dead father between us, it was difficult not to think of Thinh and Quynh lying on either side of me above the aquatic presence of the reserve-water tank.

Then I took Mother, sobbing, away from my dead father, sat her down back in the salon and stumbled with tears in my eyes to the kitchen where Sagrana stepped to me. 'For God's sake,' cursed Sagrana. 'Are you OK, man?' He threw his arms around me and we embraced strongly.

'Jesus, Sagrana, I cannot believe it. So quick.'

'Here,' said Sagrana. 'Man, do not listen to that stuff your father was coming out with. My old man was the same. They try to get it all out and they try to be hard on you because they have that tough thing in their generation and they want us to be tough guys too.'

'Yeah,' I said but he could see my father's last-minute attacks had taken the wind from me.

There was a thump from the bedroom. That ambulance idiot was forcing the trolley in there like he was at a supermarket car park.

Suddenly a presence was to our right as Sagrana and I were both embracing. With our arms still around one another, Sagrana and I turned our heads. Standing there looking at us was Tenis in a long overcoat, sunglasses still on – he removed them. The front door must still be open, was my only odd conclusion.

'Tenis.' Sagrana and I broke apart, rather guiltily I thought. 'Thank Christ you are here,' Sagrana said. 'His father,' he could only nod at me.

Tenis strode down the corridor calling behind him, 'Sorry I took so long.' He entered the bedroom and we heard Tenis say, 'What are you doing?'

The voice of the ambulance driver said, 'Waiting on the death certificate signature by a doctor.'

'Get out, get OUT.'

'Are you the doctor?'

'Yes. I am the doctor. Tenis. I am a trainee surgeon at the General and I am the family health adviser.'

'Well, I need the certificate signed.'

'This is still an emergency scene and I am in charge now. Get out! You are not required.'

The ambulance driver shot from the room but immediately lingered in the corridor then awkwardly decamped to the hall.

'Oh God,' I heard Tenis's voice moan. Sagrana and I followed – awkwardly squeezing past the ambulance man in the corridor – and we both stood at the bedroom doorway. Father had already been shifted over onto the trolley which had been lowered down to the bed level to enable this. 'When was he taken ill?' Tenis asked, quickly kneeling down by the trolley next to poor Father.

'Just at three,' Sagrana crisply returned.

'God, Lolo. Sorry. Please go out, Lolo. I need to examine your father quickly just in case. Where is your poor mother?'

'In the salon.'

'Here? She saw it all? Oh, go be with her, Lolo,' he whispered.

I left the room but Sagrana remained and I heard them whispering together immediately. I walked to the salon and I could see the ambulance driver by now lingering sheepishly in the kitchen. 'Friend, there are drinks in the fridge or make yourself coffee.'

'No, no, sir. Thank you. It is just . . .'

'What?'

'I need my trolley back, sir. If you will not be requiring it.'

'You will get it. Dr Tenis is just conducting his examination.'

I walked through to the salon. 'Tenis is here, Mama, but there is nothing he can do.'

She sat in the salon and suddenly my mother looked alone. She just nodded. We both sat hugging while she stroked my hair.

'What will we do about the money?' Mother asked.

'Not just now. You can't worry.'

'But I am worried. He has lost it all.'

'He has not lost it all. It is in the bank.'

'Those vultures will keep it if they can. Or the socialists.'

'There is nothing we can do, Mother.'

'You cannot support me now. It is all gone. You will have children to support soon. The Follanas are ruined once again.'

Tenis came striding through to my mother in the salon with his arms outstretched, 'Mrs Follana, you are inconsolable. If I could have made any difference – but I assure you not I nor any other would have changed this. It was all decided. Hospital, procedures – nothing would have changed fate.' Tenis had removed his long raincoat (I think he told me he bought it in London) to reveal a smart suit beneath. One could almost have held the suspicion Tenis had carefully groomed and changed before he came to our apartment. My mother collapsed into his arms as if he was my brother, I thought.

'Would you like me to arrange a little something to be delivered here immediately? A pill to calm your nerves?'

'No, no, Doctor. I will endure.'

'Wise, Mrs Follana. Wise. I do not condone the use of tranquillisers for grief. Terrible but natural grief. We all have to bear it, Mrs Follana. Do you both drink coffee? Mr Sagrana and I will go and make you both coffee now. No, no. Do not dare try to rise, Madame. You will not go near that kitchen. Doctor's orders! If you want a little something stronger than coffee, though, we will all share a glass soon, I think. You two sit there.'

Back in the kitchen I heard Tenis's angry voice again. 'Are you still here? This is under my control now.'

'Yes, sir, I was about to leave. May I have my trolley back? I need my trolley.'

I heard Tenis march back to the bedroom and return wheeling the trolley. 'Do you have your radio? I need to use it.' They both left.

Sagrana crashed around insecurely in the kitchen.

Then there were sounds of low talking out on the stairwell. Clicks and the sliding sound of metal tubes. They were dismantling the trolley. I heard the ambulance driver say, 'It won't fit in the elevator.' Tenis said something in reply and disappeared with the man.

After a suspiciously long time and more whispering in the kitchen, Tenis and Sagrana returned.

I said, 'If you would both sit with Mother. I must telephone Veroña now.'

Tenis held up his hand. 'Lolo. Just before you do. Once you telephone Veroña and tell her what has happened, something will have changed.'

'What do you mean?'

'Sagrana has been explaining to me the delicate situation that exists here. The bank accounts. If you telephone Veroña, suddenly someone other than the four of us in this room will know what happened.'

I looked around. 'What do you mean? The ambulance men have been here.'

'So what? They attend calls all day. They enter it in on a rough sheet. They have proved they are no experts on addresses. It is never looked at again. Only one thing matters. The cause of and hour of death entered on the death certificate which I am qualified to issue. Only I can confirm a death by law.'

'I am not following.'

'Oh Lolo,' Mother scolded.

Tenis announced, 'If I were to go to the bank with your mother in the morning – to tell the manager your father has been . . . say, feeling very unwell all evening. That we are all a little concerned for his health and, as your family doctor, I do not consider him well enough to come to the bank to give his signature, Sagrana is convinced, as a forty-year customer of the bank, the manager will immediately authorise the transfer of the money from your father's account to the dual account. Even if the bank manager requires a signature we will bring the form back here.'

'A good idea, Doctor. Or just into a café,' my mother shrugged.

Tenis nodded at her. 'Or indeed into a café, Mrs Follana. It will not be the first time, I believe, that a couple who have been in honourable business together for forty years will have duplicated one another's signature.'

Mother nodded.

'This would only be an illegal act after your poor father's hour of death and . . .' Tenis looked around the company. 'Your father according to the paperwork has not left us yet.'

Sagrana looked at me, added, 'You are looking at it down this end of the telescope, Lolo. Why will the bank be suspicious for a second tomorrow? Anybody would do what your mother will do if an elderly relative felt unwell. That in itself is perfectly legal. Besides, it in no way affects the veracity of my ledger books.'

'We are just . . . holding back time a little, Lolo.' Tenis smiled.

'So what do we do?'

'Well, firstly we do not tell anyone. Even Veroña. We make phone calls to our families saying your father has been taken ill and we will all spend the night here,' he held up a hand to me. 'And no visitors please. Then we sit out the night here together, taking good care of your mother's needs. At 8.30 a.m. myself – in my capacity as your family doctor – and your mother will go to the bank and transfer your parents' cash wealth – which they have worked hard for – from your father's account to your mother and father's dual account. We will return here and I will fill out the death certificate giving the hour of death as . . . say, lunchtime tomorrow. And we will then call an ambulance.' He held up his hands and smiled.

'Are you not risking your . . . career?'

'There are no laws being broken, Lolo. I am the law here. I sign off the death certificate. Up in the mountain villages they are signed off two, three days after death for myocardial infarction. For heart attack; natural cause like this. There will be no autopsy to challenge the time of death. The moment I write out the death certificate it will be accepted. Without being vivid in front of you, Mrs Follana, the zip bag will not be opened on your dear husband until they put him in his coffin.'

I looked at my mother. I saw her face was open to anything.

Tenis leaned towards us both and said, 'I have cancelled the call-out doctor who was heading here to sign the certificate. I am in charge now. There is just us. Sagrana and I can solve all your problems in . . .' he consulted his expensive watch '. . . sixteen hours.'

I looked to my mother.

'Be brave, Lolo,' she said and squeezed my hand.

Tenis said, 'We have one thing to fear.'

We all looked to him.

'The Solielians.' He looked at his watch again. 'And I think they will be calling at your door any minute now.'

Mr Solielian, owner of both our city crematoriums, and his mortician wife have death all sewn up in our city and have almost put their rival undertakers – the Old Rosas – out of business and soon the Solielians will prove their ultimate triumph over the death business in our city: they will literally bury their rivals, the Old Rosa.

The Solielians have many nurses at the General Hospital, and indeed ambulance drivers, on a cash-in-hand retainer to slyly phone in when any victim has been killed or any patient is about to croak. Mr or Mrs Solielian with sullen son or daughter, dressed immaculately, always get there first – sometimes just as God begins to take the soul – before families even know their loved ones are dead or on the way out.

The Solielians nearly always beat their rivals. Gone were the ugly days in the 70s when the Old Rosas and the Solielians could be found scuffling on the hospital steps or mortuary over a fresh corpse. Or the Solielians would be seen following the ambulance after a motorway accident, in their *Volkswagen Beetle*.

The Solielians have become so deadly efficient they once telephoned a family to ask where they wanted the cleaned-up body to lie in rest and the family member replied, 'What body?' They did not even know their father had died that afternoon. This resulted in a lawsuit against the hospital but the Solielians, who had virtually kidnapped the corpse, got off blameless.

Mrs Solielian the mortician visits the Old Ones, women and men in the rest homes. She flatters them. She asks the women how they like their hair. It is chilling – a harbinger of certain death – to overhear Mrs Solielian's calm voice: 'What brand of eyeshadow do you use? I do not recognise it,' and finally, 'You must have been beautiful/handsome when you were young. Do you have any photos? Do you have anything more recent?'

If the frail Old Ones are looking good that day and she can get the really senile ones alone, she sneaks her digital camera from her always-fashionable shoulder bag and takes a photo so – when they are dead – she can make them look like themselves when they were alive.

Mrs Solielian scours the second-hand charity shops of our city in her extravagant clothes and garish make-up, because in those places she can build up her own huge collection of the out-of-date and unfashionable cosmetics which old ladies use. Mrs Solielian will tell you: 'Exact make-up is important, nobody wants their mother to look like someone else when they lie in vigil. And then for eternity. I get a lot of motor accidents too. Young girls with their faces rebuilt. I need the latest make-ups for them – different hair gels and the right cheap aftershaves for the teenage boys.'

To see Mrs Solielian's glum son and daughter on either side of her, you wonder about the day they will dress and precisely replicate the garish make-up of their own mother, ready for her own journey into the next world.

The people of our city have all always lived in dread of the Solielians, but if they themselves do not get their hands on our corpses, the sullen son and daughter will.

Within fifteen minutes of Tenis's statement the doorbell rang.

'You know what to do, Lolo,' said Tenis. 'As soon as you have finished with them you call for me. OK?'

I nodded.

'You can do it,' Mother encouraged.

I walked slowly down the corridor trembling and reluctantly opened the door. In their full ghastly regalia stood both Mr and Mrs Solielian, like doom crows on our landing.

'Mr and Mrs Solielian.' I faked surprise. 'Thankfully there must be some misunderstanding.'

They knitted brows together with immediate distaste.

'Your father . . .' began that louse.

'Father had a powerfully bad turn earlier. He is being examined now by the family doctor and is very tired but he is stronger.'

'Oh?'

They were completely perplexed. They could not squeal on their sources – obviously the new ambulance driver was already in their pay – which they had become more and more blatant about down the years. I almost expected them to produce a sharpened axe, ready to finish off my surviving father.

'Our doctor, Dr Tenis, is here. I will let you speak with him.'

'Oh really, no need, I do apologise for the . . .' Solielian was trying to make for the elevator and I was almost enjoying myself.

'Dr Tenis.' I called and closed the door then walked back into the apartment. Tenis walked towards me. Slapped me one on the shoulder as he passed and tugged open the front door. 'What are you doing here?' he immediately hissed.

'There has been a misunderstanding, Doctor. We thought we heard something on the ambulance radio so we hoped we could be of assistance. I am very, very sorry . . .'

'Get the hell out of here. If Mrs Follana sees this performance you will both be responsible for her shock. That it is your business at all, which it is not, Mr Follana has had what looks like a small stroke. All sorts of chaos was perpetrated by those ambulances – total confusion. It was a disgrace. I would be more cautious about your informations in the future, Mr Soleilian.'

'Please convey our complete apologies to Mrs . . .' Solielian whimpered.

Tenis, the hero, had slammed the door on them and sneaked back through to us.

Mother and Sagrana, who had been sitting close together listening to everything, playfully and silently mimed applause, moving their hands back and forth without actual contact. Tenis bowed.

And so began the macabre night. I telephoned and lied to Veroña that Father was very unwell and we were staying at his bedside. Tenis phoned Lupe and lied to her that Father was unwell. That as our doctor and old friend of the family he wished to stay the night with my mother and me. Lupe even briefly spoke to me and wished Father and Mother the best. Sagrana phoned and whispered to his boyfriend. My mother phoned a friend from whom there was the vaguest threat of her calling round for a game of chess.

Then Mother and I washed Father's face and tidied him up. I recall all the lines and tension from Father's face had vanished in that short time and after all his busy life. I mopped his pale, cool forehead and whispered, 'So still now, Father, so still,' and I leaned and kissed that cold forehead despite his curse upon me.

So as is the custom in our land we sat: I on one side of the bed, Mother on the other, sobbing frequently and stroking Father's cold hand. Tenis took up a jaunty position on my right with Sagrana close beside him. We were hours reminiscing, there were tears from Mother, solemn and knowing nods from Tenis and Sagrana, and I too had wet eyes on several occasions but sometimes there was brief laughter over an anecdote – then a silence as we were all over-whelmed by the absolute authority of death.

The shock of Father's death and the vehemence of his attacks on me left me rattled. Yet Tenis and Sagrana revived my and my mother's spirits again and again with more and more tales from the past and teasing stories of me as a youth.

I was sent out to buy rice for four from the Dolphin (or was it the Lower Rivers?) and I carried the pan covered in silver foil back along the promenade, even nodding to the odd acquaintance as if all was normal in the world.

We four all ate around the kitchen table. Then we managed to persuade Mother to rest for a while but she found it impossible so again we sat around Father until, unable to ignore it any longer, Mother insisted on taking the wine-stained rug to the utility room to try and wash it.

Around one or two in the morning, rather sheepishly I thought, Mother came to ask if Sagrana or Tenis would care to join her in a game of chess and alas for me – I did not play – I was left out of a substantial tournament which went on all night through the quarterly tolling of the Town Hall Plaza bell.

It began in the salon but with a certain inevitability the chessboard and table were carried through into the bedroom and the games were played out beside Father, who even in death was not to be free from the accursed game he never really cared for.

After triumphing over Sagrana then finally Tenis (though I have my suspicions he deliberately let Mother win the final match on a surprise checkmate) Mother wanted to rest. She wished to lie beside Father but Tenis discouraged it.

'Mrs Follana, I have seen it before. You could fall asleep but when you awake beside your husband you can experience the most terrifying shock and relapse into grief.'

So Mother went upstairs and I lay beside her a while and kissed her forehead but when I returned Tenis nodded towards Father and said, 'Just hygienically it is not a good idea. There could be some problems during the next few hours. The bowel can come loose and other matters. It would be best if I could handle these trifling affairs.'

Terrified, I stepped quickly to join Sagrana in the salon for more strong coffee. All the same I could not help but notice later on my way to the bathroom, through the crack in the bedroom door, Tenis seemed to have wedged Father upright in a full sitting position and I am sure he was manipulating the old man's legs back and forwards. Sure enough when I stuck my head in the door on the way back,

Tenis had propped Father up against the bedhead and he had knotted a silk neck tie on him.

Tenis looked over his shoulder and said, 'Better like this, Lolo. The stomach juices run back down; I do hope you understand.'

'Oh yes,' I quickly said and fled.

When the birds began to sing again in the denuded ash trees of the Town Hall Plaza just before light, each of we men went to the bathroom to splash our faces with water and comb back our wet hair.

The metallic, blue-grey day dawned. Mother was up very bright and alert — if looking tired. I was stunned to see her wearing both the fawn suede, shorter skirt and jacket and those high heels with the coloured glass baubles which unbeknown to Mother had once been teenage favourites of Thinh and Quynh.

My throat filled with nostalgia and I had an incongruous thrust of desire as I thought of their slim limbs upright in those same shoes so many years before. I was overwhelmed with an advance of differing guilts and confused emotions. Mother looked wonderful, I must say, better than I had seen her in years.

Tenis rightly concluded that eight thirty on the dot at the bank was a little suspicious in appearance so they made it there for nine fifteen. I was to go with them as far as Cena's and drop off there. A sort of halfway-house figure. Sagrana was staying in the house as a guard on Father's corpse, only to visit the bank in a second wave if there was any resistance. Mother, arm in arm with Tenis, made straight for the bank as I followed slightly behind then I stepped into Cena's.

Apparently it went without a hitch. Mother and Tenis excitedly related all the details. The manager was full of good wishes for Father after the form was signed and the money transferred before Mother's eyes, back into Mother and Father's dual account. Tenis had slipped in a concerned frown to the bank manager, as if to say things did not look good back home.

Mother and Tenis walked back out through the new modern glass front of the bank and collected me from Cena's terrace, where I was a touch disappointed to be required so soon as I did not have time to fully consume my freshly squeezed orange juice and buttered toast. We all returned to the apartment above Town Hall Plaza together.

Mother went upstairs to lie down for a while, and Tenis washed up. I loitered, smoking, just outside the bedroom where Father lay, now on the bed. Sagrana leaned forward and nodded to something propped in the far corner. I had not noticed it. It was a piece of apparatus folded up like the trolley but smaller.

'A wheelchair Tenis got off the ambulance man,' Sagrana whispered motioning upstairs towards my mother. 'Thank God it all came off, because if they refused, Tenis was going to put your father in the wheelchair with sunglasses and a hat on, then have you wheel him along the esplanade and stand outside the bank. You were meant to wave and smile at the bank manager – indicate your father, then happily push him onwards down the esplanade while your mother explained he had fallen asleep and she did not wish him to come into the bank and join the queue, but could she please now sign for him. Tenis was quite vehement about it. But your father stiffened up on the bed suddenly this morning and Tenis was cursing that he was not bending enough to fit into the wheelchair. Now your father seems stuck longways apparently.'

Tenis signed the death certificate later that morning and made some calls to have an ambulance collect a fatality – from the more distant Regional Hospital so there would be none of the afternoon crew from the previous day.

When the ambulance crew arrived all looked normal: Father dead, Mother in tears, Tenis professional, Sagrana and I mournful. They brought up the stretcher but when they carried Father out onto the stairwell the stretcher did not fit around the building's spectacular spiral staircase.

'Wow, this guy has stiffened up quick,' said the youngest ambulance man.

They had to stand poor Father upright in the corner of the elevator but when they put in the stretcher vertically with him, there was no room left for one of the ambulance men – so they sent Father down alone, and of course at that moment, one of Mrs Cardell's grandchildren had to step out of the door on the first floor and shove the call button so the elevator stopped with a jerk, and when the kid slid the door, the stretcher fell out and Father was propped in the corner, looking like he had shot upright in the church and the pennies had flown off his eyes.

I heard the kid was back in nappies for a week after.

After Father, cancer soon took Mother from me. Her startled eyes and her morphia confusion scarred me forever as I sat by her bed week after week up at the General Hospital.

When the nurses cleaned her twice a day I would go downstairs to smoke and visit that unique, curious shop in the main lobby which fascinated me – it stocked only what, conceivably, might one day be sold in a hospital alone: pyjamas, nightdresses, towels, flowers, gift-wrapped fruit, stationery, books and magazines, sewing equipment, portable radios, hot-water bottles and other rubber goods (absolutely no prophylactics), a fold-out camp bed, dictionaries of illnesses and Bibles, make-up, shampoos, soaps, perfumes. There was something grimly honest about every item of their stock.

I had to buy a lot of perfume myself. I used to spray it on Mother's starved, sunken breastbone every few hours towards the end. She was nil by mouth by then and the diarrhoea flowed through her skeleton. I could have lifted her above my head.

Such a proud woman and so careful about cleanliness because of the hotel. No matter how often the nurses cleaned her, no matter how short we cut her fingernails, she was in great distress towards the end, the beige khaki of her own waste trapped beneath those fingernails – her face sour at her own smell. I have cursed God one thousand times.

Then with Veroña on my arm I made the inevitable return among the mausoleums and casket walls of Heaven Hill. Submitting to their inevitable victory, we allowed the Solielians to lead us all across those heights and through the cypresses to Mother's last resting place where she was shut into the wall as I will be very soon.

Ann Green And That Young Woman
Who Watched

'**D**o you feel you have lived, Ahmed?' I once asked.

He smiled shyly.

'To have made the best of the opportunities. The damned obligation of opportunities forced on you as a man. Women, girls. Then you can say you have lived?'

He showed those teeth and said, 'Every man tries to make the best of what comes his way – as you know, not all get what they want, but yes. I have lived, yes. More than some men and less than others.'

'You have experienced – lovers?'

He tilted his head this way and that. 'I am happy with what life threw my way,' he concluded, then nodded.

I told Ahmed how one afternoon on the terrace of Cena's, I met two young women: a brunette, The Young Woman Who Watched with the beautiful leather shoulder bag, who I had vaguely seen around, as one acknowledges the pretty women of our city; and then her blonde friend who was pale and obviously very foreign.

The Young Woman Who Watched only asked me if she could use a chair from my table as they were expecting company. I chatted them up a bit as one does by social obligation and even more when their female acquaintances never appeared. I bought them each a drink – nothing flashy – but for a next one I asked if they wanted French champagne, a drink which produces indigestion in me and I cannot abide – 'French champagne. For the ladies. Whisky for me,' I called cheerily to Franco. It was all very diverting – a nice fun afternoon.

The pale blonde was English, speaking hardly a word of our language so everything I said had to be translated into English language by her friend with the leather bag: and all the English things the blonde with the name *Ann Green* spoke out were made into our own language from the mauve lips of The Young Woman Who Watched.

Both were hairdressers. *Ann Green*'s parents owned their own salon back in her homeland and she had just arrived to live in our city a few weeks before. I did learn the place where *Ann* was of in England: it was named *Darlo* or *Darlow(e)*. For years I have searched and searched atlases of England trying to locate the positioning of this large northern town but I never could. '*DARLO, of course it is big town. It is in maps,*' she had loudly insisted, nodded her blue eyes quickly.

When we were all drunk I clapped my hands 'Hey. Come on then. I challenge you. I really need a haircut please.'

Amazingly, The Young Woman Who Watched just reached into that beautiful leather shoulder bag and she produced a black pouch which she unfolded: ranged within were glistening varieties of scissors and combs.

Laughing, the three of us stepped down upon the beach in front of the Imperial Hotel. It was still quite crowded in the last honeyed light of the day. I said that you always have to wash your hair first so – to their delight – without removing my shirt I shoved my head in under the beach shower, pressed the plunger and pretended to froth up a lather with my fingers. They thought this was hysterical. I took my head out of the drumming water drops – my face was wet and I had to be careful my contact lenses were not dislodged. I shook my head like a dog; the two women screamed and stepped back laughing. I was reminded of the happy days all those years before with the Vietnamese girls. My blue shirt was stained black in wet daubs. Sunbathers and groups on the beach were watching and wryly smiling at us but I did not care.

As I sat cross-legged on the sand I had to take off my sunglasses and *Ann Green* kneeled behind me with the scissors and combs. Her breasts were occasionally pushed against my shoulders when she leaned forward to comb my hair back. Sometimes *Ann Green* did not talk as she worked, she held the top of the comb between her front teeth. Her mouth was so close to my scalp I could smell the flavour of her chewing gum though I could not see her face.

Dark criss-crossings of my hair, peppered with warning grey, fell to the pale sand by my legs.

The girls told stories about their hairdressing jobs. Men they saw touch themselves under their cloth as *Ann* cut their hair. The Young Woman Who Watched recalled when short hair got fashionable, young girls of fourteen getting the first haircut of their lives who cried and wanted their long, long ponytail put in a plastic bag to take home so they would have it when they were old.

The Young Woman Who Watched translated a tale *Ann Green* slowly narrated – *Ann* used those long, appropriate catch-up pauses for the translation after each sentence, which I notice our globalised, interfering American politicians now use on television so their mad pronouncements can be translated for the non-English-speaking world.

Ann told of how a man with very long hair flowing down his shoulders came into *Ann's* parents' salon. He wanted all his hair cut off and requested his skull be shaved. *Ann* cut away all the long strands of hair then, as she shaved his skull, her electric razor revealed a lavish blue-and-red tattoo of Jesus Christ on his cross, the Christ's canted head just above the man's fringe, our Saviour's arms with punctured hands stretched towards each ear tip, Christ's crossed legs curved right down the back of that man's wrinkled neck to the tattoo's punctured feet, as the last of the tattooed man's hair fell away under *Ann's* shaver.

★ ★ ★

When my hair was cut – even though I was suffering agony from the clippings that had freely flowed down the collar of my shirt without a towel to protect it – I did not communicate that it bothered me. I took them both back up off the sand and into the old Terrace of the Imperial.

When more French champagne arrived we toasted My Haircut. I drank whisky. When I visited the toilet I took off my shirt in a cubicle and I tried to knock out as many of the itching hair clippings as I could. It just shows you to what extremes I would go to be with pretty girls for I ignored the quite terrible discomfort.

We did not leave the Terrace of the Imperial. Some delicate power made the three of us overstay for more drinks. There I was again, gaily carousing with another two females, twenty years after Thinh and Quynh were in the same place.

We shared my cigarettes and we joked together. As the day's sun in its final lethargy burned above the castle behind our position, the light down on the beach took on a delicate sheen, like a thin membrane becoming taut against everything.

I told the girls my stories of lifeguard duty on the beach.

Though I knew fine that it was, I asked *Ann* if her hair was real or dyed. It was the kind of teasing question that hints at open flirtation.

I leaned over and said directly to *Ann*'s face in a soft voice, looking into her eyes and not acknowledging her companion to my own right as she playfully translated, 'When we were in our high school institute there was only one blonde girl in the school. Tell her.'

The Young Woman Who Watched spoke it to *Ann Green* (who, pummelled but unchallenged by alcohol, had slumped a bit in her seat). We knew I was trying to seduce *Ann* but doing it through the familiar voice of her friend and I noticed how The Young Woman Who Watched ably assisted me by using the correct, low, cajoling voice, repeating what I had said into English language, even touching *Ann*'s thigh or arm as my amanuensis.

'My schoolboy friends and I in the playground, we speculated. We wondered.' I waited expectantly.

The Young Woman Who Watched again turned aside and translated, leaning over and giggling.

'It is dirty,' I whispered.

'Oh yeah.' my countrywoman's voice said to me then she turned to *Ann* and I know the words she used were: '*He wants to tell a history but very strong.*'

'What?'

I leaned over, close to The Young Woman Who Watched's leather bag which she still kept rested on her shoulder in case it was stolen, and I whispered in her ear as if the words were now directed at her – and perhaps they were as well – and not at *Ann*, 'We wondered what colour the hairs on the blonde girl's private parts were.'

'Uncle!'

'Go on, tell her.'

Laughing, The Young Woman Who Watched leaned over and said this in English, quietly and seriously, to *Ann Green*, who opened her blue eyes wide and looked at me.

'So my friend Tenis, who is a big-shot doctor now, and I, we saw this same blonde girl from high school who we both had wondered and secretly fantasised about at a café one day, going to the toilet. We both waited until she came out and then rushed together into the cubicle, locked the door and squatted, searching for evidence of any little hairs. Perhaps some had fallen off?'

'My God. You are crazy.'

'No, it is true.'

'You have a good personality but you are bad.' Pretending to be precious – or perhaps disgusted – but still aroused, The Young Woman Who Watched turned to *Ann* and translated this segment.

'Eeechhh,' went *Ann*, then said something.

'She asks what happened?'

'We found one. Or the sharp-eyed doctor did, a little blonde curly hair resting on the toilet seat.'

The Young Woman Who Watched yelped in delight.

'*What? What?*' *Ann Green* repeated, slapping her friend's thigh in demand.

Monopolising me for the whole story, her friend leaned close and said, 'What did you do?'

I whispered, 'I picked the hair up between my fingertips like this and held it close to my eyes. We kept it and we shared and worshipped it. We put it in a little plastic box of Tenis's mother, the kind used to keep a wedding ring inside and sometimes, for a price, we would open the box for a few brief moments and let one of our fellow schoolboys look at that little fair . . .' I leaned close to *Ann*'s face '. . . wire. And I cannot help but wonder if *Ann* has the same beautiful hair in that place?'

My countrywoman opened her mouth and raised her eyebrows at me. 'OK, OK, I gotta tell her this.' She held up her palm to me and turned with great deliberation to the English girl to speak.

Ann Green looked at me with a vague smile.

I said to *Ann*, 'Do not be shocked.' I indicated the bar. 'Every single man in my country thinks the same thing. We have a few blonde folk up north, even some redheads, but let us face the truth, you and me.' I jerked my hand at The Young Woman Who Watched. 'We are dark. When I was a kid there was only one blonde in our school. Now you see them everywhere. Yet each time we see a blonde woman we think it. I bet you think it too, brunette. Even of women?'

'When I was sixteen, you old pervert.'

'I tell you all men and women.' I nodded with certainty and laughed. I leaned close to The Young Woman Who Watched and I whispered, 'If you do not know already, you would be fascinated too, even now. If you would keep watch for us, I would try to show you.' I nodded out to the dark path in the blackout below the rooms of the Meliander Hotel but she did not translate this segment for *Ann*.

Darkness had fallen, like squid's ink sliding over the beach – the new cafés and bars nudging themselves along the root of the Meliander rocks let their lights sparkle then fall dark an instant as a delicate human figure slowly passed before them. The whole world seemed to be moving in harmony with me, my own blood felt as if the whisky with *Coke* I drank was some night within me.

The Young Woman Who Watched and *Ann* listened seriously – as if I were discussing a financial matter now – they did not laugh, their heads lightly befuddled by so much champagne.

Then, the bills signed on my credit card, *Ann* on one side, The Young Woman Who Watched to my right, we were walking arm in arm together with me in the middle (as in days of Thinh and Quynh) – towards the dark path.

The Young Woman Who Watched's leather shoulder bag was pushed against me as we walked, I could feel the softness of the leather on my bare arm.

'But it sometimes smells out there on the dark path,' she said, quietly.

'Of what?'

'Of dead things. Seaweed and sometimes of fish,' she whispered.

Ann asked what we were saying but I noticed The Young Woman Who Watched did not answer her.

'But *Ann* and I need you to keep watch,' I said.

'I understand,' she breathed out and chuckled.

Ann Green did not ask for translation. Quiet on my arm, smiling privately, her flat sandals snapped noisily as we picked our way past those stupid new bars which were not there in the days of my Military Service.

Beyond the bars was the dark path along the rocks beneath the Meliander bedroom windows. We were reduced to a businesslike single file by the thin, dribbled, pale line of concrete that served as a walkway among the jagged rocks and tidal fonts filled by slow accumulation of splashing waves which tossed up snowballs of froth to fill these little rock pools.

The pathway led away beneath the high walls of the Meliander

Hotel and came close to a low brick barrier topped with buckled wire but *Ann* suddenly turned and blocked my way as if she were an official.

'No,' I said, over my shoulder, to The Young Woman Who Watched. 'We have to check to make sure there is nobody at the far end who will need to come back this way.'

The Young Woman Who Watched walked on ahead past us, up the thin path. *Ann* and I immediately kissed in the dark privacy that was left behind. I impatiently reached, hoisting the long skirt fabric high on her legs with a grip of my fingers. I looked into her darkened face. I then glanced both ways. Suddenly *Ann*'s friend, The Young Woman Who Watched, was right beside us again.

'*Well, hello,*' she said in a deep voice, using English but I felt slightly embarrassed. 'Nobody is anywhere here.' She had to rub against me to squeeze past *Ann* and me on the narrow pathway – for to stray from the thin path risked stumbling, falling and grazing or soiling oneself among the undulating rocks and moon puddles. I was unsure about the proper etiquette of keeping *Ann*'s skirt hoisted while her friend passed us but I decided to allow it to remain there.

'Uncle,' The Young Woman Who Watched chuckled in an unfathomable tone.

Ann said something very quickly in English – the English speaker always talks so quickly – I could not comprehend it. The Young Woman Who Watched to my right began to dig in the darkness of her leather shoulder bag and removed the pouch. She handed me the hairdressing scissors.

The fingers of *Ann* now took over, holding up her skirt. I kneeled with the reflective scissors and a huge tension filled the air between the three of us. The Young Woman Who Watched looked down at us, leaning slightly over.

'Mother of Mine,' she whispered above.

I pulled down the white, almost luminescent underwear, stranding the stretched fabric across clearly freckled thighs. Ever so carefully

I cut the smallest tuft of hair from the blonde girl *Ann* in that darkness, trapped it between forefinger and thumb, held it up for all of us to witness then I fumbled my little clump of trophy down into the breast pocket of my blue, damp shirt. I passed the scissors – handles first – back up to The Young Woman Who Watched, who took the tools of her trade back in a businesslike way.

'I am watching,' she said in my language with a wonderful ambiguity.

It took a great deal of time kneeling there. I could hear *Ann's* toes repeatedly squeezing tight then relaxing in that dusty ground by my knees. There was the distinctive click off to our right. Not too far away at all. The Young Woman Who Watched was lighting a cigarette as she watched.

Several times, *Ann* had to adjust the stance of her bare legs which were surprisingly cold to my touch, but eventually I got the reaction we all hoped for. *Ann* just whimpered out something, in English.

My knees were agonised as I stood up trembling. *Ann* stepped aside towards the pinpoint jab of a moving cigarette end. They both crowded together over the leather shoulder bag and giggled; illuminated briefly by an ignited cigarette lighter to peer within the bag, I saw their faces close up.

Ann came limping back towards me with a sealed prophylactic held out in her fingers. I let my trousers and shorts fall to my shoes. It was challenge enough just to fumble open the prophylactic in the darkness and I could hardly see until The Young Woman Who Watched came forward helpfully with the lit cigarette lighter. A limited zone of the three of us was held in a corona of unsteady flame light.

In a leisurely way, *Ann* bent over in front of us, put her arms on the top of the low wall and rested the side of her head on her folded arms. She leaned there privately, bent slightly at her waist in the traditional wearied stance of English girls when they vomit in the early hours, propped against the sides of buildings showing their pale thighs below short skirts.

I spat to get the prophylactic onto me and rolled it down rather unsatisfactorily. Slowly, with taunting pauses while looking at The Young Woman Who Watched by my side, I elevated *Ann*'s skirt. The woman with her leather bag still slung on her shoulder kept the cigarette lighter flame illuminated a moment longer than she need have and after I slid myself fully inside her English friend, the lighter flame snapped out dramatically.

I was in the difficult condition of not having had sex for too long a time – normality, in fact – and I was overly sensitive to the extreme stimulation. Despite the euphoria, I mainly struggled not to finish too soon, holding on to her pelvic bones for moral support.

Ann uttered necromantic English words throughout it all but then I realised they were directed at The Young Woman Who Watched. This proximity acted as a violent aphrodisiac. I was almost saved because *Ann* suddenly tensed. We stopped moving but then I saw how close the other woman had moved to us – watching – and though I tried to desperately stay still, I looked directly into those cigarette-end-illuminated eyes and I can positively say – though I am a rational man – her eyes looking at me were like a force between us and induced the enormous spasm as I uncoiled into her friend.

I had felt the prophylactic come off me within *Ann*'s body long minutes before but I had continued at her as if nothing were un-toward though I knew this was morally wrong. I breathed franti-cally then I put my hand down pretending to secure the top of the prophylactic as I retreated out. Knowing fine already, I whispered towards The Young Woman Who Watched, 'Oh no. The Host. It has come off.'

'It did?' said The Young Woman Who Watched and she bent incred-ibly close, as if she might burn *Ann*'s posterior with the reignited cigarette lighter, concentrating. I could see the objective corrugation of a frown on her forehead. She spoke rapidly in English to *Ann*.

'*Aww no! Not again,*' *Ann* said, which I understood.

I shuffled to the side, suddenly irrelevant, but as *Ann* turned, she gestured aggressively from me towards The Young Woman Who Watched, then *Ann* took a step away, stooped with one arm on the wall for balance and delved within herself to try and retrieve the prophylactic.

The Young Woman Who Watched put her face close to me: 'I want to but I might feel cheap.'

'You won't,' I whispered but my desperate, insincere voice shook.

'I might not go the whole way,' she weakly lied and had *Ann Green*'s two plastic beach sandals in her hand which she suddenly dropped on the concrete path and on which she kneeled with each of her knees precisely on a sandal.

The Young Woman Who Watched cleaned me off, like a cat does to its newborn kitten, with long, unreasonable pauses between. *Ann* still had her fingers within her, and a facial expression I could perceive, as if reaching for something fallen behind a cabinet – but there was an ambiguity about her movements too. She was now also looking at The Young Woman Who Watched's mouth. Eventually the kneeling woman suddenly lifted her fingers to her nose and pinched it tightly – as if she was about to jump in a swimming pool. She took her head away from me, held her bag secure under her shoulder with one hand and spat me out again and again into the darkness off the pathway.

'Mother of Mine,' she whispered. 'I can always taste that for days.'

I was so overcome I had to sit down on the concrete path. *Ann* and The Young Woman Who Watched conferred in strangely soporific voices though The Young Woman Who Watched occasionally turned aside from her and spat out violently, several times more.

I watched as *Ann* repositioned herself, leaning her head down again against the wall. The Young Woman Who Watched placed the sandals on the ground and once more got cautiously to her knees, carefully edging her fingers inside her friend, talking to her quickly in English all the time. *Ann* gave verbal responses.

After a few minutes of those serpentine cooperations The Young Woman Who Watched placed the side of her head against her friend's pale buttock as if listening, as if that plastic within was some huge, live parasite.

They had both stopped talking. Though their act was perhaps purely medical they knew the image was powerful for me and I had my suspicions about the rhythmic motion of that hand inside *Ann*. But against my fantasy, suddenly The Young Woman Who Watched pulled the slobbery plastic from within her friend then tossed it aside, towards the slaps of sea, as if it was a stripped fish skin at the supermarket counter.

With a strange leisureliness, The Young Woman Who Watched stood and stepped out of her underwear. She used it to wipe her hands dry, which were seamed from within *Ann*, and threw the fabric aside before she would touch her leather bag. Then holding the bag secure she too bent over, in a clear copy of *Ann*'s previous stance.

The Young Woman Who Watched refused to be parted from her leather bag or risk it being knocked into one of the rock pools so as I slid into her using no prophylactic, my eyes were transfixed by the sight of that bag, which she had hung by its strap over the back of her neck. It was swinging dementedly from side to side under her face as she repeated, 'Mother of Mine, Mother of Mine.'

As the bag swung from side to side, a mobile-phone ring bleeped repeatedly within its leather. 'Mother of <u>Mine</u>,' she stressed and *Ann* let out a low laugh which acknowledged her proximity. Eventually the phone ringing inside the bag ceased, leaving the powerful, animalistic sounds of our movements which – in my mind at least – seemed to be the sound of the three of us working together, alone, to cancel and rebuff the outside world.

So this was love: manicured fingernails clenching the small nose, the leather strap of her soft bag on the same woman's delicate neck hairs, swinging rhythmically from side to side in a practical measure. For a moment in the world, a caring solidarity really existed, a mutual respect more beautiful than the diluted love of my marriages. The ideal of liberty I vowed to follow on that cinema floor twenty years before had remained my only bleak credo. A peace descended on me beneath stars, close to the surf, sprinkled by distant electric light.

Ann Green watched – her blue eyes assisted us. I held out my hand and now she touched my fingers and made me ejaculate into her friend.

I tried to continue but eventually the young woman in front sort of resigned and slowly contracted to her knees and immediately cradled the leather bag, like an infant, to the safe harbour of her bosom.

The three of us lay, aching legs out along the concrete path. The Young Woman Who Watched, breathing heavily, was delving into her bag, lighting up her oddly sombre face in the concentrated glow of her phone, checking who had called, immediately forgetting my existence with my newly shorn head lying at her feet.

At my shoes, *Ann Green* reclined, smoking. Like a processionary caterpillar, the three of us stretched out, radically adjusting our clothing, occasionally coughing. Not talking.

We stood and walked slowly back into the light of the beachfront – I felt we looked like defeated trench-warfare soldiers, immediately studying our clothing in the newly invigorated electric light for telltale signs of our dissolution.

Everything happened too quickly then. I spoiled the magic by greedily wanting more. 'Come on. I have an apartment just here.' I pointed.

They both ignored me. I was hurt and felt rejected even minutes after the feast.

'Do not dare tell anyone,' whispered The Young Woman Who Watched. She grabbed *Ann Green*'s hand and said aggressively, 'You know where to get your next haircut.'

To my surprise, but somehow relief that the magic would not be sullied further, they both walked away, *Ann*'s sandals snapping quickly towards the switched-off fountain, leaning close together with the leather bag trapped between them as if it was their baby, heads low, mumbling in a metallic Old Testament light, cast from the absurdly high street lamps.

I took myself to Mother's apartment above Town Hall Plaza. I reached into the breast pocket of my shirt where all those snipped blonde hairs clustered like an infestation of lice. From within the heart of that little wire nest I then plucked out the butter-gold circle of my wedding band to Aracelli. I rubbed it clear and placed it back on my finger.

Aracelli

Inevitably, both young women worked in the actual salon where my wife had her hair cut and had an appointment the following Wednesday. The Young Woman Who Watched actually cut my wife's hair and for that day's gossip cheerfully told my wife an edited version of her latest 'romance', which tied in nicely with my suspiciously produced late-night haircut from the previous week.

Aracelli had been separated from me for eleven days and around twelve hours (I was counting them) and she had moved into Mother's empty apartment above Town Hall Plaza. She was deciding our future. When she telephoned me at the Agency that summer morning I could hear the familiar bells tolling with the exact acoustical quality for that apartment down the phone. I had just passed those bells some minutes before on my walk from the lemon express station.

She said, 'Good morning, my husband from Hell. I need my address book from Phases, I forgot it. So damn hot I am going to the beach. Can I go out to Phases and pick it up?'

'Sure. Aracelli ... .'

'I will be gone by the time you get back. Do not come and ambush me. See you . . .' she hung up.

She was on the beach in her bikini − the yellow and orange one − by nine thirty that morning before the crowds with just a towel, sunglasses and the apartment keys around her neck on a string. She swam a few times.

For someone who did not swim so well, Aracelli had a taste for water near and over rocks which always slightly horrified me. Subconsciously I think she liked not being too far from out of her depth. I am a *scuba*-diver and strong swimmer – though weakened by years of smoking – but I always feared rocks, against which you could be dashed in a sudden wave from a ship's wake, and straps of kelp and seaweed touching and feeling for the buckles of your flippers at the ankles. I do not like the rocks by that dark path below the Meliander Hotel; they slither up, free of the surface, spilling water like huge unsteady ice trays.

That morning Aracelli had been swimming in a deceptive lull out past the Meliander almost as far as the odometer. Rocks she could have pulled herself up on must have been literally eight metres away.

She put her head back to float there for a moment, feigning relaxation which never truly exists in the sea, then she turned and started back in again. The old bay current had caught her.

I had told Aracelli before what I had learned from my lifeguard days: not to fight currents off our city if they ever caught her. Better to relax, do not be panicked by distances to shore or the feeling of profundity below you. Breathe, tread water, admit you are tired and do not be proud or embarrassed – I had heard of too many drowned macho men who were five metres from a boat of strangers and too proud to shout out. You must wave and gently hulloo to passing boats or just remove and wave your bikini top and the male lifeguards high on their miradors will quickly spot you. That current will carry you into deep water but never way out to sea – suddenly it will slacken, you might be a mile north, towards St Jordi's, but stay calm and you will be able to kick in to shore just as if it was a load of swimming-pool lengths. You will just have a long stroll home in your swimsuit.

But Aracelli was angry and frustrated. She fought. Then she panicked. The fear of being taken deeper made her swim harder and, weakening, she was soon carried around the point and the lifeguard can only see along to the odometer on the tip of the pier. He only needed to be looking the other way a moment that morning and my wife was gone. I cannot blame the lifeguard who was on duty and who the police talked to. It could have happened to me in my vigilant days it was so quick.

Poor Aracelli, she could see our city, the hard edges of the Meliander roof, the wedding cake of white fountain shielding the façade of the Imperial Hotel, the tops of the palms all down the esplanade above the yacht masts.

Now it was just helplessly sliding past her and suddenly, though it was hot weather, the wind seemed cool on her skull beneath her wet hair. She saw an old, old white-and-blue fisherman's boat with a tall tiller in the distance and she heard the rough chat-chats of its engine but already, as she waved, the first splash of water gurgled over her face and her legs trembled – panic became outright fear and she screamed.

When you scream you evacuate your lungs of air so you sink, you kick, you exhaust yourself and you understand why your face is just beneath the surface but you cannot break it. With a real push she must have got up, managed to hold her head back and get some breaths in then helplessly she put her long arm up towards the blue summer sky and waved it around and around and let out a hoarse cry.

She did it again. She could hear that fisherman's boat putt-putting. Then again. A good scream. And another, then she herself was surprised by the vivid gurgle sound that seemed to come from someone else as her mouth went under.

She went below, amazed and numb that this was happening to her, and she tried to move her legs – they were gone – just trembling jelly, so she pushed her arms around and went down. I am drowning, she thought and felt ashamed. Ashamed to be dying this way and despite it all she thought of me, and what we had.

Something hit her hard on the back and she was pushed down further. A large wave? Then violently the unmistakable sanctuary of a human arm was tight round her narrow torso but Aracelli could no longer see by then.

Voices close to her ear and shouts, warm air, the spluttered choke of the exhaust being submerged and sloshed free again and the sweet smell of fumes from the old fisherman's boat.

'Get a good hold of her for God's sake or she will go down like a stone. Hey. You OK?'

Somebody with strong hands was banging her on the back of the head. No. Hands were holding her under her arms to the side of a boat and as it rocked in the waves her own slack head was banging against it, hard, again and again. There was a swoosh, one of two men thrusting themselves up out of the water onto the boat and the frightening feeling of being alone and helpless in the water once again with depth beneath her but then more arms reached down and she was hauled up the rough wooden side of the boat. The back of her sliding thighs could feel the smooth heat of the painted gunwales as they slipped over.

'Hold her, hold her.'

'She won't come any further.'

'Lean out. A bit more.'

'OK, lovey? Are you OK?'

Aracelli nodded then she yelped because she thought she was floating back in water but in fact she was lying on the rough wood slats in the bottom of the boat, her knees up on the sides, her feet still dangling over.

Amazingly, almost instantly she felt the familiar childhood sensation of true seasickness. She suffered it rarely but as the engine putted and the boat slapped from side to side, the sweet exhaust smell and the shock made her haul her feet in, curl herself up in a foetal shell and ferociously, as if she was having an epileptic fit, she vomited out to her side, then she shot onto her hands and knees, her arms trembling, and vomited again. Not just sea water like in the movies – the salad, the fruit she'd had for breakfast: it was all returned.

'Christ,' whispered the man's voice above her.

'The rocks,' the other voice said.

The engine quickly started to accelerate.

She blinked her eyes.

'Oh dear, lovey. You want a drink to clear your mouth. We have no water,' he chuckled.

Kneeling, Aracelli spat and shook her head.

'There is water in the box there but it will be warm.'

She had breath now and pushed herself back and against the wooden sides. Something hit her thigh and she squinted. It was so bright after being beneath the surface. One man was using an empty plastic paint container to slosh down bucketfuls of sea water on the wood decking in front of her where she had vomited.

'Can you move up there? Can you move a bit?'

'Let her stay there,' said the voice behind. One had sunglasses and the other face squinted severely through the hot light.

The engine sped on and Aracelli gasped, 'I am sorry. I just got carried in the current and I panicked.'

'I saw your arm waving. Just that arm was all that was out the water of you. For ages all that was there was your arm. I cannot believe you are alive. I had to dive twice. I could not reach you first go. Had to get back up onto the damn boat to get a dive deep enough for you.'

'He is a hero this guy, lovey. Straight in he was and he had you up here.'

'I was so lucky you were passing.'

'Very lucky. Look. You better sit there now. Just sit there.'

'We just pulled you out, lovey.'

'Wow, I am all out of breath. I need to sit down here.' He sat beside her. 'Yeah, you are lucky for sure.'

She looked at him for the first time now and she turned her head. He did not look like the fishermen from the port or the villages who you could buy a crawfish or snap lobster or little sole from. The wet clothes and the wet hair. Fishermen did not wear sunglasses and they did not squint like that either. Fishermen had more lines on their face, even the young ones.

The boat was not going round the odometer of the Meliander point and straight into the Red Cross box by the lifeguard's southern mirador where I did my Military Service. The boat was heading directly out to the open sea and darker waters.

'Lucky back there. You owe me a big thank-you.'

'Me too.'

'And him too.'

She swallowed and it was hot and cracked in her mouth now. She blinked as he opened a foul beer close to her face and he held the hard cold can to her lips. Cold? They had them in a sack slung over the side on a short line.

'Take a sip.'

'According to law you are salvage, lovey. Finders keepers on the seas of fortune if you find treasure.' He laughed.

'Yup. You belong to us now, Miss. Whoa – we seem to be heading out deep here.'

The two men both sexually assaulted and raped Aracelli all that morning and all that afternoon and then for a good section of early evening too. By afternoon she was asking to be thrown in but they would not lose the sport by then.

It was so hot and exposed out there, Aracelli's principal injuries were serious sunburn all over her body and severe heatstroke with borderline dehydration from being naked all day on the well deck with no water. They fed her straight vodka. The men had kept on their T-shirts, pulling their jeans on and off at their convenience and whim so their white asses would not sunburn over the hours and hours of abuse.

Each time Aracelli tried to scream or tried to get up from the deck bottom if another vessel came close, they punched her in the stomach to drive out her breath and threatened to toss her back into the water if she did not lie down. When she vomited they threw buckets of sea water on top of her, to clean her off for the next guy.

Every hour or so they would break for vodka and beers, start up the engine and take the old fishing boat a kilometre further out, shut off the engine, drift, try a few more things on her they had thought up then start the engine and go a bit further out.

They had stolen the boat the night before. The plan was to row that old tub out, get the engine going and spend the night and day lying low around the coves. A dumb idea as it was a local fisherman's boat and they were much more in the open on the water for coastguards than for cops on land but these guys were not looking for any prizes for smartness. The one called Sanz knew boats a bit. They were both of our region. Sanz was of Piregs – up the coast on the other side of the mountain – the other guy, Buges, was from a village in the hills.

Just before they touched her, Aracelli had said, 'Will you take me back?'

'Here is our deal; I saved you and gave you your life and now I want some things back. That seems a fair exchange, does it not? You owe me your life. Or do you want to go now and swim home from out here?'

She said nothing.

He shouted, 'Do you want to go over the side now or do you agree you want to stay on the boat with us?

'Stay on the boat.'

'Right. Your choice. What will you do for me then?'

Aracelli was a social psychologist who had worked with women who had lost husbands in industrial accidents. Maybe the years of counselling helped, talking to people who have been knocked sideways. Maybe it did something to protect her from the worst or helped her negotiate something through the crackly fog of evil that the two men enjoyed.

She said she never believed in the Devil till that day but was sure she could sense him encouraging the two men.

About seven in the evening they quit on her, turned for shore and took the boat right back in, past the odometer and the Meliander rocks by the dark path. The two men argued, hopeless remorse perhaps beginning to spread through them at the sight of the shoreline and its laws. Sanz started to panic that Aracelli was so done in she would just sink and it would be murder but Buges would not take her all the way in to her own depth. He was jumpy of the lifeguards up on their watchtowers. There were still a lot of swimmers enjoying the holidays on our beach that evening.

Buges took a knife to slice them off and gave Aracelli two buoyant, polystyrene fenders to clutch in her arms over her bare, bitten breasts.

'Float with these. You needed them from the start.'

'Can I have my swimsuit?'

Sanz prised the bottom section of her bikini from the bilge water between the deck slats and slapped her face with the sodden fabric.

Sanz held up Aracelli's gold wedding ring that he had removed with his teeth earlier and which, touchingly despite me, she was still wearing.

'You are married to us now, beautiful. You want this, go fetch it,' he flipped her wedding ring over the side where it caught the light for a moment and then with the gentlest of blips, like one of Ahmed's coins, the gold ring twiddled into about eight to ten metres depth, roughly forty metres north of the Meliander rocks.

They made her get over the sea-facing side and gently lower herself down into the water. Once they saw her floating in the water it gave them both some kind of mad courage again and they taunted her about how much she had enjoyed their day together.

Their boat headed out around the odometer and away, while Aracelli slowly kicked into her own depth and the sand bottom, so soon surrounded by beautiful little children, deliriously screaming in joy on their lilos as they played in the waters; she told me it was only then, when she saw what the normal world should be like, that she almost broke down.

When the level reached her waist Aracelli kneeled in the concealing water – which was as warm as a bath after the day's heat. She kneeled the way she genuflected entering a church; she kneeled as Quynh and Thinh had in the reserve-water tank, carefully dipping themselves, their two rusted squids of blood twisting into the tank water to pass down through the Imperial Hotel pipes and taps. Aracelli kneeled to put her bikini bottoms back on.

She walked out of the water that bright evening with her arms folded over her breasts and the boat fenders. She did not even begin to cry when she found her towel and expensive sunglasses untouched on the beach where she had left them that morning. She wrapped her upper body in the towel, put on the sunglasses and, still carrying the fenders that she knew would have fingerprints, she walked up past the newsagent's kiosk in front of the Imperial Hotel to the building with the stone angels and Dr Roli's new, small evening surgery with its summer waiting room of food poisoning from defrosting, kids who have fallen on rocks and badly sunburned British teenagers.

Aracelli whispered calmly and with dignity to the nurse that she must see the doctor next as it was a police matter – the nurse, a woman, stared at her, looked her up and down.

Aracelli was permitted to step in to old Doc Roli. My wife sat down opposite him like any normal consultation; he frowned at her near nudity, the deep reddening sunburn, but still asked what he could do for her. Aracelli apologised for the trouble she brought but asked him to call the Civil Guard and explained what had happened in brief censorious terms.

That first night at the General Hospital Aracelli was on drips through needles into her sunburned arms for the dehydration. The sunburn which was general over her whole body began to lift in white, milky blister patches and the heatstroke became worse through the first twenty-four hours, making her hallucinate. She was made, in the depth of her delirium, to say crazy things to me at her bedside. Including that she hated me, as Father had also sworn on his sweating deathbed.

The blistering in various areas over Aracelli's body caused great discomfort especially during the nights. There seemed no humiliation she did not have to undergo. She was reduced to my own infantile state when I too had my entire body daubed in petroleum jellies.

There was talk of moving Aracelli to the Dermatology Unit. But the doctors decided her other prognoses were equally important.

Aracelli was on a whole selection of drugs; a mix of painkillers for her sunburned skin and tranquillisers for her troubled mind. It was an awful sight when she was free of the drips and could stand up to shuffle to the toilet, her shoulders bare under those horrific hospital gowns, the skin peeled down in deeper and deeper layers – the dirty brown of her true tan around the edging, sinking like the seashore into the pinking sheets of burn as if she had been splashed with that North American calling card: *napalm*. Her shoulders, her ears and her forehead were the most visibly affected areas of sunburn. The tops of her ears had peeled down to blood. She constantly touched at them with her fingernails, broken from clawing at the wooden deck of the boat.

In his theatre whites, Tenis came up to visit, joking and laughing all the time with her about his operations, using his easy ways and ignoring the ward doctors with natural hierarchy – although she was not his patient. Tenis excused me, whipped the curtain around my wife and did his own quick examination of her sunburn. He called for and examined the X-rays of her weak left lung which there was some concern for.

Tenis and I stepped outside the ward. He said they were treating her right and I could do nothing but let time pass. He said he would personally go then to retrieve the results of the blood tests and he explained the importance of them. It was here he mentioned the Condition, in relation to Aracelli. Also, Tenis was the first one bravely, face to face, to bring up the possibility of pregnancy because of the time of month when this attack had taken place.

I remember he cursed the perpetrators, slapped my shoulder and we both embraced at the ward door, out of Aracelli's sight.

The next day, with no explanation, my wife was moved to a single bed private ward. I later learned it was previously occupied by one of Tenis's patients who had suddenly suffered complications and passed. The pregnancy tests and the initial and later blood tests for the Condition of course proved to be negative.

What I must briefly account for are the feelings which befell me towards Sanz and Buges who both saved Aracelli's life and then took everything else as a price.

As a man who had always felt unsure of his directions in life – who had tried to fit into every cliché but did not fit into any one – I was suddenly given a clear and blinding mission.

I would die trying to kill Buges and Sanz with my own hands and if I succeeded I would then deliver myself to the police. The thought gave me an incredible peace. It all seemed so simple for those brief days of certain and sure hatred.

Those idiots were never to give me any such satisfaction. They were arrested within a week with evidence all over both them and the recovered boat which they had tried – and failed – to burn.

It made the brief trial less painful for Aracelli. They got thirteen years each.

Like love, hatred too decays and passes.

When Aracelli was released from hospital it was with joy she agreed that I could take her back home to the Phases Zone 1. It was hard for me to accept she was not ready and was understandably changed.

317

It was after she returned home and we went together for short walks that she began to pick up those little aluminium rings torn from soft-drink and beer cans which one sees discarded in the gutters of the street in any city. She really pained me by suddenly stooping to snatch up any of these rings on the street or the beach at the Phases when we took our evening stroll – no matter how disgusting – and forcing them on to her fingers. There was clearly a hygiene issue. Besides, she could not properly shower yet on account of the sunburn and I had to assist her washing carefully in the bathroom.

She became afraid she would lose those disgusting tin can rings in her restless sleep so she started to connect them all on her fingers using coloured sewing thread.

Then she had to have an umbrella wherever she went out to keep the sun off her. I can understand her aversion to the slightest sun. Anyone is the same who has endured a bad sunburn, but she took the umbrella – which was a conventional rain umbrella – out with her at night as well and shielded herself against the moon beneath it. She would also put the umbrella up to walk to a toilet inside a café. What with her scarred face with globules of white cream on it, her ring pulls and thread all over her fingers, her eccentric behaviour with the umbrella: I found it very uncomfortable – no, I will be honest, I found it embarrassing to leave the apartment with Aracelli.

I believed that going on the lemon express or a taxi to the bank, supermarket or post office was important therapy for her in returning to normality but I could hear the people of our city whispering about Aracelli's misfortunes behind me. Yes, selfish as it was I started becoming reclusive like her and agreeing when she did not want to leave our apartment at the Phases Zone 1.

I was ashamed to be seen with my wife because I began to feel guilty that I had let this happen to her. The walk to feed the stray cats in the boat became the limit of our universe.

*   *   *

Aracelli stopped eating enough because she was convinced most of her food was poisoned. Even sitting on a café terrace under her umbrella with a coffee, she looked around her constantly and said the coffee was contaminated.

I was not a cook of any sort at that time – despite the years annoying Chef and watching him in the kitchens of the old hotel. Pathetically, some nights the dishes I attempted to cook for Aracelli were so bad I had to slide them from the pan into the rubbish bin. Home food delivery was a recent innovation to our region and I tried everything to get her to eat but of course most of it was – according to her – poisoned. She would sometimes eat ice cream and she would dip North African dates – if she saw them come fresh from the packets – into the barbecue sauce that came with pizza, sealed inside a small container. As for most of the other food I had delivered? Well, the boat cats were well fed.

I suppose looking back on it we were a tragic couple then – sitting inside on sunny days, me trying to feed her slices of pears and pomegranate.

Because of the weight loss, Aracelli's parents – who always distrusted me, the suspect divorcee – backed up by the health visitor, started to insist Aracelli return to hospital. But not the General Hospital.

Aracelli silently rode beside me in the back of a taxi heading up past the cemetery on Heaven Hill, playing with the threads and ring pulls on her fingers. I had her suitcase resting across my thighs, containing boyish pyjamas – not her skimpy night vests – and a yellow dressing gown: all the temporary goods required by someone undergoing the horrific, stripped depersonalisation that hospitals depend on us to undergo. At the Phases Zone 1, I had begged Aracelli to be strong and not give herself over to them but I could not get her back.

Our City Psychiatric Hospital is situated in a pleasant cypress plantation half a kilometre down the road from the mausoleums and graves of Heaven Hill where Aunt Lucia, Uncle Luis, Mother, etc., all lie. The original old Asylum for the Insane was demolished just after democracy came – in an attempt to wash away the stigma of how the mentally ill were treated by the State during the years of the regime.

Our City Psychiatric Hospital was custom-built in the early eighties. On the very top floor is a pleasant cafeteria for staff, shifty-looking outpatients and a few privileged or escorted residents. Just below, the upper-floor Secure Wards command a fine view east and they are equipped with lowering electric blinds so any extraordinary planetary movements did not disturb the more apocalyptically inclined patients.

Male and female Secure Wards were on the upper floors, the consultancy, outpatients and alcohol/drug rehab in the middle and lower floors. At least the pleasant old gardens and fountains had, mostly, been retained and only partially destroyed for the large new car park.

It was the women's Secure Ward Aracelli was to be confined to. The definition of the Secure Ward was that inmates were a danger to themselves but not to others. I was defensive. I felt the madness of other patients was infectious and my wife would be worsened by constant contact with them. In the first week, as I timidly looked around at the human wreckage on that ward, I believed Aracelli was the healthiest of them all. She did not need to be there.

I remember I sat by her bedside those first days saying, 'Ari. Walk out, let you and me go to lunch at the Lower Rivers.' (Or did I say the Dolphin?)

She whispered, 'That was always your answer, Lolo. Go to lunch. It is a wonder you are not fat. Happiness. Why do you think so small?' she sneered.

In my early days, Matron was very strict about visiting hours though in reality there were no visitors other than me; as I became a regular and, in fact, soon a fixture, I did not have to observe the visiting hours' timetable any more. Often when Aracelli or even Beautiful Screamer – the young woman in the bed opposite my wife – were having bad nights I would sit beside them, onward into the small hours by the low spotlights next to the beds, designed only to illuminate the immediate area. Once or twice I was awoken by the elderly night nurses after dozing off completely.

I became such a regular on the women's Secure Ward sometimes I could feel jumpy. 'Still here, Mr Follana? I think you should get into your pyjamas and come stay with us full-time,' Matron called cheerily across the ward one day. Manic Coma – who never talked – Puta of Asunción, Old Mary and Beautiful Screamer all laughed with knowing delight to hear that. Even Aracelli moved her shoulders slowly in a tranquillised chuckle.

I had started sleeping over on the mattress at Mother's old place above Town Hall Plaza. Some days I would walk up the same climb Sagrana and I used to be ordered on by our physical education teacher during soccer practice. As schoolboys we could jog those lanes with still enough energy to clamber around together in the cemetery and find dark hideouts among the mausoleums. We never remember getting breathless as children. But beyond the cemetery I was soon panting and I arrived at our City Psychiatric Hospital sweating. I soon selected to only walk home downhill in the evenings. Each day I would take a taxi from Town Hall Plaza up to the graveyard car park and stroll from there to check in at the downstairs desk. The porter, who had a security clearance key, rode up in the elevator with me.

After a whole night in the ward when Aracelli was bad, I often walked down those lanes of Heaven Hill beneath the cemetery with the first birds causing commotion in the cypresses and then into the bell chimes of Town Hall Plaza where I collapsed on the mattress to sleep until I woke and returned back up the hill to the hospital.

★　★　★

It shocked and angered me that none of the inmates of the Secure Ward were ever visited. It was I who became so popular by bringing up litre-bottles of cheap supermarket lemonade in the taxi to distribute to everyone. Most inpatients had been conveniently forgotten by their relatives, who were too ashamed by the stigma of madness to visit very often. Even Beautiful Screamer could not have been twenty-five years of age but I never saw her visited once and they whispered of drugs, that her fiancé had run away, that she was heiress to a fortune so the relatives were happy to have her quietly fade away somewhere.

Beautiful Screamer sat up quietly in bed all day, reading up-to-date gossip magazines which the nurses passed on to her and which were like gold. Eventually I kept her in weekly supply. She spoke normally to the nurses. In the first week Aracelli felt me physically react when Beautiful Screamer – who I was shy to stare at – swept aside her bedclothes, pulled her long body from bed and skimpily padded off to the bathroom with her drug-emulsioned skin and spectacularly unshaven but perfect legs. She held few attractions even in those first days of celibacy. I tried to imagine Beautiful Screamer's former life with her spoiled beauty. She still held a possibility of transformation and rebirth about her.

Aracelli whispered, 'Do not get any of your ideas about that little honey opposite, she wakes up every night covered in her own faeces, screaming that dead soldiers are having sex with her.'

There were basic rules about the security key to the elevator and the need to respect washing, medication, therapy, etc., etc. I could smoke down the corridor in the glass-fronted visitors' waiting room – which was never used. I went there when they were feeding the beasts of the lower pastures and Aracelli. I could hear dishes crashing and admonitions.

At that period, in an attempt to quit cigarettes, I was smoking thin, expensive cheroots in packs of ten, which were precious – the upstairs cafeteria sold no quality tobacco.

One mealtime I looked at the magazine in the visitors' waiting room which was eighteen months out of date. The smoke from the rich cheroot fairly filled the glass box of a room. Very slowly I became aware of the batty face of an ancient patient peeking around the corner and studying me. I tried to ignore her but her old leather face kept curling round – the bright blue eyes staring at me, the toothless mouth grinning. Next thing she opened the door, slipped in and quietly shut it behind her. She stared at my cigar.

'Good afternoon,' I said.

'I was the most beautiful puta in Asunción.'

'I am sure you were, madam.'

'They say I was a nun through there. Do not believe them.'

'OK.'

'I used to smoke a cigar.'

'Yeah? In Asunción?'

'Give me one.'

'I think Matron would be angry.'

'I shall smoke it here then, with you.'

'I would get in trouble.'

'I saw your wife. She has terrible skin.'

'An accident.'

'The sun can make you like that. Was it the sun that made your wife like that?'

'Yes. It was the sun.'

'Give me a smoke.'

'OK. But if a nurse comes, give it back. It will be the secret of you and I. Shhhh.'

'Shhhhhh.'

It was amusing to see her busted-out smile and I watched her smoke. After I lit it for her, Puta of Asunción let the long cheroot remain sticking directly out her mouth without touching it and she puffed and smoked with rapid little sucks and blows which created a lot of smoke while her blue mongrel eyes smiled. She clapped her hands.

'Take it out. Like I do.' I demonstrated.

She ignored me and was blowing smoke out as quickly as she inhaled it. She was just a smoke machine.

Suddenly the door opened and I saw the creamy coils of smoke shift until she closed the door behind her. Old Mary. 'Give me one.' I gave Old Mary a cigar also and she took her technique from Puta of Asunción. Then the door opened again and Beautiful Screamer entered holding one of her magazines.

'What are you doing?' She laughed. 'Hey, give us one too.'

I immediately handed her one. She lit up as well and then Manic Coma – the handsome, middle-aged woman who never spoke and was either hyperactively walking in circles round the ward bothering no one, or asleep for days – silently entered.

It was like a smoke box within that room of glass. We were all waving our hands around so the ladies opened the door and the smoke fell out in clouds. Each one puffing smoke from an unmoving cheroot in their mouths, they formed a straight line.

'Oh no. No.' I called.

Like a procession of old traction engines they made their way up the corridor in single file, ash collapsing like bird droppings down the fronts of their dressing gowns, old cardigans or nightshirts. They entered the open ward. A shriek of welcome delight went up from the other patients.

Oh dear, I thought.

'Mr Follana.' Matron's steady voice called.

I grew to feel for them and the pains of the world they had taken upon themselves while our city lay indifferent beneath them. Puta of Asunción really had been a nun who went insane in the convent. Each seemed to have seen the world with clarity but to have carried their insight through into madness. Perhaps if we all had one pulverising insight as to the total pain in the world we too would be as they?

Old Mary took me aside one day – privately as always. I was

afraid she might suddenly reveal some intimate part of her body to me, as Puta of Asunción would hoist out a withered breast if you allowed her to succeed in guiding you to a compromised and isolated location. Old Mary lured me to the small nurses' sink. 'See that plughole?'

'Yes.'

'*Lady Di* speaks to me out of it every night.'

'What does she say?'

'She asks me what to wear.'

'What is she doing down there?'

'What do you think? She is trapped in the pipe. Go get a plumber.' She trotted away.

Restless on my mattress in the bare apartment above Town Hall Plaza, I started to have nightmares where I would be institutionalised in Aracelli's ward and never released.

It is impossible for a healthy person to constantly live with the sick of mind or body, guilty as this makes one feel. Even as I tried to force myself to share Aracelli's constant anguish I often found my mind oscillating away from her despair and, instead, caught myself smiling or reflecting on some bright, happy, innocuous thing – a fat hopping bird, a teenage couple hand in hand crossing furtively among the casket walls and mausoleums of the cemetery, a joke in the ghastly local newspaper which you could buy from the cafeteria. Even in the commitment to share misfortune I was unfaithful and a failure.

In coming months I admitted I liked to get a break from the ward – and, to be honest, from Aracelli. Every few hours I would ride down in the security-locked elevator and take a slow sauntering pass through the cypress groves to smoke a cheroot in the gardens. Especially on the increasingly rare days when Aracelli's parents and her dull sister visited – and continually interrogated me and made so obvious their distress at those other wonderful inmates.

I often strolled through the bowers and around the cloches of the garden. Every mental hospital seems to have a great garden and I have noticed, internationally, the myth exists, among all schools of profit-making psychiatry, that the insane love to commune among the fronds of nature – as if chlorophyll were a scientifically recognised cure for madness. It was only gradually I realised the pleasant gardens of lunatic asylums are – like those of old people's homes and hospices – for the benefit of the unafflicted visitors who are not full-time residents.

In the June festivals that year I arrived excited to a bustling ward. I was hulking a crate of supermarket lemonade and gossip magazines.

I was met by Matron. 'Mr Follana – just who we need to lead your mischievous gang. We are going on a little outing to the far car park tonight. Will you and your wife look after your gang? We have minibuses and cars organised.'

'Really? We are taking them outside?'

'Oh, it is good for them, just now and again.'

Aracelli and I organised them. Although it was night, I saw Aracelli was taking her beloved umbrella. With the other madwomen who were our favourites, we moved out of our ward to the security elevator and stood in deeply important silence as the porter rode us all downstairs.

Outside, at the end of the entrance corridor, Matron was organising her different wards into small minibuses. The fanatical section of druggies by the rehab centre lounged, cautiously watching the genuine lunatic fringe. They gave especial attention to Beautiful Screamer. I felt a furious stab of need to protect her from those wasters, even though my wife was probably on more medication than them.

When Aracelli, myself, Puta of Asunción, Old Mary, Manic Coma and Beautiful Screamer were next in line out of the main door there were no minibuses remaining. The grounds tractor and trailer arrived and squeaked to a halt – driven by the gardener who I recognised from my strolls in the garden, collecting his cuttings. He sat up on the tractor, smoking a cigarette.

'Get them in the back,' he called and jerked his thumb.

'Is it safe?' I asked.

'No standing.' He frowned. 'I thought you were just a visitor?'

'I am!'

He jumped from his tractor and his cigarette end glowed brighter. He watched Aracelli, Beautiful Screamer and I help the old ladies up. The old crazies did not complain for a moment. All that made it difficult to get them up into the trailer was that they refused to let go of their half-drunk bottles of lemonade. I pushed on Manic Coma's big ass then clambered aboard into the trailer myself.

I noticed they all obediently sat down against the side of the trailer and I realised they were previously familiar with this mode of transportation. The gardener put up the hinged back of the trailer and noisily sealed it with the crossbar.

I myself felt oddly excited as the gardener started up the tractor, illuminated the headlights and the tail lights of the trailer, then we moved off noisily towards the exit. We all reacted with the jerky movements of the trailer. The regulars – not me or Aracelli – all called out 'Hey!' as the trailer crossed the speed bumps on the driveway. Aracelli and I joined in and called out 'Hey!' when we crossed the last one and my wife and I, hand in hand, laughed together.

We paused at the main entrance of our City Psychiatric Hospital and the driver stuck out his arm to the right, edging forward and braking all the time so the red warning lights lit up the empty drive behind us and we all rocked back and forth; the lemonade, coloured pink by the light, swung within those clear bottles. Eventually a saloon car grudgingly braked and gave way. We swung right out on to the road with bright headlights behind us.

★　★　★

327

It was a beautiful late-June night; even through the light pollution of our entire city you could see many stars like layers of gold smoke high in the amber heights.

I looked at the odd sight of the older inmates leaning casually against the sides of the trailer boarding. They clutched their lemonade bottles with two hands to their chests like children or again used both hands to lift the drink to their mouths. I cuddled up next to Aracelli who dropped her head happily on my shoulder under that summer night. But still she suspended the umbrella above our heads to shield any moonbeams. It could have been an evening a year before when, happily drunk, we would use the imitation amusement train – towed by a small tractor with ringing bell made to resemble a locomotive – for tourists' children, which runs that kilometre of road from the esplanade to the lemon express station.

'It would be safe without the umbrella.'

'Would it?'

'Please, darling, give it a try.'

Gradually she dropped the umbrella down towards the wood boards.

'I am happy now.'

'Are you really though?'

'These are our new friends.'

'But Ari, you have to leave here and go back to the world. I have to get on with my business and we have to get on with our happiness together. We have to move on ahead.'

'Poor Lolo.' She shook her head.

'Poor Ari,' I stated bluntly.

She nodded.

'Lolo, none of what happened mattered.'

'What do you mean?'

'Only the good things mattered.'

'That is true.'

'Poor Lolo, you always needed women as your mirror and look what you have ended up with.'

'What do you mean by that?'

'You need women as your mirror.'

'Maybe, but all I want is you to come home.'

'It will not be the same.'

'Ari. The terrible thing is it will be, because I was not there that day. The way you will find what we had before is through being with me. Those guys have not spoiled me. You will find your way back to where we were through me.'

She just smiled through those nut-brown eyes.

The gardener turned us right, off the climbing ascent towards the floodlit castle and instead into the southern graveyard car park where I could see the dark tops of the cypresses across the wall which marked the limit of the mausoleums.

In the middle of the car park, guarded by a fire engine, was the usual, quite hideous effigy: the central figure a ten- or fifteen-metre wood and polystyrene sculpture.

Tonight it was a garishly coloured caricature of a national politician from a party which still happily flaunted connections to the fascist regime, to prise out the last votes of dying old men. Around the groin of the effigy's suit, daringly, almost with her back to us, hovered the enormous mouth of a blonde with spilling bosom who – because of my studies of gossip magazines beside Beautiful Screamer – I actually recognised. The blonde from trashy television had been linked with the married politician.

The faces of these figures bore the usual cheaply evoked emotion of caricature – wide eyes, booming cheeks – using the time-honoured techniques of *Fragonard* and *Walt Disney*.

A few smaller satellite effigies circled the two main ones: local bigwig councillors and politicians from the city.

Yelling to keep hands, arms 'and cocks' clear, the gardener carefully backed up right against the cemetery wall so the inmates and I were trapped in the trailer unless we clambered with difficulty over the edges of the highly sprung sides and dropped to the ground

– only lithe Screamer could have managed it easily but she was no runner. Here we were to remain.

The gardener got out to smoke and stroll around, chatting and laughing with the other minibus drivers from the hospital. I noticed he had a technique. When a demented passenger from the buses approached the gardener, he held up an admonishing figure, plucked a *walkie-talkie* from the breast pocket of his boiler suit and pretended to speak importantly into it while turning his back and walking away. For some reason the mentally ill show huge respect for *walkie-talkie* conversations and none of them pursued the gardener.

I did see the gardener look my way when he was talking to a minibus driver who I recognised as an orderly from the men's ward, still in his white coat. Since he did not care what I heard I could make out a lot: 'You should not let your bunch out the bus, man. I am never letting my lot wander from that trailer. Too much hassle; the looker who screams blue murder, she never makes a break for it but no way could I catch her with those pins on her if she took off. I am fifty next year, man. The one in the suit must be an outpatient cos I see him in the gardens muttering to himself.' (I raised my eyebrows.) 'But he thinks he is just a visitor, a businessman, and the good-looking bint with the rain umbrella thinks she is his wife.'

Fireworks began above us and their candy colours stained the rough wooden boards of the trailer. We all immediately stood or tipped our heads back – as we men, even Sagrana, once used to look up at the same time, obediently, towards beautiful Lupe Tenis the instant she appeared reading the regional news on café televisions fixed in a corner.

Even Aracelli stood and her hair fell down her back but she immediately pushed the clip which made her umbrella shoot up into place with a snap and she flicked that frame of plaid nylon above her as a shield.

No electronic ignition systems in my model region. The most

skilled and brave in the world, The Pyrotechnic (wearing a flak jacket culled from his Military Service) ducked and ran from set-up to set-up igniting them with a long fizzing touch rod – the mortar canisters threw their bombs forth, the rocket frames ignited one after another and hurled themselves towards God in Heaven.

Above us were the travelling viper hisses which seemed in a collective effort to stop their helpless fall from the sky; the spastic sparkles and the confabulation of explosions which lit their own canyons of smoke. Aracelli pointed out to me that her umbrella was not such a laughable item now as spent rocket shells or their blackened firing sticks pattered into the cypresses in front of us and tapped off the umbrella as they fell to the trailer.

Of course, for me it is impossible to see a firework display and not associate it with my father's cremation ashes being packed into the enormous rocket that burst above the waters where I first swam, shaking every window pane of the apartment blocks along our beachfront – so I am always emotionally charged by the display.

Up they went: the names of the rockets that stretched out above us in their bursts: one hundred Pepperpots, fifty of the Queen's Bloomers followed by a backdrop of ten Time of the Months, sixty Whisky and Sodas, ten Red Seas, twenty Fat Ones, one hundred Ball Breakers, ten Show-Off Parrots, sixty Roof of the Worlds, ten Constant Circles, a hundred Mosquitoes, a box of Spoons, twenty Cranes, fourteen Cocktails, ten Free Squares, forty Toucan's Beaks, four hundred Soldiers, two genuine maritime distress flares, twenty Parachutes, four of God's Laxatives and all climaxed with a yellow and a blue Satellite Buster.

Meanwhile, The Pyrotechnic had a pretty girl from the crowd light the fuse to a rocket which screamed towards the huge polystyrene effigy of the national politician and hit a trip wall igniting the crystal waterfalls and the firecrackers which hung along wires uniting the geometry like an electricity substation. The firecrackers started banging off like a firing squad, four lime tree fireworks – too bright

331

to look at – served to disguise the initial and slow ignition of the huge effigy and by the time the lime trees burned out, the sincere politician and his ancillary fellator were completely alight.

Watching something burn spectacularly fulfils a deep destructive delight – nobody is above the pure visual fascination of that natural destruction. It all has the same simplicity of certain sexual urges, instant, undeniable, then utter surety as they occur.

Aracelli and I leaned together and kissed as that politician's face – utterly certain no matter how they mocked it – his huge furrows of combed hair, his ears – all evolved into flame; his enormous polystyrene hand, which pleaded for us to include him in our lives, deliciously melted in burning globules of the purifying fire which dripped down, anointing the head and insatiable lips of his kneeling, alleged lover.

It was all too much for Old Mary: Aracelli and I kissing, the firework volleys, the burning effigy, all the lemonade – the old woman crouched and grinned, letting forth a huge puddle of urine which had to be avoided in the trailer all the way home.

In the City Psychiatric Hospital cafeteria one evening the sun was setting with a nuclear impressiveness – Aracelli was so improved we were allowed to walk in the garden together and go up to the cafeteria as long as I escorted her.

She reached across the plastic tables, our arms edging the red-topped oil & vinegar/salt & pepper self-contained plastic unit aside. We played with one another's fingers.

'More coffee?'

'With sugar.'

'How much?'

'Too much,' she smiled.

'Sure.' I smiled back but, as she sometimes would, she shyly looked away.

When I turned from the cafeteria queue to smile she was not at our table. She had gone to the cafeteria toilets. It was strictly forbidden but she had used those toilets once before. I cursed to myself that sometimes being in that mental institute was like being back in the old regime with its school rules.

I scanned around for nurses or male orderlies from the women's ward. None were around so I relaxed a bit. I remained in the queue and paid for the coffee, taking an outrageous <u>three</u> double sugar cubes back to our table. I sat down.

Aracelli did not appear at the corridor mouth which led to the men's and women's toilets. She must have gone back down to get something from the ward, I thought. All the same I began to suspect Aracelli had escaped and made a run for it. We would have to run her to ground in our city.

I stood up and walked over towards the toilets.

Outside, like the sheets I had once cast from a hotel window, Aracelli moved past the top-floor window and was gone. The movement was very quick but not as swift as you would think – I saw the head bravely faced downward, the trailing bedshirt and unmistakable yellow dressing gown hauled to the vertical.

The unique male yelp came from the table of four doctors seated immediately by the window. Me slowly turning – to look back down the toilet corridor and see that the strictly locked door up to the roof had its padlock hanging slightly askew on the plate fitting which affixed it to the wall.

I called something out – a cawed horrible sound – stumbling forward to get to the elevator and there was a gripped tension in that cafeteria for I knew off to my right more and more people were crowding to the windows and shielding their faces to look downwards.

Despite the commotion in the top-floor cafeteria nobody had communicated the news to the ground floor. Imagine – for I barely recall – my thankfully unaccompanied ride down in the elevator to collapse into the lobby and be met with complete calm: impossibly still receptionists, silent, passing staff, calm civilians. I ran at the

333

main door and pointed aggressively at the poor receptionists. 'A doctor to the car park. My wife has jumped from the roof.'

Outside, I had to look both to the left and the right for – again, odd – I had never taken the time to identify exactly where the cafeteria was positioned on the top floor in relation to the front door – the sun was well down now and the car parks in both directions were darker and lit by the unsteady, warming electric lights, no more than a novelty in that initial dusk.

The car she had fallen beside was black. Her impact had bent the top of the passenger door outwards, shattered the window and compressed the diced windscreen. But here was the worst shock: leaning over her in the oily half-light, like a succubus, was the figure of a priest (Father Garrido), close to Aracelli's stunned but unchanged pale face, as if seducing her, already moving his fingers in unspeakable condemnation over her torso with the last rites.

Unforgivable though it is – a priest, and also to be behaving in such a way near a gravely injured, delicate person – I flew through the air and I hit the priest on the side of his face with both of my Italian shoes then I collapsed against the front wheel of the car and I stood up.

A lot of blood was on my palm. It was not the priest's. It was all over the dark tarmac. Father Garrido's head had slumped forward over Aracelli's legs, his glasses flown off. I noticed Aracelli's pyjamas had changed colour from all the blood.

Then I remember this remarkable fact. Father Garrido barely glanced at me, his face was not alarmed but completely calm and accepting. He merely turned away from me and continued to administer the last rites. I actually stared at him for a moment. His demeanour was undeniably impressive and I was furious at myself for having to admire him so.

I realised I was still repeating 'No' so I stopped and screamed, 'Get away from her, she needs doctors not you, get the doctor.'

Father Garrido did not respond but I could not hit him again and, worse, I was now looking down at Aracelli and I kneeled beside the priest and cried out my wife's name.

Like a little girl giving in to a filthy pervert's advances, I felt the priest's arm go round my back and very quickly, with her face in my hands, a thumbprint of her own dark blood upon her freckled cheek, Aracelli died in front of me.

Book Three

To General Count Hullin, Governor of the Château de Vincennes.

Saint-Cloud, 25 July 1811

I have received the sentence passed on Cifenti and Sassi della Tosa. Have Cifenti executed – he is a wretched spy. In Sassi's case I agree to a commutation of his sentence. But you are to have him taken to the place of execution, and you must not produce the reprieve until Cifenti has been executed and it is Sassi's turn to mount the scaffold. I want him to see with his own eyes how a crime like his is punished.

Napoleon's Letters

The Mad *Scuba*-Diver

I told Ahmed, 'So that is how I became the mad *scuba*-diver of our city. After Aracelli's death my friends, acquaintances, work colleagues and every gossip of our city knew where I was to be found. Forty metres north of the Meliander Hotel, in eight to ten metres of water. I dived from the rocks of the dark path where I had been with *Ann* and The Young Woman Who Watched. I dived every day for those months, searching for my dead wife's lost, gold wedding ring while Kiko Bonzas and Sagrana watched over my business. Sometimes I even dived at night with a powerful torch, reasoning that gold would glisten in its beam. I admit I was deranged.

'I walked between the sunbathers in my wetsuit, carrying my tank to and from the water's edge. I would raise my hand in greeting to a new generation of lifeguards at the Red Cross hut who nodded sympathetically – next to the young lifeguard might be an admiring college girl in a bikini, with dirty soles to her feet, tipped back on her plastic chair stolen from the nearby café. I knew the lifeguard was whispering, "See that diver guy – let me tell you about him . . ."

'But I never found the ring.'

The weather had been unseasonably cold for the time of year. I decided Ahmed and I should venture forth for some air and have a fun day out. I had begun to lend him my clothes – one of my purple, very expensive silk shirts was his favourite and now I gave him a pair of sunglasses which made him appear quite raffish.

He seemed glum though, slumped next to me on the lemon express, nodding to my endless commentary. When we decamped into our city from the station I laboriously pointed out the Imperial Hotel and its mentioned features, the Meliander and the dark path below it. The approximate positioning of Aracelli's sunken ring, inshore from the odometer.

As we strolled the streets together nobody paid us the slightest attention.

So it was inevitable I took the route across Town Hall Plaza and its tolling bell and up into the lanes. Higher Ahmed and I climbed until the dark cypresses leaned over our heads on Heaven Hill – the Solielians' domain and my only future.

Ahmed and I had arrived together at the gates of Heaven Hill cemetery. The sympathetic graveyard attendant, who was not required in my youth, was still there in his hut. I always tipped him. He did not even look at Ahmed. I assume the attendant had come to terms with the fact that they were letting anyone into his grave-yard these days. It was a long time since I had visited and at least the old man had not joined his inmates whom he watched over so diligently. I had warned Ahmed how the graveyard attendant would tell us, with some lasciviousness, that he spends all his time chasing fornicating teenagers ('Satanists') from the mausoleums but with his bad leg he is so slow approaching they are generally finished by the time he reaches them and he takes that opportunity to mock the lovemaking prowess of contemporary male youth. He did tell us all this.

I led a clearly alarmed Ahmed along walls of the dead – as if through some ancient city. Small birds rose and fell towards the memorial tops at speed, darting, from cypress tree to tree. It was impossible to ignore the columns of ants on the dusty ground going about their business.

I pointed out the obvious highlights to Ahmed: the slab in the wall and final resting place of Uncle Luis and Aunt Lucia who were silent within, one on top of the other. My father's memorial stone.

The slab where my poor mother was cemented in by the Solielians. The special rusted metal clip on Mother's wall. I explained to Ahmed how – when I still used to travel – the graveyard attendant would walk out into this casket range and fix the postcards I sent to her of grand hotels, where I would later find them, faded by the sun and frayed by rain showers, months later. I emphasised to Ahmed not to consider my behaviour in any way odd; there was a lady visitor to Heaven Hill cemetery who every Sunday would sit on her husband's grave and read him the sporting pages.

And thus we came to Aracelli's resting place – a simple plaque on the wall where the Solielians had sealed her broken body in. Ahmed and I sat down on a small, raised mausoleum but with the cypress above us it was shaded and downright cold.

Ahmed suddenly asked, quite aggressively I felt, 'How did Aracelli get up on the City Psychiatric Hospital roof?'

'That poor old hospital gardener and groundsman. That morning Aracelli had taken him by the hand into the ladies' ward toilet cubicles. She pickpocketed the padlock key from him then she waited for me to escort her up to the roof cafeteria. She wanted to die that badly. The gardener had not even noticed the missing key until it was found lying on the stairs to the roof. Poor man; they say he broke down and took to drink. I blame him for nothing but the hospital sacked him and I hear they made a misery of his life. Why should anyone else suffer? Aracelli just wanted a conclusion to those choruses of suffering. But she said nothing to me. Just that she wanted sugar in her coffee. What kind of farewell or epitaph to our love was that? I guess it was just as much as my love deserved.'

Ahmed lowered his head. I knew he disapproved of me now. He judged me.

I continued our stroll. On the farthest edging of the graveyard we sat in the weak but slightly warming sun on a bench which was positioned on one of the pathways between the dead. I commented that I was hungry and wished we had taken something with us to eat.

Ahmed shook his head and said he did not believe this was an appropriate place. He was really quite angry.

After a pause I turned. 'You are not very observant.'

'What do you mean?'

'You are not very observant. Look around.'

Ahmed turned his reflective sunglasses to the sky, he looked up and down the path then he realised and took off his sunglasses. He gave me a cautionary look – again, almost aggressive. He stood up and as if in an art gallery began reading the names on the walls of caskets around us.

From the casket second up from the ground, right in front of us, he suddenly spun and looked at me. 'Follana.'

I nodded.

He stepped over. 'What happened?'

'I had not been in touch for years. We had exchanged a few forlorn childish postcards with all kinds of hollow promises. As our parents warn us, you really do always think there is so much time when you are that age. When you are your age, Ahmed, you think you have for ever. They sent me a letter daring me to come to the *Sorbonne* and study with them. Imagine. A *Polaroid* photograph fell from the envelope with the French stamps on it: them, completely naked on a bed but blurred, because in competition with the auto-timer one of them – it looked like Quynh – had raced back to the bed and jumped upon it, causing both figures to move and badly blur: legs all excitedly thrown out, almost complete modesty but dark areas between the legs – there was an intense, warm inevitability of their flesh tones, both their mouths were wide open, laughing.

'Both their fathers were some kind of diplomats in the old Vietnam, when it was a French colony. When Thinh and Quynh were nineteen at university in Paris they became party girls, drugs and scenes. They had tastes, the looks and the money to back it up.' I nodded over. 'She and Quynh attended this wild party. There was some boy there that they were both were very fond of and rivals for, so they agreed to share him. Like me. Both were determined to

342

pursue this boy but Thinh was so stoned she fell over, through a glass door in the old apartment. Her only injury was her arm but that was very, very badly cut. Yet she refused to leave the party and rebuffed all help. Several of the party members wanted to call an ambulance but Thinh and Quynh went to the bathroom and ran Thinh's lacerated arm beneath the cold-water tap of the bath then Quynh helped her wrap the arm up in a thick towel.

'Thinh managed to corner the boy in a bedroom. She insisted on them making love with him throughout that night. They continued drinking from wine bottles at the sides of the bed. Quynh explained it to me. There was blood all over their bodies. Quynh panicked and asked Thinh to stop several times but she continued and eventually Thinh just threw the blood-soaked towel aside into the corner of the bedroom. Quynh was crying but carried on with both of them.

'In the first light of morning Quynh thought Thinh was sleeping, looked into her friend's eyes. Imagine being awoken by a blood-covered Quynh screaming and that terrified boy exhausted between them. Simply bleeding to death by making love all night. There was so much of her black blood, Quynh told me, it was soaked down through the mattress of the bed. Yet the autopsy showed how glass had cut into Thinh's arm and minute fragments of this had journeyed through her all during the night, cutting away inside her veins and her arteries and soon the very heart itself so Thinh bled inside herself, the blood pressure collapsed and she died. Tenis, of course, exhaustively explained it to me.

'They decided to lay Thinh to rest down here in our city. She had once said to Quynh she would want that if ever anything happened to her because she had been visiting here when she was a little girl before I pounced on them. You know what teenagers are like. Dramatic. Veroña and I followed the Solielians through this gruesome maze and I made love with Veroña in one of these mausoleums, though I resented her for it; bashing away against the stone, I hurt her I was so angry.

343

'God, how I should have gone to Paris but my touch is surely fatal and I was too timid. They did visit our city, once again together, but Veroña and I were in the damn Capital at university. I never saw them both again. Then suddenly Quynh arrived with that translator organising this funeral. I was in a state but I could not let my heart-break show to my damned new wife who I loved as well as Thinh. Two days after the funeral I got Quynh alone. My parents had sold the Imperial Hotel but you can still gain access to the roof of it from Mother's old apartment in Town Hall Plaza, so I sneaked Quynh up there, lifting her through a hatch in the ceiling and walking over the roofs together to the reserve-water tank. She was smiling. I can still remember her perfect skin, the dark pool of her eye more delicately drawn into the curve of the skull, the flat cheekbones, still boyish figure. She seemed happy to journey to the past again. We were in peaceful silence, unable to speak because we had shaken off that perpetual translator who spoke my language with an awful accent.

Up on the wooden platform above the reserve-water tank I crazily leaned to kiss her. Rightly she snapped her head back and said, 'No.' Thinh's heavy presence was between us. We were both shaking with fear and with desire. So she sat on the wooden plat-form and bowed her neck, that of a young woman, and cried until her tears vanished among the sweating tank sides, condensation-jewelled pipes below the baby stalactites of smooth calcium which dripped from the ceiling. The pipes hissed and burbled around us. I felt I had sullied and negated another beautiful memory. Quynh returned to Paris. I wish I had left Veroña and pursued her but I did not. Quynh had children when I last heard.

Ahmed nodded. 'You are fatal, Follana.'

I brightened up. 'Nice spot. If anything happened to me, I would want to be here, under these cypresses as close to Thinh as you could.'

Ahmed looked at me. 'What is ever going to happen to you, man?'

★   ★   ★

Something had changed between Ahmed and me, as the weather between actual lovers does. The halcyon weeks in our apartment were gone; those mornings when I looked out to sea more often, wondering at Africa beyond the container ships on the horizon and felt proud of my companion. I missed the days when Ahmed and I cooked and ate steamed fish with couscous, ripe fresh pears and mangoes which he taught me how to peel using a dinner spoon; when we squeezed oranges, apples and carrots in my electric juicer and Ahmed listened to the parts of my life that I told him.

Something was uncomfortable when we returned from Heaven Hill to my apartment out at the Phases Zone 1. I presume he was suffering the oppressive Follana Effect that got to everyone in the end – including my poor ex-wives.

After a few hours I closed all the windows and sat on the calf-skin couch looking out into fading day without illuminating the interior of my dwelling, as was my habit.

Ahmed suddenly appeared carrying his dirty black bin liner.

'What are you doing?'

'Leaving.'

'Are you mad? Where to?'

'I need to go. All I ask is that I can keep this shirt. I will never be able to pay you back.'

I laughed. 'Listen, you illegal immigrant of Monaco. Stay. I will give you a job at my Agency as I have promised. You can stay at Mother's apartment if you are sick of me. If you need money I will give it to you.'

I looked at Ahmed Omar. He had no papers, no passport, no number of identification; he existed on no bank records or computer files or tax returns or governmental ledgers; this man passed through Sagrana's careful documentation of a life like a ghost. He was holy and special and it pained me to civilise him here, with our rules and timid values which in our relationship we had never shared or allowed to limit us.

'I need time alone.'

345

'This place is big enough to be alone.'

He moved to the door. I had not counted on this. I shot to my feet. 'Ahmed. Please. We have something here. We have freedom and a truth between us. Few men have that today.'

He turned round and looked at me. I had never seen him look sad before and now he did.

'I hope you do not dare feel sorry for me,' I stated angrily.

He shook his head and opened the door. 'We both need to think alone for a while,' he said, curiously.

'Hey. I will see you again? Take a set of keys, man, it's freezing cold out there.' He ignored me. 'Are you going with her?' I yelled down the stairs after him.

I felt a gluey despair that punched me in the stomach alone in the accumulating gloom of the apartments. I could not stop thinking about him. I was as obsessive as I was about a girl. Finally my door buzzer rang and I rushed to it gladly.

Young Teresa stood there, dressed beautifully, with her hair done in a new way. Her physical appearance was such a shock to me I took a step back.

Since that night weeks before when I had gone to Ahmed's lair, the sub-aqua speargun had been dropped, disarmed, into the small alcove for coats and umbrellas by the door. As Teresa dared to begin speaking to me, I turned aside from her pretentious look of concern, snatched up the speargun and – though I did not arm it – I pointed it directly into her face. She took several steps backwards on the stairwell, a slightly turned fear on her face.

'Get away from me,' I shouted.

She said my name but she still backed up to the lip of the stairway, with its irritating faded outlines of concrete boot shapes. I would need to try the wire brushes on it again.

I said, 'If you want him you can have him but do not presume you can come here, sneaking about the Phases. You are both adults.'

'Want who?' she replied, backing down onto the first step.

I lowered the underwater gun, its pointed spear to her womb.

She jumped down three stairs and stumbled. I came after her and we began to race down the stairwell together, our noisy, slapping steps echoing back upward.

I caught her at the main exit where she pulled back on the door without pressing the release button. I realised if I caught her, I would hold her and try to embrace the little fool. I shouted out in despair and hurled the gun which clattered loudly to the tiled flooring.

Teresa was out and running across the shore road towards the railway but I still gave chase and pursued outwards into the dusk.

I shouted again. I leaned over, arms on my thighs. I noticed how cold the air was and I shivered.

I had stopped and was breathing excitedly.

She had turned and looked at me but she kept walking slowly backwards. She called breathlessly, 'You frighten me.'

'Yes.'

'What is the matter with you? Are you on cocaine?'

We both stood in a cold twilight, looking at one another. Distance between us but we could still hear one another's breathing. I stood straighter and looked around me at the night air of the Phases Zone 1 which I once loved so much. It seemed illuminated by fibres of blue starlight alone.

A light went on in another apartment above, perfectly illuminating the magical, boxlike interior – a lesson in perspective. I could see the receding depth into the next room of that apartment and how the top of a distant window was visible, showing that eggshell blue of lighter, western skies above the mountains.

Behind Teresa's voice, shadows bled into the first-line lands. Up by the railway the two lights of the platform shimmered in pixels of silver. A jet trail was segmented in orange way above the crest apartments at the top of the embankment. Another light came on there. I wanted to hold my breath to hear the silence properly.

'Where is he?'

'Who? They wired in the cats,' she said.

'I know you have being feeding them,' I snarled. Then I asked, 'What?'

'They wired in the cats.'

I looked down the railway line and instead of the secret and insinuating darkness of pampas plants in the wasteland I saw a long bright wall of high, horribly virgin wire – almost shocking in its newness, unfamiliar – with white concrete poles. I began to walk towards it.

'When did that happen?' I frowned.

'The truck was just leaving.' She watched me, suspiciously, as I strode in front of her and moved beyond.

It was an apocalyptic situation. Some of the cats had fled the area during the day and they were now trapped on the outside of the wire. They clustered around me, rubbing against my calves. Other cats, which had taken refuge within the boat all day, now remained trapped on the inside of the wire. They circled suspiciously along the perimeter looking for a way out but there was none. 'You would have thought they would dig a few inches for them to get in and out in the name of Christ.' I spat, dropping to my knees hard and trying to tug up a section of the tight-fitting wire – clutching it with my hands and heaving upward.

The incarcerated cats clustered and rubbed against the wire at the sight of me on the other side. 'I will need to get those wire cutters in the basement and cut this damn thing,' I stated, but full darkness had taken over and though I could sense Teresa out there in it somewhere, I could not see her.

'Teresa?' I called softly.

'What?' her cold voice suddenly came somewhere off to the left.

'I think of you.'

Quietly her voice spoke. 'I think of you too. All the time. I wish I had stayed with you the day we had lunch. I was trying to be sensible.'

'There is stuff you do not know about me. I can explain one day. I cannot be with you and that is why I am angry.'

The boxes of light that were apartments suspended in the high airs above me were lit up but in the utter dark around there was no way of finding her.

'Ahmed!' I screamed out. 'Help me find him.'

There was no response. I cursed and strode aggressively for the basement to get my big wire cutters – the ones I bought for the park pond renovation job.

Mr Misery's Final Cocktail Hour

An hour later I rushed to the phone but sighed and picked up the receiver when I saw Tenis's home number identity in the display window.

'Lolo, wonderful news!' Lupe, Tenis's beautiful wife, sounded clear and joyful – almost laughing but with a presentiment of something profound.

'Lupe? Are you pregnant. Again?' I murmured but horribly, despite it all, I noted how my slimy voice had brightened.

She shrieked; I heard the muffled sensation of her turning aside to repeat what I had said. Then – quite clearly audible – came Tenis's bitter cackle, like a sly crow expiring.

'Come out here to the house. He needs to talk with you. A taxi will stop by.'

Forty minutes later, down in a taxi, a grumpy, yawning driver took that old National road out towards the airport with the nauseous hot-air heater full on. The stupid radio station had denuded treble sounds and annoyingly exaggerated bass voices, so much that during my journey I felt like leaning forward and asking the driver to adjust only his treble setting.

The international airport out at Lacas sat on the cold, pitch-black earth of abandoned vineyards which crowded its perimeter – the airport was hysterically lit up like a ship on a dark sea, like an aircraft carrier: the lights of jet liners escaped from its bows, and vanished into its stern; illuminated funnels, derricks, angled sub-decks and weird bollards sprouted and bristled from its bulkheads. Burned kerosene sweetened the sharp night through the taxi heater vents, airliners in mysterious pre-flight phases whined invisibly or slowly moved off, only revealing a lit-up, brightly painted vertical tailplane – huge above the lowest airport buildings.

Then we passed the bottom of the runway and we were on the lone straight out to the Tenis's seaside villa.

The taxi dumped me on the villa road and I crossed the parking zone. I was used to seeing that tarred area with ten or more vehicles parked: those evenings of the Tenis parties. Even outwith social occasions there were always the cars: a small sporty thing for Lupe and Tenis's latest expensive indulgence and frequently a small Seat or *Fiat* belonging to the house cleaners, perhaps a van of the pool or fish tank maintenance men.

That night the vehicle park area in front of the villa was empty except for Lupe's little convertible sports car with its electric roof up. The whole place had the abandonment of a mourning house. My mourning. The good-time guys and girls who were hangers-on around the place were long gone. Time for Mr Misery's final cocktail hour.

I climbed the scallop-shaped front stairway faced with glazed tiles. I saw the spiked cast-iron railings, two or three of the points broken off by clumsy delivery men bringing in the famous boat mast for the bedroom; but at each party Lupe had stuck coloured candles to the missing points so now those three specific upright iron rails were coated in a pale shroud of downward dripped, dried wax.

I pushed the modern buzzer which had the dead lens of a security camera imbedded into it. Nobody answered and I took a deep breath then buzzed once more. The door jerked in and there Lupe stood with that strange and impossible quality with which someone actually appears whom you have frequently imagined with real intensity.

I had arrived complete with the usual Homeric inflection I carry whenever I manage to make the most mundane journey. Lupe looked smaller: no shoes on; or socks. Painted toenails metallic blue. She instantly stepped outside the door to tightly embrace me but also she kissed me hard on the mouth with her small face held slightly sideways to give her lips direct access on to mine. I reacted in the usual manner of any man hit by an incongruous smacker – in other words the husband is about: instead of embracing her shoulders with my two arms I held my hands out, signing helplessness, though I did not try to draw back from the kiss too vigorously. All just as well because Tenis appeared, leering over his wife's shoulder.

'Sir Misery. Welcome to the funhouse.'

Now Lupe giggled and suddenly squeezed me so tight my breath embarrassingly squeaked out. Her hair was down, under my chin, tickling my nose. She let go, turned and sighed! I looked where her silk black hairs frothed on the back of her pale neck.

'Hey!' I managed a smile at her husband.

Still, it had felt remarkable to feel Lupe Tenis's arms around me once again, which she had not done since Eva, her first, was born. Down the years I realised I had been prey to such huge oscillating emotions for this woman that it seemed remarkable the source of my chagrin was contained in this small, tidy, almost pathetic form.

It was natural that for years I had pathetically thought of Lupe whenever I saw the replacement female newscasters on our regional television station – who never bettered her, I might add.

'Come. How are you, I wonder. You never did phone. Shush, shush.' Tenis gestured inward across the threshold; he was looking raffish, wearing thin white cheesecloth trousers and a blue shirt open far down his chest – he was suntanned but he also looked bleary. In his hand he held a large bottle of rum by the neck.

Lupe took my hand and pulled me into the grand hallway.

352

They were moving excitedly about as they crossed the hallway and I realised they were both very drunk.

'Are you not . . . cold?' asked Tenis which to my ears sounded sinister.

'So how are you?' said Lupe and she looked hard at Tenis.

'As you would expect,' I replied but I felt the first webs of a cruel fear lifting from me.

Tenis laughed and so did Lupe.

'Poor Lolo,' she said.

'You are here in interesting times,' Tenis nodded knowingly.

'Oh yes?' I said carefully.

And he led us through to the clinically lit modernised kitchen under its ox-eye spotlights – a kitchen that surely must remind Tenis of his operating theatres where he was God and played that *Turandot* and *Tosca* and *jazz*.

Again Tenis put his head forward and repeated, 'Shush, shush. The children are upstairs.' He jabbed over the rum bottle, filling four shot glasses, spilling an oily puddle on the black marble top as each overflowed, then he put the rum bottle down too heavily so the base clunked.

Lupe nodded in a determined way and picked up her shot glass using two fingers. 'Hup.'

Tenis finally turned his gaze on me then indicated the tall awkward stools which we all perched up upon simultaneously – somehow our movements reminding me of the unison of Solielian and his gravediggers enthusiastically uniting to cover my mother's casket up on Heaven Hill above our city which now lay on the horizon.

I sat between the Tenises. Already Lupe had lifted the fourth shot and Tenis sighed and filled another.

'We are having a little party, just the three of us,' Tenis blandly stated.

'Yes.' Dubiously I looked between the two of them and tried to lift the shot to my mouth without spilling it and I successfully whacked it back. It was very smooth and nicely chilled. As if I had a future, I could not help glancing automatically at the bottle label: *Mount Gay*.

Tenis looked both ways then leaned forward to the spotless silver-surfaced aluminium bread bin which he slid open. Inside were a selection of golden *croissants* and a small Asian jewel box. He opened the box and skilfully enfiladed four lines of the white powder onto the dark surface before us. Neither of them spoke but suddenly an acoustically dead electronic trill sounded loudly and Lupe aggressively snatched a mobile phone from beside her where it was charging on a stand. The tiny phone all lit up with that strangely unique artificial light.

'What?' she snapped then softened her voice. 'Oh, darling, are you not asleep?' Lupe turned to me and raised her eyes to indicate both upstairs and exasperation.

In a childish way Tenis fiddled with the four lines of white powder using the expensive kitchen knife. He whispered to me, 'Both the kids have mobile phones now; they phone from upstairs every five minutes until they fall asleep. I swear I will throw those phones in the sea.'

'No, Eva, it was a taxi. Lolo has come for a little visit. No, you cannot. You go to sleep and you can see Lolo tomorrow. Can Mama speak to Nuria?' There was a pause then Lupe said, 'Stop letting them use the phones. Well, come down and they will fall asleep,' and she hung up.

There was a long silence. Tenis leaned forward and skilfully inhaled one of the white lines of powder, then, rubbing manically at his nose and smiling, he nodded at me.

'I am sure it is best quality, Doctor, but you know I won't indulge.'
'Doctor's orders,' Lupe said gruffly and laughed. She lit a cigarette.
'My darlings. I hate competition, you know I shrink from it.'
'Go ahead, man. No competition.'
I appealed to Tenis. 'This cannot be too good for me.'
'On the contrary,' he smiled.

I shrugged, cleared my throat, sealed a nostril, bent at the waist, then attacked the line rapidly so as not to fluff it, letting it cram up my nostril. Immediately I recognised the sickly symptoms of the few times I had indulged this modish idiocy before: a burning glue acting with disturbing autonomy at the back of my throat, the unmistakable ambience of dentistry, the need to bite my tongue to stop a rush of talk.

I nodded and leaned back, smiling proudly on each side to find, as only married couples can do, they were not observing me but staring deadly at the walls in front of them. I turned suddenly. The young, attractive nanny had entered the kitchen and I quickly nodded knowingly at the remaining line of white powder.

'No, no. Easy,' Tenis said indifferently.

The nanny stood beside Tenis so her small thigh was right against his leg — actually touching, I noted — which rested on the stool and she bent, lifted a foot in a pink sandal cutely, and inhaled a line of the powder. I looked at her small nose when she stood straight beside me, I knew I was staring, quite rudely, at its pin-like nostrils. I was amazed the physiognomy of the nose seemed no barrier to this pastime. I thought a dirty thought about the girl's private parts just as Lupe drawled: 'Lolo, this is Nuria, our live-in nanny, who my husband is having full intercourse with when I said he could just fool around with her. On the way to our bed at night.'

I nodded politely. 'Enchanted,' I mumbled.

Tenis and Lupe burst out laughing.

The girl nodded to me coolly, lifted the remaining shot glass and downed it. 'I am going to bed. Eva is asleep.'

As she walked away behind us I turned to watch her departure and to look at her ass in her jeans.

'Oh yeah,' Lupe called but without turning to look at her. 'And you can give me back my vibrator tomorrow. With new batteries please.'

Tenis burst out laughing again. Shaking his head slowly and looking down at the counter in front of him.

Lupe blew out smoke. 'True, she really did borrow it and still won't give it back,' and she laughed quite cheerfully. She turned to look at me. 'So, Lolo darling. I said to him that if he was balling her, I was going out for some fun and that I fancied you. He laughed and said that you would not be in the mood because, to amuse himself, for over a fortnight he had lied to you that you had . . . this ridiculous Condition.'

I turned to look at Tenis. He was staring straight at me. 'This is fascinating,' he stated. 'Go on. Your turn.'

My face and mouth had literally gone numb. I did not know if he meant my turn to take more drink and drugs or to speak. 'Is that true?'

'Yeah!' he yelled and laughed.

'Keep your voice down, man,' Lupe said in a bored way.

I just stared at the man.

'Lolo.' He leaned fully towards me. 'Your blood is in perfect health. You are fine. I just thought I would have some fun with you for a day or so, then got carried away. Tell me how you feel. I mean really; you feel good now, right? I bet you feel magnificent. You are in good health, boy.' He chuckled. 'Low cholesterol count too, you lucky bastard.'

'Why not take that knife and stick it in him?' Lupe nodded. 'I will clean up. No, I shall have Nuria do it.'

'I have saved thousands of lives with these hands. I have the right to play around with just one or two. You or her. I am sure you have been on a little spiritual journey, yes? You are grateful to me somewhere down there.'

Maybe it was the drug but I slowly nodded.

'No.' Lupe groaned and shook her head. 'You sold out to him just like that, Lolo.'

Tenis smiled and handed me the pack of cigarettes. I took one. 'So go take her back into our city for a few days,' he ordered me.

Somehow I had put a cigarette in my mouth. Tenis lit it for me. 'Go on. You won't be disappointed.'

Lupe tapped me on the shoulder like a child would. 'He can drive Nuria back to school at the end of the holidays.' She barked a bitter laugh.

I shook my head. 'I am not ill?'

'You are not ill, Lolo, but you are as unbearable as when you were ten years old. You mistake indulgence for generosity. You never did a good thing in your life, Lolo. And then there was Aracelli.'

I felt Lupe stiffen at that but I nodded. 'I won't disgree with you.'

There was a long silence.

'What are you going to do?' Lupe suddenly whispered. 'You can't let him beat you.'

I sat.

'He is trembling,' announced Tenis.

'Take me away,' said Lupe.

Tenis said, slightly uneasily I felt, 'What are you going to do? How could you be more sure you had no Condition than that. Have her as much as you want. Lolo and Lupe!' he laughed. 'You sound like a bloody circus act.'

'The flying trapeze,' said Lupe.

'No. The clowns,' Tenis snapped.

'I won't come back,' said Lupe and shook her head.

'You can drive me back to our city,' I suddenly said.

'OK.' Lupe let out a long breath. She stood up and crossed to the corner of the kitchen where she pulled on a pair of long tan boots over her bare feet, the side zips made a dramatic, almost electric buzz as she drew each one up.

'I was talking to you,' I whispered, staring at Tenis. I stood up and walked behind Lupe's back towards the door.

'Told you,' I heard him say quietly behind me.

He did not even drive fast enough to frighten me as he usually did. In Lupe's car we moved through the runway approach lights

357

up on their suspended pylons. In the salt flats, modest shards of coast fog slashed through the headlight coronas.

'Maybe I knew all the time,' I almost whispered.

'It is coming for us all. It makes no difference,' was his only reply.

As we headed north along the National road towards our city I noted how our car headlights also lit up the reflective, trackside signs of the mainline railway which shadowed the road; they indicated train speed limits: 60 then a 40 and other incomprehensible symbols, red chevrons across white, etc.

'I did always know you were quite insane but I did not think you would go this far with your games.'

'Christ, man, I thought you were playing along. I could not believe you were so gullible. I thought it would be fun. What do you make of Nuria?' he said casually.

'In the name of God. She is just a kid.'

He shrugged and smiled.

I asked, 'Why me? Are there others not worthy of your hatred?'

'Lolo. I would have loved to have nailed one of them rather than you, old friend. I would have given a severe case of syphilis to Mendez and your sodomite best friend – not that I have anything against sodomy – could have done with something to wipe that grin off his face. However, you know those guys would have tried to sue me. They would have learned nothing from the experience. A wrong diagnosis on a blood sample could never lose me my job but, frankly, I was irritated by you and Lupe breathing on one another pathetically, without the balls to get into bed.'

'I am sorry for that.'

'You had your chance tonight, boy. I think she has lost respect for you.' He laughed. 'Hey. Did you contact any of your exes? Did you get weepy on the phone with them? I hope you have caused untold distress but now you can tell them they are all in the clear.'

'I never told a living soul,' I said quickly.

'Well I never. Selfish irresponsible bastard to the bitter end.'

'You are right. You know me best.'

As we entered the zone of high street lights near our city I was sure I saw singular rare flakes of snow settle and dissolve on the clean windscreen. I immediately thought of Ahmed.

'It has not snowed in our city since 1982.' he stated.

'Must be thick up in the mountains tonight then,' I said mysteriously.

Suddenly he said, tenderly, 'Remember when we were kids and snows were in the mountains we used to go up in Dad's van and bring home a snowman in the back? We would drive along the esplanade and throw out snowballs at the prettiest girls. It would still be warm down here and the snowman would be melting in the back. That cheat, Claudio the fisherman's son, started taking their refrigerated truck up and the blowhard would put snowmen down on the beach.'

'I remember,' I whispered.

'Times long since, Lolo. What happened to us?'

I nodded.

On the National road we drove up the edge of the esplanade's mosaic walkway: the concrete bandstand, the palms, the painted chairs neatly stacked, the hospice of the old man who I was too selfish to buy a whisky for, Cena's and the fountain in front of the Imperial Hotel.

Full-formed flurries of snow suddenly blew in off the marina masts giving the illusion of clustering around the high street lamps; balloons and concentrated gushes of the flakes created their own minute, swarming shadows on the ground beneath lenses of precise lamplight. These clouds of near weightless material seemed to reflect my interior sense of lightness and fragmentation.

Cena's was brightly lit within, its glass doors slid shut that evening to keep out the cold. Snow flurries were driving onto its awnings which the slender boughs of the palms curved up from. I craned across Tenis and mumbled, 'Wonder where the wild parrots will go in this? I need to feed my boat cats.'

359

He chuckled. I could not bear to be with him any longer so I suddenly said, 'I will stay at Mother's old apartment. Drop me here.'

As I climbed from the car I turned to him. 'I am OK?'

'Would I let you have Lupe if you were infected? I would want her back, please,' he sniggered.

'Maybe both you lunatics already have the Condition?' I offered timidly.

He laughed loudly. 'Lolo. Is there no end to you? Off you go.'

'Goodbye.'

'So dramatic!'

I shut the door and watched the car drive off in a disappointingly careful way.

Looking to my right the fountain tips were trembling, almost tinged with pink in the artificial light: the waterspouts looked like elaborate eighteenth-century wigs. I was completely stoned.

I pulled my jacket and held it shut at my chest as I dashed through falling snow – I looked up. I felt the streets of our city were vibrating with a febrile excitement: the same as when I was a child and the regime garrotted the two men up in the castle above.

I had to sober myself up and slow down my heart. I reached the main entrance at the side of the Imperial Hotel with its high curved lintel from the days of horse-drawn coaches and stepped inside once more. I nodded over-energetically to the receptionist – who I did not recognise – behind the old desk frontage and crossed the hallway by the stairs into the Terrace of the Imperial café using the residents' entrance beside the serving bar.

I heard the cacophony before I saw them: the Terrace of the Imperial was jammed with an excitable, very loud and daunting array of teenagers. They were dressed in bright anoraks, rushing to and from the bar calling to the waiters. The front door by the newspaper kiosk was wide open, letting in cold. Through the windows, youths were running then skating along on their shoes on the snowy pavement outside; an inevitable snowball banged bluntly on the glass and a table of girls turned to look at the nearest waiter expectantly.

Both television sets were switched on, one to the *MTV* and one to a loud, shouting *Hollywood*-looking movie dubbed into our language with its inevitable accents of only the Capital city.

The waiter, the one who I often granted a sorrowful look when I passed the Terrace, was at my side and seemed surprised to see me in there. 'Jesus. What is this?' I asked, my face registering sympathy.

'Two busloads for three nights. Some exchange with an institute in the Capital. They were running up and down the corridors until two in the morning. All my regulars are over in Cena's. Wish I could do a shift there too.'

I nodded sympathetically and chuckled. 'You have my condolences.'

'Thank you.'

'Some weather, eh?'

'Snowball fights in the corridors tonight.'

'Without a doubt. Look, I need water and orange juice and coffee and . . . camomile tea. And two packs of *Marlboro Lights*.'

It was so long since I had bought cigarettes in this vicinity I was pleasantly surprised to note that they stocked single packets behind the counter rather than in the damn vending machines. Behind the bar counter the waiter hit the coffee lever to free it then banged it even harder on the flip-out bin to disgorge the used coffee from the sieve fitting. The back of the waiter's glossy, black waistcoat creased as he made familiar movements: wiping the steam pipe with a wet cloth, raising the metal milk jug to it and turning the tap to boil. I did not try to talk any more over this noise. He was warming one of the widest cups with the boiling water pipe, placing the cup beneath the coffee feed – the furious hissing began, presenting the black circle of liquid in the bottom of the white cup. He placed that cup before me and out of the jug poured down a thin white rod of boiled milk from a height to generate bubbles.

As he worked behind the counter and added up with the till I looked above the kids' heads to the televisions. I noted how each cut of the *MTV* video lasted no longer than a regulation two or three seconds – otherwise it was no doubt labelled too slow by these cracklingly impatient consciousnesses.

I looked around me at the young ones. They were greedy – and very moody: the clothes, the faces, and you saw what they were greedy for: <u>life</u>. They all sat there demanding so much out of life. Quite right too, but I know this: there is only so much <u>life</u> to go around.

I tried to find any kid who was sitting still but even the girls at the tables were jutting backwards and forwards, scraping their chair legs, spinning on their bums to stare and evaluate, eyes greedily gobbling up everything around them. So, still alive then, was my only thought.

I swallowed the coffee. I gulped my water and orange juice then sipped at the camomile tea. I noted how there was no template to indicate the *Hollywood* movie was pausing for a few minutes to run commercial breaks – the movie was just brusquely interrupted mid-dialogue by a patrol of absurd advertisements; yet the movie's glittery metallic sheen seemed to seamlessly flow into these lavishly produced consumer appeals – as if the film was merely an inferior and irrelevant adjunct of the real business: commercials with their breathless, subtly desperate ideology.

'Spare a cigarette?' a cheeky lad close to me requested.

I ignored him. The sweated, self-important yet acne-haunted air of desperation around adolescent males makes me cringe with embarrassment. It was obvious he was trying to buy grass and with my wet hair and gauche, shaken appearance I must have been reduced to looking like a real possibility. I wiped my nostrils in case I had telltale traces.

'Go drink what is under the kitchen sink,' I growled in our dialect.

'Come on, mister.'

'Beat it.'

After about an hour I could take no more. I had to sleep.

Outside I let snow fall on me and flutter in my face so I blinked, perhaps my eyelashes were crystalled like Quynh Hoang and Thinh Tram's were with sea salt twenty-five years before.

I took out the flat latchkeys to the iron gate with its modern, attached inner sheeting of *perspex* to prevent waste paper and other debris being driven by the wind through the iron bars into our large stairwell area. The grand old turn-of-the-century gates had been riddled with snow along their ironwork. I pushed the gate in vigorously so I could see the snow jerk from the crossbars and a powdery quantity fell across the wet black leather of my shoes.

I tugged open the old sliding cage door of the elevator which my dead father had once descended in and I rode to the top floor.

When I opened the front door of my mother's old place and entered the corridor I stood in the bright lampshadeless light and listened. All I heard was the restlessness of my metabolism. The duplex apartment was almost empty since I'd got rid of all those crates and boxes of unread books. The furnitureless floors, white walls, white ceilings, the yellowed net curtains on each long window to the balconies gave a voluminous silence to each room. The imitation marble-tiled floors had their dustballs and creepily shifting formations of dirt behind the doors, like slime moving in a shallow tray of water as you stirred through the place.

I was standing in the main room with the pink-tinged street light outside, strangely muzzled by the moving clouds of snow. I stepped to the balcony windows and I held aside the crisp, sun-baked net curtain as if I was revealing a wildly exciting obscenity to Lupe, outside the window. Or perhaps lifting *Ann*'s skirt so The Young Woman Who Watched could see her. It was from this balcony Father had looked down on Mother and Bonat of the bandaged wrists the day they left together in a taxi with the chessboard. I noted snow was settling on the heavy flagstones of the narrow balcony.

Upstairs I took off my shoes and collapsed on the double mattress I keep there on the floor. I had poured a drink for myself believing it might help me sleep but I pushed the glass of whisky away from the mattress across the stone floor so it chattered in an irritated vibration.

Last Chapter. Titled: Last Chapter

I had been profoundly unable to sleep against my astonished, racing mind. I had wracked up in a ball and wept for an hour. I came downstairs and drank two whiskies, smoked six cigarettes – my hands flying from side to side – using the damp matches from the kitchen, stubbing each butt out on the marble floor, wearing only one dress shoe on a bare foot specially for the purpose. Then I dressed fully and from a wardrobe found Father's long, grey cashmere and wool overcoat, the very one that he had worn in Madeira that time he joked about the hearse, when I was ten. The sleeves were just an inch short but otherwise it fitted perfectly.

I urgently shoved two packs of cigarettes and the big box of kitchen matches into the side pockets. I filled a whisky glass and checked I had my cigarettes. I climbed up the stairs and walked beyond the bedroom into the boxroom.

The keys to the padlocks were in the back of the drawer of the table beneath the hatch. I unlocked the padlock and lowered the inner hatch. I removed that tray-like section of insulation and checked there was no sign of hibernating bats – for they had once settled in there. Then I used the other key on the roof hatch. Some snow fell in as I lifted it. I passed up my whisky glass, sightlessly feeling, testing and passing the glass out into cold night air, using the snow depth to fix it securely out on the roof surface. Grunting with age, I stood on the table and clambered up the short distance, clumsily hoisting myself out under a low, purple sky onto the roof of Mother's empty place above Town Hall Plaza.

I stood up and looked around the white-covered rooftops: the darker shapes of vents and fittings lifting out of the fur-like snow which retained the light of the city in a unique way. I detoured away from the edges while on the apartment rooftops, for although the edge was ten metres from where I stood, unlike the Imperial Hotel there was no wall along the drop down to the Plaza below. The Town Hall bell rang a loud, hopelessly optimistic and bright quarter.

Carrying my whisky carefully, I stepped over the low wall which divides the roof. On the old roof of the Imperial Hotel once again – for the first time since Thinh died. I took a last gulp of whisky but could not finish it and put the glass down on top of a support box for the old solar-heat panels. The glass was in centimetres of crunchy snow which would cool those remnants beautifully, I concluded. I looked up to the castle with the snow crusts trapped in crevices of the high cliff face – the low clouds that had brought the snow were breaking now and revealing again the prominent three-quarter moon. It was always beautiful here and especially tonight.

I could feel a film of sweat on me despite the cold. I reached for my whisky again and picked it up.

As I crossed a bit further to the edge of the hotel roof I suddenly reacted and squinted. My body stiffened in amazement. I could not believe my eyes at what those damn high school kids staying at the Imperial Hotel who had run riot last night had now got up to! Somehow the kids had gained access, through the 'secret hatch' I used in my youth, onto the hotel roof. I felt personally offended and a little jealous that they had violated the site of my own private teenage world.

Our penthouse in the hotel had long since been converted from residential apartments back to guest rooms, but I knew from my own curious meanderings around the hotel corridors in the years since my parents sold up that the hatch access to the roof – from our old utility room with its succession of new German washing machines – was now a top-floor laundry storeroom for the chambermaids.

These high school exchange brats who were so boisterous earlier down in the Terrace of the Imperial café must have discovered the secret hatch then sneaked up to make havoc and snowball fights because to the right they had actually constructed a small bonfire of paper scraps or something and set it alight. It was still cheerfully burning unattended!

The little bonfire's heat had dissolved the snow all around it, which lay so thick elsewhere. The dark ochre of the roof surface was visible in a defined band around the fire edges and that light – that hyper-energetic orange flame light – was seeping out over the new snow, colouring it, showing how its white centimetres did not lie perfectly level but how the wind had formed small plains and small drifts where shadow appeared along the flickers.

This strangely peaceful scene presented me with an utterly mysterious *tableau*. Why would the schoolkids light a bonfire then immediately abandon it unless their sharp young ears had heard me approach? My eyes darted to small funnels and boxes of the air conditioning and the shadows behind the elevator winch rooms but there was not a soul about nor were there any telltale footprints.

I walked carefully across the lunar roof towards the bonfire, concluding that I would skip up cupfuls of snow in both hands – the more melted slush next to the fire – then pile it on until the flames were extinguished when I would have to inform the management of what had happened.

I was anticipating how cold my hands would become, scooping up that melted snow as Ahmed had scooped the water out of the bottom of his sinking boat. I had almost reached the bonfire when I suddenly heard a familiar sound and stopped. That has done it, I thought. I could even feel the combined vibration through the roof in my feet.

The fire-alarm bells had been set off by heat convection from the roof bonfire down through the ceiling plaster to a smoke detector in a room or corridor in the hotel below.

Looking down I noticed I was not standing in snow now but a steady, heavy centimetre of slush, spotted with melted beads of large hail – like white dots of frogspawn united in a slime. I frowned. Why were the fire bells louder? The fire-bell sound seemed to emanate from the very heart of the flames. I blinked. Was I prey to some aural delusion?

It was then I saw – within the fire's white heart – the small cindered and destroyed roof cross-beam. This was not a bonfire set by teenagers on the roof. Those flames were burning upward through the actual Imperial Hotel roof – from beneath me.

'In the name of God,' I whispered aloud. I now felt the fire's catastrophic heat on my face, emerging from that white-hot hole in the roof.

Immediately my memory calculated: 91. Room 91. The fire was in the corner room directly below this roof breach and must be deeply intense to burn upward through plaster ceiling, wood beaming and the layers of roof pitch.

The snow was melting into wet, reflective slush because the fire beneath my feet was simply heating the roof, but the slow-melting area was much more extensive than just the outline dimensions of room 91 beneath me.

I turned. The snow was melting all the way back towards the rear of the hotel. The fire must have been well established through at least two or three of the side rooms in that direction.

Perhaps the fire could even spread across to my apartment building behind? I could not help my self-interested, prosaic mind oscillating from the shock to immediately reassuring itself that my current house insurance policy organised through Sagrana was valid and up to date. I felt revulsion at my timidity and my weary ties to normality. I noticed I felt no fear.

Then I heard the scream. Unmistakable: the way moonlight

shining on snow can never be reproduced, I heard a genuine scream of true terror from the voice of a teenage girl. Those screams emerged out of the burning hole itself – not the youths in the heated furnace of the Book of Daniel but a fifteen-year-old institute girl in the burning Imperial Hotel rooms below me.

At the edge of the roof I put both hands in the snow and looked down on the kiosk far below. The blue light of the inverted Imperial Hotel sign was colouring the snow along the crenulations. 'Hey,' I yelled. 'Kids. Trapped.' I whispered, 'Top floor.' As my eye ran over the human figures below, I could see a local police car and men rushing about.

I moved back to the hatch which as a youngster I had used to take us up to my secret roof kingdom. I could see no snow on top and as I lay my flat palm on the metal I felt warmth. The hatch was like a fishing boat deck covering, the roof-fitted half had a ten-centimetre lip that went flush with the top, designed to keep rain – no matter how torrential – from breaching the hatch and flooding down into the hotel.

My hand instinctively darted to the padlock and flicked. It was locked. I jumped forward kneeling – my knees wet – my hand went to the two aluminium bolts which secured the hatch to the cemented-in roof lip. The hatch was still held by bolts with four fitted securing pins on the end of each short bolt but with no small padlocks to secure the bolts. I pulled both pins and slid out the bolts, then from the wrong side I heaved open the hatch and tumbled it over noisily.

Immediately the heat and fire-alarm-bell noise arose to me with a light belch of wood-scented smoke. I peered down and could see the dull grey of what looked like neatly piled shelves of towels beneath.

I kneeled and shouted down into that laundry cupboard, almost angry. 'Here. Here. There is a way out here.'

Beneath me that door to the corridor was shut – possibly locked

– and how would my shouts be heard over the burning, structures twisting and fire bells in corridors – and screaming?

I ran, feet splashing, to the door of the reserve-water-tank enclosure and I tugged once, decisive and sharp, and waited for the stubborn resistance but the door shot back open in my hand and almost struck my face. It was unlocked. As an immediate good-luck talisman I reached out and ran my palm down the outside plaster by the door until I found the little carved indentation at one metre thirty, which Father had made when I was so young, to measure my height.

I stepped into the reserve-water-tank enclosure and reached to the familiar and distinctive light switch: military in style: the wall pipe containing its protected wire, the switch's smooth-running, up-and-down ball joint – the engaging click almost silent. The lights in their nautical metal shields came on and there I was, standing again amid the raspy dripping and small echoes of the reserve-water tank and the memory of all Thinh and Quynh and I did. The wooden frame which hovered above the water level on the left side of the tank had been clumsily painted and a mechanical jack support had been crudely inserted below the platform, submerged in the actual water of the tank itself. Otherwise the place was as perfectly preserved as my memory.

Contrary to Father's teachings I wedged <u>open</u> the door to the reserve-water-tank room then I moved rapidly between the round or crossed taps and coloured water pipes as if it were thirty years ago. I <u>closed</u> rather than opened the five floor drains with their dark, wire-meshed plugholes which had slightly horrified me as a child. Then I broke the tiny lead seal and used both hands to twist open the large drain tap, painted gloss red, which controlled the water out of a curved, brilliantly polished brass pipe, wide and dark like the pursed mouth of some river god on a baroque fountain; this pipe had a polished brass screw thread on it, large enough to have a wide fire hose affixed to drain down the tank in case of an emergency leak.

With little distinction between the on and off position, tank water frothed from the brass mouth falling on to my leather shoes and it inundated one side of my father's beautiful grey overcoat, turning it black. I raced from the tank enclosure.

Behind me a rush of water came out the reserve-water-tank doorway as high as my knees – it swept the melting snow away before it. In its enthusiasm, the wave of water moved out across the flat roof and round any obstructions into a much shallower and spreading puddle. 'Come on!' I screamed and clenched my fists as the water flooded over towards the flames.

The fire hole in the roof had enlarged and flames were now reaching higher, purple smoke launching into the skies above our city. Anxiously I watched the tide I had created. It surged on towards the fire but as the moving puddle spread across the flat roof closer to the flames, it was slowing. It almost stopped. I glanced towards the enclosure door but there was no shortage of water, it was still flooding from the reserve-water-tank room, but as it debouched on to the enormous flat roof and lost depth, its volume was not going to be great enough. The water had stopped short of the fire.

I looked over behind me. My flood was flowing backwards away from the fire hole and gathering depth up against the far side wall, beyond the hatch. Thousands of litres of water were building up on the walled-in roof but on the wrong side and to no purpose.

'The Host,' I cursed and I ran to the roof edge. Still no fire brigade but a larger crowd had gathered, looking up, their momentary faces like snowflakes. I licked my lips and glanced around desperately.

If I climbed down that hatch into the hotel laundry room . . . my mad imagination oscillated to produce gruesome fates. Even if I could climb down that wall of hotel towels or sheets what if I found the laundry room locked from the outside, where the corridor might be burning? The water lying on the roof and still flooding from the reserve tank could finally breach over the hatch lip and waterfall down upon my head. I would be trapped in that laundry room which I may be unable to climb out of. Perhaps the room would begin to fill with roof water? I would be floated up on the inundation towards the hatch with night stars tantalisingly above, pulled under by the swirling thick soup of sodden towels and bed sheets impregnated with the dried blood of a hundred virgins and with the intense heat below I would finally be boiled alive with the needy laundry like a pink lobster.

I stood closer to the roof wall with my back to it. If the roof collapsed I would be killed. I was going to live. Why should I risk my life?

There was a hissing sound that made me jump and wheel but I realised it was only the flood of water reaching the far side of the roof, meeting the snow and floating away dissolving sheets on its surface.

I began to walk away across the roof towards my apartment. I would go down to the front of the hotel and explain I had heard children still trapped on the top floor.

Then I heard it, abandoned and almost beautiful in its release – as clear and as violent as before. A single young girl scream from down below. This time I was sure it came from over the front wall of the hotel where she must have been on a balcony.

I stamped my foot. A saucer of splash shot out around my shoe. I strode to the hatch and again peered downward and in. It was so dark. I crouched, fitted my palms on to the metal lip of the hatch, took my weight on my arms, hung, then lowered my legs into the emptiness below. My feet dangled and the toes of my shoes found the sheen of linen or towels but with the shelving fitted so far inward against the wall, there was no way to swing my whole body weight forward and get a step on a shelf that could support me.

My arms were shaking convulsively. I used my feet to kick as many towels and sheets as I could down on to the floor beneath me, to break the fall.

I tried to lower myself to full length, just hanging from my hands, but my fingers could not take my weight along with the heavy, soaked overcoat. Hanging there, almost immediately my fingers painfully slipped free and I fell straight down into the dark well. I missed the shelves of towels and the ones I had kicked to the floor but my legs did take the impact well and I let myself stumble sideways, impacting with some upright vacuum cleaners. For a moment I was sitting on the floor. I could see the intense light of orange flame reflecting under the door beside me. I jumped to my feet and tried to work out my chances of climbing the shelves back to the hatch. I touched the light switch. Surprisingly the bare electric bulb came on and I was surrounded by the brilliant heapings of starched stacked towels and sheets but I could see tiny motes, black squiggles of floating ash, contrasted against the clean, pressed white linen.

Positioned in the corner shone a clean, modern aluminium extending ladder. I jumped forward and seized the ladder, pulled and positioned it so the top rested on the upper-shelf edge close to the open hatch.

I turned to the cupboard door. I knew not to put my hand on any metallic door handle. I touched the wood panelling of the door to see if it was hot and snapped away my fingers. I grabbed a towel off the shelf, wrapped my hand, depressed the handle and pushed the door.

I was surprised. I was not met with a dramatic wall of heat or a fireball, or overpowering fatal smoke – and the corridor lights were still switched on.

Shamefully, pathetically, I felt – I stuck only my head out of the laundry cupboard – like some guilty fornicator. I began bawling as loudly as I could: 'Children. Children. Girls. Here. Here. Here.' I had to register the note of hysteria in my voice – even a sort of splendid, brattish insistence that the trapped children should now present themselves to me.

I was less afraid because the escape ladder was safely positioned behind me but my adrenalin seemed to be out of control; my arms twitched unsteadily in jerky movements when I reached for something. I had not forgotten the danger of the roof above collapsing downwards on top of me. I shouted again, then listened.

The fire bells had stopped but I had not noticed when. There was no sound other than wood snapping and the strange groaning, rushings and whisperings of fierce burning as the hotel devoured itself. I held my face down, grimacing, and glimpsed a look around the corner of the open door.

The corridor was not alight but rooms 93, 94, 95 and 96 way along towards the top of the stairway were all burning. It was fascinating, I admit. I lingered for moments to see how two bedroom doors had fallen outwards with their complete cindered door frames; rich oily orange flame poured out the perfectly faithful rectangular door shapes, barbecuing the ceiling cornices. The old wall lamps from my day had their fabric singed off, hanging smouldering and withered. I saw a charcoal-black electric bulb. The curtains at the interval window were ablaze, swinging from side to side in the draughts which fires were creating and I could hear the big brass curtain rings pinging.

Glass shattered and trinkled to a stone floor. I thought it was a window but it was the glass on one of the illustration prints in the corridor: I saw the paper illustration which had been affixed beneath the glass burst into flame just from the ambient heat of a flaming doorway then turn and curl upward ferociously. A Botero copy fell vertically down the white stairwell, its frame sucking the wall.

Heading in the opposite direction I stepped out the laundry cupboard then nipped around the corner to the front-facing rooms. 'Girls, girls!' I shouted, angry now at being so endangered myself. I passed corner suite 91; rich smoke was spurting – under pressure – from beneath the door and I could see the varnish was blackening on the wood all the way round where it joined the frame. The damned windows were open inside that room, fuelling the inferno.

I stepped on to the door of 92 and used the towel to press down the handle, ready to jump back. There was some unsteady, spongy resistance from the door – signifying open windows within, which I recognised so well from my youth – yet no heat, flame or smoke burst from the gap. I pushed the door open all the way:

A girl was standing out on the little balcony – sixteen years old at the most – with her back to me, bedroom windows thrown wide open fanning the blaze, the glass panes in delicate frames secured back all the way underneath the long, green curtains encouraging combustion within the hotel; the girl stood, both arms on the metal rails, leaning over shouting and waving; her attentions were downwards to the people below, her voice muted to me.

She was nearly naked. She wore only a slightly long T-shirt with an infantile cuddly bear in repose printed on her back. She was not aware of me behind while I looked at her. Despite the perilous circumstances I was amazed it was still impossible for me not to codify and compare aspects of the girl's teenage anatomy – the legs, the buttocks which were exemplified by her stretching over the balcony railing – my whole male, coded personal reaction.

I was aware of something in my vision towards the left. From within the fierce burning room next door was a newly created fissure, several metres long but only millimetres wide, between the roof's ceiling plaster and the cornice decoration: tight little curls of a dirty pitch smoke against the white emulsion pulsed in searchingly through the solid wall.

I suddenly knew our position was bad. I do not know why or how but when I saw that smoke from the intense heat in the neighbouring room then the fresh-skinned schoolgirl with brown thighs, bare feet and the window open wide, I knew something was going to happen – damaging and permanent.

When she finally turned to me, the young girl looked beautiful and was crying, an established bright gloss of tear tributaries on her cheeks. She hesitated for a moment on the threshold between the balcony and bedroom. I presume my new presence produced an odd hallucination for her startled eyes: they looked in from the dark balcony with the flashing lights below to the interior box of yellowish, defined artificial light cast from the non-matte bulbs of the bedroom's little chandelier.

In my long, soaken overcoat and crazed hair I must have appeared an alarming figure. She was frightened by my presence even despite the more obvious dangers around her! I was offended. After the danger I had undertaken on her behalf, wildly doubtful looks of rejection transported me back to my youthful perceptions of being an outsider.

I said loudly, trying to imitate the tone of an institute teacher, 'Close the widow immediately,' I pointed. 'You are encouraging the fire.'

Again I saw her look forlornly backwards and down. She trusted those unknowables below more than me.

The girl with the bare legs held out a bony arm behind her. 'The fire engine is here with ladders,' her voice trembled but with the clear accent from the Capital city. I stepped beside her to the window and could peer down sceptically to see a red pumping wagon still manoeuvring in beside the fountain, a snaking suction hose was already tossed into the blue-painted basin to suck it dry.

'We do not need hoses, we need the ladders. That roof could fall in on top of us at any moment.'

She whimpered.

I pointed at the ceiling. 'All this side of the hotel is burning. Come with me. I have a ladder, we can walk back across the roofs to the next building.' It was then I saw the feet. 'Have you burned your feet?'

'I tried to walk on the floor and they burned. Feel how hot the floor is.'

I looked down at my own leather shoes. I bent and put my hand on the black-and-white stone tiling. I snapped my hand back. Christ. Did that not imply there was fire beneath us as well? The girl teenager had trim, bare legs but they ended in swollen feet, the edges of her heels purple and blooded where deep blisters had torn away.

'You have no shoes?'

'Got wet in the snow and I had them drying on a radiator. They were on fire. Everyone has run away.'

'I will lift you if the floor is hot. Please. Shut the window and come.'

Reluctantly she turned and closed the two sections of the window. As she slid the securing bars, instantly, like consecutive gas jets being turned down, the pressurised smoke hissing inwards up by the split cornice hesitated, meandered and aimlessly drifted.

I held out a protective hand and touched the girl's shoulder in that insinuating and at the same time controlling habit of mine. My fingers opened slightly on the smooth round ball of her shoulder leading her towards the corridor where I stepped close in behind her and I closed the door after us. It was then I noticed the door to 91 next to us was now a vertical plate of pulsating orange ember.

Either our movement or me shutting the door behind us, suction from further up the corridor or even a gust of wind from within 91 where the windows must have had the glass blown out, caused the upper half of the cindered door to fall in towards us and the girl let out a scream. Immediately the smell: those Saturday mornings with my father in the white-tiled barber's when Tomás would place his scissors by the sink then hold the burning taper close to my father's ears to singe away any stray hairs.

Behind the collapsing embers of the door came an invisible balloon of heat out of the room which made me hiss; the girl in the T-shirt and I instinctively cowered backwards.

I swung off Father's wet, grey overcoat and draped it around the teenager next to me.

'Pull it up over your head and run forwards but do not trip. On you go, little one, but quick.' To the bright furnace of the interior of 91 she held up the overcoat – like the vampire shielding itself from summer dawn as it gained the castle shadows.

I grimaced as I saw the girl's swollen feet step on red-hot cinders but she did not react. I swung off then lifted my suit jacket to shield my face, the heat was intense through just my shirt. At the corridor corner the girl in the T-shirt threw Father's grey coat to the black-and-white tiles of the corridor ahead and stood upon it. I saw the steam rise immediately from the wet fabric. I stepped up to her and grabbed the soft smooth skin on both her legs behind the knees then I swept her up in my arms. She was not heavy straight away but another step forward and I felt her burden growing. Her toes banged against the corner as we turned the corridor and she gritted her teeth.

I jerked with my head and shouted, 'In there, the ladder.' Everything seemed to be getting louder.

My impressions of what happened next are subjective. I let the girl out of my arms to the ground to prepare for the ladder climb. I was aware of her swollen feet beside my leather shoes and her suddenly taking my hand – she seemed to tremble then I realised she was screaming but I could not hear her. Before my eyes the floor collapsed. I will always remember – like an exploding chess-board – the black-and-white floor tiles seemed to lift upwards, twirling playfully. Perhaps the boiler in the basement exploded? The electric lights went out.

I turned myself and the girl beside me away. I only looked back once to see what I feared: the walls leaning inwards, methodically tipping, shelf by neat shelf, pressed linen down through the exposed and scorched floor beams into the incinerator beneath where there was just the hellish outline of destroyed rooms.

I helped the girl retreat back the few steps to Father's coat splayed in the corridor. She was screaming, quite hysterical. I kept waiting for the floor to collapse beneath us. Her eyes cluttered up with terror. Changing my voice to angry I pointed down the corridor and shouted, 'Run. Now,' and as if I were a ghost she fled from me.

I whipped up Father's overcoat and imitated her use of it as a shield, ducked passed the roaring door of 91 until I caught up with her. One would have presumed she would have retreated back for the balcony in the bedroom but she had not. She was kicking with her foot, a strip of burned skin hanging from it, at the door of 89, trying to get in.

I kneeled before her and slapped the tiles. 'Stop that. Fire is beneath us on that side of the building. You saw. But through that door there is a staff stairway one storey down.'

'I thought it was a room.' she cried out. 'The lift won't work.'

'No lift. There is no electricity. We need to run down that stairway to the floor below. If it's burning and smoky we can only do one thing. Listen.'

'What?'

'No time for talking and words down there. If we meet flame together we will run back up here. OK. Hold my hand.'

'Why not wait here? For firemen?' she whispered.

'On the floor below they will rescue us in moments. The building is falling down. We have to get lower.'

She nodded repeatedly.

From my pocket I took my packet of cigarettes and I offered the open packet to her. 'Smoke?' I casually suggested.

As I hoped, she suddenly laughed, nervously but like a sudden vomit her head jerked back and her upper body relaxed in the momentary convulsion. I took one cigarette and in mockery I bent it so it broke at a right angle and I put it in my mouth in buffoonery. She smiled. I had not seen her teeth yet.

I took her thin arm roughly. I could feel her supple bone through it. I had never felt anything so beautiful in my life. Suddenly, I longed for a daughter. 'Hold your breath all the way down because you are going to need that breath if we have to get back up. Keep your eyes closed as much as you can.'

The staff stairwell was full of white smoke, pale and rushing. I stooped down the steps holding the overcoat like a shield as if I were afraid of colliding with people dervishing upwards.

379

There was no need to keep the turns in my mind, the first, the second, the third around the lift shaft. I remembered it all perfectly. The arm I dragged behind me, forcing her to keep pace with me.

We reached the door. It was jammed. I let out my breath and moved back, knocking the girl to the stairs behind me where she sprawled in the obscurity. I threw my whole weight at the door and something broke. I fell outwards straight into a lot of flame. I heard the girl scream behind me. I had fallen but I stood up. The room opposite the staff stairway had burned out and again the door frame had fallen, blocking the stair door. My force had broken the smouldered wood but if it had been less degraded by fire then it would not have given way. The side of my jacket was on fire. I whacked at my jacket dumbly and the scorch mark simply went out.

I looked for Father's overcoat but it was lost. A bad omen. I took two steps and turned then opened my eyes. As my memory had promised me the door of 71 was before me. All was as it should be in my world. I even smiled. I violently kicked the door to 71 open and I pulled the girl in behind me.

We both stumbled forward but the layout of the room was not as I had expected.

My little companion frowned. 'The floor is hot,' she said darkly then stood on one leg and there was a crack. I jumped to grab her without thought. I caught her as if she had been seized by an alligator and I aggressively hauled her back up. I saw blood on her leg.

We seemed to be above a supporting wall for through the collapsed floorboards there was a layer of sand and rubble but to the right I saw a line of naked brick then, on the other side, wires and chains leading into the thin plaster of a ceiling – a ceiling so transparent I could see the theatrical shadows of great flame all lit up beneath it. The balcony – our only chance of rescue – was across this devastated flooring. We were not going to reach it.

380

I tried to inhale through my teeth because hot air was rushing through the shell now.

'I am scared.' She looked into my face helplessly now.

I turned my back, cuddled the teenage child in tight to my chest so the coming flame did not touch her. It felt so peaceful I swore I would never let go of her.

'I won't let go of you,' I promised. I felt my scalp sting then my lower back and I cried out, waiting for the smell of Father's barber's shop. My only thought was, 'At least Solielian won't get his hands on much of me.'

The roof slumped above us, the floor keeled and groaned. Burning debris hit the sagging ceiling plaster above and split it; there was a virulent snarl as the fire slapped on our bare skin with a painful sting. Then something fumed into steam then more replenished through the ceiling and filled my mouth with warm gritty liquid as I glanced up. I could see through the floors to the roof and the reserve tank itself, hanging high up there in space, pouring its merciful hot waterfall down upon us! Then the floor went from under us.

So I too fell down through cinder floors of the Imperial Hotel. I was not suspended by those flying carpets of pure flame that turned to steam and we descended.

As I fell I glimpsed the square concrete tube of the revealed lift shaft which was funnelling a crazy scorching, upward rush through the winch room and into the night sky high above our city.

We fell on like those forlorn bodies abandoned by technology which fly earthward from stricken airliners. I realised I was holding the teenage girl's body to me as tightly as I could. I felt my upper hands which were flush against her thin back violently impact on terrifying objects.

Through the cornices and lattice ceilings, like the old dead man in 1934 in his heavy bathtub, the girl and I in our embrace fell into the burning dining room below.

But a pressure hit my back and there was a nauseous swing then the musical complaint of disturbed, delicate glass – our fall was broken by being hooked onto the swan-necked metal and frantically chittering glass baubles of the distressed dining-salon chandelier, still suspended on a central beam – which the DC-8 *stretch series* had once hung from.

We careered one way then back the other, snagged in the garish platform. The metal arms of the chandelier made the skin on my back briefly stick to them but I did not free the girl from my clutch. This time I was remaining faithful and we joined a folding collapse of ceiling material which drew us free of the chandelier that hung sideways.

I have never had a God but I have believed in strange insight. I only saw things clearly then, suspended in a chandelier in a burning hotel! I saw the handsome face of Ahmed Omar and I recalled his words about being cast into the terrifying night sea. Ahmed had said: 'I had nothing to lose.'

There was too much flame below us. I had no strength to scream for the girl but, not knowing the child's name, I spoke aloud the name 'Ahmed.' and I spat out a forgotten cigarette butt bitten in my teeth and actually thought, Could have choked on that.

At last the human voice sounded modest and beautiful among all that noise and destruction – its hysterical drama overwhelmed by the tender cushioning puff of one human name spoken as we descended on through the middle air of this burning empire which was fabulously alight.

Old, ceiling-high curtains were quivering upwards in some sort of excited delight at their own destruction. As if they were being freed from the bind of their material shape after so very long and rejoicing in this sudden exhilarating dematerialisation.

We hit the ground with me still holding the child in a crushing hug. For seconds I felt myself begin to burn again. Then the torrent from the reserve-water tank caught up with us and collapsed on top of me, mixed with plaster, wood and tearing nails, ash and blacker, gloss cinder beams, their broken ends sharpened to spears, crashing down in a terrible soup. All fumed and was doused.

I could stand up. It was as if, like Jonah, we stood inside the blackened mouth of the whale, rivulets and waterfalls of saliva streamed from the dark shatter and buckled palate of roof above us. Poles of waters were spattering in vague circular patterns on the black heaps of debris around.

In shock the swallowed schoolgirl – so inundated in water and ash she appeared as black as Ahmed – rose from the bad dirt and held her long arms out in front of her. Without a word, as I watched, she walked away from me. In our twenty-metre fall together we had made a travelogue to this mildewed, submerged Venetian palace – the roof had poured canals down upon us.

'What is your name?' I shouted and it echoed in the destroyed dining salon.

She did not answer. I grimaced again as she lifted her young, bare leg over the teeth of a blown-out window and hoisted herself to civilised pavements.

I limped to the windows through waterfalls, warped mirrors of running water from above and stiled over and out from the Imperial Hotel forever.

I heard the huge chandelier, which had to be brought into our city by boat a hundred years ago, pulverise itself on the dining-room floor then the full orchestra of the reserve-water tank, accelerating through the cindered floors above to come down into the reception lobby.

There was nobody on my side of the street outside. My imagination had oscillated images of cheers, flash photography, Paz Vermici dashing at me with his notebook in hand. Applause louder than any for a damned French swimming-pool lifeguard.

Instead there was nobody and dirty snow. I remembered, incredulous, what the weather was like outside there after the heat of the burning hotel.

The child had lived and I leaned against the wall of the hotel. Nobody else could have done that. Nobody else knew this building like me and I had saved her.

I shivered on the shadowy side street by the old coach entrance to the hotel. They must have been expecting the whole building to collapse for the street was evacuated though I could hear great commotion to my left at the hotel front. Over by the taxi rank I saw a cordon holding back spectators but at an extreme angle so they could hardly see me. A policeman swept across the dirty snow to the lithe girl in the soaked T-shirt and embraced her figure into his arms. People encircled them excitedly. She seemed to have no connection to me now.

I flattened myself against the wall, smiling privately and sadly in my loneliness. I turned and limped up the pavement in the opposite direction.

'Get away from there. Away from there.'

'Yes.' I nodded obediently and walked ahead. A policeman frowned at me from across the road where the Major began but because it brokered no view of the burning hotel, just the smoking windows of its side rooms, there were no spectators, only this policeman and his car blocking the road. 'Hey. You OK?' he called after me but I kept going and waved one arm in the air casually.

There were two more local police cars blocking the road in front of Mother's apartment above Town Hall Plaza. Policemen were leaning on the bonnet talking into radio sets as I came out of the shadows. 'I am a resident,' I announced, almost shouting it in the sudden novelty of my voice – pointing to the gates of the apartment.

'You can't go there. Imperial Hotel is on fire next door. Really on fire. The roof just went in. They think there are children missing.'

I nodded, kept going, my arm holding my jacket tighter around me in an effort to conceal the mess of my clothes, then I was around the corner and gone.

Over the tops of buildings innumerable sirens sped to and fro. I limped quicker through the snow and suddenly slipped and fell once, called out in pain but I was up again.

I paused beneath a street lamp, looked both ways to make sure nobody was around. I was already shivering. My jacket had been burned through and I could feel a terrible spreading-out sting there, like the time a jelly-fish got me when I was *scuba*-diving. I eased up my shirt, gritting the teeth and felt the goose bumps rush my chest.

I was badly burned from the belt mark up my right side almost as high as the little nipple. The skin had lifted in a sheet and bubbled here and there like rippled plastic. And he sat down among the ashes. What a memento.

I kneeled for a handful of cold snow and doused my burned skin with it. I shuddered but there was a momentary respite from the pain then it started worse than before. No hospitals yet. I would heal. I was immune to burns as medical science and tonight had proved. In future I would stroll through the jasmine fires at the May festivals just to light my cigarette.

This had me tapping my singed jacket for some cigarettes but the Host – they must have been in Father's immolated, beautiful overcoat!

I limped my way down that side alley towards the esplanade. I saw three stray cats trapped in a doorway, utterly perplexed by snow and jumpy. They looked at me longingly but I just moved on.

The police had closed down the National road just before the fountain, which had been switched off and doubtless drained. How was I to get a taxi in this mess?

The up traffic on the National, despite the hour, was backed along the beachside at the rear of the summer cafés. Nothing was flowing the other way so the wide three lanes were hauntingly empty but for drivers who had abandoned their vehicles and walked up and back to watch the hotel burn.

'Spare a cigarette?' I asked a younger guy and his girl who were standing while she talked on a mobile phone.

'Get lost,' he said.

I almost reacted then I realised – I looked like a beggar of the streets. Like Ahmed had.

That guy with a defensive air was now looking at me with a sudden arm around his girl. He was frowning at me with a look of disgust.

'Hey. Your face!' he said.

I had walked on shaking my head.

'Spare a cigarette,' I said to two guys then I saw the taxi badges on their shirts. My hair was so crazy I saw one of the men involuntarily reach up to check if his hair stuck up madly. The other one with the moustache almost refused me with an affronted look, taking me for another street junkie, but then he recognised the dark charcoal on my suit. He looked at my face.

'The Host. Were you just in the fire? Mother of Mine! You are burned on your face.'

'No problem, I got out.'

'Jesus, you are soaked too.' The other guy started to slide off his jacket.

'No thanks, friend. Just a cigarette would be good.'

'Of course, here, here. Should you not get to the hospital? All the ambulances are the other way. On the esplanade.' He held out his packet. Lousy Fortunes!

I smacked at my burned jacket. 'I really was smoking a minute ago.' I smiled.

'Hey, you OK?' the other taxi driver put an arm gently round my shoulders. I nodded and held my head down. I looked up. 'Anyone else get it?'

'All kinds of rumours. The roof fell in so nobody knows what is happening. You should have seen the sparks from here go up in the sky.'

I leaned to the cupped cigarette lighter and inhaled the smoke.

'Your face is badly burned, man. You are badly . . . blistered. You have blood on your leg.' Both taxi drivers looked down as if they were considering a tyre. I thought they might give my leg a sharp kick to test it.

'It is of no importance. Look, can you get me out to the Phases Zone 1, quick. It is very important. I have . . . family out there. They need me. Five thousand pays the bill.' I pulled out my wallet and put the cigarette in my mouth so I could unfold the wallet to show these guys my notes.

'We are jammed in here but we could call.'

They started looking around helpless, 'We have no idea what the roads are like out there, off the National with this snow . . .'

I limped on and held up an arm. 'No problem, guys. Thank you for the cigarette. Forever grateful.'

'You should see a doctor!' the taxi driver called after me.

I moved away laughing, loudly.

The last damned lemon express of the day was running as normal despite the snow, the fire, the apocalypse behind me. It waited, engines ticking over beneath it on the slushy platform. I held my torn jacket around me and limped up the covered area. The few passengers already in the seats – most young and already drunk – stared at me and let their heads shamelessly follow my progress. The top coach was empty so I lay flat on the floor, feeling the engines vibrate beneath me as we headed out along the night coast-line, horn blowing as we nudged ahead. The hostile, dry electric heating was full on. I raised myself up on to a seat because I wanted to witness my familiar lands coated in white, the always desperately unnatural sight of snow resting on the stooped leaves of palm trees, the whole world pulled by that trailing milk stain across the clear sea into the moon-sodden surf.

I knew the guard would be making his way up the train to collect the tickets. I could not be seen now. I knew that. I could feel the blisters rising on my face. I got off the lemon express at

Disco and walked on up the track to avoid pedestrians, the train's disappearing twin red lamps ahead for a few moments then I was assisted onward by hearing the train's progress up to Kilometre 4 before me.

I was limping on past my own apartment building in the Phases Zone 1, my feet now completely numb with cold, in the buttermilk electric light of my ground-floor lobby.

I did not enter my lobby though. I kept onwards to the new wall of wire in the wasteland.

'Ahmed. Ahmed,' I screamed into the still night long before I reached the place. I ducked through the hole in the wire I had cut earlier with the clippers and shouted towards the boat. 'Ahmed, please. You are there?'

Some frightened cats arose up and looked around, above the deck level – adrift on their ocean of snow, too cautious to jump down and come meet me and highly disapproving as I stumbled noisily towards that boat wreck, only able to see by flooded moonlight on snow, ethereal, blue, eternal. 'Ahmed.'

To my left I could sense apartment lights coming on, whacking squares of light onto the winter ground.

I put my hands on the side of the boat. I climbed on the barrel that the cripple cats used to jump up and down, I swung my leg onto the deck, which creaked.

I squinted into the dark interior – like rats, cats moved urgently and the whole boat shifted a little with my weight. It smelled down in there – it smelled bad. 'Ahmed. There is no place else for you to go.'

'Welcome aboard,' came Ahmed's weak voice, speaking our language so knowingly. Suddenly I was happy.

'Hey.' I climbed down into the boat. He was lying along one split side of hull, the snow shining radioactively outside. For some reason the purple shirt was open on his bare chest. He was caressing several cats where he had sought shelter from the snow. I pushed the cats aside to embrace him. He was trembling like the girl I had just held in the burning hotel.

He said, 'What happened to your beautiful suit, Follana?' He had to take a breath. 'Did they finally try to lynch you in *McDonald's?*'

I laughed. But I could hear a breathlessness in his voice that I had ignored. 'Man. I did not know you were ill with it. Forgive me.'

'What happened to your face?'

'Never mind. Come on, we need to get you out of here.'

'But we are going to cross the sea again, Follana. I have found a sound vessel at last.'

I said, 'Yes. Set course for the Casinos of Monaco, friend. I am so sorry. You had to make it over the sea. No medicines where you are from. You should have arrived on a barge of gold, man; we should have got down on our knees to welcome you.'

I had clambered back into the snowfield and Ahmed Omar followed me as I took his hand; his skin so dark that I presume he could not be seen by the nosy old woman looking down at us from her damned apartment. I guess she saw only me, shouting, gesticulating and stumbling around my ruined boat, as if alone in the light of the moon.

I felt a helpless shuddering all over me now and assisted Ahmed for a short stretch as we walked side by side then separately ducked through the wire. We crossed that mysterious wonderland which tinkled, twinked and creaked around us.

Ahmed threw his arm over my shoulder and together we moved back towards the light of my apartment-building lobby.

'I will get you doctors, specialists. I can sell everything. You should not have let me keep you so long in my apartment telling stories.'

'I was afraid. Your Solielians will have me and I shall be up on that haunted hill.' He shook his head. 'I was finished before I made the crossing. Doctors saw me over there.'

'No. No. There are medicines here. You are in Europe now.'

'I have felt the spirit in me for days now.'

'No. I never knew until tonight. I swear.'

'Your face?' he murmured again and shook his head.

'Come on. We will get you warm.'

I turned my bubbled and lifted face away from this man and I looked in the direction we must go. One of my eyes seemed compressed above and below it. He said something. Maybe he forgave me then? I shuddered profoundly once more. I saw his lips move but though it was in my own language, I will never know what they meant.